Venice, 1368.

War hovers in the wi stake when the old doge dies. Fourteen-year-old Nico, a street urchin from the poorest Venetian parish, is chosen at random to tally votes in the upcoming election for a new leader. Uprooted from his old life and transplanted to the doge's palace, Nico becomes an alienated outsider at the mercy of scheming nobles.

Andrea Contarini, sixtieth doge of Venice, wants the ducal throne less than Nico wants to be ballot boy. Both walk a golden tightrope over treachery and deceit. When he witnesses a court clerk burned at the stake for being gay, Nico despairs. His romantic attraction to men is as powerful as his fear of fiery death and an eternity in Hell.

Taking advantage of the fraught transition in the Doge's Palace, the hostile duke of Austria pushes Trieste to rebel against Venetian domination, jeopardizing her mastery of the Adriatic Sea. The Venetian nobles split, trapping the doge between hawks rabid for war, and rich merchants desperate for peace. With his own life on the line, Andrea Contarini opts to attack decisively and end the crisis swiftly, but his gambit is sabotaged. Trusting only the boy at his side, Contarini sends Nico to Trieste to be his eyes and ears. As the Venetian commanders wrangle over tactics, Nico falls for Astolfo, the young, charismatic lord of Castle Moccò, an indispensable but unreliable ally.

Will Nico return to Venice a celebrated hero? Or will he be forever haunted, guilt-ridden, and still concealing his deepest secret?

THE BALLOT BOY

Larry Mellman

A NineStar Press Publication
www.ninestarpress.com

The Ballot Boy

© 2022 Larry Mellman
Cover Art © 2022 Jaycee DeLorenzo
Cover Photo: Frank Muzzy
Edited by Elizabetta McKay

ISBN: 978-1-64890-468-4

First Edition, February, 2022

Also available in eBook, ISBN: 978-1-64890-467-7

CONTENT WARNING and AUTHOR'S NOTE:
Discussion of sex by the fourteen-year-old protagonist. Note: In 14th century Italy, the age of consent would have been much younger than in modern days. Warnings for discussion of the torture and death by burning of a minor character for being homosexual, and the anxiety this causes the POV MC; for wartime atrocities, torture of the MC (on-page), medieval torture chambers and devices, gore, discussion of the rape of a child (off page, in the past), for a betrayal, and for bullying.

To Gerry Weisburd (Svidelsky) Mellman Polansky

(1911-1992)

Chapter One

The Ballot Boy is Chosen

Venice, January 17, 1368

I'M RUNNING AS fast as I can, but I can't catch the thief. If I don't, Alex's life is over. The necklace the thief snatched from my hand gives away the game. Alex will be exposed. Locked up. Maybe even killed because Alex's father, Francesco Barbanegra, has the temper and manners of a pirate. Alex's family is rich. Very, very rich. Richer than most nobles. But they are common, like my family, which consists of my mother, who takes in laundry. She gets paid in pennies. I understand why she wants me to be ballot boy, but that's her dream not mine. I don't want to be ballot boy. I want to be me, whoever that is.

Only heartbeats ago, Alex and I had moored our boat to the wharf and staggered ashore, covered with mud.

When Alex took off the necklace to give me—the gold dolphin on its golden chain, ruby eye glinting in the early light—the thief burst from the shed, yanked it from my hand, and took off like a demon down the deserted embankment.

"Go home," I shouted to Alex over my shoulder, "before it's too late," and I tore after the thief.

The dolphin is fatal. If the thief tries to sell it at a Rialto pawnshop, the whole world will know. I can't risk it.

Our feet slap on the mud, startling a flock of ducks. They flap their wings, burst up from the salt marsh, and take to the icy winter sky.

The thief is taller than most Venetians, with long spindly legs, no shoes, and a striped turban. He doesn't look down; he doesn't look back. He barrels down the embankment in the direction of the Customs House. My legs are a foot shorter than his, his stride worth two of mine. I suck air like I'm drowning and exhale prayers like I'm dying.

Queen of Heaven, hear my pleas. St. Nicholas, grant me thine aid.

When I manage to close the gap between us, he speeds up. No matter how fast I'm going, he goes faster. He clutches the gold chain in his fist, the dolphin dangling free, its ruby eye sparkling.

That dolphin is a pledge of brotherhood between Alex and me, the seal on our secrets, and a promise that I won't be selected ballot boy because if I am, last night was our final meeting, maybe forever.

"Please, Nico." Alex's eyes had implored me, and I could never refuse. "You've been on the sea many times. I'm thirteen years old, and my father owns great galleys, but I've never seen the sea. This could be my last chance."

"It's not your last chance."

"If you're selected, it is."

"Look at me. Do you think Ruggiero Gradenigo would pick me? I look like a muddy clown."

"Anything can happen."

Alex's pleading eyes broke me every time.

Stars filled the sky, and the moon, hovering high above the mountains beyond the lagoon, sprinkled diamonds over the water. I'd been explaining the lagoon to Alex, showing off, I guess, paying no attention to the tide. I didn't notice the moon pulling the lagoon out from under us until stranded fish danced a desperate tarantella on the exposed sandbars. A mile of mud separated us from the beacon fire atop St. Mark's campanile. We jumped from the boat and sank up to our knees. We couldn't walk, nor could we reach the shore until the morning tide swept back in and filled the lagoon. Alex would never get home without being discovered; I would never be in St. Mark's Square in time for the selection, and my mother would kill me.

I breathe in, out, in, out, in, out, pushing myself harder and harder until I hit a wall and explode and pick myself up and keep going until it happens all over again. The thief took one look at the stupid costume Mama had sewn me for selection day, all torn and wet and muddy, and he must have figured me for a drunk noble, a pushover. Mama is convinced the costume will make Ruggiero Gradenigo select me. She believes in magic. Her eye is on the prize.

He's waiting for me to collapse, this thief. He's making a big mistake. He doesn't know that every day since I turned eight, six years now, I row across the lagoon and back before the midmorning bells, and I will kill him if I have to.

He makes a move to outrun me on the straightaway in front of the old shipyard. We pound over rough planks, wobbly pontoons, and a muddy bog tangled with bramble. I'm glad he's barefoot. It must hurt like hell. He can hear my sandals slapping the ground.

The buildings crowd close along the levee. The bogs and brambles disappear under wooden docks and wharves. Merchant galleys and cogs are moored all the way to the Customs House. The ground tapers to a point where the Giudecca Canal meets the Grand Canal. Keeping running and your turban floats.

He hasn't lost me, so he squeezes between buildings with barely a foot between them, and I follow, the mortar between the bricks shredding my tunic.

The big bell at St. Mark's, the *Marangona*, starts tolling to summon the Great Council to pray for God's grace on the election of the doge. All 1,200 nobles are members of the Great Council. Their names are inscribed in the Golden Book. After Mass, Ruggiero Gradenigo, the youngest member of the Great Council, will walk out of the church, onto St. Mark's Square, and pick the first commoner he lays eyes on, age fifteen or less, to be the ballot boy. That's the law. The old doge is dead, and we can't elect a new one until a ballot boy is selected at random to count the votes and make sure the nobles don't cheat.

I squeeze out of the crawlspace and glimpse the thief's turban disappearing down a dark lane the sun never reaches. Several lanes lead into this small square; all but one dead end at the water. He doesn't know where he's going and probably doesn't care as long as he stays ahead of me. He's as desperate as I am. My heart beats a battle tocsin.

I struggle to master my breath as Abdul taught me. I'm dog-tired from fighting the moon, the tide, the mud. Sweat floods my face. The salt burns my eyes. I wipe them with my muddy sleeve, squeeze them shut, and listen. This quarter is silent. Everyone is at St. Mark's for the selection.

The thief's bare feet, bloodied from running the embankment, leave a trail winding through a labyrinth that will lead him back to me. That's how Venice is. Outsiders always go in circles, even we do occasionally outside our home parish.

The old doge died last week. He didn't last very long; he was eighty-two when they elected him back in 1365. That's old even for a doge. I was twelve then. Mama knew I was going to be selected his ballot boy. She'd worked it all out with the Blessed Virgin and St. Mark. She took to bed for a week when I wasn't selected, but she never gave up. She started praying for the new doge to die before my fifteenth birthday. I heard her, every night. First, she prayed forgiveness for wanting him dead. Then, she begged heaven for him to die. Now, she believes a miracle has happened. I'm going to be ballot boy. She knows. The Virgin interceded.

If I'm not in front of St. Mark's when Ruggiero Gradenigo selects the ballot boy, I will be dead to her. She will curse me for spoiling her miracle.

The thief backs into the little square. He doesn't see me. He sees a glint of sun on water at the end of a narrow chasm of brick. He takes off toward the water, and I get there first, waiting, as he staggers onto the wharf. On the opposite bank, mothers and their sons clog St. Mark's Square, tricked out like piglets at the Ascension Day fair, each one praying for the job I don't want.

The thief ducks between the pilings of the empty ferry dock. None of the ferries, trapped on the water, can move for all the other boats. Nobody is going anywhere. Every eye will remain on the Doge's Palace until a new doge is elected. Venice is the richest city of all; the stakes are high. Mama says anything can happen.

I charge, pin the thief against a striped pole stuck in the Grand Canal, and grab for the dolphin in his hand. But he twists free and hurls himself off the dock, crashing into a boat below. The boat rocks wildly, the passengers scream, he steadies himself. Before anyone knows what's happening, he leaps into the next boat, and the next, and the next. As fast as he can, he bounds across St. Mark's Basin toward the twin columns at the water's edge framing the Doge's Palace, St. Mark's Church, and the greatest square in the world. Executions and burnings take place between the columns, and walking between them brings a curse upon your head, which is why we call them the Columns of Doom. I saw a murderer executed there when I was seven. They chopped off his hand first, in San Barnaba Square, where he'd killed someone, strung his hand around his neck, and rowed him back here. They hung him, quartered him, and left the pieces out to dry here between the columns.

I jump from boat to boat to boat after the thief. People squawk, but I'm out as fast as I'm in, never stopping, my eye always on his bobbing turban. He scrambles up between the columns and pushes his way toward St. Mark's Square through the bodies packing the Piazzetta.

The church doors aren't open yet. The thief towers above the mothers and sons, his turban threading through the Piazzetta toward the church. Arsenal men in leather armor hold the crowd back, creating some space for Ruggiero Gradenigo to come out and pick. Mothers fight for places directly in front of the church.

The big bell tolls.

Mass is finished. The crowd surges forward, a wave of anticipation silencing them. The stones beneath our feet vibrate with the wild clangor of bells.

He made a big mistake, and now he sees just how big. Bodies block him on all sides. I elbow my way through the crush as the church doors swing open. The crowd gasps. Out of the corner of my eye, I see Mama desperately looking for me. She's furious I'm not up-front and center with her.

I leapfrog a tangled knot of eight-year-olds and their mothers, grasping for the thief's throat. He panics and hurls the dolphin over the crowd. I vault, twist, and grab the dolphin out of the air by its chain. I can't land on my feet. I come down sideways, rolling over bodies onto the cleared pavement. The guards can't stop me.

Chapter Two

My New Home

I CRASH INTO Ruggiero Gradenigo's feet. His eyes meet mine, and the crowd goes wild with cheering. They are unstoppable. They acclaim me. I clutch the dolphin so I don't lose it as they lift me onto their shoulders and march me around the square. Ruggiero Gradenigo follows me, his eyes filled with scorn, as the crowd carries me into the Doge's Palace.

I don't know what's happening, but my heart cracks in two. Goodbye Alex, goodbye Mama and Abdul. Goodbye St. Nick's, Pierluigi's boat, catching eels foaming out of the rivers, eating the baker's jelly donuts, and Mama's fritelle.

The palace guard hands me off to the youngest member of the dead doge's council. He's old enough to be my grandfather. A fringe of gray hair shows under his velvet cap. His face is clean-shaven, his nose thick, his lips thin and downward turning. He squints as he assesses me with a moneychanger's eye. The sleeves of his black velvet robe touch the floor. A gold lion of St. Mark, wings spread, paw resting on the open gospel, clasps his collar. His gold ring bears the ducal insignia. He holds me at arm's length with the tips of his bony, ink-stained fingers and steers me through the palace to his office. At his desk, he covers his nose with his sleeve as he smooths a fresh sheet of parchment.

"My name is Marino Vendramin. You will address me as sir."

He eyeballs me, head to toe, like a fishwife eying someone else's fish, and dips his quill in ink.

"How old are you?"

"Fourteen years, nine months. Sir."

"Really..."

He raises his eyebrows, wondering if I'm lying to get the job.

"Honestly, sir, I don't want this job. Throw me out of here, if you please, sir."

This has the opposite effect than intended. I disgust him, but he believes me.

"Birthday?"

"April 17, 1353."

"The day Doge Marino Faliero was beheaded."

"Yes. Sir."

They chopped off Doge Faliero's head seven months after he was elected because he'd plotted to kill all his enemies among the nobles and make himself king. Every year on my birthday, we commemorate his beheading. It's like having a birthday on Christmas. Nobody remembers me.

"Your full name?"

"Niccolò Amadeo Saltano, sir."

"Parish?"

"St. Nicholas of the Beggars. Sir."

He cocks one eyebrow. "Of course. Your mother's name?"

"MariaGrazia Saltano. Sir."

That throws him. "That's all?"

"That's her name, sir."

"Father's name?"

"He's dead, sir."

"Dead men have names."

"I don't know his name. Sir."

He stares me down, unhappier with each word.

"He died when I was a baby, sir. She won't tell me his name. Sir."

"Have you asked anybody else?"

"Nobody else knows."

Vendramin is starting to look very nervous. "You're certain he was Venetian?"

"Yes, sir. He was a bowman in the fleet. Sir."

That eases his mind. "You're a commoner, of course."

"Not one noble in our parish. Sir."

He makes a note. I don't tell him Mama says that my father was a noble. That he was bowman of the quarter-deck. Pirates killed him near Crete when he was twenty-two. His family wouldn't let him marry Mama because she was only twelve, so he swore to marry her when he came back with plenty of his own money. After he was killed, his family called Mama a whore, gave her fifty gold ducats to keep her mouth shut, and threw her out. She was a kid. An orphan. Her whole family had died in the Black Death, their bodies dumped on stinking barges. She didn't know what to do. His people said if she came back, or blabbed their name, we'd both end up facedown in the lagoon. Food for the crabs.

But Mama also makes things up. She makes up lies and then believes them to make a hard life easier. Everything she says about my father could be a fairy tale. If he had been noble and claimed me, I'd be noble. But he's dead and can't claim me. No matter who he was, I'm still just a bastard from St. Nicholas of the Beggars, so I keep my mouth shut.

Vendramin is staring at me, wondering where I've gone.

"What? Sir."

"Domicile?"

"St. Nicholas Lane, behind the bakery. Sir."

"That's enough sirs."

"You said to call you sir, sir."

"I've changed my mind. Don't call me anything. Can your mother provide two witnesses to the above-stated facts?"

"The parish priest at St. Nick's baptized me; I'm in the register. And Pierluigi, the fish vendor. I've worked for him since I was six."

He waves his sleeve in front of his nose.

"Your past clings to you."

It's true. The cats around St. Nick's follow me around all the time, begging for dinner. Vendramin finishes writing, dries the parchment and hands it off to a page, only slightly older than me, who has been holding his nose and making faces at me.

"Your mother will be notified immediately," Marino says.

"She knows. She was there."

"Official notification. You are no longer hers. You're our problem now."

I'M STILL CAKED with lagoon mud, my hair streaked with it, my fingernails black. I really do stink. Marino leads, I follow, and the page trails behind us through the echoing corridors. This palace isn't built for ordinary people; it's built for giants and makes me feel like I don't belong. Great artists have painted the walls and the greatest masons carved the stone. It's empty and quiet because we're between doges. Vendramin names each room we pass. A map comes together in my head, one I'll never forget, cataloged with all the other charts of skies, seas, canals, and streets stored in my brain.

We descend to the ground floor, behind the stables. Low stone vaults bear the weight of the palace on their squat shoulders. Outside the water door, the icy canal sparkles in the sunlight. Steam billows from tall casks of laundry. The size of the casks and the amount of water astounds me. At home, a single well supplies everyone around the square. In winter, we have to break the ice with the bucket. We are surrounded by water, but we have none of our own. The lagoon is half-salt and half-fresh, only good for fishing. We depend on rainwater collected in the wells, or else we have to buy it off ferries from the mainland. Mama has no money for water.

"I've never seen so much hot water," I say.

"Strip," Vendramin says. It's an order.

"Here?"

"And I do mean everything."

He inspects my naked body like a master builder inspecting a hull, impersonal, detail by detail. He points to the cask.

"Climb in."

"In?"

"All the way."

I've never been up to my ears in hot water before. I can float. I do a handstand, so my feet stick up in the chill air. I do a somersault, poke my head up, and shoot a stream of water between my teeth. The laundress laughs, avoiding me with her eyes, and hands me soap and a bristle brush.

"Scrub."

Vendramin is as serious as a general in battle. He only lets me out after three complete scrubbings. The laundress wraps a sheet around me and rubs me vigorously. When she's done, Vendramin steps close and taps my necklace.

"Gold and ruby. Byzantine. Possibly Roman. Where did you steal it?"

"A friend gave it to me."

"The last time I heard that excuse, the thief confessed under torture. Lost an eye for it."

The page behind Vendramin sniggers. He has been staring at me the whole time, arms straight out, piled with fresh clothes. Vendramin hands me spotless white skivvies and makes sure I put them on properly.

"Linen from Alexandria," he says. "That's in Egypt."

"I know where that is. My father sailed there."

Vendramin hands me a white linen undershirt and tucks it into the waist of the skivvies. Then leggings.

"English wool," he says. "The finest."

One leg is black, the other yellow. They fasten to the waistband of my skivvies. The colors are reversed on the velvet doublet embroidered with silver thread. Silver trims my pointy leather slippers. Vendramin shows me how to wrap the long sleeve of the velvet cap around my head. He is silent and precise. He does it once, and then I do it, exactly as he did. He doesn't bat an eye, but I can tell he's surprised. He looks at me critically and gestures me to turn around.

"It's all too small," I tell him.

"Small," he says, "but not too small. You can take it up with the new doge. Your expenses come out of his purse."

Vendramin leads me back through the palace to an empty suite of rooms stripped bare. That's the custom. When the doge dies, the people storm his lodgings and take everything that isn't nailed down. Mildew stains the wall where tapestries normally hang. Murals of sea battles or the fields of Heaven cover the remaining walls and ceiling.

"This is where your doge will live," Vendramin says. "He will bring furniture to suit his own taste and purse."

He nudges me down a corridor leading from the doge's antechamber to a wooden corkscrew of ship's stairs. They creak and groan. At the top, Vendramin opens a door carved with lions.

"Your room," he says.

I've never heard those two words together before. It sinks in slowly. The painted ceiling arches overhead, and I can walk into the fireplace of the otherwise small and unremarkable room. I can almost touch the domes of St. Mark's outside my window. Ropes crisscross the narrow bed of simple, sturdy larch planks, supporting a rolled mattress piled high with neatly folded bed linen, smooth and stiff.

"Where are my clothes?" I ask Vendramin.

"In the ash heap, I hope."

I have nothing but this uniform. That's going to make it difficult to escape.

Chapter Three

Rules and Regulations

"THIS ROOM WILL be yours until the doge dies," Vendramin says, "so you might as well make your peace with it. It may not be what you imagined, but I assure you it's more than any monk or sailor gets, and you have more privacy than the doge himself. He can't even step outside the palace without a procession. Never forget, you will be eating, sleeping, and shitting where you work, so be very, very careful not to make a mess. This is your home now."

"This may be where I sleep, but my home is in St. Nicholas of the Beggars with my mother."

"Don't worry about your mother. In exchange for you, she receives fifty ducats per annum from the state treasury. That's more than a chancery clerk or a bowman makes. She's much better off with you here than on a merchant galley."

"When can I visit her?"

"When the doge says you can. *If* the doge says you can. You're no longer a carefree boy. This is your life now, and there's a lot to learn. We can hide your rough edges until you're polished up, but from now on, you'd best hold your tongue, do what you're told, and trust no one."

"What about my friends?"

"Forget them."

"I'm not a prisoner. I have to see my friends."

"None of us leaves the palace until the new doge is crowned. After that, what you do is up to him. Some doges make you study Latin and astronomy; others make you polish their boots and trim their nose hairs. *His* duties are written in law; yours are not. You do what he says, like a horse or a slave."

I am the prisoner of a life I don't want. I don't know what happened to Alex, and I have no way of finding out. I fear the worst. The brotherhood of the crossbow is over.

Mama gave me the crossbow on my eighth birthday. She said it belonged to my father. He made his shipmates promise to bring it back to her; he wanted me to have it. It's beautiful. Mother-of-pearl inlay embellishes the stock; thin layers of laminated horn form the bow, capped at the ends with sinew. The stirrup of wavy black steel shows its age.

At first, I was so short I had to sit on my butt, put my feet through the bow, and pull with both arms to get the string cocked. Now, I do it properly, standing with one foot in the stirrup. Pierluigi, the fish vendor—my old boss—made a target from sticks and hay and a piece of painted sail. I practiced every day until I could hit it square. That was how I met Abdul. He became my first real friend.

Abdul is a slave, so technically, he doesn't count, but he counts to me. He is my brother and my teacher. His black hair and eyes contrast starkly with his parchment pale skin. He's two years older than me, a head taller, and skinny as an oar. A Venetian sea captain kidnapped him after the sack of Alexandria and sold him to the apothecary in Santa Margherita Square. Abdul is a ninth-generation apothecary's son. He knows more than his Venetian master ever will, and his master knows it too. He treats Abdul very well, sends him to make deliveries, and lets him roam the city on his own.

I was practicing on the marsh behind St. Nick's when Abdul walked down the embankment. He stopped to watch me shooting.

"Nice weapon," he said.

"It belonged to my father. He was a bowman of the quarterdeck."

Abdul laughed.

"What's so funny?"

"How stupid you think I am."

"He was!" I saw red, and when I see red, I don't stop to think. I threw a punch. Abdul slapped my forearm faster than I could see. It stung like a wasp. I fell flat on my ass.

"Never attack in anger," he said calmly. "You'll always lose. Why did you try to hit me?"

"You laughed at me. You think I'm a liar."

He looked down at my baggy leggings and pauper's shoes.

"Only nobles can be bowmen of the quarterdeck. You're clearly not noble."

"Didn't say I was. I said my father was."

"I see..." His frown softened. "You're a bastard. My apologies for laughing."

No one had ever apologized to me before. He helped me up, and brushed me off.

"May I see your bow?"

"Do you know how to shoot?"

"Better than you, I dare say." He offloaded the wooden instrument strapped to his back. It had a potbelly and five pairs of strings.

"What is that?"

"My oud." He flicked the strings with his fingers. "Like your lute, only subtler."

I exchanged the oud for my bow.

He hefted it and sighted along the stock. "May I shoot?"

I gave him a crude homemade bolt that made him smile, but he didn't say anything. He cocked the string, loaded, and pulled the trigger. Hitting the target dead center, his shot knocked it backward across the marsh.

After that, he joined me whenever he could and taught me to shoot like a Mamluk, the soldier-slaves who made themselves sultans of Egypt.

One evening, Abdul brought Alex along. Alex's eyes were glued to my bow.

"Nice bow."

"Where's yours?" I asked.

"I don't have one."

"How old are you?"

"Thirteen."

I knew that was a lie. Every boy in Venice had a cross-bow by the age of twelve. It was a duty. We were expected to take up arms if anyone invaded our lagoon. His soft white hands had never seen work, he didn't have any strength in his arms, and he was as beautiful as an angel painted in a church. His clothes were clean and fine. Everything about him said he was rich. He reached for my bow, and I yanked it back because he grabbed it like he had a right to it, which he didn't, so I figured him for a noble.

They're all like that. They think everything belongs to them.

"I just want to see it," Alex had said. That was how it started.

He always came at sunset. Abdul had taught him some basics, but it was clear he didn't practice enough. When he shot wild, it took him an hour to find his bolt in the marsh, but he never complained. He kept looking until he found it. The more I got to know him, the more I liked him. He was gentle and funny, fierce and determined. We three, Abdul, Alex, and myself, became the brotherhood of the crossbow.

I've always admired Abdul, above all else, for his calm and methodical ways. He didn't just teach me about shooting. He taught me about the trajectories of the bolts, the angles going up and the angles coming down, the properties of triangles, arcs, and circles. Alex couldn't have been more different, didn't know anything, and was enthusiastic about everything, wanting to learn it all. Watching him line up his shots, I was amazed again and again at his bright-blue eyes, the proud and delicate line of his nose, the bow of his lips. As uneasy as his beauty made me, it made me happy at the same time. When he smiled, I forgot everything else.

As soon as he found out I was a great rower, Alex begged me to take him out in a boat and teach him, which I also thought strange. Every noble house in Venice had many boats. Every fisherman and merchant and shopkeeper had at least one. Pierluigi had three, whereas being so poor, Mama and I had none. That was how everyone and everything got around. With canals instead of streets and more boats than horses it made no sense to me that Alex couldn't row.

"Don't your people have a boat?"

"Of course. Many. My father owns round ships and galleys. But they won't let me row. They're afraid I'll drown. I never learned to swim."

"How can you live in Venice and not row. Or swim?"

I thought he was going to cry.

"I was very sick," he said. "I almost died. My parents worry about me all the time. They won't let me do anything. Please teach me."

"Rowing isn't like shooting. You need more than a good eye and a steady hand. You have to be able to read the lagoon, its depths, and its moods. You need strength."

"I'm almost as big as you."

"I'm ten times stronger."

I show him the muscles in my arms and calves.

"I row fat old Pierluigi around the lagoon every morning, and believe me, you have to know more than the strokes. No matter how well you think you know the lagoon, a high tide can change it all around."

"Where do you go?"

"To Torcello. And Pierluigi has a secret place on the seacoast near Malamocco, where the old palaces got shaken down by an earthquake. They're underwater now. They belong to the crabs and fish."

"I want to go," Alex said. "Please, teach me to row."

"Only if you learn how to swim."

"Then teach me to swim."

"Fine. Take off your clothes."

He looked startled and backed away.

"Don't worry," I said. "I won't let you drown."

I walked to the end of the wooden jetty and stripped. He followed me slowly, eyes down so he wouldn't see me naked.

"You can look, Alex. You won't see anything you haven't seen before. Take your clothes off."

"I can't."

"Why not?"

"I'll swim with my clothes on."

"That's a sure way to drown. I'm going to take a piss. If your clothes aren't off by the time I turn around, you can forget about ever rowing."

He turned his back as I pissed off the dock.

"What's the big deal, Alex? Don't you ever piss?"

"Of course I do."

"Let's see who can piss farther. Abdul and I have contests all the time."

He turned squirmy and started to walk away.

"I guess you can only piss at home in a golden jar," I said.

"I piss when I want, not when you want."

"I don't give a damn. Take off your clothes, or I can't teach you to swim."

He turned away and crossed his arms. "Nico, I have something to confess. I wanted to tell you all along, but I wasn't sure I could trust you."

"Are you sure now?"

He ripped off his cap. Long silky hair tumbled over his shoulders like spools of gold thread unraveling in the sun. Framed in a golden halo, that beautiful face revealed itself for the first time to the light of day, as if a shaft of sunlight had broken through the gloom of a dark church and lighted upon an angel, or a saint, a girl saint.

He was a she.

Chapter Four

Ruggiero Gradenigo Demands to Vote

"THE GREAT COUNCIL chamber is the largest room in the world," Vendramin says.

"One hundred seventy feet long, eighty wide, fifty tall, and as you can see it's still not finished. It probably never will be. When the old foursquare castle burned down in 1172, Doge Ziani rebuilt a real palace. He created St. Mark's Square out of an orchard, which belonged to the convent of San Zaccaria. When we enlarged the Great Council to its present size, we had to rebuild it again to hold them all."

The biggest painting I've ever seen, not yet finished, covers the east wall with the holy family and more angels and saints than I can count. Jesus and His Mother are above the doge's throne, which stands on a dais below the painting. The hall is packed with nobles. Inside the hall, Vendramin leads me up one side and down the other so twelve hundred nobles can eye me.

"The very old man on the doge's throne," Vendramin says, "is Marco Dandolo, the vice doge. He is ninety and incorruptible. You have nothing to fear from him."

The nobles murmur as I walk by. A few of them clap.

"Why are they doing that?"

"To let you know you cleaned up nicely."

Vendramin leads me onto the dais. He takes the seat to the right of Marco Dandolo. I sit on a stool behind him. He leans back so I can hear him and points to the portraits high atop of the walls. "Those are doges past," he says. "As you can see, there's room for many more. That black gap is Marino Faliero's spot. You know who he was?"

"I can't forget. They chopped his head off on my birthday."

A black drape has been painted over Faliero's portrait with words written on it.

"*Hic est locus Marini Faletro decapitati pro crimini-bus,*" Vendramin reads aloud. "Here is Marino Faliero's spot, beheaded for his crimes."

It takes time for twelve hundred nobles to settle down because clerks with lists carefully check where everyone sits.

"The seats are assigned by lottery," Marino says. "So cabals can't form—gossip and conspiracy, the bane of the Republic. The clerks make sure each noble is in his proper place."

By the luck of the draw, Ruggiero Gradenigo sits directly under Faliero's spot. With his black hair pulled back and tied tight, he looks like a Roman centurion whose nose was broken in battle. He wears a black velvet robe and cap like all the other nobles, but he stands out in his own dark splendor, not as much handsome as awe-inspiring.

Marco Dandolo rises and addresses the nobles.

"In the name of the Republic, I now request all nobles under the age of thirty to vacate immediately so that we may elect the sixtieth doge of Venice."

Ruggiero jumps up.

"Unacceptable," he shouts.

That gains him every eye in the room.

"The law is the law," Dandolo replies firmly.

Ruggiero strides to the dais and challenges Dandolo.

"We made the law. We can change it."

"Be careful, young man."

Ruggiero addresses his appeal to the impatient nobles.

"Alas, I am only twenty. *Mea culpa*. But I am a noble of Venice and a member of this council. There are no greater or lesser nobles. We are all equals here. All must vote."

Scattered applause greets him.

"You will vote when your time comes," Dandolo says.

"*This* is my time."

Other young nobles rally around Ruggiero.

"We're not too young to elect senators and judges," Ruggiero shouts over the rising hubbub. "We're not too young to captain galleys and merchant ships. We're not too young to vote for wars and ratify treaties, to die on the high seas or on the bloody field of battle defending your fortunes. No, sirs. We are not too young to elect our doge."

Dandolo raises his hand to silence Ruggiero, but Ruggiero doesn't stop, even as palace guards advance on him in the unfolding scandal. Dandolo stays the guards with a simple gesture of his hand. He listens to Ruggiero patiently, his head bowed.

"It is our sacred duty, sir, as well as our birthright as nobles, to serve the Republic and to elect our doge. He won't just lead some of us. He will lead all of us, every noble and merchant and tailor and weaver and oarsman and slave. The times are treacherous. Enemies surround us, intent on destroying us. The next doge will decide our fate. Not just the fate of the old men. The fate of us all. We must all vote."

Everyone shouts, claps, cheers, or boos. Quarrels erupt on all sides. Ruggiero is out of order, but his supporters raise him onto their shoulders triumphantly.

When Dandolo answers, he no longer seems frail. "Yes, we are all equal, and none of us is above the law. Not me. Not you. Not the doge. Look above to Marino Faliero and mark the fate of one who thought he was above the law. Obey, sir, or you, too, will be charged for your crime."

ON ELECTION DAY I stand in the same spot facing the same sea of strangers. I've only seen a handful of them up close. They all know one another. Now they're all looking at me.

Vendramin ushers me to two large urns between the dais and the nobles.

"You will now see the true character of the Venetian noble," Vendramin says. "The election process is as complicated as a Byzantine conspiracy. It can take two days or two months depending on how ornery the nobles feel."

"Why is it so complicated?"

"One reason only, and this is important, so pay heed." He leans into my ear.

"The intent is to prevent any single family from seizing control and handing this throne from father to son. You heard Gradenigo. All nobles are equal. The doge is *primus inter pares*, first among equals, not because he has more power than other nobles, but because he is their elected servant, the spokesman for their collective will. He is the face of our Republic, not its ruler. He works for them. Committees rule Venice. Never forget that. And, for what it's worth, for better or worse, the doge, not the committees, gets the blame when things go bad. It's sinister and it's our greatest glory.

"Our Republic has survived half a millennium. The ducal crown passes peacefully from doge to doge without civil wars or murderous uprisings. No other state in Europe can say that. We have no tyrant. Or you could say we have a thousand tyrants who cancel one another out in committees and councils. Are you ready?"

"As ready as I'll ever be."

"Don't worry if you can't remember the procedure. I'm here to remind you."

"Don't worry. I'll remember."

He recites the rounds of balloting:

"From the Great Council, thirty are chosen by lot.

Those thirty are reduced by lot to nine.

The nine elect forty.

The forty are reduced by lot to twelve.

The twelve elect twenty-five.

The twenty-five are reduced by lot to nine.

The nine elect forty-five.

The forty-five are reduced by lot to eleven.

The eleven elect forty-one.

Those forty-one elect the doge."

I recite it back to him, word for word.

"Want to hear it backward?"

"Hardly necessary," Vendramin says. "I assume you noticed that votes are followed by a lottery and lotteries are followed by votes. Men may plot, but randomness purges conspiracy. You must also count the ballots before and after each vote. Make sure that you end up with the same number you started with."

The ballots are silver balls the size of apricots, one for each noble, separated into two urns. Thirty of the ballots are gold.

"Let it be recorded," Marco Dandolo says, "that all nobles over the age of thirty are present with the exception of Andrea Contarini. Remove his ballot from the urn."

One by one, the nobles are called forward by name to stand in front of me. I blindly draw a ball from the urn and place it in his palm. If it's silver, he leaves. If it's gold, he stays. They drop their ballots into empty urns before moving on.

It takes hours to winnow the 1,199 down to thirty men. Then I recount the ballots. It's late when I finish. I ask Vendramin if I can go to my room.

"Absolutely not. We are under lockdown. The Doge's Council has been locked in the palace since he died." Vendramin's smile is sour. "Nobody leaves until the new doge is elected. We sleep in the Senate chamber. You bed down with the others in the Great Council chamber."

I'm too tired to sleep in a room full of nobles farting and snoring. When I close my eyes, I see Alex on the wharf, muddy and terrified. If her father learns that she snuck out as a boy, there's no telling what he'll do. Her name will be shit; no respectable man will marry her. The disgrace will drive her father crazy. I can easily see him locking her up in a convent or killing her.

VENDRAMIN WAKES ME before anyone else. After Mass and breakfast, we ballot the thirty down to nine.

"They're all talking about you," Vendramin whispers. "Your ears must be burning."

As I draw ballots, I memorize their faces. Some are ancient, wrinkled and smelly. Others are middle-aged and robust, which makes my heart sink. I would be old before one of them died. The younger nobles have no chance of being elected. The doge is elected for life; old men are preferred because they don't last too long.

The nobles all dress the same, but some are shabbier than others. Some possess vast wealth, live in marble palaces, and own fleets of great galleys. Others can barely afford to eat, and their eyes are envious and greedy.

"All of them," Vendramin says, "in one way or another, work for the state. The poorest have only their government salary, men who squandered their fortunes or gambled them away. They live in debt. Scarcely a hundred are rich beyond measure and they work for the Republic out of a sense of duty. They are the real doge and ruler of the Republic. They spend their lives looking for ways to twist the system to their advantage."

Each of the nobles peers at me to see if I am like him. I avert my eyes. I don't want them seeing into me. One of them will be my master.

The man standing before me is one of the six Procurators of St. Mark. His job is to protect the church's money and the estates of noble widows. I know what he does by his robe and his ring. His gray eyes betray nothing. He stares into mine while I pull his ballot from the urn and place it in his palm. It's silver. He leaves immediately. The next noble is not particularly old. His eyes are as mean and stingy as the fruit vendor on San Barnaba Square. He would certainly buy a gold ball if I were selling.

THE SECOND DAY is long, and on the second night, our impromptu dormitory houses the forty-five nobles who will be reduced to eleven who will vote for the forty-one who will elect the doge.

As soon as we are locked in for the night, the buzzing begins. Groups of two or three men talk softly so that no one else can hear them. They keep their hands in front of their mouths so no one can read their lips. They group and regroup like partners in a courtly dance. I lie on my cot and memorize the map painted on the wall above me. Venice, at one end, is represented by St. Mark's. Constantinople, at the other end, is represented by the Imperial Hippodrome. The line between them is a golden aqueduct through which the riches of Asia pour into Europe.

Two nobles stand near my cot studying me. One, a man in his fifties with white hair and watery blue eyes, has many years on the other. They mask their faces with their hoods, so I can't see them. They watch and whisper. The older noble leaves, and the younger approaches me.

"Do you know that man?" he asks.

"I don't know anyone."

"His name is Benedetto Gradenigo. He is the uncle of the noble who selected you ballot boy."

He watches to gauge the effect of his words on me. I give him as little to go on as possible.

"Keep your pretty blue eyes open," he says. "The palace is a pit of vipers."

Chapter Five

An Unwanted Crown

ANDREA CONTARINI, SIXTY-three, the only noble not present, is unanimously elected doge on the second round of voting by the final committee of forty-one. Now, a dozen nobles in stately robes board four vessels at the palace wharf. I am among them in the same boat as Admiral Vettor Pisani and the ancient Vice Doge Marco Dandolo. We set out across the lagoon to fetch the reluctant new doge.

Horses await us across the lagoon at Fusina. Everyone mounts up except me. The captain of the guard asks me if there's a problem. I tell him I've never ridden a horse. No one thought about that; they all can ride. A smug young noble on a black stallion caparisoned in silver passes me by—even his horse sneers. "Let him walk," he says.

Venerable Marco Dandolo, seated on a massive war-horse looking like an ancient prince, stern and just, says, "We can't leave him. He is the ballot boy, the guarantor of the integrity of this election. He must present the crown to his doge."

Pisani approaches. He is a general as well as an admiral—what my father might have been if he had lived long enough. "He will ride with me."

He leans forward and swings me onto his horse behind him. "Hold on," he says. "It's a long ride."

When we arrive at Contarini's farm near the village of Gambarere on the Brenta River, the delegation forms double ranks. Pisani dismounts and walks between them, through the winter-bare farm to a vineyard gate. An old laborer covered with dust pauses in his vine pruning to greet him, his hands crusty with sap and dirt. A wide-brimmed straw hat keeps the sun off his head, his tunic and leggings made of coarse country stuff.

Pisani tucks his plumed helmet under his arm and drops to one knee in obeisance.

"In the name of St. Mark and the Republic of Venice, we greet you, Serenissimo."

The old farmer is Andrea Contarini, my new boss.

"I greet you, too, cousin," he says, "but I'm afraid you have the wrong man."

Contarini looks around at the faces of the delegation. "Old friends—and a few old foes, I see—welcome to the humble farm where I pray to live out my days."

A guard hands me the gilt chest containing the doge's *corno*, the dumpling-shaped crown of woven gold studded with jewels. I offer it to Andrea Contarini.

"Put that away," he says. "It's not mine."

The delegation circles Contarini. Dust from the road covers their gaudy cloaks. They're impatient and uneasy. Marco Dandolo speaks:

"We have known one another for decades, Andrea. We have worked together, eaten together, fought together, done business together, married and buried our dead together. I deliver this crown by order of the Great Council. Allow me to escort you to St. Mark's."

Contarini smiles wearily at Dandolo. "I'd be lying if I said I wasn't expecting you, and you'd be lying if you said you didn't already know my answer. I was nominated twice before and respectfully declined both times. This time is no different. I thank you for the honor and respectfully decline once again. Find a man worthy of the job."

"You are as modest as you are wise," Dandolo says, "but you can't decline, Andrea. You have been called to service. Venice awaits you."

Pisani signals for the others to retreat. He puts his arm through Contarini's. They walk into the vineyard. Pisani signals for me to wait by the gate. I can hear every word.

"I know you don't want this job," Pisani says.

"But you don't know *how much* I don't want it."

"Everyone knows. They're all doing cartwheels because it's you and not them, and that's not just because it costs so damn much to be doge."

"My wife is dead," Contarini says sadly. "My family is grown. I have more money than I can ever spend. My refusal has nothing to do with money. I don't have the heart for the job, old friend. I never did. I'm a decent diplomat and a successful merchant who didn't squander what he inherited. The Republic trains hundreds of us each generation, some better than others. Pick a man better suited for the job."

"Who?"

Contarini blinks, frowns, and turns away. Pisani presses his case.

"It's me, remember? Vettor Pisani. You knew me as an upstart boy, your bowman of the quarterdeck. I'm not a merchant sitting on a mountain of money. I voyaged with you and fought with you. I know without a doubt that you are uncorrupted by greed. I know you prize the common good and uphold the ideals of the Republic. I can't say that with certainty about any other man in Venice."

"Simply put, I don't *want* to be doge."

"Of course you don't. Only crooks *want* to be doge. But Venice gave you this blessed and peaceful home. Venice gave you everything. You owe her."

"I have paid and paid what I owe."

"You're the stubbornest old goat in Christendom."

Contarini lays a hand on Pisani's shoulder. "Let me tell you something I've told few men on this earth. When I was a young merchant Beyond-the-Sea, our convoy was held back after Genoa had made a series of ugly attacks. I was with a beautiful fortune-teller, a witch, some said. She told me I was very wealthy and not very ambitious, which was obvious. She said I'd known many women, and there she was right again. She said she saw politics in my future, peered more deeply, grew pale, and dropped my hand. She had terror in her eyes, and she warned me never to be doge of Venice, or Venice would pay the price. She was trembling, wouldn't say another word, and fled."

"Surely you aren't putting pagan superstition before your duty as a noble?"

"Believe what you will. I've been warned. You can't change my mind."

Head bowed, hands clasped behind his back, Contarini walks back toward the delegation. Pisani follows.

"Gentlemen," Contarini says, "I am sorry you wasted your time. I must refuse."

Dandolo meets him head on. "You can't refuse."

"Alas, I have." Contarini turns back to his villa.

"Andrea Contarini," says Dandolo, "Procurator of St. Mark, and Doge Elect of the Most Serene Republic of Venice, I am charged by the Great Council to escort you to the Golden Boat at Fusina and thence in state to St. Mark's. If you do not come, you will be banished, and all you own, including this farm, will be confiscated. Refuse, and we will strip you bare."

Chapter Six

The Sixtieth Doge of Venice

WE CROSS THE lagoon from Fusina to St. Mark's on the doge's Golden Boat. She's over a hundred feet long, thirty wide and tall, made entirely of gilded wood and beaten gold. Sixty-eight oarsmen from the Arsenal in sleeveless red tunics bend their muscular arms on the lower deck. Justice, made of gold, sits on the prow holding her Sword high. Musicians in brocade tunics play silver trumpets, cymbals, and drums. Rows of nobles in red velvet robes sit under the cloth-of-gold canopy.

Contarini is still wearing his farmer's clothes. Any idiot can tell he doesn't want to be here. The grand chancellor begs a word with him.

"Wouldn't Your Exalted Serenity prefer fresh clothes?"

"This is how they found me," he growls. "This is how they get me."

The Golden Boat glides across St. Mark's Basin and moors at the palace wharf. St. Mark's Square overflows with cheering crowds cordoned by men of the Arsenal in polished leather armor. We disembark in marching order, standard-bearers first, their silk flags flapping in the wind. Then come the trumpets, cymbals, and drums. Canons of St. Mark's in white and gold robes join the line of march, the candle-bearer behind them, then the oldest of the forty-one electors, then the grand chancellor of the Republic—the only commoner besides me—and finally Andrea Contarini, the man who holds my destiny in his crabby old hands. I follow behind him. My only consolation is that he is unhappier than I am and wants his job less than I want mine.

The rest of the nobles fall in behind us. Pisani, his horse in silver armor and silk caparison, leads the procession. The lord of the Arsenal on a white stallion clears the line of march through the cheering crowd and his men restrain the crush. Bells ring everywhere. Drums beat and trumpets blare from the balconies of the Doge's Palace and St. Mark's Church, where the four bronze horses from the Imperial Hippodrome in Byzantium paw the air above the great central door.

Contarini stops abruptly in front of the church. Everyone bumps into everyone else in confusion. He sits on the church steps and takes off his sandals. He orders guards to bring him water. They fill their helmets and he washes his feet, entering St. Mark's barefoot. I follow him across the narthex. He crosses himself before stepping inside.

Sunlight floods the five golden domes, setting fire to the mosaics. The sea of bodies and candles inside heats the winter cold. Emeralds, rubies, sapphires, and diamonds blaze on the golden altar screen.

I can't see Contarini's face but I sense something happening. His gait changes. He slows. He's shuffling. I'm afraid his heart is failing. I reach out to help him, but Vendramin yanks me back.

Contarini haltingly crosses the nave alone. Vendramin takes me down a side aisle to the marble gate in front of the high altar. Contarini's face becomes visible as he approaches. His jaw eases. All the stubborn resistance drains from his face. As he nears the altar, tears run down his cheeks.

He stops, raises his arms, throws his head back and gazes into the eyes of Our Saviour in the dome high above him. He humbly strips off his tunic, shirt, and breeches. Naked, he lies face down and presses his forehead against the cool marble, arms extended, prostrate. He kisses the floor.

The vice doge, the electors, Pisani, myself, all ascend the massive porphyry pulpit on the right of the altar. Contarini stands, naked and humble, in the vast magnificence. Two Canons wrap his golden robe around him and put jeweled slippers on his feet.

He is no longer Andrea Contarini, the old farmer in dirty work clothes who lay naked on the church floor, weeping. He is the sixtieth doge of Venice.

CHEERS VOLLEY THROUGH the nave and echo across the square. Before the high altar the doge swears to defend the honor of St. Mark and protect the treasures and patrimony of the church and the fortunes of the Republic. The Admiral of the Arsenal turns to the crowd and proclaims, "This is your doge if he pleases you."

From the church, from the porch, from the square, the voice of the people roars acclamation.

The admiral takes the standard of St. Mark and hands it to the new doge, saying "We consign on your serenity the banner of Saint Mark as a sign of true and perpetual dogeship," to which the doge replies, "I accept."

The procession forms in the central aisle of the church, trumpets in the lead. I take my place in front of the doge as we march into the square. People cheer their doge in his golden splendor.

"Go with him," Vendramin says.

I climb onto the ceremonial dais on the church steps. Guards load it with heavy sacks of freshly minted gold coins stamped with Doge Contarini's likeness. The lord of the Arsenal, trumpeters, and drummers, crowd on with us. The men who rowed the Golden Boat lift the dais onto their shoulders and carry us through the throngs in the square as the doge showers them with gold coins.

Out of the corner of my eye, I see Abdul waving a silk scarf at me.

He plows through the churning crowd diving for coins. He is trying to reach me. Just as our eyes connect, the shoulder-borne platform lurches. I stumble and grip the edge, leaning as far forward as I can. Abdul fights to get closer. He slips through a gap in the bodies, trying to tell me something. He shouts, gestures, points from his eyes to mine. The crowd swerves after a new shower of coins, and I lose him.

THE PALACE ISN'T simply where the doge lives. Our government is as intricate as the cogs and gears of a great clock. The palace is the place where everything comes together, from the doge and his council down to the Committee to Regulate the Price of Melons. Randomness may be part of every process, but everything else is precisely calibrated and tightly controlled. Behind the big council chambers, the palace is a labyrinth of offices, an armory, a chancery, a torture chamber, a prison, and a kitchen, complete with shitters, storerooms, and stables.

St. Mark's Church abuts the palace. They are separate, but there's no space between them. A corridor runs from the doge's study directly into the south transept of the church. Technically, St. Mark's is the doge's personal chapel, but it's much more than that. It is the soul of the Republic, the way the palace is the brain.

The nobles fill the Great Council chamber for the coronation banquet, along with hundreds of servers, illustrious guests, musicians, and enough food and drink for an army. The windows are open because the room is stifling on this chill winter night. Fireworks explode over the basin, filling the room with a thunderous roar.

Pisani stands when the fireworks stop, lifts both hands to quiet the musicians, and raises his goblet.

"Long live Doge Andrea Contarini! Were you to live to ten thousand years, Serenissimo, Venice would be blessed."

"He hasn't seen the new oath," someone shouts. "He may change his mind."

"He can't change his mind. He can't refuse, and he can't quit. The only way he leaves is feet first."

Everyone laughs because what they say is both ridiculous and true. In the old days, if a doge grew sick and weary, he could retire to a monastery. The ink isn't dry on the new conditions written into his oath of office preventing him from ever quitting. He can be fired by his council, but he can never resign. Unlike every other office in the Republic, the dogeship is for life.

His Exalted Serenity stands and raises his goblet.

"You all know I refused this job twice and tried a third time. I never wanted it."

Laughter fills the hall. The doge waits for quiet.

"I wish to tell you with a sincere heart I was wrong."

Silence.

"I never scorned the job. On the contrary, I felt unworthy of it, inadequate to its demands. Now I understand that the greater challenging is living up to the station fate has pressed upon me, despite my unwillingness. I accept the challenge humbly, and I swear to leave Venice better than I found her."

The nobles cheer and pound their tables with their fists making the plates and silver jump.

"Like your old friend Faliero?"

The voice hurled over the din is Ruggiero Gradenigo's. The doge answers him.

"Thirty-five of forty-one electors voted for Faliero. They are sitting in this room. He fooled us all."

Ruggiero stands. "That begs the question, Exalted Serenity. What if, like him, you too prove to be nothing more than base ambition wrapped in gold?"

Many of the nobles yell at Gradenigo to shut up. Others shout them down; they want to hear the doge's answer.

The doge charges into the fray. The Great Council, the Ten, and the Senate are horrified. Princely decorum has been shattered. The doge does it anyway and doesn't stop until he is nose to nose with Ruggiero Gradenigo.

Staring directly into Ruggiero's eyes, he says, "I stood beside Faliero on the field of battle at Zara when he led 5,000 Venetians against 40,000 Hungarians and won the day, goddamn it. He was a great man that day. A hero. *Primus inter pares.* But the heads of great men can be turned as easily as the heads of rash and ignorant young fools. Electing Faliero doge was a mistake. All our mistake. We pay for it every day. Overnight, Marino Faliero became my enemy. I testified at his trial by the Ten. Those wise men gave me voice but no vote because Faliero had been my friend, and I argued to behead him. It was the right thing to do. May God keep me honest. My only earthly ambition is to uphold my oath of office. St. Mark, grant me the wisdom to know friend from foe."

"Then give him the crown," Pisani shouts, and the nobles rise, drunk, cheering. They have their doge. They want to move forward with the business of increasing their fortunes.

"Gradenigo is still mad he wasn't allowed to vote," Vendramin says to me. "The rest of the nobles aren't here to quibble. They are happy to see Andrea Contarini manacled with golden chains."

The oldest member of the Great Council, Marco Dandolo, and the youngest, Ruggiero Gradenigo, flank the doge. I stand beside Gradenigo, carrying the chest with the jeweled *corno*. Gradenigo looks at me with a hatred that haunts my dreams.

Dandolo crosses himself and puts a white linen skull cap on the doge's bald pate. Smoothing it with experienced fingers, he kisses the doge's forehead.

"Blessings, Serenissimo. A long and fruitful reign."

Ruggiero stands behind the doge, raises the gold-and-jeweled *corno* in both hands. Placing it on the doge's head, he leans forward and whispers in his ear.

"You were right the first time. You're the wrong man for the job."

Chapter Seven

The Noble in the Square

A VOLLEY OF fireworks rattles the glass, streaking the sky with color as the nobles join the party in the streets. The doge retires to bed as soon as he can. So far, we haven't spoken. He has barely looked at me. He doesn't know my name.

It's time for me to go.

I can't wear my uniform on the streets where it will attract unwanted attention. Unfortunately, Marino burned my old clothes. The *bora*, the icy north wind, blows in from far-off Russia, but my official cloak would surely give me away. I throw it on the bed and wrap myself in my blanket. To my surprise, the inside of my fancy cloak isn't fancy at all. The rich wear cloaks lined in fur or silk. Nobody wasted a penny more on mine than they had to. Gold embroidery decorates the outside. Inside out, it looks like a student's cloak.

The old man is snoring. Silver moonlight floods the portico overlooking the palace courtyard. Guards and peacekeepers are playing dice beside the open gate to the wharf. More guards cluster around the gate to the square, joking with the drunks and whores outside. I have no easy way out.

In the palace, my uniform is respected; the majesty of the doge protects me. Outside, the silver buttons are bait for pickpockets and thieves. No one must see them or recognize me. I don't know the penalty for sneaking out. I only know Vendramin warned me against it three different times. The last time, he said, "You never know what might be construed as treason."

I don't care. Four long and terrible days have passed, during which Alex has never been off my mind. I must find Abdul. I must talk to Alex. If they want to hang me between the Columns of Doom, so be it. I can't let that stop me. We swore to protect one another. Alex needs me, and if I can't help her, then I'm truly worthless.

I saw the real Alex, Alessandra Barbanegra, one time only, on Epiphany Eve, the week before the old doge died. I was in St. Nick's Square with Abdul.

"Alex is coming with her mother," he'd said. "Mother Barbanegra is making a donation of gold ducats to poor old St. Nick's."

He was playing his oud with the pick I'd made him from an egret feather; he gave the money people dropped in his hat to the neighborhood beggars. A hubbub near the bridge from Arcangelo Raffaele, the adjacent parish, interrupted him. He set his oud aside as Mother Barbanegra crossed the bridge all rigged out in furs and jewels, her face obscured by her veil.

She squeezed a boat boy's arm as she tottered on platform shoes that lifted her fourteen inches off the ground, in hopes of keeping her silks and furs out of the mud. According to Alex those stupid shoes, worn by all the richest women, were actually a plot to hobble and imprison wives and daughters. A second boat boy carried a torch in front of mother Barbanegra. A curved dagger hung from his waist. A beautiful Circassian slave walked behind Alex's mother, doing her best to support a second veiled lady wobbling on platforms. A third boat boy followed behind them. As the second veiled lady wobbled past, she blew the veil off her face and winked at me.

It was Alex.

Not the Alex who snuck out wearing boy's clothes to shoot and practice spitting. Alessandra Barbanegra, daughter of Francesco Barbanegra, known as Blackbeard, the richest merchant this side of the Grand Canal, the son of a pirate and a slave.

Their marble palace rose opposite Arcangelo Raffaele Church. Richer than most of the nobles put together, Blackbeard was bitter that he would never be noble, never sit on the Great Council. He was born too late. A hundred years earlier, before The Closing of the Great Council, he could have bought his way in. He could have easily become a nobleman.

Then the nobles changed the rules and closed the Great Council forever. In order to become a member, your father or grandfather had to have been a member. If not, the door was forever shut. Blackbeard could never meet, debate, vote, run for office, vote for the doge, or be elected doge. He paid for a game he could never play, and perpetually enraged, his only revenge was to become richer than all of them.

Alex's velvet cloak was as green as moss in a tide pool and sparkled with gold thread and glittering gemstones. Her braids wound around her head, a blond silk turban embroidered with pearls. The gold dolphin with the ruby eye hung around her neck on a golden chain. She tried whispering to me.

Staggering pain.

I saw stars.

When my eyes opened, I lay flat on my stomach with mud in my nose and mouth. Somebody kicked me aside the way they would a dead rat in a dark alley. Everything spun. Abdul helped me up. I was about to go after whoever it was that had knocked me down, but Abdul locked his right arm around my neck, the inside of his elbow against my windpipe. He wrapped his left arm behind my head and squeezed sharply. I went limp. He had to hold me up.

"He's noble." A command, not a comment. "Back away."

He dragged me into the gathering crowd. The noble didn't notice. He wasn't interested in me. He walked up to Alex, flicked back her veil, and stared into her eyes. She blushed, not because she was embarrassed; she was furious.

He acted like he owned her and everything else in the world. We didn't exist unless he needed us to do something for him. I couldn't see his face. He was ten inches taller than me and outweighed me by fifty pounds. While I was thin and hard, he was hard but not thin; muscle filled out his tights and doublet. There was nothing nice about him.

Caterina Barbanegra, Alex's mother, stepped between the noble and her daughter. She smiled at him because that was what you did when he was a noble and you were not. The awareness that he was capable of anything was knit into her brow. She stood tall and tucked Alex behind her. Ruta hid behind Alex as the boat boys closed around, chests first.

"He wants to rape her," I said to Abdul.

"Of course he wants to rape her. She's lucky her boat boys have big muscles. Plenty of other girls aren't so lucky—pretty maids and shopgirls who don't have such protection when they go out. They're helpless against a man like that. If he's caught, he'll swear he was drunk, plead guilty, say he's sorry, pay a few ducats so she can buy a husband, and get exiled to the mainland for a month or two."

As the noble whistled his way across the bridge, I glimpsed his face. The noble who laid me flat in the mud was Ruggiero Gradenigo, the youngest member of the Great Council, who would select the next ballot boy.

Chapter Eight

The Trouble with Alex

NOBODY SEES ME sneak down the marble stairs into the palace courtyard. I stay in the shadows of the portico and slip into the stables. I see no one aside from the horses. The grooms are asleep; the guards are outside.

I startle the horses; they snort and shuffle and a couple of them nicker and show me their teeth. I circle behind the stalls to the water door that opens onto the canal behind the palace. I can get to the wharf from the water stairs, but I see a man's outline. I can't tell if he sees me. I sink into the shadow and watch. He is about my age, slightly taller, with shaggy brown hair, broad shoulders, and a sweet, simple face. He looks around, sees no one, pulls a fist-sized wooden flute out of his belt and begins to play a sad little tune. The horses' ears stand at attention. As they listen, they relax to the familiar sound. When someone shouts for him, he shoves the flute into his belt and runs from the stable.

I check twice, three times, to make sure no one else can see me before I step out onto the water stairs. With my back flat against the cold stone wall, I tread a narrow ledge to the wharf. My cloak is inside out; I pull the hood over my head, hiding as much of my face as possible, and am now covered from head to my ankles. Only my shoes show, and no one is likely to notice them in the dark. I circle behind the Columns of Doom and around St. Mark's Square, taking Merchant's Lane toward Rialto Bridge, observing every cranny, etching the map in my head.

The Grand Canal separates Venice in two parts and Rialto Bridge is the only way across. A massive wooden structure with a drawbridge at the apex, the bridge allows ships with masts to pass. I exit on the Rialto side just as the *realtina* rings, the bell of San Giovanni Elemosinario, signaling the third hour of the night, the beginning of curfew, warning everyone to clear the streets and extinguish all unauthorized fires. Ever since the Faliero conspiracy, the Ten has authorized the lords of the night and the peacekeepers to detain and question anyone on the streets after curfew. Swords and other arms are strictly forbidden. To avoid the police, I use the dark back lanes to St. Nick's.

Mama screams when she opens the door and sees me. "My beautiful boy."

She grabs me and hugs me so tight that I can't speak. She's laughing and crying, kissing my face and burying hers in my neck. She is as beautiful as ever, her eyes feverishly bright and tired-looking. Everyone in St. Nick's says I look like her, although I don't see it. Mama pinches my cheeks. "You are still as pretty as the blue-eyed cherub above the altar at St. Nick's."

"Stamped from the same mold," Pierluigi used to say, "your mother and you. Hard to say which one's prettier." I've always been several thumbs shorter than the other boys my age, a shrimp, too pretty and too short, and they never let me forget it. I gave as good as I got each time they called mama a slut, but I was always outnumbered, and they'd throw me into the sewage canal for laughs.

"Oh, I could eat you up!" She ruffles my hair and pinches my cheeks and catches a glimpse of the embroidered velvet cloak. She fingers the stitching and the silver buttons, runs her hands up and down my woolen leggings.

"Mama, I can't stay. I came for some of my old clothes."

"Old clothes. What for? These are so beautiful."

"Please, Mama. Get me my clothes."

"You're not in trouble, are you?"

"No, Mama. Clothes, please."

She fetches my work clothes, laundered and neatly folded. They're stiff from drying in the sun and smell the way clothes should, like laundry day in St. Nicholas of the Beggars, shirts and sheets and breeches flapping in the wind. I put on my old cap; the smell of the salt marsh brings tears to my eyes.

I put my clothes in a sack and sling it over my back and see a man who has been silently sitting in the shadows looking suspiciously comfortable. He smiles nervously. Mama remembers he's there and claps her hands.

"You remember Giasone? He works on boats near San Trovaso Square. We went to watch the fireworks, and then he brought me home."

"*Salve*, Giasone." I nod in his direction.

He's tongue-tied. Mama laughs and puts her arm through my mine.

"He's nervous," she whispers. "You're important now. You dine with the doge."

She sits on Giasone's lap and spreads my cloak across their knees.

"Golden thread and silver buttons," she murmurs.

"What's it like in the palace?" Giasone asks.

"I'd rather be here."

He thinks I'm joking. I grab the cloak, flip it inside out and put it back on.

"You're leaving?" Mama's smile turns into a frown. "So soon? You just got here. Sit. I made fritelle. Your favorite. Eat fritelle with us."

"I have to go, Mama."

I sound stern, and she backs off because I'm important now.

"I just wanted to get these clothes," I say. "And make sure you're all right."

"You're too important for a proper visit?"

She pinches my cheek the way she always did when I was being a brat.

"I have to go, Mama."

"I cry every night," she says. "Ask Giasone. I pray you will become a great man. The Virgin still smiles on you."

She wipes her tears and won't let go of me. I push her away to get out the door.

My footsteps echo in the empty streets. Crossing the bridge to Arcangelo Raffaele, I hear only the murmur of the tide. I see no lights in Barbanegra palace. The canal façade, two floors of arches and arcades of Istrian marble styled after the Doge's Palace, outshines the homes of all but the richest nobles. I walk back and forth along the canal, unable to see inside. The gates are locked; the courtyard is deserted. If I shout, I'll wake the whole parish. Disappointed, I keep moving.

Abdul is on the roof terrace of his master's house, playing his oud. I climb the familiar gnarly vine, eyes up because if I look down, vertigo engulfs me.

"I can hardly believe it!" Abdul rubs his eyes in wonder, sets his oud aside, and hugs me. "So good to see you, old man."

"What happened to Alex?"

"Very bad," he says. "Mother Barbanegra was waiting in the courtyard with the Circassian slave, Ruta, Blackbeard's mistress. She didn't recognize Alex, but Ruta knew all along that Alex was sneaking out and never let on. They have an agreement because Alex knows Ruta is her father's mistress, so they keep their secrets. At first, Mother Barbanegra thought Alex was a beggar boy. When she realized who the beggar boy was she went berserk. She beat Ruta, locked her in a storeroom and locked Alex in her bedroom."

"Does Blackbeard know?"

"No. He is in Ancona, for the grain. Mother Barbanegra is afraid he might kill them both when he gets back."

"I have to see Alex."

"Not possible, my friend. She's under lock and key. When it's possible to see her, I'll chalk a blue cross on the lion pillar."

Chapter Nine

Learning to Read and Write

"WHO DID GENOA send to Constantinople to bargain for Tenedos?" the doge asks.

The island of Tenedos is a constant thorn in his side. It guards the entrance to the Hellespont and the Black Sea beyond. He can't allow it to fall to Genoa, our greatest rival on the seas, at the risk of losing the Black Sea trade, and right now, Genoa is courting the emperor in Constantinople for rights to Tenedos.

"Luciano Doria," I say.

"Write it down."

"I'll remember, Serenissimo. I'm not like you. I don't need to write it down."

"For God's sake, just write it down."

He crackles with annoyance. Stony, he brooks no sass.

"I don't know how to write, Serenissimo."

"What do you mean you don't know how to write?"

"I mean I don't know how. Nobody in my parish writes, except the priest."

I just handed him all the ammunition he'll ever need to shoot me down. He does every chance he gets. I think he hates me. He's always peeved at everything, at his own life, so my life is shit.

"Can you read?" he asks.

"No, Serenissimo."

"What *can* you do?"

"I can hit a flying duck with my crossbow. I can row around Torcello and back without stopping. I know the stars and how they move."

"I don't eat duck, Torcello gives me hives, and I don't give a fig for the stars right now."

Marino Vendramin sits by the door reading, pretending to pay no attention to us. I'm on my own with His Exalted Serenity, and he's in a snit. I never know what to expect with him. Most of the time, he says nothing. I'm invisible. Or he glances at me suspiciously. At meetings and ceremonies, he prompts me with what to do next the way a hunter trains a dog. But more and more, he has come to rely on my memory, which is useful to him. I'm not sure he even remembers my name. I don't care. He's old. He can't live that much longer. The doge is quiet for a while, thinking.

"Who was your father?" he asks.

"I don't know."

"I see."

"He was a bowman. He died Beyond-the-Sea."

The doge looks across the room, halfway between me and nowhere. If he feels sorry for me, it's only for the blink of an eye. At least he's not glaring any more. He looks sad.

"How do you like palace life so far?"

The question shocks me. I don't know the answer because I don't trust him.

"It's fine, Serenissimo."

"Fine. That's it? *Fine*?"

"I don't know what you want me to say."

"The truth."

"I miss my mother."

"We all miss our mothers."

"I miss my friends."

"At least you have friends."

"Most of the time I'm bored."

"How can you possibly be bored?"

"I count ballots. I count them before the election to make sure we have the right number and during the election to see the outcome. After the election, I make sure all the ballots have the proper markings and weren't pulled out of someone's sleeve. When I'm not counting ballots, I march in processions. I miss rowing and fishing and shooting targets with my friends. I miss Mama's *fritelle* and laughing at her stupid jokes. I want my life back."

"I can't say I don't understand what you mean," he says with half a smile. "Unfortunately, this *is* your life now. You don't just march in processions and count ballots. You guard against treason and help steady the course of the Republic."

"Can't you find someone who wants this job?"

"What we want, either of us, doesn't amount to a bucket of fish guts."

Not exactly what I want to hear.

"We're Venetians," the doge says. "This is your job. You do it because it's yours. You can be great, or you can be worthless. That's up to you. But mark my words. Fate has opened doors for us that few mortals ever see. If you can't appreciate that, you're a hopeless fool."

"You don't want your job, Serenissimo. I heard what the fortune-teller said. Now we're all doomed."

For a heartbeat, I think he might hit me. I know the look. He shakes his finger at me the same way Pierluigi would when I messed up.

"Your problem," he says, "is that you know nothing. Because you know nothing, you understand nothing. Nothing at all. We're up to our necks in alligators, and I'm trying to teach you to swim."

"I know how to swim, Serenissimo."

"I don't care what you think you know. Listen and understand. Do you think you can do that?"

"Try me, sir."

"Marino, for God's sake, teach him something."

MARINO STARTS WITH the alphabet. He recites it once, and I remember it and say it back to him, forward and backward. He looks shocked and pleased. We start Latin.

Sum, es, est, sumus, estes, sunt.

Hic, haec, hoc, huius, huius, huius.

More memorizing. Read, pronounce, store in memory.

"Is the doge still mad at me?"

"He doesn't have time to be mad at you."

"He sounds mad to me."

"He's annoyed."

"I'm not important enough to be mad at. I'm just annoying. Why am I still here?"

"Fortune chooses. We do what we must."

He fetches a clean sheet of paper, writes something, and pronounces it slowly.

Forsan et haec olim meminisse iuvabit.

"From book one of Virgil's *Aeneid*. Aeneas and his crew barely escape with their lives from the burning ruins of their beloved Troy, defeated and destroyed by the confederation of Greeks. A violent storm hurls them onto the alien shores of Carthage. Stripped of every hope, ruined and dejected, Aeneas must say something to hearten his despairing troops. He tells them *one day even this memory will amuse you.*"

I recite it back to him.

He reads, "*Arma virumque cano, Troiae qui primus ab oris Italiam, fato profugus, Laviniaque venit litora...*"

And I recite that back to him, too, word for word, as if I'd always known it.

"How do you do that?" he asks.

"I don't know. I just do."

I take a fresh parchment and start copying. He watches, ready to criticize my letters or the way I hold the quill.

The *Marangona*, the big bell in the tower on St. Mark's Square, starts tolling when it shouldn't.

"What is that?"

Marino remembers something, grabs a napkin from the table, and throws it at me.

"Follow me. Quickly. You can use the napkin to cover your nose and mouth."

Chapter Ten

The Chamber of Torment

THE NOBLES JOSTLE for position at the windows of the Great Council chamber. Others fill the open porticos outside. Every eye is focused between the Columns of Doom. Hay, sticks, and logs are piled high under a wooden platform. The crowd is solid from the palace to the ends of the square. Guards with halberds corral the people. Marino covers his nose and mouth with his sleeve.

Plainchant comes from the direction of the palace dungeon. This is no ordinary procession. It's a death march. Monks in black robes with black masks over their faces chant the "*Dies Irae.*" Day of wrath. Behind them, guards drag what's left of a man. His back, chest, and hands are matted with gore and dried blood. The crowd along the wharf spits at him and jeers.

"What did he do?"

"He's a sodomite," Marino says.

As the priests chant, the executioners chain him to the stake. They throw water on him to make sure he's awake. The priest denounces him in Latin and lights the hay with a torch. The twigs flare. The logs flame. The sodomite is engulfed in fire. His screams are unearthly. The smoke spreads and people flee the smell. We run back into the palace. I'm shaking.

"The judgment was properly delivered by the Forty," Marino assures me. "The Forty argued the case. It was touchy because it happened in the palace. Benedetto, the sodomite, was one of our clerks. He seduced Antonio, a page of thirteen years, gave him two *denari* to engage in unspeakable acts, which went on for two years. One of their trysts occurred by the Great Council chamber. At trial, the boy was very touching and was given a small fine; only the active partners are burned. The boy wept and pleaded, trying to convince the court that *he* was the active partner and the man, Benedetto, was passive, which is absurd on the face of it. Nobody could expect the Forty to believe a grown man would allow himself to be degraded by a boy."

"What if the boy was telling the truth?"

"He wasn't. He recanted after seeing the Chamber of Torment. Have you ever been there?"

"No."

"Then you must. You're dangerously pretty. Consider this a caution."

He's smiling, but he's deadly serious. I don't understand what he means. I'm me. I've grown some and my leggings are too tight. Otherwise, nothing about me is noteworthy.

"You probably think you're ordinary," Marino says, "maybe even ugly, or perhaps a little deformed. Trust me, you're not. You have generated quite a bit of interest in palace circles."

"I don't understand."

"You will. And please, beware. Beauty gives you great power if you know how to use it. Great, but fleeting. If you choose to use it, use it well, and whatever you do, don't give it away lightly."

I don't know what he's talking about, and I don't want to. We go through the hall of the lords of the night to a low stone chamber with a table and several chairs. The table has quills, ink and unruly piles of parchment that Marino flips through.

"Torture is never undertaken lightly," he says. "At least four of the six lords of the night have to authorize it and then act as witnesses. Any of the peacekeepers—who are commoners—showing a special aptitude are trained in the arts of torment. They get excellent pay and bonuses, although they often end up in the lunatic asylum."

He points to a long parchment with his ink-stained finger. "Every single thing that happens here is recorded in detail. That is the transcript of the interrogation of the sodomite. It hasn't been sent to the doge yet. Since it's in Latin, we can make it one of your lessons."

He raises his eyebrows, question marks, but I don't want what it says etched in my memory. I push it aside. Marino opens the door to the Chamber of Torment, and I gag on its sick breath. The walls sweat pain and death. Low fires molder in pits. There's barely enough light to see. My knees go wobbly.

"One look changes many a mind," Marino says.

Before entering, he gathers his robe and lifts it off the floor.

"This isn't the easiest place to keep clean. Watch your sleeves."

He takes a torch from the doorway and holds it high. Ropes, hooks, and winches hang from the stone vaults. Metal cages dangle above sunken firepits. The rack and wheel are cloaked in shadow. He sees me eying a table covered with all manner of implements.

"Flaying knives," he says. "They peel the skin off face and body. That's a tongue tearer, and these are breast rippers, to tear women's breasts off. The crocodile shears"—he holds them up—"tear off a man's appurtenance. The one that looks like a tiger's claw is called a Sicilian Tickler; it rips meat off bone. The head crusher makes crushing the human skull as easy as cracking an egg."

Marino swings the torch around, but I no longer have the heart look. I turn and run.

Chapter Eleven

Returning the Dolphin

A SOUND DRIFTS down, faint and distant. The kind of tune a shepherd plays alone at night under the stars. I think maybe it's the groom, but it's not coming from the stable, but from higher up, over my head, from the attic prison.

No sunlight penetrates the lead-roofed attic; the only light is from torches where the corridors intersect. The cell doors are short, the stout timbers sealed with iron locks. I don't know who is inside. I follow the tune to the end of the corridor. The groom hunches over his flute under a window. He stops playing when he sees me.

"Why are you playing up here?" I ask.

"I don't bother anybody up here, and nobody bothers me."

He is ordinary to look at, but his playing isn't. He pipes a happy dance and smiles. His eyes are as lively as his tune. I like him, and I don't know why.

I sit down beside him. "I'm Nico."

"I know who you are."

"Who are you?"

"Matteo Bellacqua of San Giobbe parish."

"Where did you get the flute?"

"My ma gave it to me. It belonged to her uncle."

"Who taught you to play?"

"She showed me where to put my fingers. I taught myself the rest."

"How did you learn the tunes?"

"I make them up. I let the music take me away."

His eyes are brown, his lashes amazingly long. He seems open and honest with nothing to hide, unlike everyone else in the palace.

"I wish something would take me away," I say.

He lowers his voice and looks me in the eye.

"I saw you sneak out," he says. "Don't worry. I can keep secrets. I used to sneak out, but nobody cared about me. I'm just a groom. You're different. The thing is, I'm not the only one who saw you..."

"Who else saw?"

"A noble, for sure. His hood was up. I couldn't see his face."

He warns me the way a friend would. I want to trust him, then I remember the first thing Marino said: trust no one.

"Did you see the burning?" he asks.

I nod.

He scratches his head and shifts uneasily. "Do you know what sodomy is?"

"It's when you put your sword in the wrong scabbard."

He nods.

"Ever wonder why they burn you for that?" he asks.

"Because it offends God."

"They don't burn you for murder, and God hates that. It doesn't make sense..."

"You're right."

A frown clouds his sweet easiness. "Is wanking sodomy?"

"It's a sin," I say, "but they don't burn you for it."

He laughs and claps his hands. "Thank you, God, Creator of the Universe, because I'd surely burn."

"I've got to go." I stand up and brush off my uniform. "Thanks for the warning."

"You'd do the same for me, right?"

He's plays a jaunty flourish.

"Come by the stable," he says. "We can play cards or something."

One thing is certain: I have to be more careful.

His tune stays with me all the way to Santa Margherita Square. I'm wearing my own clothes, with my fancy cloak turned inside out. I whistle for Abdul outside the apothecary's shop. Two beggars are out front. One is missing a leg; the other is blind. They have a hat for coins between them.

Abdul comes out and bows politely to the beggars. "Greetings, esteemed gentlemen."

"Greetings to you, honorable exile," says the beggar with one leg. He turns to me. "To us, he's an exile, not a slave."

"We're all exiles," Abdul says. "Exiles from paradise."

Abdul drops a handful of coins into their hat. The beggar's smiles are as bright as the coins, and they heap blessings on him.

Alex's room is in the back of Barbanegra palace, atop a corner tower. From the lane behind the palace, we see light in her window. Abdul whistles like a quail, waits a breath, then repeats it. Alex returns the call.

"Is she coming down?"

"How silly palace life has made you. You must climb up to the window."

He holds out his hand for a rope slowly snaking down the brick wall. It's knotted at intervals with a hangman's noose at the end.

"I snuck it to her," Abdul says. "When I brought her mother's medicine."

He holds out the noose. "Foot in the loop. Grab the first knot and climb."

The boys in my parish climb bell towers on a dare. I can't. I'm strong from rowing; I lift my own weight easily; I can outshoot anyone, but heights and edges make me dizzy. First my palms get sweaty, and then I break out in a cold panic. Abdul knows this.

"I can't."

"Do you have a better idea?"

"I'm not kidding."

"Hand over hand," he says. "Just don't look down, whatever you do."

I want to climb. Bowmen have to climb masts. I know all that. I want to, but I know what happens every time. I slap the rope away.

"I'll die."

"I sympathize, old man. The thing is, if you want to see Alex, there's only one way in and out. Keep your eyes on her, and you won't get dizzy."

The rope is tucked into the shadow of the chimney. My heart is beating so loudly I can't believe it doesn't wake the entire neighborhood. I grip the rope so tightly it burns.

Then I close my eyes and pull myself up, hand over hand. That part is easy. I stop for breath, then hoist myself up another three knots.

Alex leans out her window. Her hair hangs around her face; her eyes blaze like beacons. I feel the power of her will, and I'm not afraid. Her eyes draw me up.

Abdul whistles—a quick, piercing note. A warning. I freeze midway up the rope.

I can't go up, and I can't go down.

Alex steps back from the window so no one can see her. Her eyes no longer suspend me. I hear only water rippling below. The footsteps echo. I can't stop myself.

I look down.

Vertigo. I shut my eyes against the sickening spirals in my stomach. I can't hold on. If I lose my grip, I will smash on the paving stones below. I will die. I suck in air and blow it out the way Abdul taught me. In. Out. I can't move. I can't swing. I can't slip out of the shadow. The rope cuts into my hands. I tilt my head back.

Blessed Virgin and St. Nick, help me. Please!

Abdul whistles the all clear.

I open my eyes. Alex is back in the window. Her eyes lock on mine and hold me steady as I pull myself up the rope. She helps me over the windowsill into her room. I have never been so happy to see anyone. She squeezes me, and her tears dampen my cheek. I want to kiss her, but I don't. She puts her finger across my lips to silence me.

She hasn't slept. Dark circles ring her bloodshot eyes. Her hair hasn't been brushed in days. Her clothes look slept in. Even her fingernails are dirty. I put my arms around her and rock her gently.

She says, "Thank God Papa's still away. He doesn't know anything."

"How much does your mother know?"

"I swore to her I only snuck out one time. She pretends to believe me because that makes is easier for her. Papa won't be so easy to convince."

"Will she tell him?"

"Not if she can help it."

I close my eyes and rest my head on her shoulder.

"I have to escape," she says.

"Where will you go?"

"Anywhere."

"But you can't."

"That doesn't mean I don't want to."

She laughs, happy I'm here. She rubs my hand in hers and watches me.

"What's wrong, Nico?"

"Nothing, now."

"Liar. You know I can tell."

"I saw a man burned between the Columns of Doom."

"Who was burned?"

"A herald."

"Why?"

"For sodomy. The boy got off. He's my age. He told the lord of the night that they were burning the wrong man, but they wouldn't believe him. Do you understand? He was willing to burn to save the other man. Why would he do that?"

"Love?"

"That's not possible."

"Why not?"

"Men can't love men like that."

"Who says?"

"The priests. And the lawyers."

"They say all kinds of stupid things. They say women can't be priests or lawyers, for one thing. Men have always loved other men. King David loved Jonathan."

"It's an unspeakable crime against nature."

"How can love be against nature?"

"It's the worst sin there is."

"The worst sin is burning a man for loving another man. Love is a gift from God."

"A gift with a lot of rules."

"But God didn't make the rules," she said. "The priests and lawyers did. Anyway, rules never stop anyone from doing anything. They didn't stop the martyrs from worshipping Christ when our religion was against Roman law. The law was wrong."

"I wish you were doge."

"They'd cut my head off."

She makes me laugh. She always makes me laugh.

"I almost forgot. I brought you something." I reach into the leather pouch strapped to my belt, press the gold dolphin with the ruby eye into her hand, and close her fingers around it. "I caught the thief and got it back. No one else ever saw it."

She smiles at it like it's an old friend she hasn't seen in a long time. "My father gave this to me; he bought it in Crete. They said it's from Byzantium. Dolphins protect ships and sailors."

Alex kisses it and then puts it around my neck. "Wear it always. To keep you safe."

She tucks it into my shirt and taps it against my heart. Then she kisses her fingertips and presses them to my lips.

I STAYED TOO long, and by the time I'm down the rope, it's almost dawn. I have to get through Rialto and over the bridge, past the peacekeepers and the thugs and the lords of the night, and sneak back into the palace.

Venetian streets are crowded during the day but empty after curfew, except near the Rialto. There, the taverns and alleys around the bridge and the markets are filled with foreigners, crusaders coming or going, pilgrims, thieves, prostitutes, freelance oarsmen, jobless workers, soldiers of fortune for hire with no place to sleep and not a penny in their pockets. I avoid the main routes even though they're quicker. The back lanes are muddy, the squares hardly wide enough for a wellhead. Here and there, dingy oil lamps flicker. The alleys all look the same in the dark. Rats skitter along the canals.

The lane twists over three bridges to San Polo, the big square where bulls and bears are baited and slaughtered during Carnival. This is the oldest part of town. Buildings engulf the streets, and streets run through buildings. The square is deserted. An altar to the Virgin burns kitty-corner from me. I wish I had flowers; the posy at her feet is dead.

Voices.

Two men near the center of the square.

I sneak as close as I can to hear what they're saying.

"They were nobles, and they got a month in jail and a fifty-ducat fine."

"Fifty ducats! That's more than I make a year!"

"The mucky-mucks are worried if they go easy on nobles, all the little people will be sorry we let them cut Faliero's head off and do something about it."

Peacekeepers. Commoners hired by the lords of the night to patrol the streets and bust up brawls.

The doge will wake up in an hour. I crouch behind the wellhead and dash to the far side of the trees. I'm halfway across when I startle a bevy of sleeping doves. They burst from the tree in a flurry of wings. The peacekeepers veer and see me. They circle, one in front, the other behind, and grab me.

"Where you running to?"

"Home."

"Which parish?"

"St. Mark's. I'm no crook, honest. Please let me go."

"What's the rush?"

"If I'm not there before first light, my granddad will tan my hide. I'm not out late, honest. I'm up early."

That gives them a good laugh.

"Let's haul him in. See how long it takes for someone to come looking for him."

"Please don't arrest me."

"Fine. Where do we take you?"

If I lie, they'll find out soon enough.

"The Doge's Palace."

"Come again?"

"The Doge's Palace."

They laugh.

"I'm the ballot boy."

"I'm Murad the Turk. Glad to meet you."

"The Senate elections start in four hours. If I'm not there, they can't vote."

I open my cloak. It doesn't take them long to recognize the embroidered lions and silver buttons.

Chapter Twelve

Quid Pro Quo

THEY TAKE ME to the lord of the night, who rousts Marino, who carries on as if I stabbed him in the back. The three of us file upstairs to the doge's apartment. Our footsteps echo down the long corridor. It's like walking to the gallows. I'm not scared when Marino knocks on the door of the doge's study. I'm glad it's over with.

"Enter," he shouts from inside. He's annoyed. This is the only time he has to himself all day, and he's not happy about being disturbed.

Marino slips in alone and closes the door behind him. I can't hear them, but I know what he's saying. The doge shouts something and throws the door open. The gold robe of state slips haphazardly off his shoulders and the white linen skullcap is askew over a storm cloud of eyebrows. He's not the doge I know; he's an angry Neptune carved in hard gray stone.

The lord of the night awaits his orders. Marino is about to say something, but the doge silences him with one glance.

"Leave us alone," he says. "Both of you."

Marino looks surprised. "Both of us, Serenissimo?"

"And shut the door behind you."

Marino and the lord of the night bow deeply. They back out of the room and shut the door. I'm alone with the doge for the first time.

"What the hell were you thinking?"

"I had to see my mother."

"In the dead of night. Wearing our cloak. Even you aren't that stupid."

"Am I a prisoner?"

"As much as I am. Do you see me sneaking out after curfew?"

"You're the doge."

"And you're the ballot boy. That was settled forever on election day. You can't sneak away from it. Try to think and act like a man of consequence. Otherwise, you render yourself useless at best, dangerous at worst. Now tell me the truth. Where did you go?"

"To see my mother."

"Why didn't you ask my permission?"

"You were busy."

"Bullshit. You were afraid to ask me."

"I wasn't afraid. I don't trust you."

His face, his posture, his color all change.

"Thank you," he says. "That's the first honest thing you've said."

He rubs his temples.

"I've been hard on you," he says. "I admit it. Yours isn't an easy job. Yours or mine. But nothing worthwhile is easy."

He tugs his gold robe tighter around his shoulders.

"I had to pay for this robe myself," he says. "They wrote it into my oath: One cloth-of-gold robe at *his own expense*. It cost more than most men make in a lifetime. They think I'm a lot richer than I am. And it's damn heavy."

"Why do you wear it all the time?"

"To get my money's worth. Follow me."

We exit through his private corridor, and I follow him up to the prison. The ceiling is so low the doge has to stoop. The stones are black with mold. He grabs a torch from its bracket and lights the way.

The black icicles hanging from the vaults are bats. When the corridor dead-ends, he kicks open a low door and mounts the torch on the wall inside.

"Men can be locked away here and forgotten forever," he says. "Adversaries, enemies, traitors, sometimes innocent victims, even the doge himself. We're playing a deadly game, you and I, and I don't think you grasp just how dangerous it is."

"I do, Serenissimo."

"No, you don't. But you will. This was Faliero's cell. He made a fatal mistake and paid with his head. He and I worked together; we travelled together as ambassadors. Arguing in favor of cutting off his head was the most difficult thing I ever had to do. But he went bad, like a rabid dog. And he knew it. At trial, he didn't try to defend himself. He confessed and requested the axe. When men in our position fall, our heads land directly on the chopping block."

He pauses to gather his thoughts, no longer angry but deadly grave.

"I apologize for the danger we've placed you in," he says, voice calm. "But no life worth living is free of danger. It may well be more dangerous *inside* these walls than out. The difference is, we can do something about it. It's our job."

"I understand, sir."

"Do you? I wonder. Marino tells me, soon, your Latin will be better than his. You've become a lot more than an illiterate boy who can shoot ducks on the wing and row around Torcello. You're apt and quick and, by all signs, unmercifully smart. Maybe I misjudged you. And maybe you misjudged me.

"I know one thing with certainty. I can give you orders. I can move you around the board. But I can only command your hands, not your heart, your routine, not your loyalty. You can help or hinder me in the great work that lies ahead. We are surrounded by enemies. Hell, our friends are enemies. I need to know where you stand, boy. Answer me one question, and I will know."

"Then ask me anything."

"How do you get in and out of the palace?"

"I sneak out through the stable, if no one is around. Out the water door, down the ledge to the wharf. Getting back isn't as easy. Obviously."

"I'm going to show you something."

He crouches through the door and steps into the corridor. He opens a door on the left and thrusts in his torch. The stairway is too steep and dark to see the bottom. The steps are stone blocks two feet high.

"There's a door to the square down there," he says. "Very secret. This corridor is considered bad luck because of Faliero. Now and then, someone comes on a dare. Otherwise, no one comes at all. You can use it to get in and out of the palace."

"Thank you, Serenissimo."

I kneel and kiss his hand.

"Not so fast," he says. "This isn't a gift. It's a quid pro quo. You must agree to my terms, otherwise this door will be sealed until the day I die."

"What must I do?"

"Be faithful, loyal, and true. Never betray me. Can you swear to that?"

"I'm not sure what you're asking, sir."

"I am asking for your oath to protect and defend me. In return, I can make you a man of consequence history will remember. Are you with me?"

"My allegiance is to the Republic."

"As is mine. There's no contradiction. Hold out your hand."

He fumbles inside his robe, pulls out a gold ring, and slips it on my right index finger. Justice sits beside the Lion of St. Mark. A ducal banner flies over them.

"This will get you out of trouble. Do you swear to be faithful, loyal, and true?"

I don't swear because I want the secret door to stay open. I swear because he treats me like I'm worth something, and he means it. He says he can make me a man of consequence, someone beyond anything I could ever have dreamed. His words touch me and inspire me to be better than I imagined possible, but not better than my mother dreamed all along.

Chapter Thirteen

A Bull's-eye

THE DOGE WATCHES me practice my handwriting.

"*Dulce et decorum est pro patria mori*," he reads over my shoulder. "To die for your country is a sweet duty. Am I correct, Marino?"

"I'm sure that's what Horace meant, Serenissimo," Marino says.

"You're making progress," the doge says to me. "We will civilize you yet. I think it's time for me to meet your mother."

Marino and I look at him with similar expressions of horror for entirely different reasons. I'm wondering how many ways Mama can find to say the wrong things; Marino has a different set of worries.

"Perhaps she could approach during one of the processions, Serenissimo," Marino says. "We can pause, and Nico could present her to you."

"No. I want her to come here, to the Palace."

"You can't invite a common woman as a personal guest."

"This boy is in my personal charge. We pay his mother fifty ducats a year for the privilege of employing his services. I wish to meet her. It's good stewardship. End of discussion."

"Where would you meet her?" Marino asks. "Where we entertain ambassadors? With your council, or with the Great Council, or perhaps the Ten?"

"Of course not."

"What do you mean, *of course not*?"

"I mean in my own apartment. The boy, his mother, and I."

"Out of the question!"

"You can be there, too, if that makes it legal," the doge says.

"Why do you pretend you don't know the rules? You reread your oath every night. In any case, it will have to be cleared with your council."

"Don't breathe a word to them. We'll apologize after."

Serenissimo turns to me and says, "We are inviting your mother to visit us, here, in our home, Sunday next, after Mass and before the Great Council meeting."

He retreats into his study, and Marino tries to resume my Latin lesson, but he can't. He is as distraught as I've ever seen him.

"Stubborn old goat." Marino pushes aside our parchments. "He's going to get himself beheaded."

"For meeting my mother?"

"For compromising himself and you and me and his exalted office."

He can tell from my expression I don't understand. He rifles around on the table for a sheet of paper, dips his quill in ink, and draws a triangle.

"This is the Republic."

He draws lines to divide the triangle into segments. In the segment at the base, he writes something. "The Great Council," he says, "the nobles of Venice."

Next, he writes in the narrower segment above the Great Council. "This is the Senate, eighty nobles selected by the Great Council, who deliberate upon policies and laws."

In the still narrower segment above the Senate, he writes again. "The Forty," he says, "the high court which enforces the laws, also elected by the Great Council."

In the narrowest top segment, he writes again. "The Doge's Council, whose only function is to counsel and restrain the doge, hence the saying, 'the doge may die, but the council lives on,' which puts the doge in his place."

He circles the point atop the triangle. "And that is our doge, who embodies the state and expresses the will of the Republic at the expense of his own. It looks very neat, doesn't it?"

Before I can say anything, he tears the paper to bits and scrambles the bits on the tabletop. He scoops them into a pile and drops the last, smallest piece—the apex of the pyramid, our doge—on top, then turns a sour look at me while fingering the torn paper. "*This* is how it really is, and then some. And each of these committees superintends subsidiary committees that conduct specific business, and every noble in Venice circulates from committee to committee to committee, and every term of office is limited to a month, three months, a year, two years at most. The most powerful nobles circulate through the most powerful committees, in and out again, because none is allowed more than one term in any position before being voted into another committee, and then another, and another. The rule is—two terms out of any committee before you can go back in. All except the doge, whose term is a life sentence atop this whirligig designed to prevent conspiracy, sedition, cabals within committees, and treachery in our ranks."

He plucks a blank bit of paper, pens an X in the center, and lays it on top of the doge.

"This is the Ten," he says, "the most feared and the most powerful of all the committees, whose sole purpose is to halt or punish treachery. And like all the other committees they circulate in and out, the most powerful of the powerful, out and in. They alone have the power to axe a doge or traitorous noble, yet they are no more permanent than the Senate or the Forty or the Doge's Council, despite wielding the power of life and death over them all and themselves. If Serenissimo displeases them, or worries the Senate, or defies the Forty, or for private and secret reasons never disclosed, the Ten can lay his neck on the chopping block as they have done before and will again, if sufficiently provoked. Entertaining guests outside the company of his council is expressly forbidden; he is not allowed to meet alone with private individuals. Ergo, he is risking everything, and for what? You visit your mother anyway. He knows it. I know it. I don't understand this foolishness. What's his point, other than pulling the tiger's tail?"

He stares down at his hands.

"Maybe he thinks he owes it to my mother to let her see I'm in good hands."

"Can't you hear how ridiculous that sounds? She is nothing. She counts for nothing. You are in the safekeeping of the Republic, not of the doge. She is a commoner of the lowest rank. No one knows who she knows, what she might be up to, what trouble she could cause. And every member of the Great Council, the Senate, the Forty, and—Blessed Virgin protect us—the Ten, will have an opinion, some fatal to him."

"I think he's just trying to be nice."

Marino sweeps the parchment tatters off the table.

"If that's so, then he's not just foolish, he's mad."

THE FOLLOWING SUNDAY, we wait in the doge's ante-chamber. I'm in uniform. Serenissimo still wears his gold robe and biretta after the morning Mass. Marino waits at the water door to bring Mama up the back stairs to the doge's apartment.

She is dressed simply and looks beautiful; she has much experience making herself look good without spending money. Her cloak is velvet and her earrings are new. She has twined purple silk ribbon and pink blossoms in her hair. She stands in the doorway, pale and trem-bling, a fragile-looking woman, twenty-six years old. Marino prompts her to bow. She doesn't know what to say.

"You didn't tell me your mother was so beautiful," Serenissimo says.

I take Mama's hand and present her to Serenissimo. He smiles, the gentlest smile I've seen on his lips, and she smiles back, her fear melting into charm.

"Address me as Serenissimo," he says to her. "Every-one else does. We're going to be informal."

Marino sits by the door, pretending to read, watching and listening. He looks like an unseen hand is shoving spikes under his fingernails.

Mama barely manages to speak. "As you wish, Serenissimo."

She flashes the smile that vanquishes men high and low, and Serenissimo blushes. His eyes linger upon hers.

"What did you bring?" he asks, noting the large sack she has dragged in behind her.

"I brought my darling boy his favorite things."

She pushes the bag toward me. I take it, and it's heavy. I can feel the crossbow.

"These belonged to his father." She addresses Serenissimo, not looking at him.

I open the sack, take out the crossbow, and show it to him.

"Is this the weapon you shoot flying ducks with?"

"Yes, Serenissimo."

He reaches for the bow, examines it closely, feels it, hefts it, and hands it back.

"It's a beautiful weapon. What else is in the bag?"

I show him my compass. He gives it the same critical eye. He taps the top, where a painted coat of arms is fading beyond recognition. He recognizes the insignia, of course. I can see it in his eyes. He flips the top open, examines the compass rose under the glass. I hand him the rolled sea chart. He opens it, lays it aside, and smiles at Mama.

"It appears his future was already charted before all this happened."

Mama slides off her chair onto her knees and kisses his fingers.

"This is his future. We are so grateful, Serenissimo."

"I'm certain *you* are. I'm not so sure about him."

"You have given him the life that was stolen from him," Mama says, and before she can say more, I kick her foot. She catches herself.

Serenissimo says, "We forge our lives from the materials Heaven presents."

"We are filled with eternal praise for you, Serenissimo," she says.

"I had nothing to do with it. It was the luck of the draw."

"It was a gift from the Virgin and the Evangelist." She casts her eyes downward, at the gold slippers on his feet.

"How are you with that weapon?" Serenissimo asks.

"I'm good, Serenissimo."

"How good?'

"Very good."

There's no reason to lie. Abdul taught me secrets about aim and concentration that Venetians rarely learn.

"Show me," Serenissimo says.

"Right here?"

Marino drops the codex he has been pretending to read.

"In the courtyard," Serenissimo says. "Your lovely mother will accompany me."

We follow him down the stairs into the courtyard.

He shouts toward the stable, "Someone set up a target."

By now, we're drawing attention. The guards all look in instead of out. There's a quiet confusion, and everything happens quickly. Two pages set up a butt of hay at the far end of the courtyard. Grooms watch from inside the stable, and nobles, gossiping before the Great Council meeting, cluster around the portico.

I assess the target—a piece of cloth with three concentric circles: outer red, middle white, and center gold.

"That's too easy," I say. "Why don't you make it challenge?"

"Choose your target," Serenissimo says.

"Got any money on you?"

"Of course not," he says. "Nor a pocket to put it in. What do you need?"

"A gold ducat."

"A gold ducat!" he calls over his shoulder, and one appears.

He hands the ducat to Marino who walks up to the target, looking perplexed and slightly terrified.

"Just hold it out," I shout to him, but he doesn't find that funny.

A groom fetches a horseshoe and a long iron nail from the stable. He fastens the horseshoe to the target and stands the ducat on top.

I've never shot with so many people watching, important people like the doge of Venice, and by now, half the Senate, and every groom, page, and secretary. I breathe deeply, remembering what Abdul said. I can have only one thought, and that thought is the ducat. I pull the bow-string until the nut clicks into place, holding it taut. I breathe on the bolt, feeling its weight and shape. I raise my crossbow. Its stock is my compass needle, aimed at the target. The bolt is the embodiment of my intention, as Abdul says. It will go where I determine. The ducat I'm seeing isn't perched on a horseshoe across the courtyard. It's in my mind.

I pull the trigger. The bolt streaks to the butt and pierces the ducat dead center.

The groom looks stunned. "You can't get more center than that," he says.

Mama throws her arms around me and covers me with kisses.

A harsh voice, bitterly sarcastic, echoes from the portico above.

"Not bad for a fishmonger's apprentice." It's Ruggiero Gradenigo. "And a bastard to boot."

Chapter Fourteen

Learning to Ride

GOING TO LIDO is Admiral Pisani's idea.

"If you want to ride a horse, go where you can ride," he says. He's surprised when I offer to row across the lagoon. We take a palace boat, sleek and fast, and I row from the palace wharf to St. Nicholas of Lido. He compliments me on my stroke.

"Why do I have to learn to ride a horse?" I ask. "I can row anywhere."

"You're right," Pisani says. "I can barely ride on the streets any more. They're too crowded. One day, there won't be a horse left in Rialto. But the doge is old-fashioned. To his way of thinking, men of consequence ride horses."

Pisani selects our horses at the fort, a charger for him, a palfrey for me. His charger is a magnificent beast; my palfrey is smaller but full of spirit. Her name is Delfín. He shows me how to approach her to allow her to get used to me. Finally, we mount and ride, slowly at first, over the dunes and along the shore.

The sea and sky are gray; you can't tell where one ends and the other begins. It's cold, and the wind blows Pisani's cape out behind him. He looks like a great admiral on his horse. There is authority in his eye, in the way he handles his reins, tucks his gloves into his belt, and cocks his hat.

"I know it's tough dealing with His Exalted Serenity," Pisani says. "He's an ornery son of a bitch. But he earned every lick of it. I've sailed with him, fought with him, whored with him. Nobody has fought for the Republic harder than Andrea Contarini."

Our horses meander along the water's edge. There is no surf. The sea is flat, the foamy edge hisses and churns up gravel and sand crabs. Atop the dunes the horses nibble the sea grass.

"Do you know where we are?" Pisani asks.

"On the lido, sir."

Pisani points south along the shore.

"A great city once stood here. You may have heard of it. Malamocco."

"My old boss, Pierluigi, the fish vendor, used to take me there to find crabs living in the ruins."

"It was our capital until the Pepin, King of the Franks, attacked us in 810. He captured Malamocco but wrecked all his boats trying to penetrate the lagoon. We learned our lesson and moved our capital inside the lagoon, to Rialto, the high banks. On Easter, in the year 1102, after the birth of our Lord Jesus Christ, an earthquake shook the entire lagoon. They thought it was the end of the world. That's when Malamocco collapsed into the sea and became the kingdom of crabs and fishes."

"Can I ask you a question, sir?"

"You can ask. I don't swear I'll answer."

"Sometimes I don't understand things. Twice Serenissimo said to me that there are two armies in the Great Council and by fighting with one another they're pulling down the house they both live in. What does he mean?"

"Imagine two galleys sailing together under one flag. One is the *Warrior King*. The other is the *Merchant Prince*. The same man owns them both, and they sail together for mutual protection against the Genoese, Turks, and pirates. But each captain has a very different idea about where they're going.

"The captain of the *Warrior King* wants a strong doge who picks his own council and has a free hand to conquer territory and rule as he sees fit. The captain of the *Merchant Prince* only wants to buy cheap and sell dear, to stay rich bringing the wealth of the East to the cities of the West. He doesn't want a powerful doge; he wants committees to govern and a doge who speaks for them. His goals are so different from the captain of the *Warrior King* that, sometimes, it's impossible for them to stick together. Together, they can hold off any enemy. If they're fighting one another, they veer off course and open themselves up to enemy attack. That's what Serenissimo means. He has the nasty job of trying to keep them together, using whatever means he can muster to steer the Republic clear of disaster. Does that make sense?"

"Yes, sir. Thank you."

I try to separate the eyes and hands of the nobles of Venice, whom I have come to know very well, into Warrior Kings or Merchant Princes.

"What about the Gradenigos, sir? Which side are they on?"

"There are three branches of Gradenigos. One is rich, one is poor, and the third is even poorer. The rich ones have produced doges. The poor ones have produced traitors. But on both galleys, you have all kinds of strange characters besides the captains. Some have very peculiar views."

"Like Marino Faliero?"

"And before him, Bajamonte Tiepolo, who led a revolt of angry nobles after the Closing of the Great Council. Warrior Kings always claim to speak for the people. According to them, the Merchant Princes closed the Great Council and ignored the people's will, becoming tyrants with a puppet doge. Under the banner of overthrowing the tyrants, the Warrior Kings wish to return to the olden days, when the doge's authority was absolute, and he ruled by the sword. That's a dangerous place to return. I think our friend, Ruggiero Gradenigo, fancies a crown on his head. Fortunately for us, he's the poorest of the lot; he can't buy or bribe the men he needs. If he had a fortune, we'd have a serious problem on our hands."

MARINO SWEEPS HIS official parchments aside and sets a codex on our worktable. The leather cover may have been red once, but it's brown with age, cracked, and stained. I reach over to touch it, and Marino slaps my hand.

"Careful. It's older than I am."

The leather binding has thick ridges where the threads holding the pages together are sewn into the spine. The leather cameo, a man's profile, has been worked into the center of the cover. Sprigs of laurel circle his head with *SPQR* stamped below him in cracked and flaking gold.

Marino taps the profile on the cover. "Do you know who he is?"

"Some old doge?"

"That's Julius Caesar, who was stabbed to death by Roman senators. This is *De Bello Gallico. The Gallic Wars*. You've had enough bits and pieces. It's time for a real story."

He carefully opens the cover and rubs his finger lightly on the first page.

"Vellum is so marvelous. To think this membrane once kept a live calf's guts inside. Do you see that pattern? Those are the veins. This is particularly fine vellum, from an unborn calf. I borrowed this especially for you from Petrarch's library.

"What for?"

"You're going to read it."

"It weighs more than I do."

"You will read it from cover to cover."

"Do I have to?"

"Of course."

"Why?"

"To learn history and style."

"I don't have time for that. I've got important things to learn."

He points to the opening words. "Read."

"*Gallia est omnis divisa in partes tres...*"

"What does that mean?"

"Gaul is divided into three parts..."

"Go on."

For an hour, I read pages filled with the weirdest names I've ever seen, tribes of Gaul, their leaders, and then the fights they have with one another and with the Romans. At the end of the lesson, Marino puts the codex in a drawer and locks it. I head straight for the door.

"Such a hurry... Off to visit the stable boy?"

"No. I'm going to the armory."

Marino starts to leave and turns back, rubbing his lip with his ink-stained finger.

"What might the ballot boy need from the armory?"

"That's my business."

"You have no business of your own."

"I need a string for my crossbow."

"You may not think so," he says, "but I'm always looking out for your best interests. I know how close you have gotten to the doge..."

"We're not *close*. He's my master. I'm like a horse or a slave, remember?"

"Andrea Contarini is my fourth doge. Four other ballot boys have come and gone. One cozies up to the cook and grows fat; another is drawn to rich nobles like a bee to pollen. Another spends his time with a groom in the stables."

"Serenissimo ordered me to ride."

"I'm not your enemy. I'm glad you found a way to be happy here among so many unhappy men."

"I'm doing my best."

"Good, because it's only going to get worse. The doge's honeymoon is over. Battle is about to resume, and we will need all our strength, wit, and skill to keep this house in order. At such times. we must be very cautious and recognize who our true friends are. And our true enemies."

He smiles and leaves without another word. I don't understand him. He's the one who warned me to trust no one. Now he wants to be my friend.

He also wants me to know that he knows I visit Matteo in the stable.

Matteo is my only friend in the palace. When I'm with him it's almost like being home for a little while. We laugh, and wrestle, and talk. He plays his flute and tells me the latest jokes. He doesn't have to read Caesar, or copy *De Bello Gallico* onto paper, or go to Mass every morning with the doge, or march in endless stupid processions. He takes care of the horses. He loves them, too, most of them anyway. He knows each one and has his favorites. He says they're like people; each one has a personality and needs to be handled differently. Sometimes he talks about his home in San Giobbe parish, and I tell him about St. Nick's. Sometimes we just lie on the roof, our bodies touching, and I tell him the stories of the constellations.

Chapter Fifteen

Hic Rhodus! Hic Salta!

IN MY OWN clothes, I can go out during the day without attracting attention. Besides, I have the ring to get me out of jams. I roam freely.

The doge always asks a thousand questions about what people are doing and saying. He misses being among people. He wants me to listen and tell him what they think. He trusts my memory and my honesty. He has to be especially careful since Mama visited the palace. His council browbeat him for the infraction of his oath but went no further. Turning her visit into a public spectacle made it hard for anyone to do anything but grumble. The Ten marked a debit in their ledger but had no reason to raise charges.

On my way out of the palace, I stop by the stable. Matteo pretends not to recognize me in my street clothes.

"You look like my old friend Nico, but you're much better looking."

"Too bad you're not."

He looks me up and down. "I like you better this way," he says.

"Me too."

He sits on a bale of hay. "I wrote another a tune for you. Want to hear it?"

As I listen, the sun glints off the canal and scatters jewels across the stone vaults.

"Like it?" he asks.

"You make the sweetest music in Venice."

He blushes as he fidgets with his flute. He has something to say, and he's having a hard time saying it.

"I was wondering," he says.

He's blushing; his voice drops. "Did you ever touch another boy?"

"Where?"

"Where it counts."

"No. Have you?"

"No. But one touched me."

"You let him?"

"It felt too good to make him stop."

He puts his arm around my shoulder and pulls me toward him. "Want to try? You and me?"

He ruffles my hair with his hand.

"I can't, Matteo."

"Why not?"

"You watched the herald burn between the Columns of Doom."

"Come on, Nico. That was different. He did the worst thing possible in the worst possible place. He was stupid.

Nobody is going to burn at the stake for priming some-one's pump or letting him return the favor. Maybe you'll have to recite six thousand Hail Marys and give up meat until St. Mark's Day. Nobody is going to catch us, Nico. Don't you want to? Just a little? It's a thousand times better than wanking."

"Yes, I want to. No, I can't."

"Let me touch you."

"I have to leave."

When I stand up, he sees my boner in my trousers.

"If you change your mind, you know where to find me," he says.

I turn away and adjust myself.

"You're not mad, are you?" he asks.

"Of course I'm not mad. I'm your friend, not your mother."

"Just checking. See you later?"

"If you're lucky."

He tips his cap and whistles my tune as I head to the secret door.

If I'm careful, no one ever notices me going in and out; it's like I'm invisible. I pull up my hood to hide as much of my face as possible. I look like a monk. In the square, I'm a free man.

There's no mark on the column from Abdul, but I head to Santa Margherita Square anyway to see what news I can find. Coming off the Rialto Bridge, I see Ruggiero Gradenigo with his uncle, Benedetto Gradenigo. They're arguing. They don't see me fall in behind them. They turn left through the arcade at San Giacomo Square, past the fabric shops that attract buyers from all over the world. They enter Blackbeard's countinghouse, where Alex's father spends most of his time when he's in town.

Men pack the anteroom, swapping the price of English wool in Flanders for how much pepper is sitting on the Egyptian docks, the state of the monsoon on the Indian Ocean, or what ivory is likely to cost in Barbary next September. Ruggiero pushes his way through the merchants and their agents, past the abacus, to the back offices, pulling his uncle in his wake.

"Wait! Sirs!"

The head clerk, flustered, bows and tries to head them off. They push past him. Blackbeard steps out of his office and signals for the clerk to disappear.

"Can I help you, milords?" Blackbeard bows reverently.

"A word or two, if you will," the uncle says. "In private."

"To whom do I owe this pleasure?"

"I am Benedetto Gradenigo, and this is my nephew, Ruggiero."

Blackbeard is so servile as to look ridiculous, an actor in a comedy.

"Please be so kind as to step into my humble office," he says.

I edge behind the abacus. I can see their backs in the pass-through, and I hear them perfectly. Alex will be hungry for every word.

"To what do I owe the pleasure of your visit?" Blackbeard asks.

"We think your daughter is a perfect match for my nephew."

I'm swept in a crashing red undertow. This is so crazy it hurts. I want to shout, but I can't. I clench my fists so tightly my fingernails cut my palms. Blackbeard just laughs.

"You've never even seen her."

"Ah, but I have," Ruggiero says.

Blackbeard looks truly surprised. "When, if I may be so bold as to ask?"

"Epiphany Eve, last, at St. Nicholas of the Beggars, on the square in front of the church. A mischievous wind lifted her veil. I gazed into her eyes. The pact was sealed then. Everything else is details."

"I know nothing about you, and you know nothing about me," Blackbeard says.

Benedetto looks at Ruggiero. "Oddly enough," he says, "I expected honesty from the son of a pirate."

"Son of a pirate and a slave." Ruggiero slaps his leather glove against his thigh.

"Like everyone else in Venice," Benedetto says, "you know exactly how much we owe the butcher, the baker, and the candlestick maker. That our slaves ran away because we couldn't afford to feed them. That we live on the crumbs of our former glory."

"Sabotaged," Ruggiero says. "Destroyed by a conspiracy of thieves and usurpers."

"I admit I don't know much about noble life," Blackbeard says. "But ordinarily, aren't matters like this settled at home, not in a countinghouse?"

"We're here to transact business," Ruggiero says. "What better place?"

"We are here," Benedetto says, "to find out how much what you want most in the world is worth to you."

"I'm a rich man; some say very rich. I'm tempted to add I have everything I want."

"All but the thing you can never have. Your line will never be noble. We can change that. We can guarantee you grandsons on the Great Council."

"You must realize," Blackbeard says, "you're not the only nobles looking for a fat dowry."

"No, we are not, but no other great house would go near the granddaughter of a pirate and slave, no matter how rich and charming."

"A slave and a whore," Ruggiero says. "What's it worth to you?"

"Gentlemen, my daughter is barely thirteen."

"Time to be married and producing noble sons," Benedetto says. "The dowry?"

"Two thousand," Blackbeard says.

"Don't be insulting," Ruggiero shouts.

Blackbeard is unruffled. "A generous sum by today's standards."

"For a cloth merchant, yes. We know what you have, so don't haggle. We can settle for five thousand ducats up front."

"That's three times the going rate."

"Cheap for the goose that lays golden eggs."

Ruggiero jumps up from his chair, and bolts out of the office. He's disgusted with the haggling. I duck behind a post as he paces around the abacus, a six-by-four-foot chessboard covered with constantly shifting colored pebbles representing transactions in wool, spice, gold, China silk, and Syrian grain. The clerk drops counters on the board faster than the eye can see, his hand a blur as he moves them from column to column.

Blackbeard says to Benedetto, "If she marries now, I'll be seventy-five before my first grandson is old enough to sit among you. *If* the first-born is a boy."

Ruggiero hunches over the abacus. "Don't waste our time, merchant," he shouts to Blackbeard. He scoops up a handful of markers from the abacus and hurls them across the room. The clerk running the lines shrieks in horror. His hands fly over the board desperate to recapture his calculations.

Ruggiero halts at the street door and shouts at Blackbeard.

"*Hic Rhodus! Hic salta!*"

I FIND MATTEO in the stable currying a fine black stallion.

"You know Ruggiero Gradenigo, don't you?" I ask.

"Everybody knows Ruggiero Gradenigo. A few think he's a savior sent to deliver us; most think he's Satan himself."

"What do you think?"

"He scares the shit out of me."

Matteo leans close and drops his voice as if the walls had ears. His breath in my ear makes me shiver. "He's not just mean. He's evil."

"What do you mean, evil?"

"He raped a girl in San Giobbe, twelve years old. Beat her up pretty bad. He can't walk around there no more. I suspect he's up to something much worse. Dunno what, but no good for sure. Yesterday afternoon, he and his buddy Hieronimo Zen see this old friar out on the Wharf. Ruggiero throws his arms around the geezer, and they talk. When he comes back, he tells Zen to forget the horses because he has to row over to Marullo's. I don't know much, but I know nothing good ever happens at Marullo's."

The stablemaster whistles for Matteo. He has to run.

"Can you come back later?" he asks.

"I'll try."

He dashes to the stable master; I dash to my Latin master.

"MARINO, WHAT DOES *hic rhodus, hic salta* mean?"

"That's easy enough to figure out."

"The words are easy, but what does it mean?"

"It's the end of a fable by Aesop. A notorious braggart returns to Athens. He tells everyone that in Rhodes he made the most amazing jump, the longest jump ever made by man, longer than any jump Athens had ever seen. If you don't believe me, he said, ask anybody in Rhodes, and they will confirm the unbelievable greatness of my jump. Tired of his baseless bragging, an Athenian finally shouts, 'This is Rhodes! Jump here!'"

"Put your money where your mouth is."

"Exactly."

When we're finished with Caesar, I ask Marino about Marullo's, and once again, his face twists into the expression of wonder and confusion I'm growing used to.

"Where did you hear about Marullo's?"

"I hear all kinds of things."

He squints and drums his nails on the table, thinking about what to say.

"Marullo's is a den of thieves where dangerous people ply their trades. Soldiers of fortune, criminals, exiles, traitors. People who don't want to be seen by the lords of the night go to Marullo's Tavern."

"Where is it?"

"On the south side of Giudecca, facing Santa Maria delle Grazia. Smart people steer clear of it."

The sun is already setting when I set out across the lagoon in Pierluigi's boat. I draw a line on the map in my head, from La Grazia to the south flank of Giudecca. I have rowed past a thousand times. In my mind's eye, I can pinpoint it exactly.

I follow the south flank of Giudecca, looking for any sign of a tavern amid the farmhouses, rowing past a run-down palace in the old style, winter gardens, and orchards near bloom behind a wall of thorny brush and low-hanging willows. Vines and bramble almost completely hide the ramshackle dock. A barely visible stairway up the hill from the dock disappears into the brush and comes out again atop the bank. I tether my boat close by and conceal it with vines.

It's weirdly quiet for a den of thieves. I imagine this might be a crowded spot on hot summer nights when the banks are thick with flowers and a fresh, cool breeze blows off the lagoon. But a chill wind rustles the tight purple buds, and nothing disturbs the silence but the plash of oars approaching, accompanied by low voices. I can't understand what they're saying. I bury myself in vines and watch the dock.

A boat, once long and fine, now in serious ruin, scrapes the dock. Benedetto Gradenigo sits inside the half-collapsed cabin. Ruggiero drops his oar and helps his uncle from the boat. Benedetto restrains Ruggiero from immediately climbing the stairs.

"Now the real danger begins," he says.

"Which danger might that be?" Ruggiero sounds angrier than usual, impatient to be on his way. Benedetto holds fast to his arm.

"Before today all we did was talk," he says. "Now we are crossing the Rubicon."

"It's about time."

Marino taught me about Caesar crossing the Rubicon River in defiance of Roman law to pursue his fate. Once the Rubicon is crossed, there's no turning back.

"My brother has filled your head with delusions of grandeur," Benedetto says. "He has ruined you."

"The only thing ruined is our name."

"Our family elected the first doge when we still paid homage to Byzantium. Our name is glorious. The men bearing it now are unworthy of it."

"Would that be you, shaking in your boots at our greatest opportunity? Stand aside, old man. When all is over, we'll give you a monastery on a nice little island of your own where you can cower for all eternity."

"It's too late for that," Benedetto says. He sounds weary and defeated. "Whither thou goest…"

At the top of the stairs, they disappear behind pines and alders that shelter the tavern from view. I grab a branch of a stout tree behind the tavern, hoist myself up, wrap my legs around the branch, then hoist myself higher, to a branch with a wide crotch hidden in the shadows. Below, a fence sags under the weight of dead vines enclosing an open patio. In the center of the patio, a fire burns in an open pit surrounded by stools hacked from tree trunks.

Benedetto places his hand on Ruggiero's chest, staying him before they enter.

"You believe my brother because he flatters you," Benedetto says. "He fills your head with imperial dreams. Take a deep breath, nephew. Think upon your hero, Bajamonte Tiepolo. He was like you in so many ways but so unlike you in the most important way. He was young, handsome, reckless, a spendthrift, and a gambler. But the little people you openly scorn loved him. They were willing to lay down their lives for him. Would anyone die for you? And even with their support, Bajamonte's rebellion was smashed in an hour. The only reason the doge didn't cut off Bajamonte's head was because he was so revered. The doge couldn't risk it. He conspicuously left Bajamonte's head on his shoulders and exiled him forever. Then we created the Council of Ten to stop any such conspiracy from ever happening again. And years later, when everything had quieted down, he sent secret agents to kill Bajamonte Tiepolo like a mad dog. All that remains, stronger than ever, is the Ten."

"Your problem, Uncle," Ruggiero says, "is that you are a coward. You have always been a coward. You were a coward in Venice, at sea, in Crete, in the Great Council. You always will be. Our name was ruined because you failed to stand up for my father and wrest our destiny from ignominy."

"Because he failed miserably. Like Bajamonte. Like Faliero."

"At least he did something besides whining and complaining. When we are again the greatest house in Venice, when we wear the imperial purple, it will be in spite of you, not because of you. And never, ever forget, if Bruno Badoer's soldiers had arrived on time from Chioggia, Bajamonte would have won. A storm blocked them. That is why Bajamonte Tiepolo failed. A blind act of nature."

"But he failed."

"*We'll* pay more attention to the weather."

A man, probably Marullo, the tavern-keeper, stands aside until their argument is over. He greets them and leads them to the fire pit to warm themselves.

Another boat approaches the dock from the direction of La Grazia and moors. A tall friar climbs the stairs and greets the Gradenigos around the fire.

"Hail, Brother Bernardo," Benedetto says. "When did you return?"

"Two days ago."

"Where are you staying?"

"The hermitage on La Grazia, as befits a humble anchorite."

Brother Bernardo wheels on Ruggiero, his face twisted with anger. "What in hell happened with the ballot boy?"

"Your great plan failed."

"How could my plan fail? It was simple enough for a bloody idiot to follow."

"Don't tell me," Ruggiero said. "You weren't there."

"How hard could it be?"

"I was blindsided."

"You knew which direction to turn. Where to look. Where the boy was standing. All you had to do was cast your eyes upon him. His father, common as dirt but uncommonly wealthy, offered thousands to have his son in the palace."

"That little bastard from St. Nicholas of the Beggars plowed into me. He caught my eye. Before I could kick him out of the way, the crowd acclaimed him. *They* picked him. Not me. Give me leave to kill him. Let them pick a new one."

"Pick a new one? Ha. That's rich." Brother Bernardo rubs his hands. "Try to imagine it. First, they would have to elect a committee to investigate the little bastard's death and another committee to examine his history for any taint of treason. The Doge's Council would appoint a commission to make rules for the selection because this has never been done before. The Senate would requisition a supplement of sixty nobles to decide if Ruggiero Gradenigo should choose again, still being the youngest, or if someone else should, perhaps the next youngest. Or three Wise Men, or six blind procurators."

They all laugh.

"Who is this ballot boy anyway?" Brother Bernardo asks.

"I told you. A bastard from St. Nicholas of the Beggars."

"St. Nicholas of the Beggars you say?"

"Yes. And if you let me kill him, he's out of our hair for good."

Brother Bernardo slaps Ruggiero so hard across the face blood flies.

"You will kill no one. Do you understand? It's time to act like a proper Gradenigo. From this moment forward, you must be, like Caesar's wife, beyond reproach. Do you understand? You cannot ruin our future with your petty vices."

"Heed the friar," Benedetto says. "Reserve your enthusiasm for major vices."

"I mean exactly what I say," Brother Bernardo says. "We can't afford to have you jailed or exiled or have your eye put out or your hand cut off for doing something stupid. Not when destiny is calling."

Ruggiero tries to make light of it. "Why are you so vexed? We weren't exactly planning on getting elected."

"Politics is war," Brother Bernardo says. "In war, you seize every possible advantage and let nothing that might be of value escape your grasp. We have one goal. To make sure Andrea Contarini fails completely and looks like a fool doing it."

Ruggiero bites his thumb. "Contarini will regret the day he was born."

Chapter Sixteen

My Fifteenth Birthday

THE DOGE HAS a glass water clock from Constantinople that rings a crystal bell each hour. That way he's always ahead of everyone. He wakes me up an hour before dawn for today's procession. Irritated and agitated, he won't listen to me.

"Serenissimo, please let me speak."

"Not now." He is unusually distracted and unkind. Marino hovers nearby, but I can't remain silent.

"Most Exalted Serenity, I heard them..."

"I said not now."

Marino steps up to inspect my uniform. The doge retreats into his closet.

"You're filling out nicely," Marino says. "Tell Serenissimo he has to buy you new clothes very soon."

"He says everyone thinks he's a lot richer than he is."

"That's what they all say." Marino counts my buttons. "At least you've still got all your silver buttons; that's what matters."

The doge returns dressed in black, looking ferocious enough to scare the Varangians who guarded the emperor of Byzantium. Huge Norsemen bred to be vicious the way stallions are bred for speed, those Varangians, and this morning, the Exalted and Most Serene Doge of Venice could make a Varangian turn tail and run home crying to his mama.

"Why is Serenissimo so grouchy?"

"It's St. Isidore's Day," Marino whispers. "Once upon a time, we celebrated a glorious naval victory on St. Isidore's day. Now, it's the anniversary of cutting off Marino Faliero's head. We celebrate the triumph of the axe over sedition."

It's also my birthday, but I don't expect anyone remembers except Mama.

The procession is bleak. Everyone wears black robes and hoods. The doge, all in black, wears no hood, no crown, only the white linen skullcap that never comes off.

We march six abreast, row after row after row. No banners. No trumpets. No joy. Drums beat a dirge, and men in black carry candles upside down.

I can see why the doge is grouchy. It's all about him, and not in a good way. The funeral procession is designed to scare him from even thinking about treason.

The drums beat slow, steady, and loud. Marino, on my left, says they're playing what they played when ten of Faliero's coconspirators were hanged, one by one, from the upper arcade of the palace while the crowd watched from the square.

The doge stops in a sea of black between St. Mark's Church at one end of the square and the church of St.

Geminiano at the other. Canons chant Psalm 129. *De Profundis clamavi ad te Domine.*

From the depths I cry out to you, O Lord.

Hear my voice and heed my cry for mercy.

We march into St. Mark's, every arch and balcony dressed for death with hanging black funeral drapes.

New mosaics cover the walls of St. Isidore's chapel in the north transept—here, St. Isidore thrown into a fiery furnace, there, across the chapel, his body tied to a horse's tail and dragged across sharp rocks. The horse's eyes blaze with demonic fire.

After a solemn Requiem Mass, Guido Morosini of the Council of Ten—who put fear in everyone—leads the doge like a prisoner to the high, purple pulpit of porphyry. The Ten roots out sedition and treachery. They employ informers and secret police and wield the power of the axe. They know where all the skeletons are buried and keep the secrets. They ordered the beheading of Faliero and crushed his rebellion, and they'll crush the next rebellion and supervise the next beheading.

"*Memento mori,*" Morosini intones.

He speaks directly to the doge.

"Look upon Marino Faliero as a mirror," Morosini says, "in which you see yourself. You are neither a great prince nor an exalted leader. You are nothing, a bag of flesh and bones, the humblest servant of our Serene Republic. Look upon your sins as debts which must be repaid, and remember, *you too must die.*"

After Mass, we march once more around the square and into the palace, where everyone important joins the doge for a feast. A papal ambassador sits on his right.

"Charming custom, that little drama," the ambassador says.

"They like to keep me on my toes. Is the emperor of Byzantium in Rome yet?"

"Our delegations are discussing details of his renunciation of the Eastern heresy, returning his soul to the one holy catholic and apostolic Church of Rome."

The Doge's Council sends Marino to stand between the doge and the ambassador so he can make a detailed report. My memory is all the doge needs, which is why he always positions me carefully.

"Can we expect a Crusade any time soon?"

"His Holiness the Pope is discussing that with the lord."

"Does the emperor know that?"

"I wouldn't presume to know what the emperor knows."

"If there is no Crusade, what will His Holiness do when the Turks overrun Byzantium?"

The papal ambassador sets down his pheasant breast and licks his fingers. "*Do you question what I do for my children?*' sayeth the Lord. '*Do you give me orders about the work of my hands? I am the one who made the earth and created people to live on it.*'"

With no answer forthcoming, the doge grows restive and excuses himself as soon as he can, requesting that I accompany him. He is irritated and ashen. He sits in his study and says nothing for a long time.

"What's the matter, Serenissimo?"

"We are Venetians first, then Christians. I distrust the Holy Father almost as much as I distrust John Paleologos, the emperor of Byzantium. Paleologos is a weak and vacillating lunatic, and the Holy Father is playing a very dangerous game. Paleologos will lose his head if his subjects rebel against submitting to the Church of Rome. One more civil war will bring Byzantium down, and if Byzantium falls, it falls to the Turk, and then we're next. Bah! It's every man for himself. We must eventually deal with Murad the Turk one way or the other. Better him, I say, than His Holiness the Pope."

From the antechamber, Marino clears his throat to let the doge know he is listening.

"Marino..."

"Yes, Serenissimo."

"Has Ambassador Bragadin left for Constantinople yet?"

"They leave with the tide, Serenissimo."

"We must speak with him before he leaves."

"Now?"

"Yes."

With Marino Vendramin out of the way, Serenissimo speaks in a whisper.

"The executioner's sword cuts two ways. Justice is one edge of the blade. Vengeance is the other, and it's far crueler. That display we put on today is to remind me that I'm one step from the chopping block if I make the wrong enemies."

"Serenissimo, I must tell you what I heard at Marullo's."

He puts his finger across his lips and shakes his head.

"Not here," he says. "When we pray."

He fumbles in the sack he carries under his gold robe and pulls out a small packet.

"This is for you."

He presses a folded parchment into my hand, sealed with his lead insignia, a privilege granted to Doge Sebastiano Ziani by Pope Alexander III for aiding the Holy See against Frederick Barbarossa.

"Open it," he says.

It is a bill of transfer giving me legal title to Delfín, my horse.

"Go see her. She's downstairs in the stable. I almost lost two grooms getting her here. Happy birthday."

Chapter Seventeen

Matteo's Revelation

I GRAB AN apple from the kitchen and head for the stable. Matteo is in Delfín's stall, calming her.

"New horse," he says. "Came last night."

"I know."

I hand him the parchment which he stares at uncomprehendingly.

"It says she's mine. Serenissimo gave her to me for my birthday."

Her ears are up, swiveling as she hears me. She smells the apple and whinnies.

"A fine beast," Matteo says, running his fingers through her mane. "Like you."

I feed her an apple, and Matteo strokes her tenderly. We stand side by side and brush her. It's stuffy in the stable. Soon we're sweating, and Matteo takes off his shirt. I watch him currying Delfín out of the corner of my eye. His back is broad and ridged with muscle. He's not a boy anymore, nor is he yet a man. He can tell I'm watching him, and he winks at me.

"You like what you see?"

He has a little hair on his chest; a fine line runs past his belly into his breeches. I turn away because I'm embarrassed he caught me looking at him. But he doesn't care.

"Go ahead," he says. "Touch me if you want."

"I've never touched anyone like this."

"That's too bad. It's fun, and nobody gets a baby. Did you ever want to?"

"Not until I met you."

"Go ahead. Touch me."

I back away. I want to, and I'm afraid to.

"You said you want to." He's closer now. Too close.

"I wanted to since the first time I saw you playing your flute upstairs."

"What are you waiting for?"

He takes my hand and places it on his chest, and I rub him lightly. His skin is silky, the hair soft as down. I pull my hand away.

"Don't stop," he says. "It feels good. Nobody can see us here."

He guides my hand down the trail of hair.

"Go on," he whispers.

"I have to go. I just came to see Delfín."

"You didn't come to see me?"

"You too."

"So touch me. It doesn't take long."

I sweat from the heat of the flaming pyre and smell burning flesh. I know each word of the sodomite's interrogation transcript Marino left for me in the doge's study.

"You've done this before?" I ask Matteo.

"Yes."

"With who?"

"My friend in the kitchen."

"Did you...spew?"

"Yes."

"Then it's a mortal sin."

"I don't care."

"I have to care."

"It would feel so much better with you. I like you better."

He nuzzles against me like Delfín looking for more apple. It feels so good I forget to breathe. He rubs against my thigh. I want to watch him. To touch him. I want to. I do. I'm afraid I'll like it too much. Afraid one thing will lead to another.

"I can't."

He puts his mouth against my ear and whispers even more softly. "Then let me touch you. Please."

He puts his hand down my breeches. "It feels like you want me to."

"I do, but I don't."

He pushes me against the side of Delfín's stall and pulls down my breeches.

"You won't do anything," he says. "How can that be a sin?"

His eyes twinkle. He rubs me softly, watching my face. He rubs a little harder and a little harder until I stop wanting him to him stop. Pleasure rises in an irresistible wave. I can do nothing but give way.

"Happy birthday, Niccolò Saltano of St. Nicholas of the Beggars."

Chapter Eighteen

Damaged Goods

THE DOGE SITS on his gold cushion flanked by the three heads of the Forty. I'm on my stool behind him. I'm supposed to remember everything, but I can't concentrate. I still haven't been able to tell Serenissimo what I heard at Marullo's.

Between Matteo and Alex, I think I'm going crazy. Letting Matteo touch me felt so good, and he says other things are a thousand times better. Of course they are; that's why we go to Hell for them. When I'm not worrying about the price of my sins with Matteo, I can't get Alex out of my head.

At the meeting's end, Marino grabs me for a Latin lesson. My hand writes, not my mind. The quill catches on the paper. A blob of ink splatters across Book IV of *The Gallic Wars*.

Marino hands me a fresh sheet of paper, and I start all over again.

"You're very clumsy today. Is anything wrong?"

"I'm fine."

"I thought maybe you were upset about something..."

He always sounds like he knows more than he's letting on.

"Why would I be upset?"

"For one thing, it appears your nemesis is about to become a very rich man."

I try to concentrate on the Romans setting an ambush for the Gauls.

"Who's my nemesis?"

"Ruggiero Gradenigo."

"How is he getting rich?"

"The noble way—marrying a merchant's daughter. The richer the better."

"Who said that?"

"It's on everyone's lips. I'm surprised you haven't heard."

"Why would a rich commoner marry a deadbeat like Ruggiero?"

"To bear noble sons."

I drop the quill. Marino isn't stupid. Why is he tormenting me? I refuse to confirm the rumor.

"It's stupid gossip," I say.

He raises his eyebrows and smiles. "The odd thing about gossip is how it has a way of being true."

After my lesson, I check the lion column. Abdul left his mark. I find him at home.

"Did Blackbeard make up his mind?"

"He's dithering," Abdul says. "Most unlike him."

"Does he know anything?"

"Not yet. He's at his mill in Treviso."

Before I'm up the rope and through the window Alex is pleading.

"You have to get me out of here before they make me marry that monster."

"Where will you go?"

"Have you heard of the Poor Clares? The priest at San Raffaele mentioned that they have a house near Padua."

"You want to go to a convent?"

"I'd rather marry Christ than Ruggiero Gradenigo."

"Ruggiero will find you and drag you back."

"Sanctuary is holy and inviolable. He can't. If he does, I'll kill myself."

"Don't say that. Your father hasn't said yes. Maybe he won't. He loves you."

"When I told Papa that Ruggiero is a beast, he laughed at me. He said all men are beasts to young girls. He also said Ruggiero is young and handsome, and that's a lot better than a fat old man with gout and two wives already in their graves. I told him I would never marry Ruggiero, so he locked me in here and said when I was ready to be reasonable, he'd let me out."

"I'll kill Ruggiero before that happens."

"You can't kill him."

"You'd be amazed how easily I could."

"No." She grabs me and shakes me. "A commoner cannot kill a noble. They will track you down and draw and quarter you between the Columns of Doom. Rats and seagulls will eat your guts. You can't. Swear!"

I say what I must to calm her fears. In the palace, that is known as diplomacy.

"I swear."

"Now that's settled, I need to escape. I can get away as a boy, but I need a boat."

A commotion breaks out downstairs. Alex presses her ear against the door.

"Oh, God. No."

She's white and trembling.

"It's Papa. If he finds you here, he'll gut you."

Doors slam. Keys rattle. Alex flutters like a bird caught in a trap.

"Behind the screen," she whispers. "He never comes in here. He talks to me through the door. They talk about me all the time out there, like I'm not here."

Her father's voice echoes in the great hall. He sounds drunk and cranky. "Where is Ruta? Where is my wife? What the hell is going on?"

"Madame took her medicine," the housekeeper shouts from above. "She is sleeping."

"Wake her up."

Mother Barbanegra is already stumbling toward the great hall.

"I warned you about drinking that stuff," Blackbeard says.

"Only a little. To settle my nerves."

"Where did it come from?"

"The Egyptian slave of the apothecary at Santa Margherita brought it."

"Do you know he talks to Alessandra? I ordered him never to come here again."

"I'm sorry," she cries. "He didn't want to come. I begged him. He's the only one who makes my medicine, and you know I can't sleep without it. He spoke to no one; I swear."

"Where the hell is Ruta?"

"What difference does it make?"

"I need to see her."

Caterina Barbanegra loses control. "Of course you do. You always do. Did you know precious Ruta is a treacherous backstabbing whore? I locked her in the warehouse. Sell her! It's all her fault!"

"What's all her fault?"

Dead silence.

"What? Nothing…" Caterina realizes too late what she has done.

So does Alex. The blood drains from her face, and she looks as though she can't breathe, that an axe is about to drop.

Blackbeard slaps Caterina. "*What* is Ruta's fault? Don't toy with me, woman."

Cornered, Caterina tells him everything in a pitiful voice choked with sobs. She tells him so that she can blame the slave who has taken her place in Blackbeard's bed.

Blind Samson pulling down the columns of the temple couldn't have roared louder than Blackbeard. He sounds like he's chewing the legs off the tables.

"She snuck *out*? Alone? Dressed as a boy? Where did she go?" He rages up and down the great hall of his palace. Caterina has no answers. "Jesus Christ! No noble will marry her now! Is she still a virgin?"

Alex shakes in every limb.

"Of course she is." Caterina's voice lacks conviction.

"Call the midwife. She can tell." He growls, a frustrated bear baited at a carnival. "I ought to kill her, for all she's worth now."

Caterina cries out and collapses on the floor.

"Get up you idiotic woman. Does anyone else know?"

"No one." Caterina's voice is barely audible.

"Are you certain?"

"Only us and Ruta—who let it happen. Sell the traitorous bitch. Cut off her nose. Throw her on the bone pile."

"Fuck Ruta! We have Alessandra to deal with."

"What are you going to do?"

"What merchants always do with damaged goods. Sell to the first buyer. From now on, she's Gradenigo's problem."

Chapter Nineteen

The Evangelist's Crypt

IT IS ALMOST Compline, the last night bell, but the doge refuses to give me his ear. He pores over the back pages of his oath, which grows longer with the death of each occupant of the ducal throne. Each page brims with restrictions and prohibitions, pulling his golden chains a little tighter. He thinks whatever he is looking for is more important than anything I have to say, and I think he is wrong. But he is the doge, and I am only the ballot boy. I can't tell him what to do.

"I pray you listen, Serenissimo. I wouldn't bother you if it wasn't important."

He puts his index finger over his lips, closes his oath, and sets it aside.

"Let's pray," he says. "In my chapel."

I imagine he suspects a clerk with quill and ink must lurk nearby, writing down every word he speaks. Within the palace walls, he rarely speaks freely to me. Lighting our way with a candle, he leads me through the corridor from his apartment to St. Mark's.

I spend most of my time in the palace, where I have grown used to the quatrefoil arches of precious marble and the walls painted with our victories. I am no longer filled with wonder. Stepping into St. Mark's behind the doge, I am filled with wonder.

I have only been here when it's full of people, and I have other things on my mind. Now, it's empty and quiet, a great golden cavern lit only by the silver moon streaming through the high windows and candles flickering on the altars. Rainbow-hued mosaic pictures on a ground of gold cover the walls and arches and all five domes. I can barely make them out. Except here and there, in a moonbeam or the flicker of a candle, I recognize Our Lord, his disciples, saints, peacocks, burning angels, shepherds, and ancient kings, their faces as human as those crowding Merchant's Lane yesterday. Behind the golden altar screen encrusted with glittering gemstones, a group of white-robed canons sing Compline. Their voices echo in the five domes, multiplying.

The doge puts his nose right up to the center of the lowest register of the golden screen, where precious gems frame three figures enameled on gold in imperial colors.

"Doge Ordelafo Falier commissioned this altar screen from Byzantine artisans in 1105," he says. "Beautiful, isn't it?"

I wait for his point. Everything with him is a lesson.

"The center figure is the Blessed Virgin, the Queen of Heaven. On her right, originally, was the emperor of Byzantium, with his empress on the Virgin's left. It is said by some that blind old Enrico Dandolo, the doge who sacked Constantinople at the age of eighty-five, changed the emperor into a doge. Not from imperial ambitions, mind you—Dandolo turned down the imperial crown—but to elevate Venice above Byzantium."

The stone steps leading down to the crypt have strange writing carved into them. They're not proper stairs, but chunks of ancient monuments piled like stairs. Below, we enter the most sacred place of all, the crypt where St. Mark is buried. Low barrel vaults bear the weight of St. Mark's Church. Bilge seeps up through the foundations. The tide must be in. Perfumed oil lamps hang from the corners of the tomb to sweeten the air.

The doge sets his candle on the floor and kisses the tomb. He rests his forehead on the cold marble and prays silently. I am privileged above others to kiss the sacred tomb of the Evangelist, but I am unworthy to be here. I close my eyes and pray.

Beloved Evangelist, protect us from our enemies and keep us strong. I ask nothing for me. I know I am unworthy. But please protect Mama from harm; she means well. Protect Alex from Ruggiero Gradenigo; she is good and brave and true. Protect our doge and the Republic, and I promise to fight for them to my dying breath.

I open my eyes to the doge watching me, his eyes sad and gentle.

"Keep looking like you're praying" he says, "and keep your voice down."

"I rowed to Marullo's tavern, Serenissimo. I heard the Gradenigos plotting against you."

I recite chapter and verse of the meeting at Marullo's. The only thing that puzzles the doge is the friar. "Who is Brother Bernardo?"

"He acted like Ruggiero's father."

"That's impossible. Marcantonio Gradenigo was beheaded on Crete. I saw the body."

"Brother Bernardo was furious at Ruggiero because someone else was supposed to be ballot boy."

"Yes, you upset their little plan."

"They want you to fail, Serenissimo. They want the Ten to cut your head off, like Marino Faliero. They said, with enough money, they could buy the people's loyalty. That's why Ruggiero is marrying Alex. Alessandra Barbanegra."

"Hmm. Faliero was married to a Gradenigo. Did you know Faliero was one of the original Ten who condemned Bajamonte Tiepolo for the same crime? Tell me, could you be bought?"

"Of course not."

"Could your friends be bought?"

"Never."

"Men with no morals think everyone else is like them."

"They're out to get you, Serenissimo."

"It's part of the job, my son. That's why no one wants it. I try to steer straight, and they try to throw me overboard."

"What are you going to do?"

"My hands are chained with manacles of gold. When they trip up, which eventually they will, when they try to bribe someone who can't be bribed, or recruit the wrong man from the Arsenal, then we will smash them."

"What did Ruggiero's uncle mean about Bajamonte Tiepolo?"

"He meant that Ruggiero is trying to make himself a hero who simple people will support. Since the Closing of the Great Council, two great rebellions threatened the Republic, the Tiepolo uprising and Doge Faliero's conspiracy. Fortunately, they both failed. Bajamonte was much like our Ruggiero. He gave voice to the violent opposition of the old houses against the upstarts responsible for closing the Great Council. Bajamonte decried their tyranny.

Note well—tyrants always rally the masses in the name of freedom in order to become tyrants themselves."

He closes his eyes and crosses himself.

"Some still think Bajamonte Tiepolo was a great man," I say without naming names. I'd heard it said more than once around St. Nicholas of the Beggars.

"He was," the doge says.

"How can you say he was a great man? He was a traitor."

"To the common people, he was their knight in shining armor. They adored him. He cloaked himself in righteous indignation to incite the overthrow of the doge. If he had won, he would have been right, but he failed, so he wasn't. Ordinary men don't dream such dreams, and greatness is no simple matter. Wasn't Caesar among the greatest?"

"That he was, Serenissimo."

"In battle, peerless, afraid of nothing, bold in the face of adversity, resolute in the face of failure, a brilliant strategist and tactician, an uncanny politician. But during his campaigns in Gaul alone, he despoiled 800 cities, conquered 300 nations, faced three million enemy in battle, took one million prisoners, and killed another million on the field. That's a lot of death and destruction to own up to, and it has been said he did it only to satisfy his insatiable personal ambition.

"Or take Enrico Dandolo. He was older than me when he became doge. He was a ferocious fighter, a crafty statesman, a wily politician, and an indomitable leader. He was eighty-five and blind as a bat when he personally led the charge that breached the legendary walls of Constantinople as if he were a man of thirty. And then he sacked the imperial city out of pure greed. Men beyond number, Byzantines, Greeks, fellow Christians, slaughtered. The streets ran with blood. The women were raped and mutilated before they were killed; the churches were defiled and stripped of their treasures; the city burned for days. For no other reason than the personal ambitions of an old man with a crown on his head. But Enrico Dandolo was a great man. Marino Faliero was a great man until he wasn't."

"Being great isn't so great."

"It's not enough to be a great man. You must also be a good man, and too often the two are incompatible."

"Was anyone ever great *and* good?"

"Doge Sebastiano Ziani was."

"How so?"

"Though his predecessor was stabbed to death by angry nobles on the steps of San Zaccaria, Ziani agreed to become doge when no one else dared.

"That's brave enough for any man. He personally led a fleet of thirty galleys against Barbarossa's seventy-five. He took them by surprise and decimated them, winning the everlasting favor of the Holy Father in Rome.

"That's warrior enough for any man. He negotiated back from Byzantium what his predecessor had lost at the cost of his life.

"That's statesmanship enough for any man. No slaughtered nations to his name, no looting nor sacking, no trail of blood, no treachery. He was the richest man in Venice. All anyone expected him to do was feast, philander, and count his money. We still say 'he's rich as Ziani' when someone is stupidly rich. He acted from a profound sense of responsibility and honor, not greed or ambition. Ziani was a man of vision, who saw what Venice needed to become and gave freely of his own money when the Republic was needy or starving. He gave his own land to expand the Arsenal, that we might have the greatest navy on earth. Out of his own purse, he transformed a squat pile of bricks into our luminous palace and gave us St. Mark's Square, the most splendid square west of Constantinople, raising the two columns to create a majestic gateway wor-thy of so rich and important a city. Making us great in per-petuity, that was his greatness.

"When he was done, he retired to San Giorgio to die and left his wealth to widows and orphans, to the poor, to war veterans and hospitals and churches. Leave *greatness* to Caesar and Dandolo and Bajamonte. It is far more im-portant, and more pleasing to God and everybody else, to be good. To be fair, and generous, and just."

"We must leave now, Serenissimo."

"Yes, yes. Just one more thing. I've given you lots of *quid*, now it's time for some *quo*. Find out who Brother Bernardo is."

Chapter Twenty

The State Machine

THE FRESHMAN MEMBERS of the Great Council await the announcement of their job assignments. They will either be minor advocates assigned to the lower courts or bowmen of the quarterdeck assigned to galleys of the fleet. A minor advocate doesn't have to be good at anything; a bowman of the quarterdeck has to know how to shoot. Although their pay is the same as other bowmen, noble bowmen are allotted space for personal cargo, which they can buy cheap and sell dear, keeping the difference.

The minor advocates are supposed to learn how the real world works. They listen to merchants squabble, adjudicate disputes, figure fines, and decide punishments. Bowmen of the quarterdeck protect ships and their cargos. They fight pirates and enemy fleets. They're noble, so they sleep in private quarters and eat at the captain's table and can never be asked to row like a common bowman.

"I can't wait to hear Gradenigo's fate," the doge says on our way in.

"He's smart to get married," Marino says. "All the important jobs go to married men. Half these poor nobles are bachelors."

"Why is that so?" I ask.

"Noble houses won't dilute their fortunes by splitting it too many ways. One son marries, creates the next generation, and administers the family wealth; the others spend their lives as monks or minor government drones with mistresses or whores or boys. It's hard to say who gets the better deal."

The heads of the nominating committees step onto the dais. The minor advocates are announced first. Seven of the freshmen nobles are assigned to the lower courts. As their names are called, they rise. Ruggiero isn't paying attention and doesn't hear his name called.

"Gradenigo, Ruggiero," the committee chair calls a second time.

Ruggiero still doesn't respond. Hieronimo Zen punches him in the shoulder. Ruggiero jumps up and shouts, "What? No!"

The committee chair looks up from his list. "What did you say, sir?"

"I'm on the wrong list."

"You're Ruggiero Gradenigo."

"As far as I know."

"Then you're on the right list."

"I am a bowman, sir."

"You are a minor advocate, sir."

"You can't do this to me. I am a Gradenigo."

"That's your problem," someone shouts. Then scattered laughter.

Ruggiero waits for silence. "By what right do you do this to me?"

"It is the law," says Marco Dandolo.

"We have too many laws," Ruggiero says. "*Corruptissima re publica plurimae leges.*"

"'The more corrupt the republic, the more laws it has,'" says Marino. "Tacitus."

"This is an affront to our house," Ruggiero says. "My ancestors were maritime tribunes when yours were digging salt. We have always been seamen, not petty clerks."

"Is that why you can't pay your butcher?"

The voice comes from a cabal of sniggering nobles.

"We can't pay for the same reason you can't—this whirligig we call a republic, like a mechanical bird from the court of Byzantium that flaps its wings and warbles when you wind it up."

He points at Fat Niccolò Dolfin. "What sort of man do you want on the quarterdeck of your ship?"

"The finest bowman in Venice," Fat Dolfin says.

"There's your mistake," Ruggiero says to the committee head. "I'm no clerk. I am the best bowman in Venice."

Hieronimo Zen leaps to Ruggiero's side.

"It's true. No one can outshoot Gradenigo!"

Fat Dolfin's face is red. "Gradenigo should be on my galley, not wasting his time in small claims court!"

The members of the Doge's Council are stiff as statues, outraged and silent, taking names. Only their lips move; the word is "treason."

The doge rises and steps to the edge of the dais.

"Nobles of Venice!"

He out-shouts them all, and they shut up. He's at his best when he's doing exactly what he's not supposed to do, such as express a personal opinion.

"In Venice, Justice rules," he says. "She sits on the prow of my Golden Boat and keeps watch over Rialto from on high. She brandishes the sword of authority. She is our guardian and our strength. We can never turn a deaf ear to demands for justice. Our judgment must always be, like hers, impartial. We must reward skill and performance above name or house.

"If Ruggiero Gradenigo speaks true, a mistake has been made, and it is our duty to set it right. I proclaim a match among all eligible bowmen. If Ruggiero Gradenigo is the best, he is a bowman of the quarterdeck. If not, the matter ends."

Chapter Twenty-One

La Grazia

"SEBO? REMEMBER ME?"

I see him on the wharf outside the palace. He's not sure who I am. I'm wearing street clothes, but he still doesn't recognize me.

He sings with three other monks in threadbare robes on the wharf near the Columns of Doom. I know Sebastiano, who we call Sebo, from St. Nicholas of the Beggars. He's a foot taller now, with a huge wreath of curls on his head that looks like a halo when the sun shines through.

"It's me," I say. "Nico. Niccolò Saltano. From St. Nick's."

"It *is* you." He greets me with a fat grin and hugs me. "You were such a little squirt. Look at you now."

"Does a monk's life agree with you?"

He nods, and his halo bobs up and down, letting me know it's the right thing for him, and he's happy with his decision.

"Where do you live now?" I ask.

"Santa Maria delle Grazia. I haven't been to St. Nick's since my parents died."

"Nothing changes in St. Nick's."

"What about your friend, the slave who plays the oud?"

"He's always fine."

"I learned so much about music from him. What do you think of ours?"

"It's not the same old plainchant, that's for sure. You sing different tones at the same time. Each voice is a separate line, and you braid them together. Amazing. And you mix the rhythm of dances with solemn liturgy. I've never heard anything like it."

"Do you like it?"

"I love it."

Sebo blushes. "Of course we can't do that in the monastery," he says. "The abbot calls it diabolical. But here, nobody cares about that. They like it. As long as we bring back lots of money, we can do whatever we want."

"Do you by any chance know a friar called Brother Bernardo? An old man, tall, with white hair and bright blue eyes. He's staying on La Grazia."

Sebo looks surprised. "I do know of him."

"Is he in your order?"

"We're Carthusians; we live in seclusion. Brother Bernardo is a hermit friar. He doesn't live in a monastery. He's supposed to live among the people on the alms of the faithful. I hear he does many things, but begging isn't one of them."

"I'd love to see your monastery."

"If you row me home, I will show you. You still row, don't you?"

I borrow one of the delivery boats from the canal behind the palace. As I row to La Grazia, Sebo still hasn't said anything, so I ask him.

"Sebo, do you know what happened to me?"

He looks puzzled. "You're taller. You don't smell like fish. No chip on your shoulder. What else?"

I flash the ring.

"I'm the ballot boy."

"No. *No!* Really? You're too old, aren't you?"

"I was fourteen years and nine months when Doge Cornaro died."

"Holy saints of mercy and forbearance. What do I call you?"

"Nico."

I row around the south flank of Giudecca and point my prow at the bell tower of La Grazia. Sebo is drunk with words because he's not allowed to talk inside. He tells me about life in the monastery and asks me about life in the palace. As we approach La Grazia, he shows me where to tether the boat, and we walk from the dock toward the monastery.

"Do you know anything else about Brother Bernardo?" I ask.

"He is a piece of work," Sebo says. "He's a hermit, but he has more visitors than the pope of Rome. Mostly from the mainland. Some of them look like nobles or soldiers. The rest look like pirates. The abbott turns the other way, so they must be stuffing his pocket."

"Are there regulars? People who come often?"

"See that window above the trees? That's the scriptorium. It overlooks the hermitage, and I'm up there a lot copying music. I see a lot of people come and go. There's one boat that comes at least twice a week."

"Is it about twenty-two feet long, faded blue, almost gray, used to be fancy but it hasn't been cleaned since the first Crusade?"

"Exactly. Yes. That's them. Why are you so interested in Brother Bernardo?"

"My cousin is going to marry his cousin. I want to know what kind of family she's marrying into."

"Believe it or not, I think he's noble. He sure acts like it."

"A noble hermit?"

"He's not the first."

As monasteries go, La Grazia is poor and small. The island was originally a garbage dump. The brick and stone were probably ferried from the mainland when chunks of ruined Roman temples could be had for the taking. Sebo is proud of it, poor and plain as it is.

The bells in the campanile ring Vespers.

"They toll for me, brother," Sebo says. "The hermitage is around the bend. Follow the footpath."

TWO JETTIES OF broken rock and boulders enclose a cove deep enough for light galleys. A hut stands on poles above a wooden dock. The shutters are closed. Vespers can be heard from the monastery.

In the silence before moonrise, a boat enters the cove, accompanied by the murmur of voices. Three men. One rows, two are passengers. They tether the boat and climb onto the dock. Brother Bernardo wears his friar's robe like a wolf wears sheep's clothing. Ruggiero isn't with them. The rower is a seaman; I can tell by his stroke. His companion isn't wearing armor, but he has soldier stamped on his gait. He starts to say something.

"Hold your tongue," Brother Bernardo says. "The monks are silent, but their ears are godlike, omniscient, omnipotent, and omnipresent."

They climb the ladder to the hut. The friar moves well for an old man. I'm not close enough to hear what they're saying.

The hut's only window faces the water. I shinny up one of the poles. The floorboards sticking out from under the walls form a narrow ledge. I inch onto the ledge, not close enough at first, and suddenly too close. This is what Abdul calls acting first and thinking later. Once I'm there, I realize there's nothing to grab on to. I press my palms against the wall and pray.

"What is the mood in the Arsenal?" Brother Bernardo asks.

"Sorry to say, milord, most support the doge."

"Of course they do. If they didn't, their mothers would send them to bed without supper."

"That's not to say there's no discontent, sir. I'd be lying if I said there wasn't."

"Discontent is the midwife of change. We must fan the flames."

"Discontent there is, sir, but not out in the open. Not yet, anyway."

"Befriend every discontented man reckless enough to act on it. What's the situation with the army?"

"Ha! What army?"

A different voice. The soldier is speaking.

"Venice don't have no army," he says. "Just a bunch of green boys and pimps in Treviso. As soon as the trouble started, the recruiters raided the whorehouses and the jails for anyone with two hands, two feet, and two balls."

"Or hired professionals like yourself."

"We follow the gold."

"Soon we shall have plenty of gold," Brother Bernardo says. "Don't let my present circumstances mislead you. The wind is changing. A hundred years will be undone in a day. We shower the people with gold ducats, and they belong to us."

"What about the old doge?"

"After Faliero, no doge counts. Contarini is a gnawed bone waiting to be tossed. Bring me thirty good men, and we can take Venice in a night."

Shit.

My foot slips. I tumble in an explosion of pain and noise, bouncing off the deck into the lagoon. I pray nothing is broken.

Heads poke out the window above me, shouting. The light from the room splashes my face. Brother Bernardo pierces me with icy blue eyes.

My legs work. My fingers work. My right arm works. My brain rattles inside my head. I know what day it is, I know my name, and I know if I don't get away from here, they will kill me. A cloud engulfs the moon, and darkness is my friend. I swim on my side in the cold, clear water, my bad arm flat against my body.

They yell from their boat as they bear down in my direction. The seaman has a powerful stroke, but he's used to galley oars, not lagoon boats. He robs himself of speed. I swim as fast as I can using both arms, the pain propelling me forward. I keep underwater as much as I can.

Close to my boat now, I yank a dead stalk from the bank, blow it clean, submerge, and suck air through it until they have passed.

Chapter Twenty-Two

Shattered Glass

I LOVE WATCHING Matteo curry Delfín. I know she likes him better than me; she sees more of him. So I bring her apples from the kitchen.

"Then what happened?" he asks.

"I stayed under water until they passed me, then I hopped into my boat and rowed like hell."

He's amazed. He squats next to me. His thighs bulge like prize hams.

"How come your thighs are so big?" I ask.

He slaps them. "I hauled sacks of grain on the dock since I was seven. Lug those up and down the embankment a hundred times a day, you'll have hams like these too."

"I wish I did."

"Can I tell you my secret now?"

We climb over the side of Delfin's stall and hide behind the haystacks where no one can see us.

Instead of telling me a secret, he starts laughing and blushing.

"I'm afraid I committed a grievous sin," he finally says. "But it sure felt good."

He busts out laughing all over again.

"What did you do?"

"My friend from the kitchen came back here with me, and he..."

Matteo looks around to make sure no one is anywhere nearby. "He played my flute with his mouth."

"Can he play?"

Matteo slaps me on the head. "Not that flute, stupid. That's sodomy for sure, isn't it?"

He looks just a little bit scared.

"Did you spurt?"

"Hell, yes."

"Technically, that makes it sodomy. Putting it in his mouth is bad, but it's a null act if you don't spurt. If you spurt, it's sodomy for sure."

I read the trial transcripts. I know the courts.

"Damn," he says. "I guess I'm really bound for Hell."

He tries to look sad, but he can't stop laughing.

"Matteo." I slap his head to get his attention. "Tell me what it felt like."

His eyes glitter with delight. "His mouth was soft and wet and warm. He sure knew what he was doing. When I closed my eyes, I saw stars, swear to God. It kept getting better and better until my insides busted open. I screamed so loud he stuffed his apron in my mouth. I guess I'm definitely going to Hell."

"I guess so."

He's so sweet it's hard to believe.

"It was worth it," he says.

"Are you going to do it again?"

"Why not? I'm going to Hell anyway. It's all I think about."

He lies back against the haystack.

"Damn," he says. "It was amazing."

"Are you going to the shooting match tomorrow?" I ask.

"Screw Ruggiero Gradenigo."

He flips over and humps the hay, laughing, his mind elsewhere.

I CHECK THE lion column. There's no sign from Abdul. I've been waiting for days, and I'm worried. I was certain there would be a sign this morning.

I go anyway.

"I didn't leave you a sign," Abdul says when he sees me.

"I have to see Alex."

"Her father is home, and the parish priest is babysitting her."

His face looks serious. Sad. He scares me.

"Why is he doing that?"

"It's like this, old man. Alex went mad."

"She what?" I grab his vest, pulling him toward me, across the table. He pushes me back.

"Don't. Shoot. The. Messenger."

"What do you mean, she went mad? Why didn't you tell me?"

"Because there's nothing we can do right now."

"What happened?"

"Remember the plants in the window that she used to tend?"

"She loved them."

"Those very ones. She attacked them with her fork. Shredded them. Her mother said if she didn't stop acting like a madwoman, they would treat her like one."

"How do you know this?"

"Ruta talked Blackbeard into letting me bring my special tea. While I was there, Ruta told me everything. Alex told her mother they couldn't keep her locked up, and her mother said they can do whatever they want until Ruggiero takes her. Alex threatened to kill herself, and her mother slapped her so hard her nose bled. Alex told her mother she doesn't want the life they gave her, that it's worse than prison."

"What did her mother say?"

"She said no one asked her how she felt when she had to marry Blackbeard at the age of twelve and he was forty-three. She said women have no choice, and the sooner Alex accepts that the better off she'll be. That's when Alex tried to strangle her mother. Ruta pulled Alex off and locked her in her room. That night, Alex broke her mirror and cut her wrists. Thank our lucky stars she cut across, not lengthwise. She lost much blood, but she's alive. She's broken, my friend, like a fragile glass."

I lay my forehead on the table. Abdul massages the back of my neck.

"Her mother dragged in the priest from Arcangelo Raffaele," he says, "because she's afraid Alex will commit a sin that will damn her for all eternity. Adultery, usury, fornication, theft, even murder can all be forgiven with the proper priest's formula, but suicide is unforgivable."

"Suicide and sodomy."

Chapter Twenty-Three

The Shooting Match

A FLEET OF senators, judges, advocates, lords of the Arsenal, and lords of the night march to the shooting match with the doge. They are all aggravated because he refuses to take the Golden Boat and makes everyone walk. He says the processions are nothing but a plot to keep him from seeing anything for himself. This is his revenge. He grumbles so only I can hear him.

"I need a hundred people to cross the square like I need the Black Death. I'm surprised they let me take a shit by myself."

Trumpeters and Arsenal men line the tops of the Arsenal walls. With so many high officeholders in attendance, the bailiff and his crew, who are supervising the match, get frantic with keeping everything by the book, which shooting contests never are. As we arrive, the contestants' families stand on their benches to watch the procession.

"One of the great wonders of the world, our Arsenal," Serenissimo says. "Three hundred years ago, it was eight acres total with enough gear to handle twenty boats. Now, it's four times that size, with ten thousand shipbuilders, master-builders, foremen, carpenters, caulkers, sawyers, rope-spinners. The pride of Venice."

"Why did so many nobles want to come today?"

"You saw the scene Gradenigo made. Big money is riding on this match."

Trumpets announce the contestants. One by one, they march in front of the dais and bow to the doge. Their names are checked off on a list, their identity is vouched for, and they are assigned to eight-man squads.

A bailiff checks the target, a man-sized torso with a heart the size of a gold ducat painted on the chest in the center of white, yellow, and red circles. Ruggiero is in the last squad. Drums beat. A trumpet announces the first squad. The bailiff checks off each contestant and makes sure his bolt is stamped with his family coat of arms.

The contestants cock, load, and aim their crossbows. The bailiff drops a red flag, and the bolts streak toward the target. The bailiff pulls the losing bolts and throws them aside, leaving only the winner in place.

The crowd cheers. Drums and trumpets summon the second squad.

Flag down.

Bolts scream toward the target. Two miss completely, one hits in the white, two hit in the yellow, one in red, and one hits just under the heart but not significantly better than the first squad winner.

By the time Ruggiero's squad is called, only seven bolts remain in the target, none worth calling a bona fide bull's-eye. Ruggiero's crossbow doesn't have fancy cranks or winches. It's trim and fierce, like him, tailored to his long arms and broad shoulders. He places his foot in the stirrup, cocks and loads, raises his arms, elbows out, sights along the stock, then drops the weapon to his side like he already won.

Flag down.

The bolts scream.

Two hit near the heart. Ruggiero still hasn't pulled his trigger. The bailiff glares at him. Ruggiero bows to the doge, raises his bow, and shoots. He's so full of himself, he doesn't compensate properly for the wind. His bolt pierces inside the heart but slightly high and off-center. Technically, it's a bull's-eye.

The bailiff removes all the other bolts and points at Ruggiero's. The crowd cheers. Ruggiero turns to the committee.

"I told you I'm a bowman, not a clerk."

He bows. Not a gracious bow; a snotty bow.

The doge leans into my ear. "It's hard to believe he's the best we have."

"He's not. He's the best of the nobles."

The bailiff is about to pull Ruggiero's bolt when the doge raises his hand. The bailiff freezes.

"Can you beat him?" the doge asks me under his breath.

"Are you the doge of Venice?"

"You are the best of our nobles," the doge says to Ruggiero. "But most Venetians aren't noble. Will you accept the challenge of a commoner? Not for the job, that's yours by right. For the title only? Best bowman from Grado to Cavarzere."

"I accept only to prove that we are noble because we are best. May I ask Your Exalted Serenity who challenges me?"

"My ballot boy."

Ruggiero laughs out loud. I stand forward.

I don't have my bow with me. Cristoforo Orio offers me his. I heft it to feel its weight and sight along the stock to see if it's true. It's not mine, but it's a classy weapon.

I bow to the doge. I even bow to Ruggiero because I'm learning how to play this game. I take my position, lock the stirrup under my foot, cock, slide a bolt into the channel, and lift.

"Was that your best shot?" I ask Ruggiero.

"If you can beat me, I deserve to lose."

The wind is light, from the northwest. My hands are sweaty. I cross myself.

St. Mark and St. Nick, steady my hand and clear my eye.

I breathe in and out. I see Abdul in the crowd and imagine Alex laughing when she hears the story. Closing my eyes, I clear my mind. Opening them, I arrange my field of vision as Abdul taught me. I aim, adjust for the wind, and pull the trigger. The bolt streaks straight and true, splitting Ruggiero's bolt in two.

The bailiff pulls Ruggiero's bolt from the target, throws it to the ground, and calls me forward. He raises my arms, shouting, "Niccolò Saltano of St. Nicholas of the Beggars, the best shot from Grado to Cavarzere."

The crowd chants "Ni-co. Ni-co. Ni-co."

Ruggiero lunges at me with his dagger. Cristoforo Orio tackles him and pulls him off course. They hit the ground in a burst of spit and blood.

AFTER THE MATCH, a cross in blue chalk on the lion column alerts me to news of Alex. I zigzag, right, left, right, running my ass off all the way to Arcangelo Raffaele. Is Alex back from the dead?

She definitely looks better. Her skin is still ashy, but the circles around her eyes are gone. Her hair, braided and twisted and pulled back off her forehead, makes her eyes appear seven times bigger than usual. She turns her face so I won't see her crying, and embarrassed by the bandages on her wrists, tries to hide them in her sleeves.

"Thank God, you're alive," I say. "You can't imagine the nightmares I've had."

"I'm so sorry." Alex throws her arms around me.

We sit on the floor under the window, side by side, our fingers laced together.

"I was afraid you forgot me," she says.

"How could I forget you?"

"You have Matteo now."

"Matteo is my friend. You're my soulmate."

I raise her wrist to my lips and kiss the bandages. "You told me I couldn't kill Ruggiero because I'd be drawn and quartered. You said you couldn't live with the thought that I died for you. Did you forget that? How do you think I could live, knowing you did what you did without giving me a chance to help?"

"I wasn't thinking," she says.

"I know."

"Can you forgive me?"

"If you can forgive me for making you feel forgotten," I say. "Just think, Ruggiero must leave before he can marry you. He got his place on a galley. No time for a wedding."

"I heard Papa arguing about it with his uncle," she says. "Where is he going?"

"Alexandria. His convoy leaves in one week, and Serenissimo swears Ruggiero will be on it."

"How long will he be gone?"

"They can't return until the pepper ships from India unload. October at the very earliest."

"Thank God. Thank God. Thank God. Nico, swear to me that I'll be gone before he gets back."

She flushes with color. I catch a glimpse of the old Alex. She squeezes my hand desperately.

"Swear, Nico. Swear, and I promise I'll never do anything stupid again. Swear to help me escape."

"Escape to where? And how?"

"We'll figure it out. Nico, Nico, Nico, I sank into the darkest depths of my soul, down with the worms, down where there is only fear and more fear until I had to end it, and it still didn't end, so I had to let go. As soon as I let go, I rose back up to the surface. I'm alive. I'm clever and strong. I will find a life. Not this one. A life I want. So I apologized to my mother for being so crazy. I brushed my hair and dressed nicely again, and then she started acting normal."

"Your mother—normal?"

"Well, normal for her. Not as scared of me. I even started talking to Papa. I told him I don't hate him, and I'm not ungrateful. I said I would do whatever he wants. I talked about wedding dresses and how he must fix up that dreadful old Gradenigo palace. I kept at it until he sent the priest home, so I must be a good liar."

"It's late, Alex. I have to go. Thank you for coming back."

"Wait. Nico. You didn't swear...to help me escape."

"I swear."

She strokes the dolphin around my neck, kisses it, and presses it against my heart.

"Get me a boat," she says. "Set me free."

After I climb down, the rope disappears back into her window, and she closes the shutters.

I'm in a state, not looking where I'm going. I slam into a drunk stumbling off the bridge. He shoves me out of his way with a snarl I'd know anywhere.

Ruggiero doesn't believe his eyes either. "Everywhere I go, there you are," he says. "What the hell are you doing here?"

"Following you."

"I think you've been sniffing around my bride again. You and that yammering half-wit slave you run with."

He grabs me and pulls me against him. "I should have killed you at the shooting match."

He fumbles for his dagger.

"Kill me," I say, "and Brother Bernardo will kill you."

He stops dead. "What did you say?"

"Brother Bernardo sounded like he meant business. You know, at Marullo's."

"What the hell..." He's pushes me into the wall, his knife at my throat. My ring won't help me now.

"You're not just an idiot," he says. "You're dangerous. What else do you know?"

"I know you were supposed to pick someone else as ballot boy, and Brother Bernardo was burned up about that. I know the Ten can roast Brother Bernardo over a slow fire for what I heard. And I know you can't kill me, no matter how much you want to. I sure as hell wouldn't want to be in your shoes if you do."

"You're right."

He stops. Laughs. Sheaths his dagger.

"Goddamn you. Stinking little mongrel bastard. You're right. Don't let it go to your head. You'll end up dead soon enough. Ugly dead. So ugly even the vultures will pass you by. And you can be certain someone else will hang for it. But not me. And not now. My beautiful bride awaits me."

He spits at me, swaggers up to the gate of Barbanegra palace, and bangs with both fists. A torch flares upstairs. Caterina Barbanegra steps onto the balcony overlooking the gate. She recognizes him immediately.

"What do you want?" she asks.

"Let me in, woman."

"You have no business here."

"I want to kiss my beautiful bride good night."

"She's not your bride yet."

"Oh, tell me please, mother dear, that she is still breathing? I am so worried."

"I don't know what you're talking about."

"Surely you do, lady. Everyone else in Venice does."

Caterina is visibly shaken. "Leave. You have no business here."

"Not before I kiss my darling Alessandra."

He glances back at me and up at the frightened woman in the portico. He bangs the gates until his fists are bloody.

"Open the goddamn gates. I must kiss my bride."

Caterina Barbanegra has no fondness for nobles in general. She hates Ruggiero.

"Come back when she's yours," she says, "and not before."

She signals into the courtyard. The gate swings open, and two oarsmen step out. One is as big as an ox; the other is bigger. They carry heavy wooden clubs studded with iron spikes called "morning stars." A slave slams the gate behind them.

Ruggiero staggers back. He looks at me, at the oarsmen, at Caterina Barbanegra.

"You bloody bitch. This isn't over yet."

Chapter Twenty-Four

Thunder in Trieste

AT THE MEETING of the Doge's Council, Marino sits next to Serenissimo taking notes. I sit behind them, listening intently.

These men aren't afraid to stand up to the emperor of Byzantium, the king of Hungary, or Murad the Turk, himself, but they fear Genoa like the devil. Genoa is the only other sea power in Italy with a navy to rival ours. They fight us for trade routes, conspire to cut us off from the Silk Road trade, and hate us more than we hate them. The doge, however, sees things differently. When he suggests the greater, more immediate danger is Lord Carrara of Padua, they cluck like so many hens about Genoa.

"But Genoa is caught in a trap of her own devising," the doge says, struggling to rein in his temper. "Rival factions killing each other right and left make Genoa impossible to rule, so the strongest among them, in their monumental stupidity, begged Bernabo Visconti of Milan to act as their lord until they can manage themselves. Unfortunately for them, but fortunately for us, Visconti is hip-deep in his war against the pope and can't afford to let Genoa do anything stupid with the Holy Father, the dukes of Austria, and King Louis of Hungary all ravening at his hells. Visconti chokes Genoa with a tight rein, so until they figure out how to free themselves from their savior, we need not worry about them. We need to worry about our ruthless and ambitious neighbor, Lord Carrara of Padua."

Marino interrupts Serenissimo with the same impatient voice he uses in my Latin lessons when I have strayed and he needs to get me back on point. "Nevertheless," he says, "the question before us is what to do about the chancery scribe accused of passing transcripts of Senate meetings to his contact in Genoa."

"Torture him. He'll confess," says Bruno Badoer, a Gradenigo cohort.

"He'll tell us *something*," the doge says. "God knows what."

I hear it first because I'm a lot younger, and my hearing is a lot better than anyone else's in the room—a sound like distant thunder echoing through the palace, raised voices moving closer. The rat-a-tat-tat of boots on terrazzo floors grows louder and louder until everyone in the room stares at the door.

Three sharp raps.

"Who goes?"

"The Lord of the Night."

A guard opens the door.

The Lord of the Night bows deeply. "May I?"

"Please. Enter," the doge says.

The Lord of the Night approaches and bows again. "Our embassy has returned from Trieste, Exalted Serenity."

The Lord of the Night steps aside. Two nobles enter, bow deeply, approach, and bow again. Mud dirties their embroidered cloaks and silver-trimmed boots and gloves; their matted hair and haggard faces testify to the desperation of their flight.

"What news from Trieste?" the doge asks.

"They refuse to fly our flag, Exalted Serenity. Tore it to shreds in the square."

The room is so quiet I can hear the grand chancellor farting from across the courtyard.

"Esteemed councilors, Exalted Serenity, nobles of the Most Serene Republic of Venice," he continues, his voice weak and shaken. "Our face has been slapped in public by foulmouthed swineherds and salt diggers."

"Who refused, exactly, to fly our flag?" The doge clearly can't believe his ears.

"The rectors refused, the council and the judges refused, the peasants shaking their pitchforks at us refused. They spat in our faces. We were lucky to get out alive."

"Let me be clear," the doge says. "They threatened your person?"

"They most certainly did, Exalted Serenity, after swearing they would never fly our flag again. When the rector said the will of their people was to be rid of us, the crowd cheered. Absent the bravery of our captain and bowmen, we would never have made it back to our ship without bloodshed."

"Have they gone mad?" The doge is incredulous and irate. "They can't do that. They are bound by treaties."

"I reminded them of the treaties," the envoy says, "by which we are sovereign over their shabby little seaside salt pan. They said the treaties are no longer binding."

"Flaming heart of Jesus! We own the gulf. The name says it all. Gulf of Venice. We alone keep it safe for their sorry excuse for a fleet. They don't even have a fleet. They have fishing boats and fat cogs to smuggle salt past our patrols. Have they entirely lost their reason?"

The veins stand out on the doge's forehead.

"They said it is no longer the Gulf of Venice," the envoy announces. "As far as they are concerned, it is the Gulf of Trieste."

"The gulf is ours because we cleared out the bloody pirates who made the entire Adriatic a charnel house of rape and pillage."

"They also complained bitterly about our royalties, Exalted Serenity. They refuse to pay us another cent on salt traded in their port."

A tall, beak-nosed noble, Federico Cornaro, says, "Obviously, they're bluffing."

Cornaro's father is the sugar king of Cyprus, reputedly richer than Ziani. Federico has a reedy voice and sounds like a man who knows what he's talking about.

"They know exactly what we're thinking," he says. "They know we don't want a war because we have no men to fight one, and we can't afford one anyway. They don't want a war either. They want the revenue from the salt trade, untaxed. They are children throwing a tantrum. Offer them sweets to quiet them and remind them how expensive it is to raise an army and fight a war. Better yet, bring them here. Let them plead their case. Feed them soft-shelled crab and Cretan wine. Find common ground."

Bruno Badoer rises, red in the face. "Give in now," he shouts at everyone, "and you might as well give them the keys to the Customs House."

He always uses those same words about any outsider challenging our dominion.

"Nobody said give in," says Federico Cornaro. Badoer does not intimidate him. "We're talking about negotiating."

"Negotiate my fat hairy arse!" Badoer roars. "Mark my words. Invite them to table and they'll soon be eating our soup."

"There are times," the doge says, "when a show of strength is necessary to make sure they understand they do not want us as an enemy. Organize men-at-arms and cavalry. March our flag to Trieste. Tell them to hang it, or we'll hang them. Then bring back their negotiators to hammer out an agreement."

"Objection, Exalted Serenity." Disappointed, the noble stands firmly in dissent. "Profound objection. With all due respect, Serenissimo, you do not make decisions. We make decisions. I don't think your order accurately expresses the will of this body, and we can overrule you. Most men I see here favor a diplomatic solution. We will request an embassy from Trieste with men empowered to negotiate terms."

Bruno Badoer once again springs from his seat.

"They spat in our faces. You can't talk that away. We have to smash them before we lose the gulf and everything else along with it."

In a rare instance, Badoer and the doge are on the same side and in the minority, as it happens. The doge is outraged but holds his tongue as he's overruled.

BY THE TIME the doge and I are alone, it's very late.

"Follow me," he says.

"Are we going to pray?"

"We're going somewhere else tonight."

He stuffs a sack with fat white foot-and-a-half long candles from his private closet. The candles testify how rich he is; he never runs out, and these candles are so expensive people leave the half-burned stubs in their wills.

He stashes the sack under his gold robe, takes a small candle from the table, and hands it to me.

"Don't let it go out."

The guards in the Hall of Maps outside his antechamber are dozing. We duck left, behind the Senate chamber and committee rooms. No one sees us. The atrium facing St. Mark's Basin is silver in the moonlight. Palm trees in porcelain pots from the court of Kublai Khan stand between Roman statues of muscular athletes and voluptuous goddesses. On cold days, the nobles come here to gossip and twist one another's arms instead of standing outside in the arcade. This is also where the sodomite herald and the boy were caught *in flagrante delicto*.

The doge opens the door to the Great Council chamber. The entire east wall behind the dais, over 200 square feet of it, is filled with a single painting depicting Paradise, with Jesus Christ placing a crown on His Mother's head in the center. The nobles' benches have been moved away from the windows overlooking the water. A vast quantity of supplies litters the floor and covers a long trestle: rags, plaster, roots and stones for pigments, trowels and brushes, jugs and bowls, paper and charcoal, and pins. Another picture is in progress on the wall. The doge sets his candles on the floor in a semicircle and lights them from mine. I think I hear someone behind us, but I don't see anything.

"I think someone is following us, sir."

"Marino," he shouts, "go to bed!"

He winks at me and holds a candle up to the painting.

"Have you looked at this painting?"

"Can't say as I have, sir."

It's at least forty feet wide and twenty feet tall. There's no way I can see all of it in the dark. During the day, I'm usually behind the urns and don't pay attention to the walls. The doge holds his candle close to the fresco and highlights some of it for me.

"Tell me what's going on."

"St. Mark's Square is filled with people."

"Who is this?"

"The pope?"

"Pope Alexander III."

The doge lowers the candle. Another man lies face down in front of the pope, his forehead touching the paving stones. He wears armor, but his helmet is off. Yards of curly red hair fan out around him. His scepter lies on the ground beside him. The pope's foot rests on his head.

"Any idea who he is?"

"A king."

"Frederick Barbarossa, the Holy Roman emperor. The year is 1172."

"Why is the pope stepping on his head?"

"It's an act of submission. Next, Barbarossa will kiss the pope's foot. They were bitter enemies, and Barbarossa lost. He is surrendering."

He moves the candle to the left.

"Who's that?"

"The doge."

His gold robe and dumpling-shaped *corno* give him away.

"Doge Sebastiano Ziani, nicely framed between the Columns of Doom. Of course, they weren't the Columns of Doom then; that came later. To Ziani, they echoed the columns on the Golden Horn in Constantinople—his way of saying we had surpassed Byzantium."

The doge pulls a bench against the wall. "Stand on the bench and look at Ziani's face."

He holds the candle high so the light falls on the painted face. "Does he look familiar?"

"No, Excellency."

"It's Lord Francesco Carrara of Padua. Our best enemy."

"How can that be?"

"Guariento di Arpo is painting this fresco. Next to Giotto di Bondone, he is the finest painter Padua has yet produced. He put Carrara's face on the doge. Nobody seems to have noticed."

Serenissimo stands back and sets his candle down. Shadow swallows the painting.

"No one?"

"Some admit a passing resemblance if I point it out. Others say paintings never look like the people they're supposed to represent, and there's certainly truth in that. The painter just shrugs. He says no one could show him what Ziani looked like."

The doge sits on the bench, his hands on his knees, looking off into darkness.

"It's a sign," he says.

"A sign of what, Excellency?"

"Carrara's face on the doge? It's obvious to me. The fortune-teller was right."

DELFÍN MISSES OUR rides on the Lido, and I don't see her often enough. I feed her apples, curry her, lean my head against her silky red-brown coat and talk to her, but she's edgy until Matteo shows up. Then she relaxes. She's always happy to see him. I am too.

When he saunters in playing his flute, I can forget everything going wrong. We climb over the backside of Delfín's stall to our den in the hay. He plays a new tune on his flute.

"What do you think?"

"It sounds like a drunk bird singing his ass off."

"Is that good or bad?"

"It makes me want to fly."

"Sounds good to me."

He spreads a horse blanket on the hay. We lie on our backs, close our eyes, and he plays again. Delfín whinnies because he's playing her song.

"I saw my kitchen friend again."

"Did you sin?"

"Actually, I think technically speaking, it wasn't a sin."

"What did you do?"

"I put my pecker between his thighs. Humped him. How bad can that be?"

"Did you spurt?"

"I sure did."

"Then it's a sin."

"I should have known. It felt great. Not as good as before but pretty damn good, and it's hardly a sin at all, wouldn't you say? Want to try?"

"No, thanks."

"I'm starting to think you don't like me."

"You know I like you."

"Let me show you. The sin is mine. Then if you want you can try on me."

He pulls off his tunic and drops his trousers and his breeches. I've never seen him naked before. He's a boy on top and a man below, with chestnut hair from his loins to his ankles. He grabs me and pulls me toward him, then presses my fingers between his thighs.

"Feel that, and then say no."

I pull back, and he wrestles me, pins my wrists to the blanket, his face in mine.

"Just once, Nico. You liked it when I touched you."

"I *know* I'm going to like it, Matteo. That's why I can't."

He lets go, his face annoyed and sad.

"I saw Hell," I say. "I saw it, and I don't want to go there."

"When did you see Hell?"

"I was seven. I stole some coins from Pierluigi, so he took me to see the Last Things—Death, Judgment, Heaven and Hell—in the church on Torcello. Have you ever been there?"

He shakes his head and pulls up his breeches.

"Pierluigi explained it to me. Our Savior was sitting among the holy and the wise while the earth and the sea yielded up their dead. The Book of Life was open at His feet because we're all judged by our deeds. He separated the righteous from the damned for all eternity. *Dies irae.* Day of wrath. Fiery angels with pitchforks threw the damned into the lake of fire. Princes and emperors and kings sent screaming into the lake of fire alongside thieves and murderers and whores and infidels. No earthly power could save them from everlasting torment. So Pierluigi said. But the real torment isn't the fire, Matteo. It's being separated for all eternity from everyone I love, from my mother, from Alex and Abdul and Serenissimo."

"Hey, what about me?"

"You'll be in Hell with me."

We hear voices out by the stalls. Matteo whips on his tunic and jumps back into Delfín's stall.

SERENISSIMO SUMMONSES ME and sends me out again to put my ear on the street, as he likes to say. To hear what the little people, the real people, are saying in their unguarded moments. The sorts of things he never gets to hear. I put on my street clothes and head out through the main gate of the palace.

Guffo, the one-handed beggar from St. Nick's, sits near the hospital across the square from the palace. I've known him all my life, way before they cut his hand off for stealing a pig from the butcher in San Pantalon.

"Good day, fair prince." He pats the ground next to him for me to sit. I squat behind a pillar where no one can see me. The stump of his right arm rests on his knee. His cap has a few coins in it.

"People don't see me," he says. "I'm a ghost. I don't exist."

"I didn't exist before I became ballot boy."

"How do you like it?"

"I have a lot more to worry about now. What's the word in the arcades today?"

"The word of the day is Trieste."

"What about Trieste?"

"War. You look surprised. Don't you know about it?"

"Yes, but nobody else is supposed to know."

"Only the Ten keep secrets, even from each other. It's old news. Everyone already has an opinion. Knock Trieste down and build our kind of place. Buy them off. Negotiate with them. Hire Turks to slit their throats. Go to war. Don't go to war. You name it; somebody thinks it, the sort of shit you hear at the Swordfish."

"What's the Swordfish?"

"If the Great Council had an evil twin, that, my fine young prince, would be the Swordfish."

"Where is it?"

"Around the corner from the big whorehouse at San Canciano. Stay away if you know what's good for you. Poke your nose in the Swordfish, and you might lose it."

ACROSS RIALTO BRIDGE, in San Giacomo Square, a misfit with a long beard harangues anyone who will listen. It goes on every night. He pays no attention to the curfew bell; he strides around the square. He looks like a mad monk and sounds like a university student.

"Citizens of Venice, is this how our Republic is supposed be? The doge's robe is worth a fleet! Federico Cornaro could melt down his silver belt and pay the national debt. How about your pocket? How much is in there?"

Men with nowhere to go stop and listen.

"It's wrong, brothers," says the orator. "It's not God's way. The Lord said, it's easier for a camel to pass through the eye of a needle than for a rich man to get into Heaven. Why do we put the greatest sinners in the highest places of honor?"

Ruggiero Gradenigo steps out of the shadow and confronts the orator. "What would you have us do?"

The orator inspects him from head to toe. "Which 'we' are you talking about, milord? I say to hell with you nobles if we can't at least feed our families while making you richer."

"I'm poorer than you, my friend. For every rich noble, ten more live on crumbs. Less than a hundred of them reap the riches."

From the dark porch of San Giacomo church, another voice shouts, "Burn the bloody palace down. Start all over. We did it before."

"Who remembers our popular assembly," the orator shouts. "When the big bell rang, every Venetian who heard it came running. We were the government. We elected the doge. Why did we allow them to replace our popular assembly with their Great Council?"

Another voice: "What if another Faliero makes himself king?"

"They'll chop off his head, just like the last one."

Ruggiero steps forward. "Faliero plotted against the very men who closed the Great Council. Was that so wrong?"

The orator stands nose-to-nose with Ruggiero. "I love nobles the way a dog loves the stick you beat him with, but I don't want to kill them. I want jobs for starving men."

"Oh, you'll have plenty of jobs," Ruggiero replies. "You'll soon be going to war."

"Rowing in peacetime is war enough," says a grizzled oarsman.

Peacekeepers begin weaving into the crowd.

"I'm not against Venice, and I'm not against war. I'm against starving," the orator shouts at Ruggiero.

Ruggiero says, "I'm not against Venice, and I'm not against war. I'm against a cabal of greedy nobles turning our Republic into their own private mint."

Men cheer. The peacekeepers tighten ranks. Their leader shouts, "Empty the square or fill the jail."

The orator leaps into the crowd beside the Peacekeepers. "By whose order?"

The peacekeeper brandishes his sword. "By her order, that's who!"

Ruggiero slips out of the square with his crew. The rest of the mob grumbles and disperses. The peacekeepers drag the orator and a half-wit away. I follow Ruggiero.

The Swordfish is hard to miss. The sign hangs beside a smoky torch. A blue swordfish, tail down, sword pointing up, looks a lot like a man's plumbing primed for action. Ruggiero's crew knocks a bunch of drunks off their stools and takes their places. I keep my face covered with my hood, my head down, and fade back as best I can.

Pietro Obizzi, another freshman noble on the Great Council, eyes Ruggiero's strange crew. They're men of the sea for sure, but I'm not sure which one. Their clothes look Venetian; their faces tell a different story. Oarsmen from Cyprus. Hired soldiers from Crete who don't ask questions and take their money up front. Mainland thugs.

The tavern is too noisy for me to hear. I edge as close as I can without being seen.

Pietro Obizzi looks like a big curly-haired baby. He'll look like a baby when he's an old man. A stupid owl. He throws the butt end of a stale loaf of bread at Ruggiero and hits him on the head.

"I hear you made another rousing speech, Gradenigo. I can't wait to hear you when the Ten stretches you out on the rack."

Ruggiero looks puzzled. He taps the guy next to him on the shoulder. "Since when do piss pots talk?"

Obizzi puts his foot on Ruggiero's bench. "When shitholes give speeches. What about Trieste, Gradenigo?"

"Trieste? That should take all of about two days."

"But will we be allowed to loot?"

Ruggiero throws up his hands. "You know the rules," he says. "No looting Christians."

"But losers are losers."

"You ought to know."

"What's up your sleeve?" Obizzi asks.

"I'm going to be on the first galley out of here." Ruggiero is on edge, glancing around, looking for someone.

"How's your little bride?" Obizzi goads Ruggiero to do something legendary.

Ruggiero just grins. "As tasty as a fresh-shucked oyster."

"How would you know? You never even kissed her."

"I don't need to. Everybody else has. Ask anyone."

He's seen me all right. He's goading me now.

"You're full of shit, Gradenigo."

Ruggiero catches my eye, winks at me, and smiles.

"Alas, the seal is already broken," he says. "All the fun's been had. The well is open to all comers. Anyone can drink."

I dive across his table. Three of his crew block me and hold me back.

"Don't you recognize the doge's butt-boy?" Ruggiero asks.

He grabs my wrist and brandishes my ring. "Anybody else have a ring like that?"

Men push close, grabbing, arguing. Punches fly. Not about me. Not about anything. Too many men, too much temper, and everyone goes off at the same time.

I plow into Ruggiero, pinning him against the wall. I want to kill him, and this is my chance. I don't care what happens to me. My hands go straight for his throat. He fumbles for the mercy-maker on his belt, the thin blade designed to slip through visors to pierce eyes and brains or penetrate vulnerable spots in armor to deliver sudden death.

Men see the blade and go crazy. They swarm Ruggiero and hurl him back against the wall, head first. He slides down, dead weight. I'm about to close in when a brute weighing three hundred pounds hurls me across the room.

The barkeep whacks heads willy-nilly with a club. A squad of peacekeepers fights their way in the front door. Swords and daggers flash.

Peacekeepers block the front door, and a pile of bodies blocks the side door. I take my chances with the side door because the peacekeepers in front are working their way toward me. I shoulder bodies aside until I can put one foot flat against the wall and pull the door with both arms. The peacekeepers close in, herding the rioters across the room with a wall of shields, Roman-style.

The side door creaks open, an inch at a time. I hold the bodies back with one foot while I use the foot against the wall for leverage to open the door. When I can squeeze through, I yank my legs after me and roll into the alley as the bodies inside tumble back to barricade the door.

Chapter Twenty-Five

The Praetorian Guard

AFTER I REPORT to the doge about Rialto and the Swordfish, he says, "I need to visit the Arsenal. By myself. Without eighty nursemaids and trumpets and drums."

"You can't do that, sir."

"You sound like Marino. I don't care if I can't. I have to. No procession. No witnesses. A man among men. You've had plenty of experience out and about. I consider you something of an expert. It's time to put it to good use and get me the hell out of here."

"I am an expert, Serenissimo, but I'm also not the doge."

"The doge isn't going. Andrea Contarini is."

"Serenissimo, with all due respect, Faliero's end started with a secret meeting between him and the lord of the Arsenal."

"That's a chance I'll have to take."

He disguises himself as an old sailor with bits and pieces from a scrap shed. I'm amazed at the difference an eyepatch makes. With his hood covering most of his face and the eyepatch over one eye, I wouldn't recognize him on the street. He starts to strap on his sword. He's doge, and I can't tell him what to do, but I have to say something.

"The sword is a serious liability, Serenissimo. It's illegal. It will draw the wrong kind of attention. If certain people find out what you're up to, they might chop your head off."

"Stop worrying."

"I'm not worrying, Exalted Serenity."

"You never stop worrying."

"Take this instead."

I grab a wooden crutch off a pile and hand it to him. "No one gets arrested for a crutch. If we run into trouble, you can use it as a club."

"If we run into trouble, it won't matter." He draws a finger across his throat.

The shops and windows along the Strand are shuttered. People don't notice us. The doge stops in the middle of a bridge to listen to the sound of oars echoing underneath. A boatman sings a song of love betrayed. Bells peal, near and far, the last until morning. The wind rustling through the trees sounds like rushing water.

"Listen," he says. "The music of life. Great God in Heaven, I do miss it."

The brick walls of the Arsenal rise straight out of a canal on our right. On the left, wooden houses with flat roofs lean against one another. Gardens leap from roof to roof, and each house has a boat tied in front. The windows are dark. The neighborhood sleeps until the big bell sends them to work, turning forests of trees into fleets of galleys.

The lord of the Arsenal locks the gate at night and opens it in the morning. Once the gate is locked, no one is supposed to go in or out, but Guffo told me about a back gate by the Convent of St. Mary of Heaven that's never locked. The Arsenal men use it as a shortcut to go home.

The Arsenal wall is taller than the trees beneath it and the trees are so dense they conceal the brick, but we easily spot the iron gate that is closed but not locked. Inside, we ferry across a small lagoon on a pole raft to the opposite bank. The stench of boiling pitch bites our nostrils. The doge breathes as deeply as if it were sweet perfume.

"Our dominion rests on the ships we build," he says. "These men are our Praetorian Guard. Every noble could vanish, but as long as there's an Arsenal, there's a Venice."

Thin fog drifts across the water. Ship sheds and warehouses glow with banked fires that color the fog red. Forests of larch and oak and fir stacked in pyramids line the warehouses. Hulls line the banks of the interior canals, changing, shed by shed, from bare skeletons to fully planked vessels. Nearby, laborers twist hemp into rope and hew trees into deck planking, masts, and spars. Every peg and hinge and gear is made by men whose uncles and grandfathers also made them.

"We're in," I say. "What now?"

"Find Orsino Bellarosa, lord of the Arsenal."

He taps his eyepatch. "Remember, I'm blind in one eye and not much better in the other. Lead me around and let me do the talking."

At peak times, during Crusades or wars or when the merchant fleet returns, the Arsenal runs twenty-four hours a day with all hands on deck. Now, money is tight. We're not at war. The Arsenal is as quiet as it ever gets.

The doge approaches a lonely caulker stirring a cauldron of pitch used to seal the hulls. His eyes are open, but he looks asleep. We startle him.

"Who are you?" he asks.

"Carlo Fontana," the doge says hoarsely. "Mapmaker. This is my boy, Niccolò."

"What's your business here?"

"I'm looking for Orsino Bellarosa. I'm told he's here tonight, but we've been wandering around for an hour, and we haven't seen him yet."

"How do you know him?"

"We fought together Beyond-the-Sea."

"He's making his rounds, and he hasn't been here yet, so if you stick around, he'll turn up. He don't follow a fixed route, that one. He follows his nose."

The caulker touches his nose and winks. His ancient smile reveals toothless gums, and the little hair he has resembles a fringe of ash and soot around his shiny pate. He sits in his chair upwind from the cauldron and makes space for the doge.

"How many ships have you caulked?" the doge asks him.

"Too many to count."

"You are a true patriot and hero. What do you think of our new doge?"

"Dunno," he says. "Takes a while for them to show their true colors, I guess."

"Faliero lost his head after only seven months," the doge says.

"Weren't he a piece of work? I remember him like yesterday. Mean son of a bitch, he was. Slapped the sawdust out of the bishop of Olivolo for coming late to Mass. Strange business. Doge one day, the next day, head chopped off."

The doge nods and stares at the glowing embers. "The first thing a doge needs to know is who his friends are," he says.

"Only thing I know," says the caulker, "is I wouldn't want to be doge."

"Hell, no." The doge laughs. "Great Christ in Glory, save us all from that."

Another caulker hears us laughing and heads our way.

"Having a party, Giorgio?"

"*Salve*, Michele".

"Who are these?"

"This is Carlo Fontana, mapmaker, and his boy, Niccolò. They're friends of the lord. Hoping to catch up with him tonight."

"He's two stations down. I'll take them."

He leads the doge without recognizing him. We pass through a warehouse containing a half-finished hull to another filled with every size and shape of saw known to man. The lord is taking inventory.

"Visitors, sir," Michele calls out, all smiles.

The lord wheels around.

"*Visitors*?"

One glimpse of the lord's scowl sends Michele in hasty retreat. The lord unsheathes his sword and strides toward us, blade first.

"Who the hell are you, and how did you get in?"

"Don't you remember me, Orsino Bellarosa? Tyre. *The Primrose.*"

Seeing only an old man on a crutch with a boy, he sheathes his sword. The doge lifts my hand, shows him my ring, and silences the lord with a finger across his lips.

"Can we go somewhere and reminisce?" asks the doge.

"This way," the lord says. He leads us to a secluded shed.

"You can't be who I think you are," he says.

"Then I guess I'm not."

The doge removes his hood and lifts his eyepatch. The lord immediately kneels, takes the doge's hand, and kisses it.

"Exalted Serenity."

"We'll speak briefly, and as soon as I leave, I was never here."

"As you wish, sire."

The doge pulls him to his feet and puts an arm around his shoulder.

"War clouds are circling our lagoon. The Republic is in danger."

"She's always in danger, sire. That's why we're here."

"You may hear many strange things in coming days. Who do you trust?"

"His Exalted Serenity, Andrea Contarini, the doge of Venice."

"You will fight to defend and preserve us in the name of the Republic?"

"I will, sire, to my last breath."

"My orders are your command?"

"They are, sire."

"Swear your loyalty in the name of Jesus Christ, on the gospel of St. Mark, by the grace of the Blessed Virgin."

"I swear in the name of Jesus Christ, on the gospel of St. Mark, by the grace of the Blessed Virgin that I am loyal unto death to the doge and Republic of Venice."

"For whom do you speak?"

"I speak for myself, for my family, and for the men of the Arsenal."

Chapter Twenty-Six

Rebellion in the Ranks

THE VENETIAN AMBASSADOR to Byzantium has returned and he's scared out of his wits.

"The Turks have overrun Greece," he warns the Senate. "They'll reach Italy soon if we don't stop them. Serbia and Bulgaria will fall next. Byzantium has nothing left beyond the walls of Constantinople."

Ancient Marco Dandolo addresses the ambassador. He speaks like he walks, measured and indomitable.

"For his own reasons, which are God's, the Holy Father in Rome is reluctant to call a Crusade."

The ambassador's face crumples. "Then Byzantium is lost."

Voices echo in the corridor outside the Senate chamber, closer and closer.

Three sharp knocks at the door. The captain of the guard shouts: "Who goes?"

"The Lord of the Night."

The captain steps back, signaling the guards to open the doors. The Lord of the Night bows and steps aside. A hubbub erupts outside as Hieronimo Zen and a soiled bowman enter, supporting a sailor with bloody bandages who can barely walk. Behind them, surrounded by peace-keepers, three frightened men cower, obviously not Venetians. The guards shut the Senate doors against the growing furor in the corridor. The Lord of the Night is out of breath.

"Just arrived, these men. From the gulf squadron, Exalted Serenity. From Trieste."

The bowman kneels and bows his head to the doge. Marino Vendramin slides a chair under the wounded sailor. The Lord of the Night points to the other three men.

"And those poor excuses for men are ambassadors from the Council of Trieste. They tried to beat us here to spread their lies, but our brave men outran them."

The doge turns to the Venetians. "Tell us what you know," he says.

"Exalted Serenity, I am bowman on the light galley *Primavera*," one of them says. "This is Maffeo Soranzo, oarsman. We were patrolling the gulf near Trieste for smugglers and the like. Our captain is...was...Enrico Bembo. Until the Triesters murdered him."

The doge raises his hands to silence the tumult in the room.

"Murdered him?"

"Shot him through the heart, Exalted Serenity, along with six others of our crew. Two nights ago, after the second night bell, we spied a fat little cog sneaking out of the harbor, riding low in the water like she was heavy with contraband, salt most likely. We wouldn't have seen her but the moon was so bright. We overtook her easy enough and hauled her back to Muggia, where our fleet moors. We locked up her captain and bowmen. The rest of them ran like rats.

"We moored *Primavera* alongside the cog to keep an eye on her. It was my turn to sleep, so I stretched out on a bench and pulled a tarp over me. A big mob of surly Triesters, brutes all, wakes me up, mad as hell, seamen the lot of them, boarding the cog. They had just tore down the jail and freed their captain."

"Where was the rest of our squadron?"

"On patrol, Exalted Serenity. My captain orders the mob to stand clear of that fat-bellied piece of shit—excuse me, sire, those were his exact words—but before they were all spoke, a bolt split his chest from as close as you are to me. Went clean through him and took his insides with it.

"The Trieste dogs kept firing while they raised sail and took off back where they come from. Seven of ours died. We couldn't stop them. They got away, tub and all."

A sob shakes his shoulders. He's tired and humiliated. The doge turns to the Trieste ambassadors, and they cringe in his glare.

"How does Trieste respond?"

The wounded sailor shouts, "Don't listen to a word they say. Those Triesters ain't done right, Exalted Serenity. Not to our way of thinking."

A storm rattles the Senate doors, thumps and thuds and angry outcries.

"The nobles of Venice demand entry."

The captain of the guard draws his sword. "This is a meeting of the Senate."

"Venetian blood was shed," booms back from the corridor. "It is our right and duty to demand why and how."

The captain looks to the doge for instruction. At his nod, the captain opens the doors. Six guards with crossed halberds can't control the flood of nobles.

"Send to the Arsenal for men," the doge shouts.

Marino weaves through the chaos to call reinforcements. Nobles clog the stairs and fill the corridors, trying to force their way inside. The Senate chamber can't hold them all. They hoist Ruggiero Gradenigo on their shoulders to speak for them.

"We demand this meeting be moved to the Great Council chamber," he shouts.

"By what authority do you make this demand?" the Senate head shouts back.

"There are sixty senators," Ruggiero shoots back. "Add the Ten, the Council of Forty, and the Doge's Council, that's one hundred and twenty more or less. I speak for the others, the majority of nobles. By our own authority, we demand that this meeting move to the Great Council chamber."

"Treason," Marco Dandolo shouts over the uproar.

"Then right is treason," Ruggiero replies, "and treason, right."

More nobles whistle and cheer for Ruggiero. The boots of the palace guard echo loudly on the marble stairs. Swords drawn, two more columns of guards line the stairs and corridors. The first unit circles the Senate chamber.

"We're nobles, not criminals," Ruggiero says. "Order the guards to stand down!"

"Withdraw, and they will stand down."

"We will withdraw when this matter moves to the Great Council chamber."

Another senator speaks out. "Serenissimo, noble senators, these are the admirals of our fleet, the captains of our galleys, our bowmen in battle, defenders of our dominion. They must be heard."

Nobles start chanting, "Coun-cil! Coun-cil!"

I know the doge wants to open the debate. He favors the gladiatorial Great Council to the constipated Senate. In the Great Council, anything can happen. It gives the doge more freedom to break rules himself.

Guido Morosini speaks for the Ten.

"I hear no treason," he says. "The Senate can vote to convene the Great Council by ringing the bell and carrying this matter over at any time *if it so desires*."

The disgruntled nobles chant, "Vote! Vote! Vote! Vote!"

"All in favor?"

"Secret ballot!" Senator Pietro Trevisan shouts, outraged.

The opposition roars, "*No!*"

Trevisan stands firm. "We vote for the doge by secret ballot. And the Senate. And the Forty. And every major appointment and committee. We vote which way to wipe our asses by secret ballot, and we all know why. So the ghosts of dead battles don't haunt us. This is no different."

"Secret, public, silver balls, we don't care," Ruggiero says. "Just do it before we're as old as you."

It's the fastest vote I've ever counted.

"By forty-six to twenty-five with one abstention, the Senate moves this meeting to the Great Council chamber."

"Ring the bell," the doge says. "Summon the nobles."

When everyone is seated in the chamber, the doors are locked. The Arsenal men have arrived, looking meaner than the palace guards. The doge addresses the ambassadors from Trieste.

"What does Trieste say for itself?"

The ambassadors look worried they won't make it home alive. One is a fat butcher, another is a tall, skinny priest, and if the third put on an apron, he could pass for a red-faced dockside tavern-keep. The butcher is tongue-tied. The priest hides behind him. The tavern-keep recites memorized lines.

"The rectors of Trieste wish to express their sincere apology over this unfortunate accident."

He gets down on his knees.

"We apologize before God and man and wholeheart-edly beg the forgiveness of the Exalted Doge, the great Senate, the nobles and citizens of the Most Serene Repub-lic."

The ambassadors get down on their knees. They touch their foreheads to the floor.

"That's it?" the doge asks.

The ambassadors look at one another, mute. Finally, the tavern-keep stammers, "What's done is done and can't be undone, Exalted Serenity."

His mouth keeps moving, but he's out of words. I can't tell if his face is wet with sweat or tears. Probably both. He stands and helps fat Hector to his feet. Hector clasps his hands in prayer.

"We beg forgiveness, Exalted Serenity, for a terrible mistake. What those men did was wrong, but nobody or-dered them to do it. You can't make our council responsi-ble for what common criminals do on their own."

"Yes, we can," the doge thunders. "We demand you deliver to us the criminal ship and its contraband, along with the captain and the bowmen who murdered our men, to stand trial before our Forty. Your leaders must swear allegiance to this Serene Republic and immediately fly our flag as per our several treaties. We also fine you one thou-sand silver marks for each treaty violation. Do you accept these terms?"

The ambassadors are as white as a nun's underwear. The priest wrings his hands and grovels.

"Most Exalted Serenity, we throw ourselves on your mercy. We were sent to express our profoundest apologies. We have no authority to make promises."

Angry nobles whistle and boo and stamp their feet. The doge motions for the guards to surround the ambassadors from Trieste. He addresses the nobles of Venice.

"Gentlemen, by what right do we hold Trieste?"

Voices rise up from the hall.

"They begged us to protect them!"

"To protect our gulf," says the doge. "The sea is our dominion."

Warriors boo, concerned with holding territory, while merchants shout their approval, concerned with mastery of the seas. The Great Council splits.

"Trieste is small and weak," the doge says, "as we once were. Great princes surround them, scheming to seize their port, as did we, once."

He looks from face to face to face among nobles he has known all his life.

"I say we have no right to hold Trieste against her will, but the sad truth is that without us, Trieste falls to our enemies. If that happens, we lose the Adriatic. If we lose the Adriatic, we lose all."

More applause. The members of the Doge's Council scowl. He is committing a doge's greatest sin, speaking his own mind and not the thinking of his council. He knows, and he doesn't stop because he is winning his audience and their support is his only hope.

"Nobles of Venice, if we become thieves, we have failed, but we can never allow thieves to steal what is ours. Trieste isn't the enemy. She is caught between us and our real enemies. Let us convey our demands and pray the rectors of Trieste heed our warning."

Ruggiero jumps up on his bench. "Who here cares what they want? It's not their decision. It's ours. They didn't ask permission to murder our captain and crew in cold blood. Hang these bakers and fishmongers from the Columns of Doom. Let Trieste know we mean business."

The butcher, Hector Canciano, kneels before the doge and raises his arms in prayer.

"We beg Your Exalted Serenity, spare us."

The nobles roar, hungry lions. To deny the ambassadors safe return is a declaration of war.

"Four days," the doge shouts. "You have four days to return to Trieste, to fly our flag, to bring us the cog, its cargo, and the captain and crew who slaughtered our men with no provocation. If you do not, we will blockade your harbor and starve you to death. We'll keep Hector Canciano as hostage. If you others aren't back in four days, you'll find him hanging from the tower in an iron cage."

Ruggiero elbows his way to the ambassadors from Trieste. "Tell your city the nobles of Venice aren't all frightened old men. You will pay! An eye for an eye."

Arsenal men circle Ruggiero. Hieronimo Zen shouts, "An eye for an eye!"

The nobles take up the chant. The doge leaps into the fray like Caesar in the heat of battle. He's not an old man any more.

"Yes, gentlemen," he says. "We can wage war. And we can win. But remember, each and every one of you, war isn't cheap. It costs more money and more lives than we can afford. Don't dare complain when we tax and levy and fine. It's time to empty your purses. Victory comes dear."

Ruggiero hoists himself on the shoulders of the nobles crowded around him.

"To Trieste!"

RUGGIERO'S NAME IS on everyone's tongue, from the palace arcades to the Rialto to St. Nicholas of the Beggars. No one, high or low, lacks an opinion on his triumph over the old men, how he stood up to the Senate and the Forty and the doge. He is separating himself from the nameless, cowardly pack of poor nobles. He is becoming the Champion of the Hopeless, the Advocate of the Powerless, the Protector of the Weak.

Alone in his chambers, the doge's words spew like lava from a volcano of deep disgust for Ruggiero and everything he represents. "You see what he's doing don't you? It's naked ambition. He needs to be a hero. Nobody follows a deadbeat. People follow heroes, and right now, Trieste is his chance to be a hero, and I can't stop him. I made him bowman of the quarterdeck. Now he looks so patriotic that gullible common folk and weak-minded nobles are blinded by his Roman nose, seduced by his voice, thrilled by his passion. They would follow him off a cliff and never see it coming."

Marino winks at me. "*Fere libenter homines id quod volunt credunt.*"

"Caesar," I say. "'Men generally believe what they are inclined to believe.'"

"Gradenigo is a mad dog," the doge snarls.

"Of course he is, Serenissimo," Marino says. "But apparently, a very winning mad dog. Suddenly every noble in Venice wants an invitation to his wedding. They want to see what Barbanegra's money is doing for the Gradenigo palace, and they can't wait to see the bride. They've heard so much about her."

"I've had it up to here with our nobles," the doge says, rubbing his forehead.

Marino touches his thin lip with his ink-stained finger.

"Gradenigo is definitely shaping up, sire," he says. "His style and rhetoric have improved tremendously. He gets more like Bajamonte every day. Who's been tutoring him, I wonder?"

"Brother Bernardo of the Hermits," I say.

Marino swings in my direction. "Who?"

"A hermit friar with a big mouth and fishy friends."

Marino is genuinely puzzled. I know something he doesn't.

"We must investigate this golden-tongued hermit friar."

"We have," the doge says.

"Where is he?"

"He disappeared as soon as we started investigating."

THE NEXT AFTERNOON Bartolomeo Bon, head of the Forty, addresses the Doge's Council. "Benedetto Gradenigo claims that Ruggiero's imminent departure for Trieste is punitive and vindictive."

Marco Dandolo is annoyed and impatient. "He's a bowman of the quarterdeck. He must go."

"No war has been declared," Bon replies. "The uncle contends that Ruggiero's upcoming marriage is well known. A hasty departure means postponing the wedding until he returns, causing hardship for both families."

The doge scowls and snipes. "Should we set aside our crisis until after the wedding?"

Bon persists. "The uncle contends a pattern of systematic harassment is wreaking irreparable damage to their house."

"Great Bleeding Heart of Jesus!" The doge sounds like his finger got caught in a door. "What hardship? Barbanegra is feeding them lobster and covering their palace with fresh white marble."

Marino loses his patience. "Simply put, they can't have it both ways. Ruggiero might have been a rich and happily married minor advocate living in the newfound luxury of Gradenigo palace. Instead, he caused a riot—two riots—and is leading the charge to Trieste. Now his uncle is complaining that Ruggiero is being forced to leave as part of a conspiracy to thwart their fortunes. Bowmen follow orders, sir, not social calendars. This complaint is void."

"Let us pray," the doge says to me as soon as the meeting is over.

We kneel in the crypt, kiss the Evangelist's tomb, cross ourselves, and pray.

"At least that gets Gradenigo out of our hair," the doge says after his paternoster.

"He can still rape her when he gets back."

"Once they're married, it's no longer rape."

"It will always be rape."

"However, her father's will is sovereign."

"I can't let him do that, sir."

"Enough."

"Serenissimo, I can't..."

"I said enough."

His voice rolls through the silent crypt like thunder.

"Right now, I'm worried about the fate of the Republic," he says, "and you're worrying about a little girl. You swore an oath of loyalty to me and to this Republic. This nonsense stops now."

"I'm sorry, sir, I..."

"You're not sorry. You hate me because she is all that matters to you. Hate me if you will, but make sure you understand why. Things have been easy up to now. You put in your time on the job, visited your friends on the side, did a few odd jobs for me. I didn't stop you. I gave you the key. But things change, sometimes very suddenly, and when they change, we must change, just as suddenly. The wind shifts, and we trim our sails according to how the wind is blowing and not how we wish it was blowing. At times like these, men of consequence set aside every-thing—their personal ambitions, their friends, their wives and children—to do what duty demands, without question and without hesitation. Is that clear?"

"Yes, Serenissimo."

"Then tell me what I said, in your own words."

"I worry too much about Alex and not enough about my job."

"That's not what I said. Let's try again. Like it or not, we have responsibilities, you and I. We steer the course for a hundred thousand people who count on us to make their homes safe, ensure they have honest jobs, and enough food to feed their families. It is our sacred duty to provide those things. Sometimes that's all we can do. Sometimes all we can do isn't enough. Either way, it's all that matters."

"I know, but sometimes it's hard, sir, to..."

"I know it's hard, damn it. It's hard for me too. I'm not doing this to be mean. I'm trying to wake you up.

"Listen to me. If you're brave enough to make history, this may be your best chance. Don't throw it away on a girl sold into a bad marriage. You have the opportunity to stand beside me at the helm. We are on uncharted seas, you and I. Clouds hide the stars. We have only history to temper our ambition and principles to guide our judg-ment. Our mission is to steer our endangered ship through treacherous straits during the worst possible storm without shattering on the rocks."

"*Hic Rhodus*, sir. *Hic salta*."

Chapter Twenty-Seven

The Envoy from Castle Moccò

THE HALL OF the Ten is small because not many people go in and most of them don't leave the same way they went in. It is somber, with dark wood and black upholstery. The Last Judgment takes up an entire wall. Bodies of the damned burn in the pits of Hell, while Heaven rains grace on the saved. In the lower right-hand corner Doge Andrea Dandolo and his council gaze into the face of God.

Today, everyone is fidgety. The table where a clerk usually sits is empty. Marino takes the notes. He knows he can count on me to help him.

Finally, the knock on the hidden door that we've been waiting for. "May we?"

"Please enter."

The lord of the Arsenal and a lord of the night usher in a bundle of cloak and hood with no face to be seen. As soon as they shut the door, he sheds his camouflage.

"Most Exalted Serenity," the lord of the night says, "may I present Giorgio Barozzi."

"We know Barozzi from Crete," says the doge. "He used to be one of us."

Barozzi kneels and kisses the hem of the doge's robe.

"I still am, Exalted Serenity. I may work for the lord of Moccò, but I am a Venetian first, last, and always. I am humbled and amazed that Your Exalted Serenity remembers me."

He remains on his knee in reverence.

"We always remember the men we fight beside," the doge says. "You were one of the best swordsmen on Crete. Why have you come?"

"On behalf of Astolfo, lord of Castle Moccò."

Voices crescendo. Astolfo appears to be very unpopular.

"Make no mistake, noble lords of Venice. Astolfo is no enemy of yours," Barozzi says. "He fought for Venice both in Crete and against Hungary."

"Which side is he on today?" asks the doge.

"That's up to you. I beg you allow me to tell you why I am here."

Reluctant thumbs go up; the doge nods agreement.

"In years past, it was Astolfo's honor to fight for the Republic," Barozzi says. "Now, he is lord of Castle Moccò. Astolfo recognizes no sovereign over Moccò but himself. As you also know, there are only two trade routes through Trieste, one from the south to Istria and Dalmatia, and the salt road to the north. Castle Moccò controls the salt road and, thus, all traffic from Germany, Austria, Hungary, and points east seeking access to the Adriatic."

"We are aware of the importance of Castle Moccò," the doge says.

"Of course when I say the only routes in and out, I'm not talking about merchants and goats. I'm talking about armies with baggage trains. Nothing passes without Astolfo's permission. The men of Castle Moccò are a disciplined legion worthy of Caesar himself."

"We've heard them called many things," Marino says, "but never a disciplined legion."

"I know Castle Moccò and its men," Barozzi says. "Believe me, Exalted Serenity, Moccò is impregnable."

"So they say."

"I know," Barozzi says, "that the city of Trieste sent ambassadors here to apologize for killing your captain and crew."

"We heard their apologies and responded."

"Did you know they also sent envoys to Leopold of Austria, Lord Carrara of Padua, and Louis of Hungary, begging for armed assistance against you?"

"I suspected as much."

"If Moccò stands with Trieste, Trieste can withstand an attack, even a siege. If Moccò stands with Leopold, ten thousand Austrians will drive you out of Trieste. If Moccò stands with the Serene Republic, Leopold will never reach Trieste, Trieste will fly your flag, and your position in the gulf will remain unassailable. That is to say, Most Exalted Serenity, Castle Moccò can decide who wins."

"What does Astolfo want in return for his support?"

"That Castle Moccò remain his alone for as long as he lives. He has no children and intends to have none. He has no interest in what happens after he dies. But he is young, and he wants to remain the sovereign lord of Moccò for his natural life. In exchange, he pledges to support the Serene Republic in this dispute."

"Germanic armies are fierce," the doge says. "Astolfo has, what, 1,000 men?"

I remember Caesar's description of the Germans—naked, thick-necked brutes with swords and javelins in their fists fording icy rivers.

"Leopold's army is large," Barozzi says, "but it is full of fresh recruits, country bumpkins hungry for the loot the recruiter promised them. Fertilizer for the grape-vines."

"Then why do we need Astolfo?"

"Because your galleys are useless against the walls of Trieste. One of Astolfo's men is worth a hundred of Leopold's best. Here, you have the opportunity to avoid an expensive war entirely. If you agree, Astolfo will parley with the Council of Trieste. He will assure them that, together, Moccò and Venice will safeguard Trieste's prosperity as long as they continue to honor their obligations. If they refuse, Astolfo will drive them out in sackcloth, with ashes on their heads, and hand you the keys to the city."

"We thank you for this visit, Giorgio Barozzi," the doge says when he has heard enough. "We will consider Astolfo's proposal and advise."

"Exalted Serenity, when you wish to contact Astolfo, send your envoy to Castle Moccò with this, and he will be received with full hospitality."

Barozzi hands the doge a silk pennant. He then bundles back up in his cloak and hood and leaves. We wait in silence until a second door closes below.

Ancient Marco Dandolo eyes the doge.

"You know Astolfo of Trieste?"

"Of course I do."

"He's a thug," Dandolo says, "a common highwayman."

His dusty old cheeks flush with color.

"He was acquitted of all charges against him," the doge says.

"That doesn't mean he didn't do it."

"He did it," Bruno Badoer says. "And more besides, when he was younger. Which of us didn't do things when we were young we wish everyone would forget?"

He looks directly at the doge when he says that. There are plenty of rumors about Andrea Contarini's wild youth.

"Far be it from me to judge a man for the follies of his youth," Dandolo says. "I merely raise it as a bellwether of the man's character."

Marino is dumbfounded. "Why on earth would we not expect him to have made the same offer to Leopold, to Carrara, and to Trieste?"

"During the rebellion in Crete," the doge says, "I saw Astolfo surrounded by the worst of the rebels and hopelessly outnumbered. Single-handedly, he hacked his way through cavalry and infantry to rally his panicking cohort and turn the tide from retreat to victory for the Republic."

"That's how reputations are made," Marino says. "Every mercenary has his own Crete to back up his claims. They trade on reputation. That doesn't make him honest or trustworthy. The men of Moccò are a band of renegade heretics who listen only to Astolfo and have no regard for man, law, or God."

"Not necessarily a bad thing in war," Badoer says. "Pay him what he wants."

"I don't see a problem," says Egidio della Fontana, who is simpleminded, so everything seems simple to him.

"The wind turns, Egidio" the doge says. "The wind turns."

"What is our decision?" Marino's quill is poised.

"Promise him everything, give him nothing, and watch him like a hawk."

TWO DAYS LATER, the Doge's Council meets. Marino hands me a letter from Trieste. The wax seal is still unbroken.

"Please read it to our colleagues."

I break the seal. Thank God the scribe who wrote it had a legible hand.

I clear my throat and look around while the old men get comfortable. Most of them don't know Latin. They pretend they understand and nod, but even if they ever knew, they've long forgotten. That's what clerks and priests are for.

I read slowly and properly pronounce a galley's worth of empty phrases. Behind the tortured evasions, the message is simple, and it's not good.

The doge understands Latin. Now and then, he raises his finger for me to repeat something he didn't catch or I misread. When I finish the letter, the doge looks at the faces of his council. He reveals nothing. He watches to see what they have to say. Nobody says a word because they have no idea what I just read.

"Thank you, Niccolò," Marino says. "Now summarize in your own words the meat of what you just read." He spins his finger. "Skip the fat. Cut to the bone."

"The Council of Trieste refuses to decide anything until Hector Canciano, our hostage, is there to consult with them. Until then, they refuse to fly our flag. Furthermore, Odoricus of Prebissa, speaking for the Council of Trieste, disputes our entire protest."

Bruno Badoer slams his fist on the table. "He disputes the murder of our men? Hang the bastard."

"How about diplomacy?" Marino asks, playing devil's advocate.

Old Marco Dandolo shakes his head gravely. "We are beyond diplomacy. We are at risk of losing Trieste to our enemy. The question is, which enemy?"

"Genoa of course," Badoer says. "It's always been them and always will be."

"Genoa is incapable of doing anything at present." Marino gives Badoer the look he gives me when I say something stupid. "It is a cauldron boiling over with civil strife. They had to call in an outsider with an iron fist before they killed one another. They can do nothing."

"Not to sharpen it too keenly, the doge of Genoa will soon be overthrown," says our doge. "We will deal with his successor later. Whichever of our enemies seeks to gain from this imbroglio must strike quickly. We must stop it before it gets out of control."

"Precisely," Marino says. "For Trieste, this is simply about salt and money. They want to keep our taxes and duties for themselves. If we blockade their port, they can't make a cent. Lay siege to their pocketbook, and they'll see reason soon enough."

Badoer leaps back on his high horse. "Bollocks. That takes too long. Starve them out. Burn the bloody farms and vineyards all the way to Friuli. They'll sing a different tune."

The doge raises both hands for silence. These men may regard him as a gilded figurehead, but they obey the formalities they have smothered him in.

"The buzzards are circling," he says. "We must dispatch an army and a fleet to smash the rebellion before our enemies rally to their aid and attack us. We must move lightning fast, strike decisively, and end this now."

"Now, Exalted Serenity?"

"This very heartbeat. Surprise is our greatest weapon. Instruct Captain Michiel and Admiral Molino to storm the wall. They will not lay siege, they will not blockade, they will not reconnoiter endlessly. They must immediately smite the enemy with a mighty blow, win a quick victory, and fly our flag over Trieste, leaving no doubt who holds dominion over the gulf."

Chapter Twenty-Eight

A Fatal Day

INSTEAD OF A lightning attack and quick victory, our army and fleet do exactly what the doge ordered them not to. They dig in to make a career of it. Claiming it is impossible to launch an immediate and decisive attack, the army starts building a wall around the existing one, a behemoth of a wall, while our fleet blockades their harbor, settling in for the winter with no decisive action.

On April 3, 1369, we receive word that the captain general of our army built his camp at the confluence of several mountain streams, which flooded in the spring rains, costing us men and ruining our weapons. The doge is closer to the axe than ever. By early summer, the army is still begging for more arms and men, while we, all the way in Venice, can hear the tread of Leopold's armies crossing the Alps.

Having expected a quick victory, our people are demoralized by the long and costly siege. The longer this siege lasts, the more it costs, and the more unpopular the doge becomes. Money is easy to raise on the eve of victory but impossible in the middle of a stalemate. The mighty lion of Venice can't bring mongrel Trieste to heel.

In August, the Ten meet with the doge and his council to stanch the wound. A spy from the north reports that Leopold of Austria has agreed to arm Trieste against us. A second spy reports that Louis of Hungary is anxious to get in the game and champions Trieste.

The only boon is that the stalemate keeps Ruggiero a hundred miles from Alex. As long as he is in Trieste, she is safe.

The Ten couldn't make it any clearer that they hold the doge personally responsible for our public humiliation. He didn't order the siege; in fact, he forbade it, but now, he's responsible for it anyway.

One thing is clear. We're stuck, and something must be done.

The doge studies these angry and impatient men whose eyes are already convicting him of treason.

"Enough," he says. "This stops now. Our commanders have failed utterly. They are traitors."

Bruno Badoer rises. "Are you calling Domenico Michiel, captain general of the Republic, a traitor?"

"For the everlasting love of merciful God," the doge sputters. "He sets his camp on a flood plain and then complains about flooding after wasting the dry months on a useless wall that should never have been built. Stupidity of that magnitude is tantamount to treason. They brought this disaster upon us."

The doge pulls his robe tightly around him.

"Mark today," he says. "This is no ordinary day. It's not like yesterday or the day before or the day before that when nothing memorable occurred. No, gentlemen, today is of a different order, a fatal day, one worth a century of ordinary, indistinct, unremarkable days. Such days tower above others. They are celebrated and remembered throughout time. Today, we define ourselves and create our legacy. What we do this day will count when countless others are long forgotten. Immediately recall Admiral Molino and Captain General Michiel and appoint leaders to end this ruinous farce."

Bruno Badoer, always a bellicose old-line warrior, the descendent of Roman legions, of late has become an apologist for General Michiel's failure. Michiel is a clansman by marriage. A public disgrace would damage both their houses. Badoer takes a deep breath and swallows his pride, hoping to snatch the fish from the flame.

"What more could any man have done, Serenissimo?" he asks.

"Follow orders."

"In his judgment, the situation was unfavorable to immediate attack."

"We didn't send him to judge; we sent him to follow orders."

"If we doubt his judgment, why did we send him?"

"To attack."

Marco Dandolo, usually a reliable ally, frowns at Serenissimo. He has grown weaker in breath and voice. "Summer is already waning. Soon winter will be upon us, and the dread *bora* blows harshly on Trieste. Perhaps it might be better to await a more propitious season."

"We cannot wait." Serenissimo is adamant. "We must win before winter. We must win before our enemy snatches Trieste and marches on us. We look stupid and weak. It's too late to change that, so let them think us stupid and weak. They won't suspect the blow we deliver. Appoint Bartolomeo Bembo as captain general of the army and Taddeo Giustinian as admiral of the gulf. Round up every bowman and able-bodied man to march under our banner. Smash this rebellion and cut Leopold off at the knees before he reaches our gulf."

Badoer scowls and shakes his head. "Bembo is not the man to cut anyone off at the knees. He makes Michiel look like Caesar himself."

"Who then?" Marino asks, quill in hand.

"There's only one man for the job. Paolo Loredan."

The doge looks around the room. Everyone nods agreement.

"Objections to Loredan?" the doge asks. "I have none. He is a good man and a gifted general. Are there any objections to Taddeo Giustinian as admiral?"

None.

The doge wanted Loredan all along and was fearful he couldn't get away with naming both leaders. Loredan was so obviously the right choice that Serenissimo let Badoer champion him. In return, he got his choice for admiral. He would have preferred Vettor Pisani, but Pisani is in the Aegean.

"MOMENTOUS MORNING," THE doge says to me after the meeting. "Let us pray."

In the Evangelist's crypt, he crosses himself and hikes his gold robe out of the bilge seeping through the stone floor.

"You once asked me why I always wear this robe," he says. "The answer is because it's so goddamn heavy. Pounds of gold beaten thin and wrapped around miles of the strongest silk thread, all woven into splendor and then embroidered with more gold and precious stones. It weighs a ton. I feel it day and night. From the moment I took office until the moment they lay me out on my bier, I will bear its weight, the weight of history.

"Any idiot can ruin his own life; it happens all the time. Sometimes he ruins his wife's life, too, sometimes his whole family, and on rare occasions, his entire clan—like Marcantonio Gradenigo. Very few men get the opportunity to ruin an entire nation, and I am one of them. I wear this robe so I never forget it."

"The responsibility isn't entirely yours, Serenissimo. You share it with others."

"The price of failure is my head, not theirs."

"You were elected to lead, Serenissimo. Now you're leading."

"I wasn't elected to lead. I was elected to wear a crown and pay for a gold robe, to keep my head high, my mouth shut, and agree with my council, the Ten, and the Senate. Ruggiero Gradenigo was right. I am the wrong man for the job. But I will lead, damn it, despite these chains. I will not be remembered as the doge who lost the Republic. Are you ready?"

"For what?"

"To be Giustinian's bowman. He needs you more than I do."

Chapter Twenty-Nine

Baptism at Sea

A FULL MOON soars high over the Adriatic. Our galley, *The Lion of Venice*, glides smoothly across calm seas at an easy eight knots per hour. There's no sound but the plash of 120 oars. Our admiral, Taddeo Giustinian, pores over his charts. He's noble, but he's a man of the sea. He puts on no airs, and he expects the same. A fat ruby glitters in the pommel of his sword, which has seen a lot of action. The scars on his face and hands attest to battles fought on land and sea.

"General Loredan is already in Trieste," Giustinian says. "I didn't want to wait for morning to depart."

He traces a line across the gulf on his chart, east and north to Trieste.

"Barely a hundred miles as the crow flies," he says.

"It's the farthest I've ever been from home, sir."

"Pray this weather holds. The gulf is a man-eater when Boreas blows, the wind of the dead, so-called. Boreas can blow the trees off the mountains, and beware anything in his path, houses, barns, Venetian galleys."

I set my compass on the table. Giustinian runs his finger over the three faded dolphins on the lid and flips it open.

"This compass is well used. Where did it come from?"

"My father left it to me when he died, along with my bow."

Giustinian dips his quill in ink and updates his log. As he works, I study the navigation charts—portolans—over his shoulder, committing to memory what I don't yet understand. When I've finished that, I sit alone in the prow.

The silvery surface of the Adriatic undulates gently from horizon to horizon, with no sign of land in any direction. Numberless stars form a web of diamonds studded with fiery constellations slowly drifting across the dome of heaven. Majestic. Terrifying. Exhilarating. The enormity of it humbles me and fills me with an unfamiliar serenity. Not the serenity of the Serene Republic, but a deep serenity, sincerely serene, serene in itself and everything it touches. I could laugh and cry. I don't know what to call this miraculous sense of wellbeing that feels like eternity and lasts but an instant.

A worried-looking sailor approaches and fingers his cap nervously, waiting for the admiral to recognize him. Giustinian finishes his entry and looks up.

"What's on your mind?" he asks the sailor.

"I don't like the look of things, sir."

"Why not? The sky is clear and the sea is calm."

"The thing is, sir, the current is pushing us wrong, toward Grado. Might be better to head there, drop anchor, and push on when things turn right."

Giustinian ices over with a disappointment he cannot hide. "General Loredan is already in Trieste. Every hour we lose increases his danger. If we keep up this pace, we can reach Trieste before Matins. What does Girolamo have to say?"

Girolamo da Burano's wrinkled face may be fifty, but his body isn't. He's shorter than me and weighs fifty pounds more, all muscle. Gray lightning bolts streak his dark beard and unruly hair. His tough skin, as brown and weathered as his leather vest, is stretched thin over thick muscles. He rolls his blue cotton pants over his knees because his calves are the size of melons. A perfect rowing machine and a stern taskmaster, our captain of the oars scowls at the prospect of rowing all night against a contrary current. It takes the swagger from his stance.

"I think we should make for Grado and push on at first light."

"That adds six hours to the journey." Giustinian's scowl matches Girolamo's. "We're not dogging smugglers. We're at war."

"Aye, aye, skipper." Girolamo nods solemnly. "That's what we're here for."

Giustinian walks the 128-foot-long gangway, the spine down the center of our galley, with thirty rows of benches on either side splayed like ribs, two men to a bench, all armed. The inboard oarsmen have pikes at their feet, and the outboard oarsmen carry stones and slings. In addition to the hundred and twenty oarsmen, we have caulkers, carpenters, a cook, the helmsman, riggers, a basket boy, and six bowmen including me.

Giustinian stops amidships and blows the whistle around his neck. The men raise their oars in unison. With the lightest of winds and no plashing of oars, utter silence rules the sea.

"Listen up, men. I'm no Cicero, and I'm not going to stand here and speechify. Girolamo says he doesn't trust this contrary current and wants to make for Grado and push off at dawn. I've known Girolamo a long time, and I respect him like a father. But this time, I think he's wrong, and here's why.

"Outside the walls of Trieste, General Loredan and his men are scanning the horizon for the first sign of us. We lack men there, and those we have are poorly armed. We all know why. At Muggia, across the bay from Trieste, the gulf squadron sits idle, waiting for us because their former admiral won't budge. Whether he's a traitor or a coward, the Ten will decide. Meanwhile, our oarsmen, our bowmen, our helmsmen, our sailors and sappers and caulkers and cooks—a thousand strong, all armed—can't fight the goddamned fight because without me, no one will lead them. They are becalmed, and we are the wind to fill their sails and carry them into battle.

"I, Taddeo Giustinian, admiral of the gulf fleet, can't wait even one more hour. Fuck the contrary current. Fuck caution when the fate of our Republic rests on us. I cannot and will not fail my doge. I refuse to leave our fleet leaderless and afraid to fight.

"If you believe strongly with Girolamo that we should head to Grado and wait for dawn, so say now. I won't stop you because unless you believe in what you're doing, you can't do it. '*Possunt quia posse videntur*. They can because they think they can.' What say you?"

"The army's been stuck there for a year," shouts an oarsman, "and they ain't dead yet."

"The Austrians are nowhere near Trieste, sir. That's when the trouble starts."

"Nothing's gonna happen until we get there. You said so yourself."

The men speak, and Giustinian listens patiently before he speaks again.

"A hundred years ago, off the nearby island of Curzola, our magnificent fleet, ninety-four vessels, met the

Genoese with scarcely sixty vessels. We should have won. I won't waste breath on the details of how the Genoese kicked the feathers out of us and routed us utterly, destroyed our fleet, and took our men captive, but you all know they did.

"Our defeated admiral, Andrea Dandolo, the doge's son, a valiant seaman crushed by fortune, wore a prisoner's chains. Imagine what went through his head on the long journey to Genoa—the grief and the shame. He knew he was about to be marched through the streets in chains, spat on, reviled and ridiculed. He alone would bring more shame than all the others combined, shame on our families, on our city, on our Republic, and he couldn't do that. Instead, he bashed his brains out against the hull to spare us the humiliation of his public disgrace.

"That was a man. That was a prince. That was a Venetian. That was honor, conviction, courage. How dare we balk at our duty. Turn away from it? I say, no. On to Trieste. On to victory."

"On to Trieste!" Girolamo shouts. "On to victory!"

The amen chorus rises and fades quickly as 120 backs bend to the rhythm of ten knots per hour.

I would row if I could, but every seat is filled, and for each man, the effort is personal and fierce. I sit beside Giustinian, yearning to be helpful, but he is lost in his charts of the gulf.

"Have you read Virgil?" I ask.

He looks up for a moment. "Of course. *The Aeneid* is the story of our people."

"Maybe your people. I'm not so sure about mine."

"You're Venetian, aren't you? Your people too."

He winks, and I'm happy at the brief flash of a smile on his face before he goes back to work.

I lie back and observe the stately procession of constellations. Afar, at the eastern horizon, clouds begin spilling across the sky. The moon is still bright, and we're at top speed, but the clouds come faster than we can row. They condense out of nothing and eclipse the moon and stars.

Then the fireworks start. Giustinian jumps up without a word and heads aft.

Lightning strikes so close it singes my ears. I smell it. The sky crackles with deafening thunder. The sea bucks like a rampaging stallion as big as the world, throwing our *Lion of Venice* off high swells into churning troughs until we're completely out of control. The *bora* whips the sea into a frenzy. We stash our crossbows below deck. The oarsmen fasten themselves to their benches. All is in God's hands.

I lurch from bench to bench toward Giustinian on the poop deck. Every light in the world has gone out. My ears ache with the storm's roar. By the time I get to Giustinian, he is strapped to the lantern post.

"Secure yourself, boy. Have you never been in a storm before?"

I lash myself to the rail near the helmsman, the first mate, and a carpenter fighting to hold the tiller lest it snap off, sending us spinning in crazy circles.

THE STORM PASSES as suddenly as it came. In its wake, the sea is as smooth as silver satin. We are battered, exhausted, and thrown off course. The men, reprieved from death, row like hell. Giustinian is scribbling in his log when I doze off, and sometime later, a crazy dream startles me awake. Giustinian is showing Girolamo our position on a *portolano* that looks like a spider's web. I don't know if I slept for the wink of an eye or an hour. Giustinian, still poring over his maps, doesn't appear to have slept at all. The moon has shrunk to a moldy grape. My eyebrows are icy, and my teeth chatter in the cold. The stars say it is two hours to dawn. In the distance, a light twinkles on the shore.

"Muggia," Giustinian says, "our destination, three miles from the walls of Trieste."

Muggia: a bright beacon burning in a stone tower at the base of a rocky peninsula jutting into the sea. As soon as we dock, the exhausted crew passes out on their benches, covered with tarps.

I hustle to keep up with Giustinian because his legs are so much longer than mine. We don't stop until we reach the central warehouse on the wharf. Giustinian rings the bell to summon the men of the fleet.

Standing at Giustinian's side—far from the doge and the urns of silver ballots and the splendor I have come to take for granted—the doge's gold robe weighs heavy on my conscience. Here, we are leaders. We're not allowed to be tired or demoralized. Nothing matters but victory.

The men assemble quickly, half-awake, edgy, and uncertain. They fill the big warehouse, grumbling, coughing, laughing, nervous about the new admiral. They clear a space amid the boxes and barrels. Giustinian stands on a crate so everyone can see him, an eagle in the torchlight.

"By the authority of the Senate of the Serene Republic and of his Exalted Serenity, Doge Andrea Contarini, I hereby relieve Sir Crescio Molino of his duty as admiral of the gulf fleet, which responsibility I now assume."

Molino steps aside, sheepishly silent. He's probably relieved he's not dancing at the end of a rope. At least no one leads him out in chains. His fate will be decided elsewhere. His crews don't seem sorry to see him go. All eyes focus on Giustinian.

Ruggiero Gradenigo stands in the rear. He gives me the evil eye, but I don't care. As long as I can see him, Alex is safe.

"Some of you already know me," Giustinian says. "You know I don't make or take excuses. I have one master, our doge. We are here to serve the Republic. The orders I give are as absolute as the orders I receive. Those of you who don't know me yet will find out soon enough. I am not here to assign praise or blame. I am here to smash the rebellion and raise our flag over Trieste."

Cheers break out and quickly ebb into respectful silence. This is not the Great Council. These men have more respect for their admiral than all the nobles together have for their doge. The fleet is grateful for leadership. It gives them hope.

"We rowed through hell to get here," Giustinian says, "and we're lucky to be alive. Thank you, St. Nicholas and St. Mark, who protect us. My crew needs rest, and my ship needs repairs. Right now, I need a galley and a crew to take me to Captain General Loredan before the morning bell rings. Are you with me?"

The men answer as one and push forward. Giustinian counts them off, and when he has enough oarsmen, he dismisses the rest. The warehouse clears fast. As the men file out, Giustinian taps two captains on the shoulder. Each has a bowman with him. Giustinian greets them and pushes me forward.

"This is Niccolò Saltano of St. Nicholas of the Beggars."

The first captain shakes my hand and introduces his bowman of the quarterdeck, who bows to Giustinian and nods at me. The other captain, I know. Hieronimo Zen. I recognize his massive bush of brown curls. He's almost thirty and still carries his baby fat, only now it's as solid as cured ham. He has a smile on his lips and in his eyes. He looks like he's never had a bad day.

Zen bows to Giustinian and really means it. "This is my bowman of the quarterdeck, Ruggiero Gradenigo."

To me Giustinian says, "Hieronimo Zen was the youngest member on my galley crew during the St. Titus rebellion in Crete." Then he turns to Ruggiero.

"*Salve*, Gradenigo. I knew your father and grandfather."

Ruggiero bows. I can't tell if he's happy about that or not.

"If I may, sir," Ruggiero says, "what's the ballot boy doing here? Did we come to vote or fight?"

"He is bowman of the quarterdeck on the *Lion of Venice*."

"Hmm. I thought only nobles could be bowmen of the quarterdeck, sir, but he's barely a man and common as dirt."

"He is here by the order of His Exalted Serenity. You may remember, he's the best shot from Grado to Cavarzere."

Giustinian was at the match; it's a slap in the face to Ruggiero's arrogance.

Ruggiero holds his tongue; he smiles at Giustinian, bows, tips his metal cap to me, and stands behind Zen, who is a head shorter and a foot wider. Ruggiero must play a different game. We're at war now. Different rules apply.

"How soon can we leave?" Giustinian asks.

Chapter Thirty

Beneath The Walls of Trieste

THE SUN BEATS us to Trieste, and the enemy sees us as soon as we see them. We moor in the harbor between the city wall and our army's camp. We're out of range of flying boulders and flaming pitch, but bowmen crowd the parapets of Trieste, firing storms of bolts and arrows.

Ruggiero leans close. "If you get too close to the wall, they pour boiling oil to fry you and ground talc to blind you. Let's go."

"Where to?"

"To kill as many of them as we can."

He jumps into the two-man basket at the base of the galley's mast. A flaming bolt sticks in the mast and splashes fire on the deck. An oarsman scales the mast while two others cover him with shields. He yanks the bolt and hurls it into the sea. I jump into the basket with Ruggiero and beg St. Nick to keep me from puking. Zen grabs two shields and shoves them after us. He and a big oars-man pull the ropes, and we rise.

Sweat runs down my forehead. I grip the basket so my knees don't buckle. Flaming bolts set our galley afire. Black smoke stings my nose and eyes. I wipe them so I can see.

"Crying already?" Ruggiero asks.

He points to the man he's going to kill, raises his bow, aims, and shoots. The bolt hurls the body off the parapet.

"You're pretty good with hay and ducats," he says. "Let's see you kill a man."

He points one out for me, a body with neither face nor name. A fellow with a family, a small field, some goats, and a dog named Iole. Or he's my age and hasn't even lived yet. It's my duty to kill him. My hands shake. I have to take a shit. He's not a painted pennant. He's a person like me.

Ruggiero yells, "Kill him before he sets us on fire."

My bolt smashes into his stomach, hurling him from the wall, a pile of broken tin.

He's dead. I killed him.

Ruggiero has already killed another. And another. He's pointing out guys who are asking to be shot. I cock and load. I kill another. Ruggiero is ahead of me, and I want to catch up, ablaze with vengeful fire. They are my enemy. I want to kill them all. I'm a bowman. That's what I do, better than anyone else. I kill another. And another.

I no longer care about their names, their farm, their goats, their dog named Iole. I'm killing for the doge and St. Mark. I'm killing as many as I can while their flaming bolts scorch my ears and set fire to our galley below.

"What's happening?" I shout to Ruggiero.

"Someone's lowering the fucking basket."

"Why?"

I want to keep killing.

Zen is at the bottom. We don't have a chance to say a word. He pushes us forward shouting, "This way, this way."

Soldiers protect us with shields as we jump from the jetty into a tunnel of shields, stumbling every time a bolt or a stone strikes one of the shields, which is often. Hides soaked in vinegar cover the shields, dampening the flames. We crouch and hustle. At the far end, Giustinian, Zen, Ruggiero, and I emerge behind the wooden palisades of our army's camp, out of range of enemy fire.

Paolo Loredan, newly appointed captain general of the army, awaits us in his tent. He doesn't look happy. He's handsome, younger than Giustinian, with sad eyes, curly brown hair, and a square jaw buried in a week's worth of beard.

"Is it as bad as you thought?" Giustinian asks.

"Worse. Trieste is like Venice, an armed *comune*, and when the bell rings, everyone comes running—men, women, children—ready to die. Our best men are demoralized. Our cowards have already deserted. The rest remain because the alternatives are worse."

"Can they fight?"

"They have to. They're all we've got."

"I've got a fleet ready to fight like hell."

"Fine vessels, your fleet," Loredan says, "fine and useless. There's a double wall twenty-two feet high around the city. There's a street atop the wall, behind the parapets, running all the way around, wide enough for wagons with mangonels and trebuchets. Twelve towers in all. Three flank the main gates and guard the harbor. The whole damn place isn't worth a pig's testicle, and it's walled up like Byzantium."

Loredan's lieutenant speaks out.

"At least in Constantinople, the boats can get close to the wall," he says. "You can raise your ladders and towers, swing your spars around, jump onto the damn parapets, and kill the bastards with your dagger and sword. Here, the wharf is too wide for any of our gear. They blind us, burn us, and shoot us full of holes before we reach the wall."

"What about your machines?" Giustinian asks.

"Haven't breached the walls yet. The damage we do by day they repair by night. Squads of them. We're loyal Venetians, sir; we're ready to die for the Republic. But when we're all dead, that wall will still be standing."

"And if we can't get in?" Giustinian asks.

"Then we fall on one another's swords," Loredan says. "Michiel and Molino were cut for not breaching the walls. If we don't, we might as well be dead."

"We were sent here to win. That doesn't necessarily mean breaching the wall. As long as we win, we followed orders. The question is how do we win?"

Silence.

"All right. Why haven't we won yet?" Giustinian asks.

"Because they fight like demons," Loredan's lieutenant says.

"They fight the way we fight anyone who invades our lagoon," Giustinian says. "They're no better fighters than we are."

"No, but they built a bitch of a wall," Loredan says, "and we built another wall around it."

"The wall that keeps us out keeps them in." Giustinian measures his words carefully. "They're prisoners of their own wall. Their supply lines are cut. They haven't been properly provisioned for months."

"They must be starving by now," I say.

"They can still cock their bows and boil us in oil, so they must be eating something."

"Cats and rats," Giustinian says. "They're not fighting because they're braver than we are or better fighters. They're fighting because they believe that tomorrow or the next day, ten thousand Austrians will come marching out of those mountains to drive us into the sea. That's what gives them the courage to fight another day. As long as help is on the way, they'll keep fighting. Take away their hope, and they lose."

"Then how do we stop the Austrians?" the lieutenant asks.

EVERYONE AGREES WE can't stop Leopold of Austria without Castle Moccò on our side. I bear Lord Astolfo's pennant, and I am authorized to speak for the doge. With Loredan's agreement, Giustinian selects Ruggiero and Zen to accompany me—Ruggiero because he speaks the language and Zen because he understands army men.

"In the meantime," Giustinian says, "we starve the city. Cut the hands off anyone caught smuggling contraband into Trieste."

"What about the women and children?"

"Cut off their noses. Niccolò, you know His Exalted Serenity's intent."

"I do, sir. When do we leave for Moccò, sir?"

"As soon as you can."

Zen and Ruggiero are on their way out the door. I start to run after them.

"Saltano," General Loredan shouts. "Niccolò."

He knows my name. I'm not just the ballot boy any more. I'm a warrior.

"Yes, sir."

"Come with me. I have something for you."

He takes me into the stable, and I hear her before I see her. As soon as she senses me, she starts whinnying like a hyena.

"Delfín, my beautiful friend."

I nuzzle her. She's mad I have no apple.

"The doge figured you'd need a reliable horse up here," General Loredan says.

We're almost out the door when Giustinian orders us to catch some sleep. Reluctantly, we comply and leave at dawn. By noon, we have made a wide arc around Trieste and begun the ascent to Castle Moccò. All around us, the slopes are charred, uphill and down.

"What happened here?" I ask Hieronimo Zen.

"We burned every vineyard, farm, and shit shack from Moccò to Moncolano."

"He's never been to war," Ruggiero says. "He doesn't know how it works."

"Neither have you," I say.

"Haven't I? Tell him Hieronimo."

"Crete, 1364."

"I was your age," Ruggiero says. "I went to visit my family, and I walked into a bloody insurrection. Ask me about war..."

Zen and Ruggiero ride ahead. I follow them in silence, haunted by the men I killed. Watching them fall from the wall over and over sickens me with an incurable fever.

"This is Via Flavia," Hieronimo says to hear himself talking. "The Romans built it all the way to Emperor Diocletian's palace in Dalmatia."

Limestone cliffs jut up from the foothills, jagged white scarps eroded by rain and sculpted by the wind. A plateau behind the cliffs ends abruptly at the Alps. The canyons between the cliffs are thick with oak and spruce and pine. Toward midday, we ford a river and water our horses.

"Rosandra Gorge," Hieronimo says. "The Salt Road follows the Rosandra. Castle Moccò sits on a spit, high up, where Moccò Creek splits off from the Rosandra."

I note everything on the map in my mind. Brush grows in thick tangles on either side of the road. Farther upstream, the limestone walls close in. The road has been worn into the stone by the feet of men and mules bent for centuries under loads of salt.

Halfway up the mountain from Trieste lies Bagnoli Superiore, a bunch of burned-out buildings with charred vineyards, and beyond it, the chasm swallows us again. Trees thrust straight out of the rock cliffs like broken arms. They cling to the sides of the cliffs and jam their roots into the stone, fracturing it. Birds drop seeds, and falling pinecones lodge in the crevices; the rock sprouts trees. Crown of thorns bushes, leafless and spiky, crowd the base of the cliffs. Birds we can't see make a racket as we approach, go silent as we pass, and make a racket again once we've gone.

Zen disguises his chainmail cowl and steel breastplate with a Trieste tunic he stole from a dead body. The visor of his helmet is open. Ruggiero slings his crossbow over his back; his quiver hangs from his saddle. The pommel of his sword pokes from underneath his stolen Trieste tunic with a bloody hole back to front. He wears no armor under the tunic, just a red velvet jerkin, black leggings, and a steel bowman's cap. I'm a drab sailor in coarse wool, my crossbow under my saddle blanket. We pause to water the horses and study Hieronimo's hastily sketched map.

"We're here," Hieronimo says. "There's Moccò. We need to get from here to there without anybody seeing us."

"Let them see me," I say. "I represent the doge of Venice."

"That may get you a glass of wine and a kiss in Venice, but these hills are crawling with vipers, Triesters, mercenaries, spies, Austrians, Paduans, Hungarians, Genoese. They kill Venetians for the fun of it," Ruggiero says.

"What are you thinking?" Zen asks him.

"Avoid the main road. Tack south and east where nobody will see us, work our way to the top, approach Moccò from the crest, and meet the mighty Lord Astolfo."

Eying the crest of the limestone cliffs, Hieronimo scratches his head.

"How the hell do we get up there?"

"Follow some dumb-ass donkey trail. Like we did in Crete."

We follow a hoof-beaten path up a defile so narrow we couldn't see it from below. Delfín kicks up rocks and sends scree skittering down the cliff. I accidentally brush against a bush and a thorn an inch-and-a-half long rips my sleeve. I snap it off the branch and put it in my pouch to show the doge. Another thorn pricks Delfín's flank. She starts to bridle, so I force her to the opposite side of the path where there are no thorns but nothing between us and the valley floor dropping farther and farther below.

A few deserted-looking huts cluster by a creek. Below them, the gulf glitters in the distance. Behind them, a line of tall pines marks the crest and the road to Moccò. A distant church bell rings Nones, the ninth hour of the day.

Hieronimo taps his map. "Welcome to Bottazzo."

We dismount and drink icy water from the stream.

"If you gentlemen will excuse me," Hieronimo says, "I am going to relieve myself in Mother Nature's lap."

When Hieronimo pops back from the trees, he has a relieved smile on his face.

"Now," he says, "I can ride forever. Think we'll reach Moccò before dark?"

"Before Vespers," Ruggiero says.

We ascend to the crest, riding behind a screen of tall, pungent pines, the dusty trail carpeted with their needles. Castle Moccò is hard to miss in the distance. A solitary tower juts up from an isolated rock spur shaped like an arrowhead. We dismount and tether our horses. Ruggiero hunkers at the edge of the cliff to study the castle, which appears to be surrounded on three sides by air and with no one to be seen.

"Fat lazy bastards." Hieronimo points and laughs. "We could take the whole place right now, and they wouldn't know till we woke them up."

We hear a grunt we don't understand.

It's not one of us.

Chapter Thirty-One

The Lord of Castle Moccò

THREE SOLDIERS IN chain mail hauberks rope and tie us before we can say boo. They bind our hands and march us to Castle Moccò like the losers we are. Our horses follow behind, except for Delfín who runs clear of the enemy. Shrieking like a she-devil, she disappears into the trees. She will stay hidden and wait for me.

"I am the official envoy of the doge of Venice," I repeat over and over.

No response. Laughing and joking with one another in the local tongue, the men of Moccò prod us like lost sheep. More akin to Caesar's Germans than Italians, beefy, with ruddy complexions and giant strides, they do one thing, and they do it well. No pack of thugs, these, but professional warriors who capture us with easy grace. Giorgio Barozzi spoke true when he praised Astolfo's men to the Doge's Council at our secret meeting; they are awe-inspiring. Any one of them could lift Hieronimo Zen over his head and hurl him into the canyon without breaking a sweat.

Squat and ugly, Castle Moccò does not compare to our palaces. Made from odd stones of all shapes and sizes, as if no one had time to sort them and pieced them tightly together in unruly ranks, this castle couldn't be more different from the proper brickwork and fancifully carved marble I'm accustomed to. But Moccò has nothing to do with a lord's comfort. Born as a Roman *castrum*, a bare-bones military fortress, it guards the most important road in the region. Blunt and to the point, Moccò has wasted no resources on carvings and gold leaf. Giant oaks, six to a side, form the gate, flanked by two open-topped towers. The ramparts running atop the castle walls meet between the towers. Stout parapets protect the bowmen.

The triangular courtyard juts into the gorge, with a tall tower at its apex. The main torrent of the Rosandra runs to the left. Moccò Creek, smaller, flanked by a narrow road, splits off to the right. Stables, kitchens, and a mess hall line the gorge side, with the barracks and armory along the creek. The keep rises three floors, and the tower behind it pokes higher into the sky, a crow's nest of stone up top.

The men of Moccò jeer and laugh at us as our captors drag us through the courtyard to the keep. Mostly young and engaged in either working, gambling, or sparring with swords and shields, the garrison whistles and shouts insults. I am mesmerized by these fighters, so fierce and powerful, so polished and unafraid, even in sport, to draw blood or die.

The keep, dark as the meanest hovel in Venice, shows no windows, only slits for bowmen, through which the wind whistles mournfully. Low fires smolder in fireplaces big enough for wrestling matches, and torches have

scorched the bare walls black. The great hall fills the center of the keep, with three open stories so dark at the top
that the roof beams are obscured.

Our captors prod us through the great hall to the
tower behind the keep. Astolfo's quarters, wedged between narrow rooms and a shitter on the ground floor,
would never stir a sane man's envy. Our captors knock on
the wooden door, open it, thrust us face down onto the
stone floor, and plant their feet on the backs of our necks.
We can't even see the lord of Moccò.

One of them tells Astolfo something I don't understand.

"What did he say?" I ask Ruggiero on my right.

"He says we're dressed like Triesters, but we stink like
Venetians."

Astolfo stands over us. I can only make out his leather
boots turned down at the top. I don't hear his voice, I feel
it, like the firm tone from a large and resonant bass viol.
"Why are you snooping around my castle?"

"We weren't snooping," I say.

"What do you call it?"

"I'm an ambassador from His Exalted Serenity, the
Doge of Venice. These men are my bodyguards."

"Why are they wearing Trieste on their chests?" Astolfo asks.

"We didn't want to attract attention."

"You attracted mine. I'd fire them if I was you. They
did a lousy job."

He hunkers over me and studies my eyes. His hand
engulfs the side of my face, his right forearm a braided
bundle of muscle under smooth golden skin tattooed with
infidel writing. His chest and arms strain his chainmail
hauberk; gold chest hair bursts through the silver links. A
leather eyepatch covers his right eye. His left eye, startl-

ingly green and alert, pierces me with the intensity of an eagle. He doesn't look like a thug, a cutthroat, or a thief. The eyepatch threw me for a pulsebeat or two, but he is absolutely the most beautiful man I have ever seen.

"Allow me to stand," I tell him. "I can prove what I say."

I look up at him. His bare thighs show between the hem of his mail and the top of his boots. A master sculptor chiseled him from rugged granite the color of honey. His thighs make Matteo's thighs look like twigs. If Matteo is half man and half boy, Astolfo is a man and a half. A strange smile plays across his lips.

"Go ahead," he says. "Prove it."

I stand and pull the pennant from my tunic, never taking my eyes off his.

"This is the pennant Giorgio Barozzi gave my doge."

Astolfo snatches it, glances at it, and drops it on the table behind him.

"Why didn't you say so in the first place?"

"I told your men."

"They don't understand your tongue."

"They understood. They didn't care."

Astolfo gives orders to the men who brought us. One of them leaves, the other two stand beside Ruggiero and Hieronimo Zen still facedown on the floor. His men pull off their chainmail cowls and attach them to leather belts. They stand at attention, left hands gripping sheathed swords. Not as beautiful as Astolfo, but cut from the same mold, the unruly auburn hair of these twins of Hector and Achilles tumbles down their backs. Astolfo circles Ruggiero and Zen.

"Are you noble?" he asks them.

"We are noble-born," they answer proudly in unison.

Astolfo shakes his head and looks at me. "I can smell nobles. What about you, boy?"

"As common as rain."

That wins me a pleased smile. "How is it a common boy speaks for the doge?"

"I'm his ballot boy. I keep the nobles honest."

He laughs as if I made a joke. "How did you get saddled with that thankless job?"

I point to Ruggiero. "Ruggiero is the youngest noble on our Great Council. On election day, he picked me at random from a crowd of common boys."

Astolfo grins as if I'm an idiot. I don't even know where my words are coming from. His beauty muddles my mind.

"Picked randomly, by a Venetian noble." He smirks. "You're very funny."

He orders Achilles to bring a chair for me. Ruggiero and Hieronimo stand, their hands behind their backs. Astolfo's eye rivets me. More than anything, he looks like a fallen angel with red-gold hair to his waist. He reaches behind his head, pulls his hair back tight, wraps it around and fastens it with a silver pin. The short sleeves of his hauberk slide back and I can see the golden hair in his armpits. His muscles flex with each movement.

"What message do you bring from the doge of Venice?"

"His Exalted Serenity asked me to tell you that you must immediately block the Salt Road to Leopold of Austria and open Castle Moccò to our army."

"*Must?*"

"Yes."

"Or?"

"Or you become an enemy of the Republic."

"And that's supposed to scare me?"

He looks at Hector and Achilles. "Did you hear that, boys? The doge of Venice is threatening to attack us."

They laugh, and Astolfo looks back at me. No smile on his face. "We are to be conquered by those Pygmies stuck in the mud outside Trieste? Is that supposed to scare me? Or are you planning to row your galleys up the Rosandra?"

"I'm only the messenger. My charge is to deliver the message and return with your answer."

"You *were* the messenger. You're my hostage now."

Behind the beautiful face is the steely will of a man who doesn't like being told what to do. Wildly, I wonder what it is to be a man of Moccò.

"You are bound by the laws of war to ensure my safe return," I say.

"There you go again. Your laws mean nothing at Moccò. Astolfo heeds no superior. I make the rules here."

Hieronimo speaks up. "I know you, Astolfo. I fought with you in Crete. You are a noble warrior."

"Your name?"

"Hieronimo Zen, bowman on *Fortuna* under Taddeo Giustinian, now my admiral. We're still on the same side. The doge is offering you what you want if you stand for Venice."

"That's clearly best for Venice, but what's best for Astolfo?"

"It's better to have Venice at your side than at your throat," Ruggiero says.

Astolfo examines Ruggiero's face. Then Hieronimo's. Then mine. He doesn't say anything. He takes in our faces and bodies from toe to crown, and our eyes, especially our eyes, and knows all he needs to know.

"Lock them up," he orders Achilles and Hector.

Chapter Thirty-Two

Ruggiero's Confession

HECTOR AND ACHILLES prod us down a circular stairway to a dark cellar. Locked in one cell, we sit in the gloom on rancid straw.

"I'm glad I took that dump when I did," Hieronimo says. "Otherwise, you would be wishing you were dead."

Keys rattle. Hector yanks the door open and gestures to Hieronimo, who stands up. Hector jerks his thumb for Hieronimo to step out into the corridor. Ruggiero leaps between Hieronimo and Hector. He shouts something in their tongue. Hector whips his sword around as if it were light as a feather and backs Ruggiero against the wall with the razor-edged point at his throat.

"Take it easy, Gradenigo," Hieronimo shouts from the corridor. "I've got everything in hand."

Ruggiero says something to Hector, who nods and locks the cell door behind him.

"What did you say to him?" I ask.

"I told him if he messes with my captain, blood will be shed."

Ruggiero lies on his back chewing straw and jiggling his leg, angry and impatient. They took our gear away, so he doesn't even have his mercy-maker. All we have between us is our bare hands. Lucky for me, he's not acting like someone who wants to kill me right now. He's too busy figuring a way out, and I might be useful to him.

"You know what's funny?" he asks.

"What?"

"You trust Hieronimo, and you don't trust me."

My turn to laugh. A gut-buster.

"Go ahead. Laugh." He grins sheepishly. "I don't blame you. All you see is a nasty prick who threatened to kill you a couple times. You aren't going to believe this, but I was just messing with you. Sometimes I talk tough and play rough. I'm an asshole; when I drink too much, I do stupid things. By now, you're getting to know my moves, and I'm getting to know yours. So how is it you don't know shit about Hieronimo, and yet you trust him?"

"The friend of my friend is my friend. He believes in the Republic, and he's loyal to the doge."

"I bet I believe in the Republic more than both of you."

"Bullshit."

"The difference between us is I believe in the Republic and you believe in Andrea Contarini. I believe in the office, and you believe in some old farmer who'd rather be pruning fig trees. If he's a doge, I'm St. Mark. There were great doges before, and I respect them—Orseolo, Ziani, Dandolo. Men who understood power and how to use it. Men with a vision for Venice. Your Serenissimo is a little man doing a big job badly. Not that it matters; he can't do shit anyway. You know that. He has to make an appointment to fart. The whole arrangement stinks. Committees run him, and there's nothing he can do about it. His own so-called councilors veto him right and left. They can fire him, but he can never quit. Their so-called Republic is nothing but a private club to make a handful of rich men richer. They keep everyone else running around in circles, too busy with elections and committees to pay attention to what's really going on. Hell, you see it every day. You know what I mean."

He's infuriated. Not at me or the doge, but at the machinery of the state. And there's a certain truth in what he says.

"But this shit between you and me, it's not about that. It's about Blackbeard's beautiful Alessandra, the little girl with the biggest dowry in Venice. What I don't understand is how someone as smart as you could think you ever had a chance with her?"

"I don't, but I love her anyway."

"Too bad for you. Her father has been planning to marry her off to a noble since she was born, and we made the best offer, fully guaranteed. A noble stud pumping out noble heirs. Honestly, I don't give a shit about her. She's pretty enough. Maybe she's sweet; I don't know. All I want is her daddy's gold. She's not my type, and believe me, I get all I want of what I want."

"Raping girls in San Giobbe?"

"You heard about that. Don't believe everything you hear."

I can't go there with him. Not here. Not now.

"What do you think of Astolfo?" I ask.

"He's a very bad boy. He's everything you think I am, times ten."

Footsteps outside. Keys jingle. Achilles opens the cell door. There's no sign of Zen, and the Moccò men don't answer questions.

"Where's my captain?" Ruggiero shouts, ready to fight. "I'm not going anywhere until I know where he is."

Hector knocks him on his ass, and they drag him away.

I'M ALONE FOR the first time since I left Venice, and I'm coming unglued. Everything crashes inward, crushing me. I don't know who or what I am anymore. Yesterday, I wasn't a killer. Today, I am. I killed men and boys, and I wanted to kill more. That crazed compulsion still lurks in my blood. Then Ruggiero starts making scary sense, and I can't get the old Ruggiero back, the one I hate. I don't know if I was wrong all along or if Ruggiero was just practicing a speech on me, more fancy words to woo the weak-minded.

Maybe I've got it all wrong. Maybe I don't know a damn thing.

Maybe I never did.

The truth is, that's not what bothers me most. Something else is burning me up.

Astolfo.

He has lit a fire in me I've never felt before. It must be lust. As soon as I saw him, I wanted to get all tangled up with him. I like Matteo well enough; he's funny and sweet, but he's nothing like this. When I close my eyes and see Astolfo—the intense green of his eye, the line of his jaw, the curve of his shoulders, the flare of his thighs, his tattooed forearm and powerful hands—he raises a riot in my blood. Astolfo even eclipses Alex with her trousers and sleeves rolled up, her lean muscular arms at the oar, her gorgeous hair blowing free.

Which means I'm doomed.

My yes is louder than my no. My lust throttles my virtue.

I'm doomed, and I'm damned.

I easily stopped myself from committing grievous sins with Matteo. Astolfo makes me want to commit them over and over and over again.

Keys in the hall.

The door opens.

Achilles nods. It's my turn.

They lead me to the lord of Moccò.

A fire blazes in his den. The air, hot and thick, smells of men without women in close quarters. I'm damp and feverish, like I haven't slept in a year. Astolfo's sweat glitters in the torchlight. He looks weary, drunk, excited, all at the same time. He sprawls in a throne carved to his measure from the trunk of an oak tree. His chainmail hauberk lays on his table. A red fox cloak hangs around his shoulders, his chest bare. A silver belt cinches his linen breeches. He wears nothing else besides the soft leather boots bunched around his ankles. As he turns toward me, the fox cloak slides off his shoulders. The flames in the hearth turn the hair on his chest and legs to a golden fleece and set fire to the jeweled pommel of the dagger stuck in the arm of his throne like a symbol of office.

Hector shoves me into the wooden chair facing Astolfo; Achilles tethers my wrists with leather straps. Their lord leans forward and watches.

"This one is different," Astolfo says to Achilles so I can understand him. "A nipper."

"A pretty nipper at that." Achilles surprises by answering so I understand.

"I'm no nipper. I'm a man."

"You're the doge's boy," Achilles says.

"I'm the ballot boy, but I am now a man."

"Barozzi was right," Astolfo says. "Black hair and deep-blue eyes. A beauty. Innocent eyes, a fine young body, and a smart mouth."

"He got that right," Achilles says.

When I open my mouth to say something, Astolfo covers it with his hand.

"I'm thirty," he says. "I've been around a lot longer than you, and I know a lot more. Don't even think about bullshitting me."

He takes his hand away.

"Why would I?"

"Well spoken." He smiles appreciatively. "Out of loyalty to your doge."

"Loyalty to my doge demands I speak the truth."

"What does he want here?"

"To subdue Trieste, enforce our salt monopoly, and secure the gulf."

"What about Castle Moccò?"

"As long as you're with us, he's happy that you remain lord of Moccò."

"Is that so?" He looks at Achilles, who shakes his head.

"Not hardly," Achilles says.

"Every prince," Astolfo says, "in Austria, in Hungary, and each and every one of your squabbling Italian tyrants, including the doge of Venice, covets Castle Moccò. We control the Salt Road. Only the price they'd have to pay prevents them from trying to seize Moccò. My men aren't bumpkins recruited from farms and whorehouses, or hired scrappers who have no idea how war is fought. I handpicked professional warriors, as strong and fierce as Spartans. I'm their lord, but we fight and share as equals. We're Brothers of Moccò. Before us, the mightiest armies tremble."

"'Brothers of Moccò.' You sound like monks."

"We are, in our way. Monks who fight instead of pray. But we don't fight for God. We fight for ourselves. When we're not fighting the enemy, we fight one another to stay sharp, and when we're not training, we make love."

He watches for my reaction, moving closer. His shadow falls heavily across me. The space between us crackles, lightning without thunder.

"The brothers of Moccò are the finest in the world," he says. "They put the Varangians of old to shame. Who does the doge have for soldiers?"

"Men of the lagoon."

"Lagoon men are sailors. I mean foot soldiers and cavalry."

"Men from the countryside."

"My point exactly. Bumpkins. The best money can buy, which isn't much. You can't trust men who fight only to loot and rape and move on to the next war. My men are as loyal as they are strong and as disciplined as they are fierce. Venice will lose against us."

He's as close to me as he can be without touching.

"We won't lose," I say.

"Not *we*. Venice. You're not Venice. At least you don't have to be. I like you. I see possibilities. I think maybe you're a brother of Moccò, and you don't know it yet."

"I'm loyal to the Republic."

"I hear things, even way up here. Things about you and the doge. Things that happened while you were still fishing for anchovies. Things nobody will tell you, except me. *You* interest me. Not Venice. You. I could use your so-called bodyguards as saddle blankets for all anyone cares. You're different."

He touches my chest lightly. "You count."

"You lied to us. I don't bargain with liars."

"I lied. The doge lied. The council lied. The captain lied. The bowman lied. We all lie."

"What are you going to do with us?"

He doesn't answer right away. He looks at me, his mouth halfway between a smile and a frown. He likes me, but he's sad that I'm so stupid.

"Not *us*," he says. "You. What am I going to do with you? That's the question. The doge is soft on you. I'm told he sent your horse with his medallion on the bridle. You're valuable."

"No, I'm not. My first day on the job, someone told me everyone remembers the doge, but no one remembers the ballot boy."

That makes him laugh.

"The same man told me, emperor or slave, every man has a boss."

"Most men, yes. Astolfo, no." He raises his forearm and runs his finger over his blue tattoo. "Do you know what it says?"

"No."

"It's Turk for slave."

"Were you a slave?"

"A Turkish pirate tried to make me his slave."

"How did you escape?"

"That's a story for another time. But any man who wants to be my boss better not be afraid to die. I'm not."

"I'm not afraid to die."

That surprises him. He studies my eyes to see if it's true.

"Is that so?"

He stands close and puts his fingers around my throat. He's not smiling any more.

"What will the doge do next?"

"I don't know."

He squeezes my throat until tears stream from my eyes.

"Tell me what the doge has in mind, and I'll show you what we do for fun at Castle Moccò."

He relaxes his grip. His face is so close I can smell his breakfast. His breath sets my ear on fire.

"I'm no mind reader," I say.

"You don't have to read his mind. He tells you everything, especially when you *pray* together. I know about that too."

Did Ruggiero tell him, or does gossip really travel this far?

"You probably know him better than he knows himself," Astolfo says.

"I don't know what his intentions are."

"Have it your way."

He raises my chin and positions his right thumb and index finger on my throat.

"Such a fragile tube. Why would something so important be so delicate that I can crush it with two fingers."

He squeezes slowly until I can't breathe. His fingers are strong as steel. He releases my throat. My body violently sucks in air. I hack and gasp.

"That's what drowning feels like," he says.

I can't talk. I have no voice, just cords rasping.

"Tell me what your doge has up his sleeve."

He squeezes again, steady and relentless. Everything blurs at the edges. His face vanishes in a swirling darkness. I'm floating. I don't feel his fingers any more. His words are meaningless. His voice disappears. I hear only distant thunder and feel a quiet peace.

Floating in the darkness, I say goodbye to everything. The further the world fades, the less I give a damn. I'm truly unafraid until a Titan throttles me. My teeth and bones rattle. Light shatters my darkness.

I'm on the floor, flat on my back. Astolfo straddles me, his knees on either side of my chest. He sticks his finger in my mouth to sweep my tongue aside, covers my mouth with his, and blows his breath into my lungs the way he'd inflate a pig's bladder.

I want to keep floating in the darkness, but he won't let me. He slaps my face and comes at me, lips first, to inflate me again.

He tastes sour—fear and excitement.

"You're crushing me."

"You're alive!"

He takes my face in his hands and kisses my lips.

"Welcome back."

He grins, laughs, jumps up, and bellows because I'm breathing. He was truly afraid he'd killed me. He yells for beer. He says he's so hungry he could eat a boar. Pressing his ear to my chest, he listens to my breathing until satisfied it won't stop. Then he lifts me off the floor and carries me into a small adjacent chamber, lays me on a simple bed, makes sure I'm comfortable, and stays until I fall asleep. He follows me into my dreams, and when I open my eyes, he's snoring in a chair in front of the fire. As soon I stir the slightest, he stirs. Warrior reflexes. He pours me a goblet of warm beer.

"Drink that. It will put hair on your chest."

The brew is crisp and bitter. He throws me a chunk of bread from the table. He points at the oily boar. I stare at the floor and wonder what I don't remember.

"You really don't know anything, do you?"

He sits up in his chair, bread and boar in one hand, beer in the other. His mouth is full of meat and crumbs.

"If you knew anything, you would have talked before I killed you, right? Unless you want to die."

"I said I'm not afraid to die. I didn't say I want to."

He treats me differently now that I have survived the ordeal. That makes me more like a brother. He eats more meat, hardly chewing, and washes it down with beer. His manners aren't any worse than most of the nobles at free palace suppers.

"Your loyalty is impressive," he says. "I honor that. You should forget Andrea Contarini. He's history."

"And the Austrians aren't?"

"Not yet."

"You think Leopold is better than the doge of Venice?"

"I told you, no boss for Astolfo. I'm not marrying Leopold. We're using each other. We each get what we want, and he goes home."

"You trust him?"

"He needs me to protect his conquest here."

"Is he smart?"

"He doesn't have to be. He was born with a crown on his head."

"Is he brave?"

"His kind watches the battle from a nearby hill, close but not too close."

"Then Venice will win."

"It doesn't matter if he's brave or smart. That's what generals are for. He's marching hundreds of knights, a thousand cavalry, ten thousand foot soldiers. The battle will be on land, not at sea. How can Venice win?"

"Can I take your answer to the doge now?"

"I told you you're not going anywhere. You're too good to lose."

"At least let my men go. You said yourself they're useless."

"That they are, but why should I set two Venetian nobles free for nothing?"

"To carry a message to my admiral and our doge."

"What message?"

"They will believe whatever I write and seal with my ring."

I flash the ring. He holds out his hand for me to take it off and drop it in his palm.

"You'll have to cut it off," I say. "It carries the authority of the doge who gave it to me. My admiral knows this seal; he'll know if it's been broken. Do you have parchment and quill?"

Parchment, ink, and quill are quickly brought in. He watches as I prepare to write the note.

"What are you going to write?"

"I'm sworn to tell the truth."

"Then tell them that as long as I control Moccò, you are well taken care of. As for Trieste, I wish them luck in their battle with Austria, but I'm betting on the winner."

Chapter Thirty-Three

Prisoner of Moccò

ZEN FOLDS HIS arms over his chest, plants his boots, refuses to leave without me.

"Orders are orders. You heard the admiral. We can't go back without you."

He means every word. His loyalty is honorable. Handing him the sealed parchment, I pull rank.

"In the name of the doge and Senate of Venice, I order you and Gradenigo to take this message to Admiral Giustinian."

Ruggiero nods and winks at me. He's ready to go. "Have a good time with Lord Astolfo," he says.

Two grooms bring their horses from the stable, along with their weapons and gear. Zen looks tearful, but he has no choice and must leave. Ruggiero is more concerned with checking his gear to make sure it's all there.

Astolfo puts his arm around my shoulders as the gate closes behind them. "Being a hostage isn't so bad," he says. "Let me show you my castle."

Two squads of men spar in the courtyard like the gladiators who got sacked for eating the wild lions for breakfast. It's only practice, but their swords are bloody.

We climb the stairs at the base of the high tower. Up top, I'm smacked with the cold emptiness. I stagger. The Rosandra glitters in its gorge hundreds of feet below. The wind whips around the tower. My knees buckle. I press my back against the wall until the spinning stops.

Astolfo looks surprised. "What kind of bowman are you? You act like you've never been in a crow's nest."

"This is ten times as high."

"Bah. There's Muggia, across the water, Moncolano in the far west, and there's Duino. Trieste is straight down the gorge."

I inch along the parapet feeling like I'm falling. I grab Astolfo's arm and put my head down. When I concentrate on my breathing, the world stops spinning. I bless Abdul for this wisdom. Astolfo steps behind me, grabs my waist with both hands, and hoists me up, over the parapet. I almost shit myself. I shut my eyes. Wind roars like a thousand drums beating the charge. Astolfo shouts in my year.

"Lean forward. On your left, the little tower below, that's Santa Maria in Siaris. They ring the bells you hear."

He won't set me down until I say something. I open my eyes. The vista washes over me like a tidal wave, the sparkling blue-green gulf, the craggy white cliffs, the water falling from a twisted peak down to the thick pines in the valley far below.

"It's beautiful," I shout.

He sets me down, presses against me, and wraps his arms around me, a bulwark against the wind.

"You might learn to love Moccò."

"Love it or not, my duty is with my doge."

"Bottazzo, where you watered, right down there. I see everything. Nothing goes by I don't know about. I watched you assholes all the way from Bagnoli. My one eye takes in more than most men ever see."

We climb down from the tower and walk the ramparts.

"Moccò is impregnable," I say to Astolfo. "You can keep everybody out, but it's like the walls of Trieste. It also locks you in. How could you provision under siege unless an angel comes down from the sky in a flaming chariot?"

"We don't need angels in flaming chariots. The supply line was taken care of a thousand years ago. Moccò is built on a Roman fort."

He needs say no more. I know Roman forts better than he does.

In the courtyard, the men who have finished sparring loiter around fountains carved into the wall. They guzzle the gushing water and wash their faces and their wounds. They do it every day. The most common things are the most frequently overlooked. These men are accustomed to water gushing up from solid rock, filling troughs and basins. To me, the flowing water is the most important element of this scene. It means the water comes from higher ground through pipes with sufficient pressure to push it up into the courtyard—evidence of a subterranean aqueduct.

Two sides of the triangular castle are flush with the arrowhead of cliff they stand on; there's nothing around them but air. The Rosandra plunges hundreds of feet below. The only way in or out of Castle Moccò is along the base of the triangle, where two towers with a barbican flank the gate. To the left of the gate, the Salt Road from the Alps descends Rosandra Gorge to Trieste. To the right, the trail along Moccò Creek falls off steeply.

The men scattered around the stables and the armory are cleaning, polishing, chewing straw, gaming. Crossbows line the barracks wall. I walk over to inspect them.

"May I? This one's a monster."

I pick one with a huge cranequin. A bolt shot from this bow could pierce three or four men as easily as a skewer pierces woodcocks.

"Can you shoot?" Astolfo asks.

"I'm the best shot from Grado to Cavarzere."

"Show me."

He hands me the crossbow I admired. "Six more of these are pointed right between your big blue eyes so don't try anything stupid."

I nod to the bowmen targeting me from the rampart. Astolfo hands me a bolt.

"How brave are your men?" I ask.

"None braver."

Three men are playing cards nearby. I reach between them, pick a king of swords, and show it to Astolfo. The king sits on his throne, brandishing his sword. A medallion hangs over his heart.

"Right there," I say, tapping the king's medallion with my finger. It's a hell of a target, even for me, half the size of a ducat. I pray to St. Nick to help me now. The fate of Venice rides on my shot.

"Who's going to hold the card?" I ask.

Mouths open but say nothing. The men who stopped sparring and everyone else who has nothing to do are all mute. Astolfo snatches the card and stands against the wooden gate.

"Fire away, ballot boy. I hope you shoot as good as you talk."

The bow is a thing of beauty. I crank until the string almost breaks. I examine the bolt, feel it, breathe on it. I judge the speed and angle of the wind blowing around the tower, all as Abdul taught me. Astolfo holds the card straight out to his side. He's not nervous. He winks at me. I could shoot him, but then we'd both be dead, and nobody wins. He knows I won't, just like I knew he wouldn't kill me last night.

I load the bolt, raise the bow, and sight down the stock. I don't see Astolfo, or the walls, or the towers, or the gate. I see concentric rings inside a deep cone whose tip rests on the medallion over the king of sword's heart. I am a Mamluk, and the crossbow is my obedient servant. My bolt rips the card from Astolfo's hand and sticks it to the gate. The men come running as Astolfo holds up the card.

"Straight through the heart."

He beams with pride. I'm his new toy.

The men pass the card around, gaining me everyone's respect. That always comes in handy.

When Astolfo takes the crossbow he says, "I have much better weapons than this. You will be happy here."

"Who said I'm staying."

"You have no choice. You are my hostage as long as it pleases me. Why would you want to go?"

"My doge needs me."

"Do you need him?"

He hangs the crossbow on the wall and orders the guards to open the gate.

Day and night, six men stand watch in the towers flanking the gate. Ladders on the inside wall ascend to the rampart at regular intervals. Stone ramps run from each side of the courtyard up to the rampart for easy transport of machines on wheels, catapults, and trebuchets. Rope lies in tall coils near the ladders, along with iron pulleys for raising and lowering arms and ammunition. Stacks of javelins and shields line the walls. Horses whinny from the stable where a farrier hammers on his anvil beside a stone forge.

Outside the gates, out of earshot of the watchmen, Astolfo and I sit on a stone bench overlooking Moccò Creek Canyon. Sprawling in the bright sun and icy air like a lizard on a hot summer day, Astolfo shields his eye from the glare.

"Is it true what they say about your palace?" he asks.

"Is what true?"

"Nobles bugger boys on the palace stairs."

"He wasn't a noble. He was a clerk, and they burned him alive between the Columns of Doom. The boy said..."

"What?"

"Nothing. It doesn't matter."

"Tell me what the boy said."

"The boy said he was buggering the clerk, not the other way around."

Astolfo laughs. "Cheeky nipper. Any nobles ever touch your bum?"

"No."

"Never?"

"Never."

"You're not a virgin, are you?"

He watches. He waits.

"You are." He laughs. "Lard and skewer me, boy, you're in your blazing prime. What are you waiting for?"

"The right man, I guess."

I tell him I'm weary and need to sleep. He takes me back to the chamber beside his. I sprawl on a pallet, close my eyes, and roll toward the wall. He watches me until he thinks I'm sleeping and then goes about his business. He wants me awake and eager.

Assuredly, a way out can be found. The real question is, do I go or stay?

In the complete stillness of the room, no one knows what I'm doing or not doing. Right now, no one cares. Surrounded by the men of Moccò, I am absolutely alone. I'm a prisoner, and I have never been so free. My balls throb with painful longing. I'm alone with images of Astolfo still fresh in my eyes and no one to see or hear me. I yield easily to the dream; it's the reality that scares me shitless.

Face down, I lower my breeches and grind my hips into the fur blanket covering the straw. It's agony, and it's bliss. I burn hotter hearing Astolfo's voice nearby; it vibrates down my spine spawning images of Astolfo's arms and chest glistening like cloth of gold. His pungent breath, spicy and provocative, envelopes me as the weight of his body presses down. He'll show me Moccò fun, he said. Like wild beasts. He crushes me in his arms, drunk with desire. I taste his mouth again. I suppress my groans of ecstasy as I spill my seed.

I'm out of breath and drenched with sweat. My head throbs, and the fur blanket sticks to my soiled belly. The stench of sin clings to me. My only hope is to escape before I lose my eternal soul. I want to sin with Astolfo so desperately that I hate myself for it.

Astolfo interrupts my tossing and turning. He mounts a fresh torch, sets a jug of beer down, and sits beside me.

"Hungry?"

I sit up. "I'm thirsty. What hour is it?"

"Late. The night monks are getting ready for Matins at St. Mary in Siaris. Everyone here is asleep."

He hands me a mug of beer, and I drain it. He leans over and kisses my neck so tenderly I could cry. I put my

arms around his shoulders. My hands explore the landscape of his back. He kisses my face, my chest, my ears. I
try to stay true to my purpose, but his body is a bible of
forbidden pleasures I'm desperate to discover.

Chapter Thirty-Four

The Aqueduct

THE LINE BETWEEN yielding ground and losing advantage is very fine. The lay of that line depends on which I want more, to escape from Astolfo or to sin with him. If I want to sin, I need only yield. If I want to escape, he must trust me so that I can take advantage of his vulnerability. I must appear to yield while playing for advantage. When he thinks I have yielded, he will yield to me. Then I can vanquish him. But I'm in uncharted territory without border markers to tell me when I've gone too far.

So when he kisses my mouth, I have to decide which side of the line I'm on. And when he kisses my throat and the palms of my hands, a starving man diving into a feast, I have to know if I'm still in control, waiting for his point of maximum vulnerability, or if I have already yielded, ready to go wherever he takes me. He can't miss my crazy boner. He appears to trust me, smiling as he yanks off his breeches, drops his guard, and leads with his passion.

He's on all fours, straddling me. His hair brushes me lightly and sets everything it touches on fire.

"No," I say.

He stops. He looks into my eyes, puzzled.

"The other way," I say.

He is stunned. I haven't seen this expression on his face before. He doesn't want to show his surprise, or yield too easily, but he does want to. I can tell because it's not what he expected and that excites him. He doesn't say no. I move aside, and he lies face down on the bed.

I straddle him and lean forward, massaging his shoulders to relax him while I ease my right arm around his neck until the inside of my elbow is over his windpipe. I gently pull his head back toward me, kissing him so he's not suspicious, and press my lower body against his as I grip my right arm with my left and squeeze his neck between them. Sudden. Hard. Just as Abdul instructed.

Astolfo bucks, trying to throw me, so I squeeze tighter. Hard. Harder. And hold until he collapses. The longer and harder the pressure, the deeper the stupor afterward. Too long, and men die. Abdul and I practiced on each other. I know when death is near.

His good eye rolls back in his head. He drools, his jaw slackens.

I release him. He's asleep with one eye open. I don't have much time.

I tie him to the bed with stout square knots and gag him, careful not to block his breathing. I want him to live, to appreciate what I've done.

In the barracks, hammocks hang from the rafters and pallets line the walls. The dank stench of a legion of sleeping men permeates the airless stone vault. The men are out cold, to be roused at first light and not before. I crawl through the barracks low and slow, snatching any clothes that might fit as I go.

I snatch a stout bow and a quiver stuffed with bolts from the wall outside the barracks to see me through until I find my own. I also need apples from the kitchen. They will attract Delfín a lot faster than my scent. I pray she's still waiting. I pray she still has my own bow, bolts, and compass.

Pipes from a subterranean aqueduct run up through the kitchen wall, providing water for both the interior and exterior troughs. The aqueduct below the kitchen must run beneath the courtyard and gate from a mountain stream high above Castle Moccò. I spot a sack of apples near the kitchen door, stuff several in a pouch, and strap it around my waist.

At the far end of the kitchen, a stairway descends into darkness. I seize a torch from the top of the stairwell and descend into a cavern hollowed from solid rock by Roman hands. The cavern has three doors. I don't bother with the first whose stench tells me it's a shitter. The second door leads to an armory stuffed with weapons collected from defeated armies.

The third door opens into the aqueduct tunnel itself, dug through bedrock. The water pipe, lead, two feet in diameter, runs through the tunnel on stone trestles. The pressure in the pipe increases with the height of the water source and pushes the water up into the troughs of the kitchen and courtyard.

The space above the pipe allows me to crawl on my hands and knees up the steep grade. The crossbow won't fit. I chuck it. But I manage to stuff the apples into my clothing. I set out with no idea how to go through the dark tunnel angling upward. Every hundred yards or so, light beams down through a shaft to the surface, dug by the Roman engineers to track the path of the aqueduct.

Slime covers my hands and feet, making it almost impossible to maintain the traction I need to keep moving upward. I must constantly correlate the distance below the surface with the landscape twenty feet up, on the mountainside. I don't want to go too far; I need to be close enough to Moccò to find Delfín and far enough to get out before they start looking for me.

Chapter Thirty-Five

An Unexpected Meeting

CLIMBING THE SHAFT I have chosen in the aqueduct, I pray Delfín hasn't wandered too far. Once I'm on the surface, I don't dare whistle or call for her. I spread pieces of apple along the bank of the stream where she is wont to nibble grass and wait until she comes my way, using her nose to scour for greenery. Little grass is left, so she smells the apple all the more easily, then she smells me. My bow and quiver still hang from her saddle. She nuzzles me, and I lead her along the trail to the three entwined pines I noted on my way in. I want to gallop to Muggia, but only the weakest moonlight slips between the trees. I can barely see the path, so I walk, leading Delfín downhill, twisting and turning toward Bagnoli.

Delfín suddenly stops and won't budge. She senses something I can neither see nor hear, calling to her far more strongly than Muggia calls me. I can't pull her my way. She rears, frustrated. I give her slack and let her lead.

Through a break in the trees, faint moonlight falls on boulders piled high at the base of the cliff. Delfín pulls free and runs to the boulders. She stops and nudges something.

I follow her. It's a body. Face down. A hole ripped through its back.

The bolt is stuck in a tree behind him. He must have been standing on the boulder. The shot threw him forward. His blood pools around him; little can be left in his body. I touch his hand. He's barely alive. He turns his face to the moonlight.

Blood mats his wild halo of unruly auburn curls.

"Hieronimo, can you hear me?"

His body twitches at the sound of my voice.

"Can you open your eyes?"

He's trying.

"Who shot you?"

One eye opens. He sees me. His eyelid flutters.

"Do you know who shot you?"

He twists to fix both eyes on me. His index finger moves ever so slightly, right to left, left to right across my palm, as if shaking his head no.

"Am I Niccolò Saltano?"

His finger barely moves, up and down, a nod.

"Did you see who shot you?"

He drags a diagonal path across my palm. Not a nod; not a shake. He stares at my face, his eyes sad as the life flickers out.

"Was it Ruggiero?"

His eyes open wide.

He is heavy. Inert. Dead.

I've killed men from the safety of a bolt's distance—strangers without faces, men with metal visors hiding their faces. This dead man is Hieronimo Zen, my country-man and comrade. I can't stop my tears. He exhales his soul on his last breath, leaving an inert empty husk.

I have no time to bury him, but I can't leave him exposed. I stuff his body into a crevice and cover the opening with broken chunks of limestone to keep wild beasts from desecrating him. The body is no longer the Hieronimo I knew; I grasp that. But when the trumpet sounds and the dead arise, at least he won't have been gnawed by wolves or wild boars. Before I leave, I pull the bolt from the tree hoping it will tell me who shot him.

Delfín runs like the sirocco from Bagnoli to Muggia. We're half-dead by the time we arrive. I go straight to Giustinian on the poop of the *Lion*. He is so surprised and happy to see me he throws his arms around me and lifts me off the deck before setting me down in his chair.

"Zen is dead," I say.

"I know. Gradenigo said they were ambushed."

"How did Ruggiero get away?"

"He can tell you himself."

Giustinian sends for Ruggiero, who can barely mask his shock at seeing me.

I blurt out, "You killed Hieronimo, you bastard."

"That's the kettle calling the pot black," Ruggiero says.

I fly at Ruggiero, but Giustinian grabs me with both hands, holding me back.

Ruggiero smiles at me. "You're crazy; you know that?"

"You shot Hieronimo in the back because he knew something you didn't want anyone else to know."

"You make shit up," Ruggiero says, "and then you believe it. You saw the big guy give us our gear and cut us loose. We were ambushed halfway to Bagnoli. Two cowards from Moccò. One of them shot him in the back."

"Why didn't they shoot you?"

"They couldn't see me. Like an idiot, Hieronimo had to climb on a rock to piss. I told him to cut it out, but he said he liked the sound. Next thing I know, he's flying off the rock."

"That's bullshit."

"Why would I kill him?"

The old Ruggiero is back, the one I knew was there all along, the one I hate.

"You don't need a reason. You're crazy."

"You're the crazy one, my friend."

"I have the bolt that went through Hieronimo's heart. That will tell us who shot him."

Giustinian snaps. "Enough. Both of you."

He's upset that Zen is dead and out of patience with both of us. I hand him the bolt from my saddlebag. He cleans the gore from its grooves and examines it carefully. It's as long as my forearm, with a square metal head tapering to a sharp two-inch point. The bloodstained fletches are made of wood.

Giustinian shakes his head. "It's not one of ours. Ours are larch with leather fletches. This is aspen and willow." He holds it under my nose. "*M* for Moccò, here, scribed into the point."

"Ruggiero could have grabbed one of their bolts."

"Right, and donkeys could sing Mass," Ruggiero says, "but they don't. Your buddy Astolfo watched us like a hawk. We didn't leave with anything we didn't walk in with—swords, crossbows, quivers, horses all saddled up.

All by the book, except the ambush. Astolfo is twisted. I wouldn't put anything past him."

Giustinian dismisses Ruggiero and holds me back. He waits until no one else can hear us before he lets loose.

"Don't ever do anything like that again. You'll get us both killed."

"Do what?"

"That bullshit with Gradenigo."

"With all due respect, sir, it's not bullshit."

He grabs me and shakes me to make me listen.

"Stop it. Now."

He is no longer my friend. He is no longer my commanding officer trying to get something very important through my thick skull. He is the angry god of the Old Testament appearing out of the whirlwind.

"You can't accuse a noble of treason and murder. Not in public. Not even with proof. Not where anyone can hear you."

"I know what I saw."

"What you *think* you saw. Listen carefully. Ruggiero Gradenigo is a noble. You are a bastard commoner. There are hundreds like you on the docks any day of the week, except you happen to work for the doge, shoot like a marksman, and read Latin like a priest. These nobles could know he did it, and they would still go after you first. The men who hate Ruggiero most will be his staunchest defenders against a commoner. They look after their own, like him or not. No one will be able to help you. Not even the doge."

"I need to know why he killed Hieronimo."

"People love to talk. Here, as much as in Venice. Some would rather gossip than gamble. Your vendetta against Gradenigo gives them plenty of fodder. You, Ruggiero, Alessandra Barbanegra. A fountain of gossip. Some of them talk about your influence over the doge and how he treats the Gradenigos like shit. Some say you only give gold ballots to people on a secret list. None of them will mourn you."

"It's all lies."

"I would still have to swear before God and the Ten that Gradenigo's behavior in Trieste has been exemplary. You could almost say he's a new man."

Chapter Thirty-Six

The War Council

PACING IN FRONT of the war council in General Loredan's tent, Giustinian explodes in frustration. "The men won't stand for it."

He's immediately ashamed his temper outpaces his patience. He drops his voice. "They'll all desert before they build another wall."

"We can't block Austria with galleys," Loredan says. "They're marching through the mountains, by land, not by sea. We *can* build a wall across Via Flavia."

Loredan and Giustinian have been going at it for nearly an hour. They are at loggerheads, neither willing to yield, both fearing for their heads in different ways. Loredan is the first to notice when I stand.

"May I speak, sir?"

"Sit down." Loredan dismisses me with a flick of his hand. I implore Giustinian with my eyes to weigh in on my behalf.

"What harm is there in it?" Giustinian asks General Loredan.

"Do we have time to let every sapper and carter speak?"

"His Exalted Serenity chose you to lead this army," Giustinian says. "He chose me to lead the fleet. He chose my bowman to carry Astolfo's pennant and be our embassy to the lord of Moccò. Do you doubt His Exalted Serenity's judgment?"

Loredan must choose his words carefully. "I have never doubted Serenissimo."

"He also ordered us to waste no time building another wall. Allow Niccolò to speak."

"He's a ballot boy, for Jesus's sake. He wears a velvet tunic and counts gold and silver balls."

"I turned sixteen on April 17, sir, and I am a man."

"Yes, yes, yes, we know. Legally you are a man," Loredan says. "As green as early corn. You know nothing of war. You are wasting our time."

"Don't be so quick to judge what he knows," Giustinian says. "Who was the greatest leader on the field of battle?"

"Julius Caesar, I suppose," Loredan says. "But what has he got to do with the price of salt in Trieste?"

"Have you read Caesar?"

"No," Loredan replies. "I had neither the time nor the inclination."

"Niccolò has. I daresay he has not only read Caesar, but he has studied Caesar, and I might even go further and say he understands how Caesar thought. How he, over and over again—outnumbered, with dead legions piled at his feet—met the advancing enemy and pulled victory out of the jaws of disaster. Is that not so, Niccolò?"

"Yes, sir. It is so."

Loredan scoffs. "You don't learn war from books."

"No," Giustinian says, "but you learn what has been done before, the outcome, what might be done again. Strategy and tactics are a way of thinking, which all too often we learn in the heat of battle through monstrous mistakes that cost men's lives. To scorn what can be learned from history may be a worse mistake."

"What could Caesar possibly have to say about the imbroglio in Trieste, the Austrian army crossing the Alps as we speak, and the merry lord of Moccò threatening and promising everyone? Can we please deal with the matters at hand?"

"Let him speak," Ruggiero says, hoping, I suppose, that I will make a fool of myself quoting Caesar and sounding green and stupid. "He has the doge's ear, ergo, he has mine."

"Let him speak," others say.

"Go ahead, little man" Loredan says. He smirks like I'm a trained dog who does tricks for biscuits.

"Seven thousand Romans faced a massive army of Gauls," I say. "They were outnumbered eight to one."

"Yes, yes, we've all heard the story," Loredan says, impatient and unkind.

"I haven't," Giustinian says, which I know to be a lie. "How many of you have?"

No man raises his hand.

"Continue."

"Caesar's legions were exhausted and edgy. Caesar knew he couldn't attack the Gauls head on any more than he could repel or survive an all-out attack. He knew that without doubt. He ordered his men to wander around aimlessly, looking as defeated and frightened as possible, to walk in confused circles, to start one thing and leave it for another as if in a daze, to look anything but what they were—brave and battle ready. They did what he said because he was Caesar, not because they understood why. Caesar knew that above all, everything rides on the certainty of the leader, so he gave his orders, and they obeyed. The Gauls saw a bunch of sorry weaklings walking in circles, and they believed what they saw. So certain were they of their victory that they put off their attack until the morning. Before dawn, when the Gauls least expected it and were least prepared, Caesar rallied his men and delivered a single overwhelming blow, assaulting their camp and breeching their palisade. The Gauls panicked, leaving their dead behind. The Romans carried the day. Caesar didn't outman the Gauls or outfight them. He outsmarted them. That's what we must do."

"How do we outsmart Leopold and his ten thousand men on the march?" Loredan drums his fingers impatiently on his shield.

"We don't outsmart Leopold, sir. We outsmart Astolfo and let him do it for us."

Loredan has no easy reply. He stares, silent, thinking. Giustinian frowns at the tack I'm taking.

"Astolfo lied to us," Giustinian says. "He killed Hieronimo Zen and would have killed you and Gradenigo. We can't trust him. Gradenigo, you talked to him. Give us your assessment of Astolfo."

"I think the lord of Moccò is a bully and a braggart with a great big mouth, surrounded by a mob of losers just like him who do whatever he says. But we could never take them, sir. The men of Moccò are as much fighting machines as mangonels and trebuchets, and Castle Moccò is impregnable."

"Not impregnable," I say, "not entirely..."

Even Ruggiero looks puzzled. "What the hell are you talking about?"

"I didn't leave by the front gate, sir. Castle Moccò started as a Roman *castrum*, and beneath it is a deep tunnel dug by Roman legions for a subterranean aqueduct, including air shafts to the surface every hundred yards. So there is a way into Moccò, but it doesn't matter. If we weaken Astolfo, Austria will occupy Moccò and take Trieste, no question, because we won't be able to stop them. Moccò is the key to stopping them only if Astolfo agrees to oppose Leopold's army."

Ruggiero leans across the table to scoff at me. "Astolfo won't fight Leopold under any circumstances. He said as much. He'll fly the Austrian flag, open his gates, and let Leopold advance to Trieste. He'll count it as a favor Leopold owes him. I agree with the general. A wall across Via Flavia will block the Austrian army from marching on Trieste. We can hide our men at Bagnoli with axes and swords, attack the Austrian flank, and annihilate them."

Giustinian shakes his head. "Throw in all twelve of our horses, and we still can't defeat ten thousand Germans. A hastily built wall won't hold for a quarter of an hour."

"Sir, if I may..."

"We heard you," Ruggiero says. He turns to Giustinian. "Please make him shut up, sir."

"He also spoke with the lord of Moccò," Giustinian says. "Speak, Niccolò."

"I would stake my life on one thing. Astolfo only wants Castle Moccò. He's not mad with ambition. He doesn't want to be emperor of Byzantium or doge of Venice or king of the world. He wants to be lord of Castle Moccò until the end of his days."

"He advised Leopold to support Trieste against us." Ruggiero spits into the dirt.

"He told me the only side he's on is his own. If he favors Austria, it's because he thinks Austria is going to win. If he thinks we can win, he will favor us. I'm certain we can change his mind."

"How are we going to change Astolfo's mind?" Giustinian is losing patience.

"I will present a failproof plan to destroy the Austrian invaders," I say as if it were the easiest and most logical thing in the world.

"You had your chance with Astolfo," Ruggiero sneers. "That didn't go too well."

"I didn't know what to do. Now I do."

Giustinian is visibly alarmed. "I can't allow you to go back to Moccò." He looks at me like I'm crazy. "You barely got out. Why the hell would I send you back?"

"To win. Astolfo is right about one thing. We need him to win. Together, we are invincible. Going to Moccò and returning, I memorized the terrain. There are ways..."

Giustinian hesitates. "If something happened to you, His Exalted Serenity would chop off my head."

"Astolfo will listen to me, sir."

"Your plan is that good?"

I pull Astolfo's pennant from my tunic pocket.

"His Exalted Serenity trusts me."

Loredan's brows are knit, his fingers clenched into fists, knuckles white, his eyes cast down in deep humiliation.

"And what is this plan?"

GIUSTINIAN RELUCTANTLY AGREES, and Loredan, even more reluctantly, yields. He cannot argue with the pennant, entrusted to me by the doge, designating me his embassy to the lord of Castle Moccò. No sooner has Giustinian agreed than he refuses to let me go alone. I tell him it's a criminal waste of manpower to send men with me. Giustinian's warrior mind prevails over the counsel of his heart. He warns me not to do anything stupid.

"You've been there before, so you know what you're up against. If you can save us, save us," he says. "But for God's sake, don't martyr yourself. Be smart. Caesar smart. I swore to Serenissimo I would return you home alive."

"What about Ruggiero?"

"You worry about Astolfo. Let me worry about Ruggiero."

"God bless you, sir. I have every intention of returning home and serving the doge for many years to come."

He needs to hear that from me. My honest eyes incline him believe it. I don't know how or where this will end, but if I save the lives of my countrymen, my own life won't have been totally worthless. Even if I stay with Astolfo, at least Venice will be victorious. The only certainty is that if Austria wins, I have an appointment with the axe, alongside the doge.

I DON'T TAKE the Salt Road. Instead, I take Moccò Creek Canyon, the route I discovered when I escaped. A low-hanging fog shrouds the leafless trees whose branches scratch the sky's gray belly with dead fingers. Neither flower nor leaf hides the gnarled shrubs along the roadside, known as *spina-christi*. Crown of Thorns. Their long thorns are curved at the ends, fiercer than eagles' talons.

Compared to the Salt Road, Moccò Creek Canyon, twisty and narrow at the opening, straightens in the middle for a long climb at an uncomfortably steep grade. On my right, a sheer drop growing deeper as we ride higher. On my left, the limestone cliffs rise upward. The trees are winter dry. The stratagem is an ugly thought, but simple. If Astolfo listens to me, we will drive Leopold back to Austria, his name forever stained with the blood of his army. Our men won't die in vain. Venice will triumph, and Astolfo will keep Moccò.

If.

I travel slowly, committing every detail of Moccò Creek Canyon to memory. By the time I near the castle, I can draw the route blindfolded.

The men of Moccò must see me by now. I'm on official business, carrying the Standard of St. Mark. They'll see the banner before they recognize me. If they play by any civilized rules, they can't shoot an embassy bearing a standard.

As I round the final bend, a hundred bowmen lining the parapet aim their bolts at my heart. Astolfo stands atop the barbican housing the gate. As soon as he recognizes my face, he looks surprised, angry, and annoyed. I dismount and slap Delfín's butt. She remembers this place, and it doesn't make her happy. She trots across the road and hides in the trees. I plant my standard before the gate.

"You've got a lot of nerve, ballot boy."

"I trust you, Lord Astolfo."

"So you bound and gagged me to demonstrate how much?"

"I had no choice."

"Neither do I."

"I beg your patience and your ear. I have a plan, sir, for us both to win."

"And the doge too?"

"Everyone except Leopold."

"How stupid do you think I am?"

"If I thought you were stupid, I wouldn't be here. I think you don't want a spoiled Austrian prince with a premature crown looking over your shoulder."

His grimace fades, but his heart still seems hardened against me. Astolfo first. Always. I step closer, take off the doge's ring and hold it up.

"I pledge this to you, sir, as surety for the sincerity of my heart and the honesty of my intentions."

"I don't give a tart's fart for your heart or intentions. I don't need you or Venice."

"It's me, sir, Niccolò Saltano. I know how we can win."

"Too bad I don't give a shit about you."

Despite the freezing air, I open my shirt to bare my heart, kneel, and stretch my arms out toward the lord towering over me.

"Then kill me, sir. Here and now. Without this victory, I have no life worth living, so take it, please."

"What the hell do you want, boy?"

"A parley. You and me."

The gates swing open. I rise, enter, and they slam shut behind me. Astolfo walks the ramparts to the keep as I cross the courtyard. A hundred crossbows follow me. Astolfo waves them off, and their stirrups hit the ground.

He takes me into his lair and throws a fox cloak around my shoulders. "Talk when your teeth stop chattering."

He pours mulled wine into a pair of goblets and sets them on the table. "You sure know how to get a man's attention."

"You don't make it easy."

"I never expected to see you again."

"And here I am, like a bad penny."

"You're lucky you're so pretty. Did you miss me?"

"Like I miss confession."

"I missed you. I missed everything we didn't do."

"Be serious, please," I say. "We have a chance to do something great, sir. Our names will be celebrated in the chronicles, the ballot boy and the lord of Moccò. I know how we can stop Leopold, cut him off at the knees, just like the doge ordered, and send him home so that it will be a long time before he ever thinks about coming back. Give me your support in this plan, and you'll never have to worry about Moccò again."

"A smart man always worries. Keeps you on your toes. Where do you land in this make-believe?"

"The only thing I'm sure of is that the doge will honor his word as long as he lives. He faithfully rewards loyalty. That's the best you can ask from any prince."

"I could ask for a prince who doesn't already have one foot in the grave. How long can he last before nobody-knows-who succeeds him? On the other hand, Leopold is eighteen. He could be around for a long time. It's his first war."

"Let's make it his last."

Chapter Thirty-Seven

Leopold of Austria

ASTOLFO SITS BACK, his jaw clenched, his mind ripping like a bolt through all the possible outcomes. Fingers interlaced, thumbs twirling, he works things out like a clerk at the abacus.

After a while, he says, "I underestimated you. You're a wicked little bastard. Can I have a kiss now?"

"I have to go back to Muggia."

"You're not getting off that easy."

His kiss is intended to make an indelible impression, and it does, but I hold my ground. I take off my ring and the dolphin necklace for the first time since Alex fastened it around my neck and hand them to him.

"These are my pledge. You know I'll be back for them."

Astolfo lets me go because he believes that I want Venice and Astolfo to win for my own gain. I focus solely on the plan because I don't know if I want to make Venice strong and secure, or if, in securing Moccò, I will have Astolfo.

I reach Muggia before dawn. We divide the men Roman-style into eight-man squads. Ten squads make a century; the squad leaders report to the century leader. Six centuries make a cohort. We set three cohorts under Ruggiero to build the barricade where Moccò Creek crosses Via Flaminia. The other three cohorts, under Girolamo and me, take the Salt Road.

Under cover of darkness, Giustinian's galleys transport the army from the walls of Trieste to the mouth of Rosandra Gorge. My cohorts include caulkers, sappers, sailors, and oarsmen. Our horses and mules pull wagons piled with hammers, saws, rope, and provisions up the Salt Road. Cauldrons of pitch hang from poles between men's shoulders. We must find a cave and start cooking.

We're shivering when we set out, a long column of men forging into the cold, dark canyon. By midmorning, Moccò's prow splits the sky above us. Girolamo da Burano jumps onto Delfín with me, and we ride slowly while Girolamo scrutinizes the canyon wall for weaknesses.

"Hold up," Girolamo says. He dismounts and scrambles straight up the cliff, hand over hand, slaps the rock under a ledge above the road, and climbs back down.

"That ledge is barely hanging on." He points to where the rock is deeply fissured. Full-sized trees grow on tons of limestone thrust over the Salt Road like a mistake. Evergreen roots splinter the rock. Girolamo crosses himself.

"St. Mark be with us," he says. "This here's our spot."

He scratches his chin and sizes up the volume of stone.

"If we knock that ledge down, it will block the Salt Road with a pile of rock too high for armored men and horses to pass."

"How do we do that without killing ourselves?"

"Watch and learn, boy."

He analyzes the rock, the nearby trees, the fissures and crevices deforming both the ledge and the cliff. A wrinkle in the canyon wall blocks our view of Moccò from here, which also means they can't see us. Girolamo scales the ledge, stomps around, listening, and then shouts down to me.

"We have to build a platform to work the ledge and use baskets to get out of the way when it comes down."

"How long will it take?"

"We built siege towers in Alexandria in two hours, but we had the lumber ready-cut. This don't have to be pretty. Thirty-two men to a tower and the same number on the ground. Dispatch a couple squads to fetch every pulley and ladder in the fleet. Make sure these laggards run both ways so it don't take till doomsday."

The men, weary from hauling supplies into the canyon, groan at having to run down and back again loaded with yet more gear. Girolamo gathers them around and hands them over to me for a proper exhortation.

"When the Gauls sounded a call to arms," I say, "every man dropped whatever he was doing and ran to the town square. It was their custom to torture the last man in, torture him unmercifully until he died. No one wanted to be the last man in. No one stopped to fasten his sandals or take a piss. They ran like hell. That's what we're asking. The price isn't torture; it's defeat. We count for nothing if we fail. The reward is the safety of our homes and families, lest Leopold sack our parishes, burn our homes, rape and murder our families. Only we can stop that from happening, so when I say run like hell, I mean run like hell."

As they take off down the canyon, Girolamo puts his arms around me and squeezes.

"You surely gave them hell. Not bad for a ballot boy."

Girolamo selects tall pines for the towers and shorter trees to plank the platform. The men attack them with saws and axes. When the trunks are felled and the branches hewn, we lash the tall trunks together and raise them like masts on either side of the ledge. The wooden platform between the towers stabilizes them. When the runners return with pulleys and ladders, we haul the ladders onto the platform and secure them to the cliff. Then our men climb the ladders with spikes and hammers to mount winches and pulleys to hoist their baskets above the platform when it collapses.

Girolamo strips down to his breeches and works up a sweat despite the cold.

"When the rock starts to come down," he says, "we hoist ourselves up in the baskets. You won't see us till the dust clears."

Nobody's complaining about the cold anymore.

"Stop!" Girolamo shouts and waves his arm. "Stop! Now!"

Work stops. Sudden silence. We listen.

A trumpet.

A sapper shinnies up the tallest tree standing, then shouts, "From Moccò!"

"Astolfo's a clever one," Girolamo says. "If the Austrians hear Astolfo's trumpets, they have to reply. When Astolfo hears their reply, he signals back, meaning they've entered his territory, and they'll be here right quick."

The trumpet call goes unanswered. The men go back to work.

"Your towers and platform look like the scaffolding on the Doge's Palace," I tell Girolamo.

He puffs out his chest, proud as hell. "Who do you think built those, Maestro Stands-on-his-head-and-re-cites-Latin-backward?"

Trumpets from Moccò sound again. Girolamo whistles, and we halt to listen for an Austrian reply.

"No reply," the sapper shouts from his treetop.

The crew tests the pulleys, raising and lowering barrels and logs before they hoist themselves in baskets. Two squads on the platform batter the ledge with axes and sledges to shake the low-hanging fruit onto the road below. We wrap our shirts around our faces to protect us from dust and shards flying from the splintering rock. Soon our backs and arms ache. We're banging so loudly we don't hear a thing.

The sapper high in his tree throws pinecones at our heads to quiet us.

Moccò's tantara finishes after sounding twice. The sapper points toward Moccò. Girolamo climbs down from the ledge and tears around the bend to see what he can see. I catch up with him as a flag unfurls atop Castle Moccò. Two broad stripes, red on the bottom, white on top, to greet the arriving guests.

Girolamo spits. "Austrian devils. Moccò must see them."

"What shape are we in?"

Girolamo doesn't waste time answering me. "What the hell are you waiting for?" he shouts at the men.

He clears everyone off the ledge except his men in baskets. They drive stakes into split rock, forcing cracks to fracture. Girolamo is an admiral commanding his fleet. He pinpoints the critical faults and directs his men's blows. Streams of gravel and scree spill from beneath the ledge.

The Moccò trumpets sound. Girolamo waves his arms, and the men halt.

This time, we can hear the faint reply. The Austrians are near.

Girolamo and his men pummel the ledge with unrelenting brute force, pounding in fat spikes, stakes, spars, and branches, anything hard enough to splinter the stone.

An earsplitting crunch. The ledge loses its purchase and snaps. The pulleys squeal as Girolamo and his men hoist their baskets above the raging fall of shattered stone. The collapsing ledge buries the Salt Road under a limestone torrent that bursts, floods, ebbs, trickles to an eerie quiet, and ends as abruptly as it started. The Salt Road is impassible.

Austrian trumpets blare brightly as the dust blows downhill toward the gulf. Everyone on the ground cheers Girolamo, and his men wave from their baskets, flexing their muscles proudly.

Delfín is uphill where the air is clear and quiet. While the men hustle to hide our gear in a cavern, Girolamo and I ride the crest toward Moccò. I tether Delfín behind a screen of shrubs perched above the bend where the Salt Road from the north meets Rosandra Gorge. Castle Moccò is directly in front of us, and the Austrians march directly below. Drums beat slow and steady to keep everyone moving. The men slog wearily, their horses foamy with exertion, hooves and boots raising clouds of purple dust.

A knight wearing fifty pounds of silver atop a steed wearing another hundred pounds of steel heads the column. His standard flies the flag of Tyrol, a fierce red eagle, crowned, its head circled with laurel, its sharp talons extended. The feathers on its outstretched wings are daggers.

Beside the standard of Tyrol, Leopold's personal duchy, another knight bears the standard of the counts of Habsburg. The house of Habsburg has ruled Austria for centuries. Their standard, a snarling red lion, rampant on a field of yellow, has bared claws, and it, too, wears a crown, blue like its claws and sharp tongue. The lion's tail is a devilish pike, razor sharp, raised to strike.

Behind the standards, three abreast, row upon row of armored knights ride armored steeds, their helmets on, their visors closed. We needn't whisper; they hear nothing. Their standard-bearers stop at the gate of Castle Moccò; behind them the line of march jerks to a halt in disorderly ripples.

The knights plant their standards in front of the gate. The trumpets of Moccò blow a tantara as Astolfo appears on the parapet to greet his guests. He wears his ceremonial armor, his chest covered with a Roman-style silver breastplate. The Romans embossed their breastplates with muscle to make their bodies more godlike. Astolfo doesn't need to. His bare arms and shoulders are godlike. Silver and bronze greaves cover his legs from ankle to knee; his magnificent thighs are bare. He wears no helmet. His hair streams behind him, as distinctive as any standard.

"Who approaches?" Astolfo shouts to the knights below.

"Leopold III, duke of Austria and lord of Tyrol."

"Welcome, great Prince." Astolfo bows to Leopold. "We humbly extend the hospitality of Castle Moccò."

Leopold holds his helmet under his arm. I can see his face clearly. He looks like a rich kid on his father's horse. He makes all the right gestures, but he's too small for them.

"All he's thinking about is a big mug of beer and a proper shit in private." Girolamo snickers. "Eighteen years old. His first war."

"He's only two years older than me."

"At your age, he married the duke of Milan's daughter. Her grandmother is Anna Gradenigo, the old doge's wife."

"The Austrian invading us is married to the great-grand-daughter of the doge who reigned over the Closing of the Great Council?"

"Exactly."

"Are they related to Ruggiero?"

"Third cousins twice removed." He spits. I can't tell if he's serious.

Leopold and his knights file into the castle courtyard. The cavalry tethers their horses outside and pitch tents in front of the barbican, while the infantry collapses along the Salt Road, too tired to raise tents. They build fires to cook their dinner under the open sky.

I watch and pray. If Astolfo keeps his end of the bargain, I can keep mine.

CAESAR SAYS AMBIORIX, the Gallic chieftain, lied to Roman Generals Sabinus and Cotto when he advised them that a huge army of Germans was on its way to destroy them.

Sabinus and Cotto fought over what to do. Cotto said no Roman based his strategy on the word of an armed enemy. Sabinus replied that the Romans were weak and outnumbered. Why stand alone, he asked, when they could decamp, as Ambiorix suggested, and unite with the other legions? Sabinus accepted that Ambiorix was doing them and Caesar a favor, thereby saving his own ass. Sabinus won the argument.

While the Romans worked all night to break camp, Ambiorix and his Gauls barricaded the sides of the pass the Romans must pass through. The weary Romans marched at first light. As soon as they were deep in the barricaded pass, Ambiorix closed the front and rear. The Romans had nowhere to run. They were massacred.

We do our desperate work by moonlight. I counsel Girolamo to order the men to grab saws, swords, axes—anything that cuts—and shields to protect themselves.

"Who are we fighting, maestro?" he asks.

"The bushes. Watch out. They're sharp."

The *spina-christi* take their toll until we learn our way around them. We're bloody by the time we hack the bushes to pieces and separate the pieces by size. We pile our carts high with the longer branches, lash them down with rope, and send them to Bagnoli. Ruggiero's men will cover their barricade with thorns. Any man or beast trying to breach the barricade will be forced to tangle with them. An armored horse is like an alligator, its soft belly unprotected. The thorns will tear them open.

Once the carts move out, we face a mountain of shorter branches. The men's stomachs growl for food, and they grumble loudly about fatigue, cuts, and the cold.

"What do we do with these?" Girolamo kicks the mountain of short branches.

"Separate them into bunches by size and crush the bunches into balls."

Nobody moves a muscle, their eyes wide with mutinous thoughts. They think I'm a madman.

Girolamo laughs out loud. "Seriously, maestro?"

"That's what the shields are for," I say. "Compress the branches and lash them with rope. They don't have to look pretty. They just have to fall."

The men balk, but Girolamo has learned to trust me.

"Show me just what you mean, maestro," he says.

Girolamo and I wrestle a bunch of branches with our shields, compressing them while two sappers bind them with rope. It looks like rubbish, but it bounces downhill. Girolamo grabs my shoulder and hugs me.

"What the hell are you waiting for?" Girolamo shouts to the men. "You saw what to do. Do it!"

As we work, the bundles of thorns grow rounder and rounder, more like balls, which we coat with pitch and set aside to dry.

Our guards watch Castle Moccò from crow's nests in the trees. They report that Astolfo is throwing Leopold a banquet. The smell of roasting meat and fowl makes our stomachs rumble so loudly we're afraid the Austrians will hear us. After the banquet, Astolfo gives Leopold a torch-light tour of the ramparts, the keep, and tower. The camp-fires twinkling along the road go out one by one like stars at dawn.

Our men take refuge against the icy night in a lime-stone cavern, eating cold meat and drinking beer, too excited to sleep.

"There's so damn many of them," a caulker says. "I couldn't even see the end of the line."

"So there's a lot of them," Girolamo snaps. "However many there are, we do the same thing. We fight to victory or die."

"Or," I say, "we don't fight them at all."

The men look at me, all confused because they know their orders come from me.

"Caesar's Ninth Legion was deep in hostile territory, surrounded by the most ferocious Gauls…"

"Are you still spouting that Caesar shit?" Ruggiero slaps me on the back like he's glad to see me and hunkers beside me, haggard but smiling.

"That barricade." He shakes his head. "I've got to hand it to you. It's diabolical. I didn't know you had it in you. We covered the entire barricade and some of the road with thorns. They'll be ripped to shreds, every man and beast trying to cross. The admiral wanted us to check on things up here."

"We're waiting to give the signal," I say.

"Look who we caught snooping." Ruggiero whistles.

Two guards drag in a prisoner and throw him at our feet. Giorgio Barozzi, the Venetian who pleaded Astolfo's case before the doge, gets up on his knees.

"I have a message for Admiral Giustinian from the lord of Moccò."

"He's a fucking spy," Ruggiero says. "I say hang him."

"I'm no spy. I bear a message."

"What's your message?"

"With all due respect, sir, the message is for the admiral."

Ruggiero smacks him back down to the floor. "You're so full of shit it's coming out your nose."

Barozzi wipes his bloody nose with his sleeve. "That's Venetian blood, sir. I am Venetian first and always. I joined Astolfo when he fought for the Republic in Crete, and I stayed with him because he is a great leader who respects his men."

Ruggiero unbuttons his doublet and pushes up his sleeves. "I guess I have to beat it out of you."

Barozzi has no official position on either side. No laws apply. He's nothing, a prisoner, a casualty of war, and he knows it. He grovels before me.

"I'll tell you the message," he says. "Alone."

Chapter Thirty-Eight

The Stratagem

"MY LORD ASTOLFO," Barozzi tells me, "wishes to re-mind Admiral Giustinian that the ballot boy has unfin-ished business at Moccò and pledged to return after the battle."

"That's your urgent message?"

"Yes, sir."

He would say or do anything to save his own skin. I have no idea why he's here, and I don't believe a word he says. I do know I don't want him to know what we're do-ing.

"Take him to Giustinian," I tell Ruggiero.

Pale and sweaty, Barozzi doesn't want to go with Rug-giero, and can't refuse.

As soon as they leave, we try to grab an uneasy rest. When the bells of St. Mary in Siaris ring Matins, no trace of pink lightens the eastern sky. I ride Delfín over the crest and watch Moccò from above. Bodies soon stir in the castle. Knights stagger into the courtyard in their breeches to take a shit and wash their bums with ice water before putting their armor back on. No sign yet of Leopold or Astolfo.

After the second bell, Astolfo escorts a sleepy and disheveled Leopold onto the rampart. Leopold wears his crown to remind everyone he is a Habsburg. He points to the Salt Road. I can't hear what they're saying. It's like watching a puppet show in St. Mark's Square.

Astolfo shakes his head. He steers Leopold to the west rampart, pointing out Moccò Creek Canyon on the opposite side of the castle from the Salt Road. He most certainly advises Leopold to surprise us by taking Moccò Creek Canyon instead of the Salt Road. Leopold shakes his head emphatically and shouts for his generals, who run out half-dressed, still clutching bowls of porridge and hunks of blood sausage. The generals bow to their sovereign, who demands their counsel. They duck into the castle to dress, and Leopold paces the courtyard.

The generals return in military tunics. They unfurl maps and trace their route. Astolfo shakes his head. On the map he circles the upper end of Moccò Creek, alongside the castle. He follows the line of the creek, showing Leopold and his generals how Moccò Creek Canyon comes out behind the Venetian line at Via Flaminia.

I know what he's saying. I could have written his words for him.

Astolfo explains to the Austrian generals that the Venetians expect them to take the Salt Road. The Venetian line crosses the Salt Road at Bagnoli, with flanking detachments on either side of Rosandra Gorge. If the Austrians take Moccò Creek, they can surprise the Venetians from the rear and demolish them in an hour.

The palace has taught me that the first rule of politics is never to be seen letting someone else tell you what to do.

The Austrian generals scoff at Astolfo because it's not *their* plan. They pull Leopold aside and argue among themselves. Leopold's personal councilors, his equerry, and the bishop of Merano join the confused parley.

The second rule of politics is to never be directly responsible for anything.

Astolfo appears decisive, passionate, virile, and commanding—everything Leopold isn't. He must terrify Leopold, who paces, argues, twists his crown, and bites his nails; losing terrifies him more than Astolfo, who plays his part with brio. I can't hear him, but I can read his body like a book. It's no skin off my nose, he says. I have spoken my mind. I can't tell you what to do, and I'm not responsible for your decision.

By now, the Austrian generals must be worrying about their own asses. They pass the burden of responsibility to Leopold as their liege lord. Everyone looks at him. Their fate now rests squarely on his slumped shoulders. Like the doge of Venice, he doesn't want his first war to be his last. He crosses himself and prays.

At that very moment, a peasant bursts through the trees. Crossed halberds block him at the castle gate. He shouts desperately to Astolfo, making as much noise as a man can make.

Astolfo sprints back to the barbican above the gates. "What the hell do you want?"

"God's mercy, Noble Lord. There's been a terrible rockslide, sir. A big one. It buried my people."

"Where?"

"Above Bagnoli, Great Sir. Two of my sons are trapped under limestone. In the name of God, I beg you, help them." He falls to his knees in prayer.

Leopold's generals dispatch runners down the Salt Road to verify the rockslide. By the time the Austrian troops are ready to march, the runners return, verify the rockslide, and argue about how big it is and how long it will take to clear.

His resistance broken, Leopold orders his generals to take Moccò Creek Canyon.

The bells of Santa Maria in Siaris ring Sext as the Austrian vanguard begins their descent. The knights on armored horses clank down the steep and rocky incline. Never was armor a more painful burden for man or beast.

Leopold's attendants prepare a cloth-of-gold pavilion on the rampart overlooking the canyon from which Leopold and Astolfo observe the army decamping.

When the castle gate slams shut behind the knights, the cavalry and foot soldiers form a long file and slowly follow them down the narrow canyon trail.

I whistle softly for Delfín, and she trots through the trees to where I stand. She paws the ground impatiently and sniffs the air. She knows we're waiting, not what we're waiting for.

By the time the baggage train at the Austrian rear enters Moccò Creek Canyon, Santa Maria in Siaris rings Nones. The Austrians must be worrying about losing light before they reach bottom.

I dig my heels into Delfín's sides, and we race to my first station. The Austrian foot soldiers must be groaning with pain from the long, steep downhill grade. People dread climbing uphill, but a long downhill under arms torments the calves and hamstrings.

I ride to my battle station and set fire into the first ball of thorns, which flares up and singes my lashes. I load my bow and shoot a bolt into the ball, transforming it into a flaming missile tumbling into the canyon. Soon screams rise up. I shoot a second flaming ball of thorns into the canyon, the signal for our men stationed along the ridge.

A wave of fireballs cascades into Moccò Creek Canyon, from rear to front. The din mounts, from scattered screams to a tumult, a desperate roar, and the crashing and scraping of collapsing men and metal. Unable to go forward or back, locked in place by a wall of rock on one side and a cliff on the other, hundreds are thrown, pushed, or jump off the cliffs fleeing the infernal fireballs. Dry brush and barren trees catch flame. Waves of terror echo through the canyon. By now, the barricade at the bottom is slicing the bellies of any knights' horses that went the distance.

I sink to my knees under the weight of the scent and sound of so much death.

I am responsible for these screams of men who can't escape, slashed by burning thorns, plummeting, flaming to the canyon floor or crushed beneath stampeding feet and left for the fire to consume. What I see is no picture on a church wall. It truly is Hell.

In the heat of the rising flames, I close my eyes, bow my head, and pray.

Queen of Heaven, hear my plea. St. Nicholas, grant me thine aid.

I have sinned, and my crimes make me unworthy of your grace. I beg you, take my life as remission for my sins; I offer it willingly if only you will bless my father, may he be in Heaven, and my mother, may Heaven await her. Bless Alessandra Barbanegra, who is all things good, and Andrea Contarini, who is all things wise. Watch over my friend Abdul, free him from bondage to achieve his greatness. And please, do what you can with Matteo Bellacqua; he may occasionally sin, but his heart is good.

Bless them, Holy Mother, and do what you must with me.

Before I stand, two mountains of metal come crashing down, enraged eyes blazing through the slits in their helmets. Red eagles on their chests tell me everything I need to know. One smack in the face from a metal gauntlet puts me down.

Chapter Thirty-Nine

Astolfo's Chamber of Delights

ASTOLFO AND LEOPOLD retreat deep inside the castle to hide from the smell of burning flesh.

The angry knights who ambushed me drag me in and drop me at Leopold's feet. The gash where they hit me is still bloody, and my right ear feels stuffed with wax.

I only recognize Leopold by his robe and crown. The baby face I witnessed before the battle has collapsed under the weight of burning bodies. His eyes are feverish, tormented by the scale of his defeat. Astolfo stands behind him, poking the fire and scattering herbs on the flames to mask the stench of death. He glances at me and turns back to the fire. For all anyone can tell, he's never seen me before.

Leopold quizzes my captors, never taking his eyes off me. They are surely telling him that I lit his army on fire. He runs his fingers through his matted hair. He fidgets with his crown, his fingernails gnawed and bleeding, and stares hate into my eyes.

"He pretends he doesn't speak our tongue," Astolfo mutters to me under his breath, "but his wife is Milanese. Watch what you say."

Two guards hold me fast.

"Who burned His Majesty's army?" Astolfo asks at Leopold's behest.

"The victors."

Astolfo slaps me for my insolence. "His Majesty wishes to know the name of the man responsible."

"I don't know."

"You have no idea who devised this devilish ambush?"

"I was just following orders."

Astolfo translates my answers. Leopold spits a reply, and Astolfo reassures him calmly and quietly. He lifts my face so they can both look into my eyes. Leopold jiggles his leg and nibbles his bloody finger. Astolfo continues questioning me.

"A man devised this plan. We want his name."

"Julius Caesar."

Leopold doesn't need a translator to understand that. He snaps at Astolfo, but he's staring at me.

"*De Bello Gallico*," I say to Leopold. "*Liber Quintus. At hostes, posteaquam ex nocturno fremitu vigiliisque de profectione eorum senserunt, collocatis insidiis bipertito in silvis opportuno atque occulto loco a milibus passuum circiter duobus Romanorum adventum exspectabant...*"

"You speak Latin..." Shocked, Leopold speaks Latin to me.

Now that we understand each other, I continue.

"*When the greater part of the line of march had descended into the valley, which had previously been fortified, they harassed the rear and hindered the van, giving battle in the worst possible place.*"

"How old are you?" Leopold demands.

"Sixteen."

"I was duke of Austria at your age."

Astolfo doesn't understand us. He turns his back to Leopold and whispers to me. "He wants me to torture you. Talk to him about that."

"Caesar says nothing of fire," Leopold snarls at me. "Whose idea was the fire?"

If I lie, he'll torture the truth out of me. If I tell him the truth, he'll torture me for burning his army.

"What difference does it make? They're dead. They're not coming back."

"Make him remember," Leopold tells Astolfo.

Astolfo drags me deeper into Castle Moccò.

"Where are we going?"

"Astolfo's chamber of delights."

"You can't do this," I say. "He lost the battle. I am the victor. He has no right."

"He's duke of Austria, with powerful allies. If he suspects I had anything to do with this, he'll be back with a hundred thousand soldiers to kill me. If I kill him, his brother will march over the Alps, destroy me, take your port, and my castle. Venice couldn't even breach Trieste. She'll be no help against a hundred thousand Austrians."

"But we won. I am the doge's embassy."

"Shut up about that if you know what's good for you."

Leopold comes down the stairs behind us carrying a white candle. The bishop of Merano accompanies him to make sure my torture meets the standards of the Church.

Astolfo's chamber of torment is smaller than ours, but the sight sickens me. My hopes collapse. My courage fails.

Astolfo holds my arms behind my back and whispers in my ear. "End this now. He knows the sight of this can crush any man's will. Give him a name."

"It was me," I shout. "I lit the fire. It was my idea."

I shout so everyone understands. Astolfo fumbles for the first time.

"That's crazy," he shouts back because he wants me to live.

Leopold is offended, as if I called him an idiot. "No boy devises and executes such a plan. Who are you protecting?"

"I swear on my mother's soul."

"Stupid boy. Fuck your mother. How could I possibly believe you?"

"Because it's true."

"Put him on the wheel," Leopold orders Astolfo. "Then we'll get the truth."

Astolfo strips off my tunic and shirt; the duke's men pull off my leggings and breeches. They spread-eagle me on a seven-foot wheel. Every tender spot is exposed. I am about to suffer for what I did. Maybe it must end this way because I have become a monster. I open my mouth to shout that I am telling the truth, but Leopold stuffs it with his handkerchief.

"This is how we do it in my country," Leopold says.

By birth, he outranks everybody, and he wants Astolfo to torture me. No one can stop him.

Leopold and the bishop sit facing the wheel in straight-backed chairs. After binding my wrists with leather straps, Astolfo rotates the wheel until I'm upside down and cinches straps around my ankles. After turning the wheel again, we are face-to-face. His sorrowful visage says that no matter how sad this makes him, he has to do it to save himself. I can't hate him. He is the Angel of Death sent to deliver me.

An argument ensues with Leopold over flaying knives and Sicilian Ticklers. Astolfo selects, instead, a cat-o'-nine-tails, showing Leopold the steel claws braided into the knotted leather. Arguing that I am part of the victorious army, Astolfo says it would serve Leopold well to keep me alive. Leopold and the bishop ignore him, testing the sharpness of the claws. The bishop nods approval.

"This is going to leave scars," Astolfo murmurs. "I'll go as easy as I can."

He's guilty and anxious and sweat from his armpits drips down his sides. When he hesitates too long, Leopold shouts for him to get on with it. I'm stretched tight as a drum. Astolfo raises his arm and snaps his wrist. The claws rip my flesh, the eagle tearing its way to Prometheus's liver. Bloody stripes blossom on my chest and stomach. I can't scream without choking on the gag. Leopold claps, shouts, and the lash strikes again. Again.

Again.

Pain snuffs the light.

Blackness.

A disembodied hand scrawls in blood across a black curtain.

Dies Irae.

Day of Wrath.

Flagellants chant, stumbling along the wharf, metal-tipped flails raking their backs, spattering blood.

Dies irae, dies illa...

This is the day of wrath.

I am naked and alone, begrimed with dead bodies. Ravens swoop down and rend my flesh with their beaks and talons. The darkness echoes with an even deeper sound, the endless hopelessness of eternal torment.

Solvet saeclum in favilla.

The world dissolves in ash.

I stand before the Eternal Throne.

The Book of Life is open to the page where my deeds are written, and I am the hand, writing, the author of the acts upon which I am judged.

Domine ne in furore tuo arguas me neque in ira tua corripias me...

Neither in rage nor anger punish me, O God.

I am who I am. That is no sin.

The gag is pulled.

Light blinds me. My throat aches. Leopold claps at the sound of my pain, and I scream because I can.

"Next he will pull your nipples off with red-hot pincers," Leopold shouts. He pinches the air with his thumb and forefinger. "No man endures that. Only saints."

A harsh banging on the door startles everyone.

The door flies open, and two haggard Austrian knights drag Giorgio Barozzi between them. His tunic is singed, his leggings ripped, his boots caked with mud and ash. The Austrians drop him in front of Leopold.

My eyes are open, but everything is a blur. The bloody stripes across my chest and stomach sting so badly I can scarcely breathe.

This body screams in pain, but it's not me. I don't remember me. I don't feel like anyone. Something happened in the darkness. I blink away the sweat and blood so I can see. The artery pulses in Astolfo's neck. He's surprised to see Barozzi and pretends not to know him.

Barozzi plays along with Astolfo. He can't take his eyes off my bloody stripes.

He kneels and delivers a brief message in the German tongue to the broken boy wearing the crown. I don't know what he says, but Leopold's face caves in further. He looks a thousand years old, as gray as the ashes of his army. He leans on the bishop of Merano, and they whisper together before gesturing to Astolfo, who cuts me loose, lifts me off the wheel, and sets me on a table so his surgeon can dress my wounds.

"Only scars," Astolfo whispers in my ear. "No disfiguration. Scars are honorable."

He holds me down while the surgeon applies poultices and bandages.

"I'm sorry," Astolfo says. "I had no choice."

"You made your choice," I say, and he flinches because I've hurt him.

"You didn't help yourself," he says. "You could have stopped it sooner. You could have told him it was Ruggiero Gradenigo."

"That wouldn't have stopped him. He wanted my blood, and you gave it to him."

Barozzi leans over the table, his face caked with human soot. "You look like shit," he says.

"Look at you. Fresh as morning dew."

"I was at the barricade," he says. "As soon as the Austrians panicked, Giustinian sent me to fetch you from Moccò Canyon. The trees were on fire. Bodies exploded like drippings off a spit. Then these clowns found me and dragged me here."

Leopold snarls over his shoulder to Barozzi. Bowing deeply, Barozzi replies with what sounds like a list of Austrian names. The list is long. Leopold turns back to his advisors.

"The Austrians hold one prisoner," Barozzi says. "You. Venice has two hundred of Leopold's knights. Giustinian is offering to exchange Leopold's nobles for you, safe and sound. I don't know what humiliates him more—that so many highborn Austrians were captured or that you're worth the lot of them."

Without a word, Leopold stumbles up the stairs, an old man, one arm on the bishop of Merano and the other on Astolfo.

Barozzi is a man without principles. He would as soon lie as tell the truth. I can't believe a word he says. He watches the surgeon finish my bandages.

"Let's get out of here," he says, "before they change their minds."

He helps me up the stairs to the courtyard.

"You'd best wash your face before you attract flies," he says.

I rinse in a marble basin running ice water. Barozzi talks to one of Astolfo's men. He finds me a dead man's shirt and leggings, but I won't part with my old tunic. There are still apple bits in the pocket. I no longer notice the blood splatters. Everything is blood-splattered. The land is blood-splattered. The creek would be blood-splattered if it didn't run so fast, flushing its stains into the gulf.

I am surrounded by charred faces and burnt limbs. The dead are heaped in piles. The living stagger and collapse among them. Men of Moccò, faces wrapped in wet cloth, use pitchforks to sort the dead from the dying. This is worse than the wheel. God, grant me peace.

"You won a great victory," Barozzi says. "Tomorrow, the rectors of Trieste give Loredan the keys to the city. Your commanders are giving Leopold a day of truce to bury his dead before he must march home with what's left of his army. Giustinian is waiting for you. You're the hero of Trieste."

"Hero of Trieste." I'd laugh if it didn't hurt so much.

"Can you walk?"

"Help me. My horse is out there somewhere."

He throws my arm over his shoulder and helps me through the gate. Farther uphill where it's quiet, Delfín has found unsinged forage. I whistle for her and take the apple bits from my pocket.

Chapter Forty

Checkmate

BLACK SMOKE FROM Moccò Creek Canyon makes me puke over and over again. When there's nothing left to puke, my body tries to push my stomach out my mouth.

I recognize the stench of human flesh. I remember it from the sodomite burning between the Columns of Doom. But this is worse, multiplied by thousands. I don't know how many soldiers burned in the ambush.

I arrived from Venice a week ago. I'm only sixteen, and it feels like I've been here twenty years. I try to recollect myself, but I am no longer me. I ride a horse, read and write Latin, and I have killed, over and over and over again.

The oily ash blows sideways like dirty snow. I recognize that too. Marino taught me about how Aeneas had watched the flaming ruins of Troy. Everything he ever loved, his home, his city, his future, up in smoke. The poi-soned cloud billowing up from Moccò Creek Canyon is my Troy.

I am still called Niccolò Saltano, but whatever I was, I no longer am. The life I knew has vanished. I'm a sinner bound for Hell, but can Hell be any worse than this?

Delfín whinnies and paws the ground. She can hardly breathe, and she's about to bolt. Giorgio Barozzi, a traitor and a coward, pukes into the canyon.

Below us, the trees dissolve into gray and orange cin-ders; higher up ash dusts the landscape like the first snowfall. The path isn't wide enough for two men side by side. I boost Barozzi onto Delfín. He groans like a mar-tyred saint, glad he doesn't have to walk.

I strip off my shirt and soak it in the stream that's burbling as if nothing has happened. I wrap the shirt around Delfín's muzzle, cover her eyes, and lead her up-hill, away from the smoke and ash. She walks as delicately as an acrobat on a tightrope. I tell her everything is going to be fine. She knows it's a lie as well as I do.

After a mile, the path slews around a cliff. Scree makes the ledge slippery and unstable. Rocks skitter into the chasm, spooking Delfín. I lead her with a firm hand, and she shits at each sharp turn.

Wind rips down the canyon flushing the ash and stench out to sea. Fresh air fills our lungs. Delfín shakes off my shirt, throws her head back, and sucks the clean cold sky through flared nostrils. Barozzi begs for water. A creek crosses the road, and we stop. Across the valley, a silver stream plunges a hundred feet into a forest of ever-greens.

I help Barozzi dismount and prop him against a tree trunk. Delfín works her way uphill nibbling anything green. The roar of the wind fades, and the bright winter sun shines through tattered clouds. I hunker down beside Barozzi.

"Where's Ruggiero?"

He looks blank. Blinks.

I lean closer to his ear. "He was taking you to the admiral. Remember?"

Barozzi nods. Shrugs. "Back to Venice. To get married." His chuckle turns into a racking cough.

My last hope catches fire and burns. I swore an oath that I would beat Ruggiero back to Venice. What happens there without me is too heinous to consider.

"When did he leave?"

Barozzi shakes his head weakly. "He couldn't wait for the boat. Rode home."

The sun ducks behind the cliffs, and the air chills in a trice. My shirt is still wet, but I put it on anyway, fasten my tunic, and cinch my crossbow on my back. I would give anything for one of Astolfo's fur blankets.

Barozzi rests against the tree, his legs splayed in front of him, eyes closed.

Nothing stirs. The canyon is utterly silent. Time stops.

It's all wrong.

A bolt screams past my ear, pierces Barozzi and pins his heart to the tree behind him. His jaw drops. No words. Blood pours from his mouth.

The shooter steps out of the trees wearing an Austrian helmet and chain mail. On his tunic, a rampant red lion on a yellow field—the arms of the counts of Habsburg—claws his chest. His crossbow swings at his side. I clutch mine.

I have three bolts left. I only need one. I slip my foot into the crossbow's steel stirrup. Before I can cock the string, another bolt whizzes past, parts my hair, and slams into the tree behind me with a splintering thud. I roll behind a boulder.

Silence.

His boots crush dead twigs and branches, raising ash and dust. He rounds the boulder, his next bolt aimed squarely at my head. If I move, he shoots. "Checkmate," he says.

The closed visor of his helmet muffles his voice, but I understand him clearly enough; the German in scorched armor speaks my tongue. He walks like a man who lives for moments like this. A renegade. The war is over, and his side lost, but he loves the game too much to quit. I've got a bolt in one hand, an uncocked crossbow in the other, and I can't put them together to save my life. If I move, he nails me between the eyes.

So I stand up. "What are you waiting for?"

I put my foot in the stirrup of my bow. "Go ahead. Shoot me."

He gestures for me to throw my weapon aside.

"Come and get it." I'm cocked. I fumble for my bolt.

Instead of shooting, he lunges at me, swinging his bow like a club, catching me in the shoulder and knocking me against a tree. He raises his visor.

Goddamn.

What did Marino call him?

My nemesis.

"Don't look so disappointed," Ruggiero says. "Were you expecting Astolfo?"

"He's a better man than you."

"We had a long talk, Astolfo and me. He had a thousand questions about you. We see eye to eye on a lot of things. Except you. That idiot still wants you back. Too bad I got you first."

"What will you tell Giustinian?"

"I did the best I could, sir, but the renegade coward was mad with grief."

"He won't believe you."

"No. But he'll act like he does. It's his job. Of course, I'll have to tell him you were a sodomite but that won't surprise him. I'll tell him that rat, Barozzi, got there before I could stop him. He was crazy jealous, lusting after Astolfo, and he knew Astolfo preferred you. I put a hole through him, but it was too late to save you."

He throws his helmet on the ground; it clatters down the canyon. "Anyway, I won't be shooting any holes in you."

"You're here to play pitch-penny?"

"My plan doesn't include bolts." He picks up my bow. "How do you know this was your father's?"

"Mama told me it was his."

"I wonder what he does without it…"

"He's dead."

Ruggiero smirks. "He wasn't dead the last time I saw him."

No matter how bad things are, don't ever be fooled into thinking they can't get worse.

First, there's the screaming inside my head: If he's alive, he doesn't want me. Why didn't he ever care to know me? To be near me? To love me? Why did he try to kill me?

Then come other questions, each with a sharp claw like the whip Astolfo used to torture me. Did he always hate me? Does he know what I am? Does he know what I have become?

I lunge at Ruggiero because I want him to kill me. He whacks me again with his bow. I topple and crash on my back, paralyzed like the poisoned dog I saw in St. Nick's Square. My limbs are useless; they dance to somebody else's music. I flail on the ground in blind rage. Ruggiero digs his boot into my chest to keep me from going over the edge, and the screaming pain of his heel on my stripes knocks me back to my senses.

Ruggiero looks spooked. "What the hell was that? Some kind of fit?"

"Wrestling an angel."

"Looked more like a demon to me."

"Where is my father?"

"Near Venice; very near."

"Who is he?"

"You saw him."

"When?"

"At Marullo's."

"Your Uncle Benedetto?"

"Uncle Benedetto was never inclined to make babies. He's more like you."

"...Brother Bernardo?"

"Yes, Brother Bernardo. Marcantonio Gradenigo."

"What are you talking about?"

"He's my father too."

"Your father is dead."

"Right. Just like yours."

"This is bullshit."

"Don't ask if you don't want to know the truth."

Everything spins out again.

Ruggiero grabs my shirt and pulls my face to his. "He didn't die on Crete, you idiot. He faked it. He found some poor Greek slob about his size, switched clothes, chopped off the Greek's head, put his ring on the Greek's finger, tied the body to a horse's tail, and let the horse drag it through the city. He kicked the Greek's head off a cliff into the sea, never to be seen again. Everyone except that self-righteous cunt, Contarini, swore the body was Marcantonio Gradenigo."

"Who was your mother?"

"No whore like yours. She was a Byzantine princess, as plain as a donkey's ass. All she did was pray. He hated her, but she bore him a son before mysteriously dying, which made no difference since her father was deposed by the son he deposed. She had lost her value. He prefers little girls anyway, like your mother.

"He is a monster—that's a fact—but a brilliant monster. Very cunning. I was never more to him than a good-looking stud to give his revolution a pretty face. Then you came along. Prettier. Younger. A better story. And working for Doge Andrea Contarini. He figured you out in two winks of a Greek whore's eye. Everything changed. Suddenly, I'm nothing but an asshole, and you're the prince of Byzantium."

"I see why you hate me."

"No matter what I do, you manage to make me look like an idiot."

"I don't want any part of his plans. He raped my mother and tried to kill me."

"More than once. Trust me. But what really kills me is you don't yet understand that what you want doesn't matter. He'll twist you around until you want what he wants. You have no idea how persuasive he can be."

"I survived torture. He can do nothing to me I can't endure."

"Not your flesh, asshole. That's nothing. No, no. Your mind. That's where you don't stand a chance, little brother. I know. From personal experience. And that's why it's either you or me. There's not enough room in this world for both of us. I was supposed to come up here, make myself a hero, and ride that home to my wedding bed. You fucked it all up."

"Being a hero's not hard. Burn up an army."

"That was brilliant; I give you that. There's no stopping you. You're the hero of Trieste. Nobody gives a rat's ass about me anymore, not even my own father. Your father."

His words snap shut like a trap. He caresses the dagger in its tattered scabbard. I am familiar with his eight-inch mercy-maker, a slender double-edged blade designed to slip between armor plates or into helmets to deliver the death stroke. Encircling the jeweled pommel, a snake devours its own tail.

He leans over me, opens my shirt. "Where's the dolphin?"

"Astolfo has it."

"Shit." He pounds the ground in fury.

"What does it matter?"

"It's Papa's, and he wants it back."

"That can't be. Alex gave it to me, and her father gave it to her."

"Marcantonio Gradenigo, your father, left it on the Greek's body for identification purposes. Blackbeard bought it from a Jew merchant who snatched it from the gravedigger who tore it off the body. Fortunately, I got the dagger."

He doesn't see what I see behind him, so I need to distract him.

"What are you going to do to me?"

"I thought you'd never ask." He grins wide, a galley's beam, his rage over the dolphin eaten up by a new fire in his eyes.

"First, I'm going to tie you down and open your chest with his dagger."

He unsheathes the dagger, raising it up the way a priest elevates the Host. "Then, I am going to open you up and cut out your heart. You'll be alive long enough to watch me eat it. Watch your heart become part of me. Think of it—my soul and yours rolled into one. You will render me invincible, and I will rule."

His eyes are ecstatic.

Chapter Forty-One

Triumph in Venice

I feel her presence in the rustle of trees as Ruggiero raises his dagger to open my chest. I keep my voice as calm as I can so I won't spook her right away. Ruggiero, drunk on the sound of his own voice, doesn't hear her ambling gently forward to reconnoiter.

As soon as she is close enough, I let out an unholy scream. She rears up in panic and comes crashing down. Ruggiero twists so violently his dagger sticks deep into his thigh. He screams as she rears again, crushing him. When he tries to rise, she kicks his body backward over the cliff and it plummets through smoldering trees.

I BREAK INTO a cold sweat remembering, safe in the Doge's Palace. I get the sweats, mostly at night, and sometimes, the shakes when something triggers the smell of burning flesh. I've given up trying to make sense of it all. I can't. I still get a hard-on when I remember Astolfo's chest against mine, his arms around me. I live in a fever.

The way things used to be is mysterious to me now. I know exactly what happened, but not how it felt. I am different. I am a Gradenigo.

Matteo can't figure out why I'm not happy, being a celebrated hero and all, and there's no way to tell him. He couldn't possibly understand. His father wasn't a monster. He'd never killed men, had never been tortured, had never felt the weight of Astolfo's body or the doge's golden robe.

Before the victory celebration, I go over every detail of the events in Trieste with the doge and Anzolo Tron, who is now the youngest member of the Doge's Council. Marino's term is over; he's on the Forty now, daily trying cases. It's a good job for him. He tries to be fair. Serenissimo and Tron pore over the notes and maps I made for them.

Outside the palace, Venice celebrates victory. Decked in streamers and confetti, she has never been more beautiful. The nobles have never been drunker. The people have never been merrier. This cold winter night will forever commemorate our victory. My victory. Fireworks cascade down the sky. Bonfires light the square as bright as afternoon. Acrobats juggle fire, athletes somersault and stack up into tall pyramids, musicians fiddle and beat drums, and people dance as if they never had a care in the world and never would again.

In the morning, the palace guard clears our procession route through the mob as we march around the square to the church. The silver horns and golden trumpets, the gold standards flying red silk flags with golden winged lions, the colored robes in precise ranks, the silver sword held aloft, and the gold umbrella held over the doge all remind me of Caesar's triumphs.

Victorious Roman generals were awarded triumphs after great victories, spectacular parades through Rome. Their order of march, like ours, never varied. The Roman Senate came first, followed by trumpets, followed by wagons loaded with all the loot from the losers. After the spoils came musicians, then the animals to be sacrificed to the gods, then the standards and ensigns of the conquered army, followed by prisoners, often thousands. Behind them, their leaders walked in chains, and behind them the victorious general rode in a golden chariot drawn by four white horses. He was called "imperator" and wore a gold robe like the doge's. In his right hand, he held a laurel bough, in his left, a scepter, and on his head, he wore the laurel wreath of victory. Directly behind him, a slave of the lowest station held a gold crown over his head, repeating over and over again into his ear: *hominem te esse, memento mori.*

You are nothing but a man. Remember, you must die.

I am the hero of Trieste. I march in front of the doge with a laurel wreath around my brow. Loredan and Giustinian are men of the hour, marching behind the doge and in front of the nobles arrayed in descending order of importance despite all being equal. All sins are momentarily forgiven. We don't need slaves whispering in our ears to remind us we are mortal. We have breathed the ashes of men. The captain general and the admiral look grim and sober, relieved it's over. Giustinian appears weary to the bone. Loredan may yet dance tonight.

Two Viscontis from Milan are the doge's guests at the banquet, along with the Della Scalas from Verona. No Paduans. Not a Hungarian or German in sight. The pope's ambassador sits near the doge. After the last toast is made, the doge rises to leave. He suggests we pray before retiring.

In the peace of the Evangelist's crypt he says, "You made me a liar."

"How?"

"This time, the ballot boy will be remembered and the doge forgotten."

"I doubt that I will be remembered or you forgotten, Serenissimo."

"I haven't had a chance to thank you."

"Thank me for what, sir?"

"For saving my neck. Otherwise, I'd have an appointment with the axe."

"Don't thank me. You're the one who made me read Caesar. Thank Caesar."

"I could force my dim-witted nephew to read Caesar, but I doubt he would have delivered so decisive a victory. No buts, and don't contradict me. Take credit where credit is due and accept my gratitude as graciously as it is given."

"Of course, you're right, Serenissimo. Thank you for your gratitude."

My words are empty. After all, he only loves me because he doesn't know who I am.

"Is there anything else I should know?" he asks. "That you couldn't say before?"

Nothing that I could say now. "Ruggiero Gradenigo was a traitor and fool, Serenissimo. I'm glad he's dead."

"You're certain he is?"

"As certain as I am of anything. I had to know without a doubt, so I scoured the hillside for hours and didn't stop until I found his dagger in a pile of ash and scorched bones."

"Then there's an end to it. A wasted life. Take comfort that demons also die."

"He told me I'm his half-brother and that our father lives."

"I saw Marcantonio Gradenigo's dead body."

"The body wasn't his."

"Then where is Marcantonio Gradenigo?"

"He calls himself Brother Bernardo."

"The hermit friar?"

"That's what Ruggiero said."

"Do you believe him?"

"I don't know, Serenissimo. Do you?"

He studies the despair in my face and nods.

"You knew all along, didn't you?" I say.

"I didn't know, but I suspected. It would seem everyone suspected, and none dared speak of it. I know he's not the father you imagined or wanted, but that's water under the bridge. That was all a boyhood dream."

"My mother's lies."

"Be glad you were spared his hand. You created yourself in this world, and you did fine without him; you always will."

"His blood still runs in my veins."

"We aren't our fathers. We are ourselves."

"Ruggiero said my father wants me for his prince of Venice, or Byzantium, or the world—whichever nightmare currently bubbles up in his brain. Ruggiero said he is very persuasive."

"If he comes anywhere near you, I'll crucify him between the Columns of Doom."

"But what if I turn out like him?"

"Great God and all His Angels in Heaven. You are nothing like him. You are the perfect opposite. You are a hero and justly so. Don't forget it."

I can't tell him how Astolfo makes me want to sin. I won't lie, but I leave things out. I only tell him how Astolfo came to our aid.

"Duke Leopold refused to take Moccò Creek Canyon, which would have spoiled our ambush, so Astolfo smuggled his cook out of the castle dressed as a peasant. As if on cue, the cook charged the gates, yelling about the landslide."

"The landslide you created."

"Yes. Leopold was stupid enough to try the Salt Road against all warnings, but the cook did him in. Leopold caved. Astolfo led him into our ambush."

The doge nods. "In Crete, our Astolfo was a marvel to behold and impossible to control. He was younger then, even more incorrigible. His balls were legendary."

He studies my face intently.

"You left a boy and returned a man. Wiser. Sadder. Wounded in spirit. War does that. I'm sorry it happened the way it did, but sooner or later, all men of consequence must make their peace with war."

Tears run from my heart to my eyes and down my cheeks. I can't stop them.

"I'm so sorry we stole your youth," he says. "Neither of us wanted this, but you can't escape destiny. It's who you are. You must accept it, as hard as that may be."

"As hard as the oak upon which Andrea Dandolo beat out his brains."

"Don't be so dramatic. Dandolo lost his battle. You won in Trieste, and that's nothing to be ashamed of. I know how quickly the exhilaration of victory vanishes. I know the bitter aftertaste of battle that lingers forever. I know the horror of death up close. I have felt everything you feel."

No, he hasn't. Not everything.

He fumbles in his pouch, and takes out a packet. "I almost forgot. This came to you from Moccò."

He hands me the packet. My ring and necklace are wrapped in parchment with a note scrawled in bad Latin by a crude hand.

Dixisti te venire. Omnes ego feci pro vobis.

You said you were coming back. I did it all for you.

Chapter Forty-Two

Mama Tells the Truth

I DISGUISE MYSELF on the street. Not because I'm ashamed. I'm the hero of Trieste; everyone knows me. That's why. They recognize my uniform, my ring, my eyes. They cheer and lift me up on their shoulders and carry me wherever I'm going. They buy me wine and toast me and kiss my cheeks and pat my butt. Their enthusiasm is genuine. I understand. But I don't want to be recognized.

I hide under my cloak, cover my face, and keep my eyes down. Stragglers from my victory party still throng the streets, drunk and disorderly. I'm not drunk, and I don't feel merry. I am covered with sin and ash.

The bakery behind Mama's house is cranking out fritelle. The smell fills the street and makes me seven years old again, waiting for Pierluigi to pay me so I can buy one. Mama's window is wide open despite the cold. She never needs a fire. The bakery oven keeps her warm all winter. In summer, we slept outside so we wouldn't melt.

I look in the window before going in, something else I always did as a kid.

Mama's fists are on her hips, elbows out, the way she always gets when she's spoiling for a fight. Her back is to me; she's facing Donabella, who I've never seen in our house before. Donabella was born in St. Nick's, but she now runs a whorehouse in Rialto, with money to spare. She wears at least six layers of clothes because it's fashionable: shifts and tunics and over-tunics and robes with slashed sleeves. She's too businesslike to wobble on platform shoes. She doesn't care if her hems get muddy. A knife scar disfigures her left cheek, such that her mouth couldn't look tender if she tried.

"He only wanted to pay you for your silence," Donabella says.

"I gave my word."

Donabella pulls a pouch from her sleeve and dumps gold coins into her palm. She shows them to Mama, then slips them back into the pouch, tightens the string, and offers it to her.

"I don't want your money."

"Don't be stubborn, MariaGrazia. Take the money."

"Why does he still bother with us?"

"Take the money. It may come in handy."

Mama bites her thumb at the money. Donabella shrugs and tucks the pouch back into her sleeve.

"Another thing," Mama says. "Never come here again. Now my house stinks. I'll have to scrub for a week to wash your stench away."

"Without me and my stench, you wouldn't have a house. You'd still be sleeping in the alley with the Greek whores."

I leap through the window as Donabella bolts out the door. I start to give chase, but Mama grabs my wrist and won't let go. Donabella's hasty footsteps fade to silence.

"No kiss for your mother?"

I kiss her cheek and stand back.

"Did you hear what she was saying?" Mama asks, slipping her little girl mask over her face.

That's when it hits. She is only twenty-eight years old—twelve years older than me.

"What nerve she has..." Mama says.

I don't answer. I wait.

"Pay her no mind," Mama says. "She's crazy. I haven't seen her in years, and here she comes out of the blue talking nonsense."

She knows I'm waiting. She stops. She looks into my eyes. Her eyes fill with all the sadness of the world.

"What, Nico? What?"

"You lied to me."

"When did I lie to you?"

"Every day of my life."

She slaps my face, acting offended to mask the gall of being discovered.

"My father isn't dead."

She drops the pretense and picks up another one. "That's stupid. Who said that?"

"Ruggiero Gradenigo."

Her body sags like a sail losing wind. "Bah. What does he know?"

"More than me. He is the only person who would tell me my father's name."

"Why would you listen to Ruggiero Gradenigo? He's as crazy as his father."

"Why was the whore giving you money?"

"That's no way to talk. You're a man of the Court now."

"Answer my question."

"I didn't take her money, did I?"

"Answer me."

She lowers her head and stares at the floor. All pretense falls away until I no longer recognize the person in front of me.

"For never telling you his name," she says.

This may be the first time she has ever told me the truth.

She sinks into a chair, shaking her head. Becalmed, we bob in the current. I hold her hands.

"Speak his name."

"Marcantonio Gradenigo." She cringes pronouncing it.

"Why did you tell me lies my whole life?"

"He said he would kill us both if I told you the truth."

"Why?"

"How should I know why? He is a demon with twisted thoughts. He tried to kill you when you were seven months old and I was still living with Donabella. She's the one who introduced me to him when I was a little girl playing with dolls, an orphan whose family all died in the Black Death. Donabella told me he was a rich noble who would take good care of me if I was nice to him. So I was nice to him, and he raped me. Many times. And then he was gone.

"I didn't know I was with child until Donabella figured it out. She thought it would be worth some money. But his family... Ha! They were ruined, fighting over the last ducat. They threw her out. He showed up again seven months later. He gave her that scar on her face with his mercy-maker. He was going back to Crete, and he didn't trust me to keep the secret. He didn't want you around. He had another son, a real son, a legitimate son. He came to kill you. Donabella fought like a Fury. She was covered with blood, screaming, when men came—Pierluigi, and the baker's boy, and Guffo, the beggar. Gradenigo swore if I ever revealed his name, he would tear off my skin and roast me on a spit. Me, you, anyone I told. The last I saw him, half the parish was chasing him."

"Are the crossbow and compass really his?"

"Yes. I kept them because I thought they might be worth money."

"Did he hand them to you himself?"

"I found them wrapped in a sheepskin outside the door. I recognized them straight off. So I kept them."

"He hated me. He tried to kill me. Why would he want me to have them?"

"How could I know? The mind of a madman is impossible to understand."

She was a child when he destroyed her and while she tried to raise me. She'd been dealt a terrible lot. I believe she meant well. I have no choice but to forgive her.

I ROW PAST Gradenigo Palace. It's empty now. Benedetto Gradenigo moved in with a widow, a rich commoner with a fine house of her own who feeds him delicacies and prays every night that he will marry her and move her into his pink palace.

Work on the palace stopped as soon as Ruggiero died. The scaffolding is still up. Along the façade, arches of white Istrian stone face the Grand Canal, framing windows of clear Murano glass seen only in the richest palaces. A thick carpet of moss covers the unused water stairs.

I try to grasp that this is my ancestral home, to make that feel somehow right, but it never will be.

ALEX'S MOTHER DOESN'T really look at me. It would be impolite to notice the scab that still runs from my eyebrow to my jawbone, inflicted by the Austrian knight's steel gauntlet. She looks slightly over my shoulder as if she's talking to someone next to me.

"We haven't seen you in a long time," she says.

She still doesn't see me. She sees the fighting ballot boy, the hero of Trieste, not Niccolò Saltano, bastard of St. Nicholas parish.

"It's an honor to welcome you to our house." She bows.

When I was a shrimp from St. Nick's, I wasn't even allowed through the warehouse door. I didn't exist. I wonder if she knows all the things I've taught Alex and all the places I took her while I didn't exist. Maybe she pushes all that into the abyss of her mind the way I push Astolfo and the Austrian army down deep, along with Ruggiero, and my father, and all the other things I don't want to remember. Maybe that's all growing up amounts to. Learning to forget, to shut down, to quiet your rage and your shame, and do your duty.

"May I see Alex now?"

"She has been waiting to hear from you since first word of the victory."

Mother Barbanegra leads me upstairs to where Alex is seated outside in the portico, her back to the sun. A wide-brimmed straw hat covers her head, with the crown cut out. Her hair fans out over the brim to catch the sun, a long golden fringe shiny with the lemon unguent noblewomen use to lighten their hair.

She sits with a stiff smile on her lips and makes pleasantries. As soon as her mother leaves, Alex tears off the hat, grabs my hands, and kisses them.

"I can't believe you're here. Thank God you're alive."

"I'm glad to see you too."

"Is Ruggiero really dead?"

"Yes."

"I was afraid to believe it until I heard it from you."

"Delfín kicked him off a cliff."

She crosses herself. "God be praised."

Alex lightens in the blink of an eye; a terrible weight lifts from her features. She studies me quietly, drinking in my presence.

"Isn't that Ruggiero's dagger?" she asks. She touches the pommel with her finger, then pulls her hand back as if it bit her.

"That's how I knew he's really dead. He would never leave this dagger behind."

She puts her arm though mine and lays her head on my shoulder.

"Another funny thing about Ruggiero," I say. "He was my brother. Technically, my half-brother."

Her mouth moves without words as shock registers in her eyes.

"I'm a Gradenigo," I continue. "Isn't that hilarious? My father is Marcantonio Gradenigo. He raped my mother, and I was born. He is a monster, and I am his son. Me and Ruggiero—a pair of monsters."

"Who told you that?"

"Ruggiero."

"He probably lied just to be mean."

"I asked my mother. For someone who lies so much, she's terrible at it. I guess once you're onto her game, it doesn't work."

"I don't believe it."

"I have my father's eyes. Same shape. Same color. Ruggiero hated me because I got our father's eyes, and he didn't."

She squeezes me and strokes my back to comfort me, as sweet as it is useless. "I'm so sorry," she says.

"For what?"

"Everything." She laces our fingers together.

"Something else happened in Trieste," I say. "Well, a lot happened in Trieste. It's hard to untangle it. I killed boys younger than me. I burned an army to ash."

"Would it be better if we lost and they killed us all?"

"No, but I'm the one with dirty hands."

"You did the right thing."

"But that's not all that happened..."

"What else could there possibly be?"

"I fell in love. No, not love. Lust. I lusted, Alex. For the first time in my life, I was consumed by lust—for the lord of Castle Moccò. They call him Hairy Astolfo because his hair is down to his ass when it's not bound up for battle."

Alex presses closer. "Is he handsome?"

"He's magnificent. A warrior in body, mind, and heart. He makes his own rules. He seduced me, and the more I tried to fight the temptation, the stronger it grew."

"Did you do anything?"

"He covered my mouth with his and blew the breath of life into my body. We kissed. He carried me in his arms. I wanted more. I wanted everything."

"But you didn't do anything else?"

"I couldn't."

"What a shame."

"I had to get back to my ship, to my admiral, to my doge. I had to win a war. And because it offends God. I don't want to face eternity alone in torment."

"Didn't you already offend God with Matteo?"

"Matteo is a boy. We play games. Astolfo is a man with a man's appetite. I would have gladly committed the worst of sins. I would have done whatever he wanted."

"What are you going to do?"

"I don't know."

Alex bursts out laughing.

"What's so funny?"

"Nothing. Everything. You want to love a man, but you aren't allowed to because it offends God; I can love a man with God's blessing, and I offended God by refusing."

"I'm a sodomite, Alex. I always will be."

She wipes the tears from my eyes with her velvet sleeve and snuggles against me.

"I don't care about any of that. I don't believe God cares. I love you the way you are because that's you. You're going to be fine. You're smart; you'll figure it out. You will. Now, it's time for the other thing."

"What other thing?"

She pulls back, looking sad and hurt. "You forgot. My escape..."

"I didn't forget, exactly. I didn't think it mattered anymore. Ruggiero is dead. You can stay in Venice."

"No, I can't."

She presses her lips together, then opens her mouth to speak, and once again nothing comes out.

"Why can't you stay in Venice?" I ask. "You can twist your father around your little finger."

"I don't believe my ears."

"Well? It's true, isn't it?"

"Lust must have fried your brain. That, or you never understood anything about me."

"I understand more than you think. You're spoiled, Alex. You smile and bat your eyes, and expect everything to go the way you want. Only, sometimes, it doesn't. Sometimes we can't have what we want. Sometimes we get Hell on Earth if we don't watch out. Life is hard enough for me without having to worry constantly about where you are and if you're safe."

"I see. Thank you for explaining. This is about you." She turns her back like she did when she told me she was a girl. "You're selfish, Niccolò Saltano. You only think about yourself."

Boom.

The echo.

What Mama always said.

You're selfish, Niccolò Saltano.

I am selfish. Monstrously selfish. Like my father and my brother. Worse yet, I suffered for nothing. I haven't changed a bit. I'm the same selfish monster I always was.

I tug Alex's arm. She takes another step away.

"I'm sorry, Alex."

"For what, exactly?"

"For being so selfish."

She turns around and looks into my eyes to see if I mean it. I fall on my knees and speak from the depths of my heart.

"I am sorry, Alex. I was being selfish because I love you too much. The way Mama loves me. Of course you have to run away. It's the only way out of this prison of shoes like stilts and never going farther than the next parish for the rest of your life and being forced to marry a man you don't love. And you're so smart, Alex. It's too terrible to compass."

"I can do sums and write now," she says. "If I dress like a boy, I could be a ship's clerk or a merchant's agent."

Selfishly, I want her safe with the Clares. I want it for me. We agreed to that. I fight to remember who I am and who I'm not.

I take a deep breath and try to smile. "You were going to seek holy sanctuary with the Poor Clares."

"Of course," she says. "For a while. Not forever. I'm not ready to trade one prison for another. You told me our hopes can fly as far as our courage takes us."

"That was Caesar."

"Caesar may have told you, but you told me."

"Please don't torment me. I would die for you. Remember that."

"And I for you. My father will be in Ancona for three more weeks. I can't be here when he returns."

Chapter Forty-Three

Farewells

"ARE YOU GOING back to the big guy in Trieste?"

Matteo is sad and jealous.

"Because if you are, I'm sure gonna miss you."

"Not as much as you'll miss Delfin."

That makes him smile. "At least she loves me back," he says.

"And you'll say nothing to no one." I don't need to remind him, but I do anyway.

"They can flay me and splay me; my lips are sealed."

He whips out his flute and starts to pipe a tune.

As for my doge, what could I possibly say to him? He'll think I'm selfish and dishonorable. I'm breaking the oath I made him. I'm deserting my post and shirking my responsibilities, actions unworthy of a man of consequence. But I'm not a man of consequence. I'm a sodomite on the road to Hell.

I don't have much to pack. Alex's necklace is always around my neck. Only the clothes on my back, the crossbow, and the compass are mine. The nearly vanished gold leaf on the compass lid has yielded up its mystery. Three dolphins flying over a wave. The Gradenigo arms before the family split in three.

I'm leaving the doge's ring behind. I'm no longer worthy of it. Instead, I wear Ruggiero's dagger the way the doge wears his golden robe—to remind me, always, of who I am and how treacherous life can be.

The *bora* lashes Venice with hard rain, and the swollen tide pushes the canals up over the streets and squares. The celestial zodiac hides behind black clouds crackling with lightning. I strap my pack to my back, cover myself with the tarp I keep in the dark stairway, and exit into the square where no one pays any attention to me. They're all huddled by fires, rolling dice and drinking, trying to stay warm and dry. Within two hundred yards of the palace, my feet are soaked. The water is up to my ankles. In places, it's up to my knees. My hood and cloak are sopping; at least my pack is dry.

The sky flashes white. Thunder rattles the shutters. The wind hurls clay chimneypots to the street. I pray the storm will abate. It's a long way to Padua.

The driving rain floods my boat. I stow my sack in the shed, grab a bucket from the dock, and start bailing. The rain refills the boat almost as fast as I bail it out. I take Pierluigi's sail and lash it over the boat to keep the rain out while I bail.

I hope Caesar was right—that we can go as far as our courage takes us. In exchange for Heaven, I get Astolfo's body for earthly consolation and Hell as my eternal reward. There's no way out. The priest at St. Nick's said wanting to sin is as much a sin as the sin itself. Whether I do it or not, I can't stop wanting it. Nothing slakes the desire. Pretending I don't feel it is Hell right here and now.

When I've bailed as much water as I can from the boat, I row to the apothecary at Santa Margherita. Abdul's shutters are open. I climb the gnarly vine to his terrace. Inside, he sits cross-legged, playing his oud, eyes closed as he plucks the strings.

He senses my presence and sets the oud aside. "I guess, dear friend, this is goodbye."

I start bravely but soon choke up and cannot speak.

"Not goodbye," Abdul says. "Until I see you again. But before you must go, may I say something?"

I nod, and he fixes me with his no-nonsense stare.

"To the best of my understanding," he says, "you can run away from many things but never from yourself. We take ourselves along wherever we go."

"The difference is that at Castle Moccò, nobody wants to kill me for what I am. Here, the priests and lawyers think I'm only fit for burning."

"They don't understand God any more than you or I do. God is infinite, beyond our limited capacity to grasp. We catch glimpses if we're lucky, signs to decipher and follow."

"The signs these priests and lawyers see tell them to burn me alive."

"And they are wrong, aren't they, my brother? But you will find such men wherever you go. You are very clear about what you are running from, but I am interested in what you are running to?"

"A life that is impossible here."

"Do you truly believe your destiny is to be a renegade warrior in the mountains? I'm surprised you would fancy a life of fighting and killing the way nobles hunt boar, for no purpose, as an end in itself until you are weary and re-gretful."

"I haven't thought that far."

"You see, that's the problem, the peculiarly Nico thing—do first, think later, when you only have time to be sorry. I say, before you go, be certain of what you want your life to be about, your true destiny, your reason for being alive."

"And what's my reason for being alive?"

"I can't tell you. No one can. You must struggle to find it. Anything given easily is easily forgotten. Your purpose hides behind all the empty blandishments of this world, waiting for you to open your eyes to the simple reality of its truth. Try, try, try, try, fail—fail, fail, fail, and then, just when you're ready to chuck the whole thing, what you have been searching for ambushes you, like Moses stumbling upon the burning bush. Then you catch fire, and those flames burn away all the vanity and greed and igno-rance that was blinding you. At last, you then understand what you must do and not do. You have your compass and rudder, without which you fritter your life away, a raft bobbing in a storm, lost forever."

THE DOWNPOUR HAS slackened to a drizzle. We hustle to the boat and fight the swollen canals. I moor as close to Barbanegra palace as I dare without calling attention. The armed boat boys no longer guard the gate now that Rug-giero is dead.

I whistle our old call, three sharps, two longs, three sharps. Alex replies, two sharps, three longs, two sharps. She darts out the side gate and splashes down the lane, drenched by the time she reaches the boat. The hood of her heavy green tunic covers her face so that only her eyes show. She's stuffed her gear into a leather bag slung over her shoulder. Her crossbow, wrapped in a saddle blanket, hangs from her other shoulder with her quiver and bolts. She is as wiry as any teenage boy.

"Send messages to the apothecary," Abdul tells her. "Not too often. No need to attract attention."

Alex bursts into tears. She wants to speak and can't.

"Look at you, silly Alex," Abdul says. "Chin up. Act like a boy."

I don't know what he's talking about. I'm crying too. He takes Alex's right hand, places it on top of mine, and places his on top of hers—the sign of the brotherhood of the crossbow.

"We will see one another again," he says. "Our destinies are deeply entwined."

"UGH. DISGUSTING." ALEX spits bilge into the canal. "There's six inches of water down here. I'd much rather row."

She's sprawled on the deck behind our sacks.

"Be quiet. It's stupid to hide if you then bitch so loud they can hear you on Torcello." I throw the tarp over her and starting rowing to the House of Poor Clares at Arcella, a mile from the Roman gate of Padua. Protected by holy sanctuary until her father stops looking for her, she has time enough to figure out where to go next.

I stand aft, rowing with both oars, fighting wind and wave. The tide is so high I have to be careful not to lose the channel that takes us to the Brenta River.

Two men rowing parallel to us pick up speed and give chase. They shout, and I ignore them until they cross my path at an angle, cutting us off.

"Thugs," I tell Alex. "Cover up and don't move."

I secure one oar and hoist the other like a lance. They're young and stupid, but I'm caught in their trap.

"If you're headed to the mainland, it'll cost you," says the muscle standing on the prow. He's tight and wiry, with several teeth missing, and his coarse black hair blows wildly around his head.

His boss, younger still, taller, blond—a piss pot admiral—can't be older than Duke Leopold.

The muscle hooks his oar inside my boat and pulls us close. "Two against one. If you're smart, you'll give us your purse and go in peace."

When I throw him the pouch of gold at my waist, he sees the gold dolphin with the ruby eye around my neck.

"I'll take that too."

"Like hell you will." I grip my oar tightly.

The muscle opens his vest so I can see his curved Turkish sword.

"Is that all you've got?" I ask.

"It's more than you've got."

Alex throws back the tarp, her bow cocked and loaded.

"Look again," she says in her boy voice.

Alex's bolt slices the muscle's shoulder and pitches him into the water. She chose to wound, not to kill. She has learned well.

Their boat rocks wildly. I jab the boss in the stomach with my oar. He stumbles and grabs it to keep from falling, so I jab again, harder, doubling him over. I then yank the oar free, swing it back over my shoulder, and whack him into the waves.

Alex grabs their oars from the water. Wind and current carry their boat away from them while I row like hell. We throw their oars overboard near St. George in the Seaweed, a monastery island halfway to the mainland.

"I thought I told you to stay hidden."

"You needed help."

"I'm captain here. You disobeyed orders."

"Shut up," she says. "And hand me a fucking oar."

It takes no time at all to get used to each other's rhythm and hit our stride, rowing in fluid unison toward destiny.

Dawn triggers my first sharp pang of remorse. Gripping me like a cramp in my calf, a manageable ache becomes a screaming pain.

Back at the palace, Delfín is waking up, anxious for her apples and a quick trot down the deserted strand before I go with the doge to morning Mass. He has been up for an hour. He's probably wondering where I am. In another hour, he'll seriously start to worry.

The sun slowly climbs the sky behind us as we row upstream toward Padua. Everything grows clearer with the light. Simple and straightforward.

I'm running so I don't have to tell the doge who I am.

What I am.

That's what I'm doing. Cowardly bullshit.

Yes, memories of Astolfo make me spring boners, and no, I can't stop thinking about him, but I know I do not love him, not after I saw him stripped of pretense, a beautiful, selfish man. He's not what I want. But I do want a man the way other men want women. Just not Astolfo.

That's who I am. Niccolò Saltano, bastard of St. Nicholas of the Beggars; part Gradenigo—the bad Gradenigos—and all sodomite. Whether or not I go to Hell is up to God and me. But I am more than my sin. If I choose, I am a man of honor and not an oath breaker, a man of consequence if I'm willing to face the consequences. Only a coward would run from the doge without telling him why. I certainly owe him the respect to allow him to make his own decision instead of banishing myself.

I can see him sitting in his study, his gold robe heavy on his shoulders, alone and surrounded by treacherous allies and ravening enemies. The Turks are storming Europe. Our enemies—Genoa, Padua, and Hungary—are plotting against us. They will eventually unite. Trieste only diverted our attention and sapped us, just like the doge said it would. The future of Venice is at risk.

I cannot run from that.

Serenissimo needs me; he's the first to admit it, and I need to be there for him. I need his steady hand and forgiving heart. I swore my oath on the crypt of the Evangelist because I believed in what we must do. If I run now, everything becomes as meaningless as the ash of dead men.

I set down my oar. Alex keeps rowing, hypnotized by the rhythm of her stroke. I take off her golden necklace and fasten it around her neck.

"This protected me when I needed it most," I tell her. "Now it will protect you." I kiss the tips of my fingers and press them on the dolphin.

"Won't you need it at Moccò?"

"I'm not going to Moccò."

"Where are you going?"

"Back to the palace."

"What are you talking about?"

"You have to run, Alex, to disappear entirely. Your father will search from Grado to Cavarzere because he must save face. Seek holy sanctuary so he can't touch you. That's the only way you'll be safe.

"But I can't run. Moccò isn't my destiny. It's a dream gone sour. I'm taking you to the Clares because I must. Then I must go back. My duty is to stand with the doge for Venice."

Chapter Forty-Four

The Feast of the Ascension

"OUR LORD JESUS Christ rose from the dead and walked the hills of Galilee for forty days before he ascended to Heaven," Marino says.

He came early for the ceremony to fuss with my new uniform.

"That's what Ascension Day means to most Christians but, of course, not to us Venetians. Here, Ascension Day celebrates the victory of Doge Pietro Orseolo over the Narentian pirates. His fleet set sail on Ascension Day, 997, to solidify our dominion over the sea, and every year since, on Ascension Day, we have a wedding. Any connection to Our Lord is purely coincidental. It is the day the doge marries the sea with the ring given him by the pope of Rome."

He runs his finger over the gold embroidery of my blue velvet tunic.

"Fits like a glove. Now I must be on my way. Be careful with those buttons! Count them like ballots, before and after."

The buttons are gold, a gift from the doge, stamped with the lion of St. Mark standing with one paw on the wall of Trieste. The doge understands our nobles; he gave me a deed certifying that the buttons are mine in perpetuity.

His Exalted Serenity descends the stairs to the palace courtyard with Admiral Vettor Pisani. They both wear gold robes for the procession, a pair of emperors. I had no idea Pisani would be here. He grips my arms and squeezes me, his smile brilliant, his hands steely and proud.

"When I left, you could barely ride. I come back, and you're a hero."

"Don't believe everything you hear, sir."

"Remember," he says, "the sea claimed you first. You're a bowman of the quarterdeck, but I see an admiral one day."

"See how he blushes, Vettor," the doge says. "That's what I like about him."

After Mass, a legion of chanting canons followed by trumpets and drums leads the procession to the Golden Boat. The bells in St. Mark's square are deafening. The crowd cheers happily. Everyone in the procession wears gold, from the grooms carrying the long bells of trumpets on their shoulders, to the canons carrying jewel-encrusted crosses of silver and gold, gospels studded with precious gems, and censers streaming perfume.

Pisani hoists the symbolic silver sword aloft, huge and heavy, and he makes it look easy. His strength informs his character. I don't know if he's changed, or if I have, but seeing him now is like seeing him for the first time. His profile reminds me of Caesar's silhouette on the cover of *The Gallic Wars*.

Pisani isn't beautiful the way Astolfo is beautiful. His manly features are stamped with stern and gentle grace, but the set of his bearded jaw says he can handle anything. He is devoted to the doge and to the Republic. He risks his life not because he has contempt for it but because it seems so little for his homeland to ask of him. Like the doge, he is unencumbered by personal ambition; he measures the value of actions by how much they contribute to the common good.

As the Golden Boat slowly crosses the lagoon to the Adriatic, thousands of boats decorated for a wedding fan out behind us, filled with flowers, lanterns, and pennants. Every bell in the city rings as we pass. Beyond the Arsenal, the bishop of Olivolo's barge joins ours.

The canons on the Golden Boat sing, "Hear us with favor, O Lord," and the bishop responds from his barge, "Grant us safe passage, O Lord, and all who sail the sea."

At the mouth of the lagoon, the bishop's barge circles the Golden Boat three times as he blesses it and everyone in it, sprinkling holy water with an olive branch.

Trumpets pierce the wind as the bishop pours an urn of holy water into the sea and blesses it. The doge kneels, and the Primate raises the golden wedding ring on high for all to see. He hands it to the doge, who stands and ascends the stairs to the open window behind his throne.

"*Desponsamus te, Mare, in signum veri perpetuique dominii.*"

We marry you, Sea, as a sign of our true and perpetual dominion.

As soon as he tosses the ring into the sea, men and boys in loincloths dive after it. Whoever finds it, keeps it.

The doge sits on his golden throne. I can barely hear him over the din of pealing, chanting, blaring, drumming, and clanging.

"That should hold us for another year," he says.

"Best wishes to the groom, Serenissimo."

Later, after Pisani has apprised him of the situation in the Aegean, the doge suggests that we pray before bed.

"Are you all right?" he asks in the privacy of the Evangelist's crypt.

I thought my happy face was fooling him. Obviously, he knows me better than I give him credit for. He never asked me about my mysterious absence when I pirated Alex to Arcella. I assumed he didn't want to know any more than necessary about my private affairs. He has always respected my silence, just as he has always been fair and honest with me. I owe him the same.

The truth is, I'm too scared to tell him the truth. I love him and trust him, so it makes no sense, but that doesn't quiet my fear. I'm poised at the point of no return, and I'm too afraid to speak.

"Why would my father give me his crossbow and compass?" I ask Serenissimo.

"Men are unfathomable," he says. "Why does anybody do anything?"

"It means he wanted me to have them, but why?"

"You've heard me speak of signs," he says. "The fortune-teller. Carrara's face painted on the doge. These are meaningful, like a ship's telltales warning us the wind is shifting. To my way of thinking, he gave you the bow to keep you safe, to keep you alive, and he gave you the compass so that, when the time was right, you could find him. But that is only one old man's opinion. Is there anything else you want to tell me?"

"Things happened in Trieste, Serenissimo, that I'm struggling to understand."

"After the horror of battle, the kings of the old Bible, in their wisdom, gave their exhausted warriors a long period of solitude and seclusion to cleanse their bodies and spirits. You have been savaged and scarred by your initiation into the world of men. It's not easy. It takes time. I feel the heaviness in your heart, and I know nothing I say can make a difference. The pain is still too fresh. Speak your heart, but please, believe me when I say it will pass."

"The sadness passes, Serenissimo. The scars remain."

"Let the scars remind you of what you have overcome, not what you suffered."

I try to hide my trembling hands. I'm so dry my tongue sticks to the roof of my mouth. I remind myself I have survived torture and faced death. But I don't know if the doge, who loves and trusts me before I tell him, will love and trust me after I tell him, and that frightens me more than torture.

"There is something else, Serenissimo."

There. *Alea iacta est.* The die is cast. I have crossed the Rubicon.

"I know there is," he says, "and I can't figure out what's taking you so long to get it out."

"I'm afraid, Serenissimo."

"You can't let that stop you. I certainly didn't teach you to be a coward."

"No, sir."

"I know you, my son. I have seen your best and worst, so believe me when I say nothing you tell me can substantially change how I feel."

I take a deep breath, exhale, and talk fast.

"I was about to run away because I couldn't tell you..."

"Tell me what?"

"I am a sodomite, sir. At least I think I am. No. I know I am, sir. I am an unrepentant sodomite."

He looks at me with grave concern. "That's a harsh word."

"I desire men, Serenissimo. I do. Men like..."

He smiles and raises his hand. "Spare me the details."

"There are no details, sir. I haven't exactly done anything yet."

He looks sincerely puzzled. "Then why are we having this conversation?"

"Because I want to, Serenissimo, as much as I have ever wanted anything."

"I assume you've had ample opportunity..."

"Yes, sir. I have."

"Then why haven't you?"

"I could not bear to be separated for all eternity from those I love."

He places his hand on mine. "Why must you always put the cart before the horse?"

"The desire is too strong do deny any longer, Serenissimo, and that means doing it, and that means going to Hell."

"Ah, how well I remember the power of youthful lust. Overwhelming, isn't it? It is a thing of beauty to treasure and enjoy and a source of grave danger to every one of us, disorienting, dizzying. I have committed many sins in my life. What man of consequence hasn't? Who's to say which sin is worst?"

"The priests and the lawyers, Serenissimo."

"Bah! Hang them and what they say. Matters of the heart are strictly between a man and his conscience. No one else knows what's wrong or right for you, and I don't believe we are judged on individual acts but on the aggregate of our lives. Our sins will be placed on one side of the scales of Eternal Justice and our virtues and accomplishments on the other, and our fate lies in the balance. From what I have seen, you have nothing to fear. Of course, you are always harder on yourself than anyone else is, including God Almighty."

"With all due respect, Serenissimo, I'm speaking of the gravest of sins."

"Damn it, boy. You're young. You have your whole life in front of you. Don't let any man tell you how to live or how to love. Hell, Julius Caesar ran off with King Nicomedes IV for a lengthy honeymoon. Didn't Cicero call Caesar the Queen of Bithynia? Do you honestly think he cared what anyone thought? Don't live in fear. Live in hope instead. Do what you know is right and learn how to defend yourself when judgment comes."

"I'm sorry, sir. To do this to you. Our lives are already so complicated."

"Great Weeping Soul of Jesus. Listen to yourself. You have nothing to be sorry about as far as I can tell, at least not yet, and even if you did, it wouldn't matter. When the time comes, we will negotiate a treaty. I've had plenty of experience doing that. I can even judge certain crimes—theft, treason, piracy—but I am in no position to judge another man's sins. I have my own to account for. What I do know, as sure as I know my own name, is that you have an honest heart and a generous soul. Be true to them, and you'll be fine. But please—and this one thing is more important than everything else—don't do anything stupid. When the dick gets hard, the mind gets soft. I know this from bitter experience."

I put my arms around him and hug him fiercely.

"Is that all?" he says. "Because this old man is tired."

Before leaving, he pauses and turns back. "Before you consider running away again, talk to me first, because we have history to make. Which reminds me. Pursuant to our quid pro quo. I can't talk to Pisani one-on-one, as you know, but you can. I have a message for his ear only. Tomorrow."

MATTEO, A SACK slung over one arm, waits for me at the mouth of Malamocco channel and helps me pull my boat onto the beach. Delfín whinnies because she knows there are apples in her immediate future.

The full moon transforms night to silvery day. Matteo rides a borrowed horse as we gallop across dunes and the hard wet sand, racing the wind along the shore.

I win, not because I'm a better rider, but because Delfín is a much more spirited horse than the farm nag Matteo's brother loaned him. Matteo doesn't care. He's as happy as he can be. He tethers his horse, tears off his clothes, and runs into the surf, baying at the moon. The sirocco, unusual so early in the year, has warmed the air and water. Matteo wraps himself around me and pulls me into the waves. We pretend we're dolphins and swim to one of Pierluigi's oyster beds. We bring back armloads of oysters which Matteo shucks with his knife.

The warm wind blowing off the sea dries us, and we curl up on the sand, naked and drunk on oyster nectar. I say yes this time, and we make love until we're spent and sweaty.

"I'd say that was worth at least eleven thousand paternosters and six hundred thousand Ave Marias," Matteo says.

"One for each time we struck gold."

We lie on our backs looking up at the stars.

"Do you love me?" he asks.

"Why do you ask that?"

"To see if you feel the way I feel."

"You love me?"

"I think so. Sometimes. I was damn sure when we struck gold at the same time. But now I'm not so sure. You're such a jerk the rest of the time."

I turn my back to stare out to sea. Matteo bites into an apple, leans around, and offers it to me.

"Do you?" he asks. "Love me?"

I bite the apple and hug my knees.

"We have fun together," I say. "Isn't that enough?"

"I'm not handsome enough, am I?" He looks genuinely sad.

"Don't be silly. I love how you look. I love your eyes when you smile. I love the music you make. I love boatloads of things about you. That's why we're such good friends."

He looks away. "You want someone smarter."

"No."

"Then what? Because whatever it is, it's not me."

The truth comes easily because Matteo is my friend. "I want someone older."

"Like Astolfo?"

"Like Pisani."

First, he looks shocked, then, he laughs and tousles my hair.

"Not a chance. You're damn fine, but he's not that way."

"I don't mean *the* Vettor Pisani. I meant someone *like* Pisani."

"There's only one Pisani."

I punch him in the shoulder, hard. He kisses me to let me know he's not mad and plays our song on his flute.

Chapter Forty-Five

Becoming Me

THE HOPED-FOR peace after our victory at Trieste vanishes as quickly as the pea in a shell game. Sensing our battle fatigue, Lord Francesco Carrara of Padua—our putative ally and relentless enemy—is rattling his sword.

General Giustinian, uncomfortable with bearing bad news, stares at his hands as he speaks. "Carrara is building new forts on our land, pointed directly at us."

Serenissimo squirms on the ceremonial stool that follows him wherever he goes. The stiff gold cushion irritates him even more than the stool. I half expect him to growl, a lion with a thorn deep in its paw.

"What did that jackal have to say for himself?"

"That the land is not ours, and he would be a bad prince if he failed to protect his people from such an aggressive neighbor. As for diverting rivers to flood our crops and garrisons, he said he won't be held responsible for acts of nature."

"Acts of nature my ass. He dug those channels and directed the floods to specific targets each time."

"Of course he did, but he swears otherwise."

"'Don't believe your eyes; believe what I say.' That's Lord Carrara in a nutshell."

"He's really hopping mad about Sant'Ilario."

"Sant'Ilario? Holy Saints of Mercy and Forbearance. We built that abbey centuries ago."

"He claims jurisdiction over the island upon which the abbey sits, so he will adjudicate the case of the wife of Padua abducted to Sant'Ilario."

Serenissimo shoots to his feet. "Go. Now. Tell him he'd better be ready to fight. Niccolò, row the general to Sant'Ilario. I want to hear every word."

We leave within the hour, Giustinian and I, in a fast, trim boat, no men-at-arms, no horses, no guards. Only a handful of fishing boats ply the channels between Rialto and terrafirma, usually crowded at midday.

"What's going on?" I ask Giustinian.

"We blocked the waterways. No traffic between Padua and the lagoon."

"That's undeclared war."

"That's right."

Sant'Ilario has seen better days. The abbey and its distinctive tower still cut a fine profile, but salt marshes choke the wharf and threaten to swallow the island.

"It certainly looks bleak," I say.

"The abbey boasted fine orchards and vineyards until the lords of terrafirma dug canals and diverted the rivers. Now, brackish lagoon water poisons the orchards and spawns new marshes, leaving the whole damn island fit for nothing but salt pans, which is probably what Carrara had in mind all along. Salt lurks at the root of everything."

"*Radix malorem.* I thought money was the root of all evil."

"Same difference. The cities of terrafirma can't get enough salt. What they don't eat, they sell at a markup upstream. Our salt monopoly built half the palaces on the Grand Canal. Everyone loves our salt and hates us."

We dock unnoticed. Angry voices from the abbey's chapterhouse volley across the silent cloister. As soon as we enter, silence.

"I am General Taddeo Giustinian, and I come at the direction of His Exalted Serenity, the Doge of Venice."

"We know who you are. Why are you here?"

The emblem of the house of Carrara, a four-wheeled red cart splayed on a field of white, emblazons the speaker's tunic. "I am justice of the peace for this district," he says.

The abbot cowers in the corner, quiet as a mouse facing a hungry cat.

Giustinian steps forward. "Where is Giocomo da Mazzorbo?"

"Awaiting trial in Ezzelino's tower."

The notorious tower, built by the infamous tyrant who ruled Padua before we put the Carraras on the throne, stirs dread in the fiercest of men.

"Giocomo da Mazzorbo is a Venetian citizen," Giustinian says. "We try our citizens."

"Not this time. He was captured right here, and he's ours."

"Where is Giovanna Buzzacarini?"

"Restored to her family, I'm happy to say."

Somber-looking men-at-arms wearing the red cart of Carrara stand at the ready behind their leader.

"I'm glad you're happy," Giustinian says. "But this is our abbey, our land, our territory, and our jurisdiction. We demand the immediate return of Giocomo da Mazzorbo."

"That won't happen."

"We'll see about that."

We leave because two men, unescorted, can say no more. We accomplished our mission. On our way back to Venice, Giustinian tells me the story.

"Giocomo is madly in love with Giovanna, as only a young man can be. Giovanna's father long-ago matched her with a Scrovegni of the banking clan and forbid her to marry Giocomo. According to her father, Giocomo stole Giovanna away in the dead of night with half the household goods in tow. The city militia gave chase and caught them at Sant'Ilario, where they sought sanctuary. You heard the rest. Lord Carrara sorely needs a message that this will not stand."

I REPEAT THE scene verbatim for the doge.

His eyes bulge, as if he might explode, but he doesn't. Instead, he says, "It's Fat Thursday. I have more important things to do."

Carnival has been roiling in the streets and squares for a week. The crazed hilarity culminates on Fat Thursday.

Just as Venice turned the feast of the Assumption into a celebration of our victory over the Narentian pirates in 997, we turned Fat Thursday, the feast of revelry and indulgence before the solemn Lenten season, into a celebration of our victory over the Patriarch of Aquileia and his twelve canons in 1162. The patriarch's ransom—twelve pigs, one for each canon, twelve loaves of bread, and a bull—is paid yearly in St. Mark's Square.

The doge, in his golden robe and jeweled biretta, first conducts a trial of the twelve pigs in the hall of the lords of the night. Wooden models ring the hall representing the patriarch's castles and fortresses. When the doge pronounces the guilty sentence the lords of the night release the pigs into the square. The crowd chases them, squealing and frantic, until all twelve are caught and handed over to the butchers lined up in front of St. Mark's. The pigs are slaughtered, their bleeding parts handed out to senators, the loaves are distributed to prisoners, and the bull is cruelly baited, slaughtered, and roasted. The ducal procession then escorts the doge back into the hall of the lords of the night.

This is Serenissimo's favorite duty. Sledgehammer in hand, he smashes the wooden castles with gusto, shouting out the names of Lord Carrara's fortresses. "Oriago! Borgoforte! Solagna! Gambarare! Mirano!" Sweaty and exhausted, he smashes the last. "Campo San Piero!" Happy, we retreat to his study.

"You look fatigued," Serenissimo says. "Go to bed."

"Can you silence the revelers outside?"

"That I cannot do. Forget bed. Enjoy the fireworks. Drink wine and make merry like everybody else."

But sleep eludes me. I don my cloak and step out of the palace into a madcap topsy-turvy Venice. Peacekeepers dressed as thieves spit at fruit vendors dressed as priests, and priests dressed as students get drunk and eye the whores. Oarsmen dressed as ladies sneak into convents, and barmaids dressed as lads dance with the daughters of rich merchants. Twenty bands of musicians pumping out dance tunes compound the pandemonium. Amid the bonfires, young men create giant pyramids with their bodies, vendors hawk everything from sausage to indulgences, pickpockets run wild and everyone gets drunk. I buy a mask from vendor across the square and turn toward San Zaccaria, my ears ringing, to escape the noise.

Carnival dogs me until I reach the twisted cul-de-sacs behind the church of San Martino, in the shadow of the Arsenal. Fewer revelers crowd these narrow lanes, and I can cross bridges without using my elbows. I stop midway across a bridge uncertain where to go. I should get drunk and dance like Serenissimo said, but I don't know how or where.

Candles flicker on a votive altar to the Blessed Virgin, guttering torches flank the high Arsenal wall, and a bonfire flickers in the nearby square. A blessed hush envelopes the canal. As a gondola glides slowly under the bridge, the gondolier sings a plaintiff lament of betrayed love to a pair of maskers tangled in the dark cabin, their feet sticking out the windows, their moans echoing across the water.

A tall masker watches me from the far end of the bridge. Masked faces look alike, but his body says he's looking for something that might be me. His long legs, fine torso, sturdy neck, and louche posture hint at hidden treasure. Ordinarily, I would not be so easily tempted, but on Fat Thursday, anything goes. I don't worry about my personal safety as much as the desire roiling my blood.

I descend the stairs at the far end of the bridge and walk past him, keeping a slow but steady pace through the twisted lanes behind San Martino. Closed shutters turn a blind eye on the oil lamp that should light the darkness but has been snuffed. Beyond the public bath house, the lane straightens for several blocks with neither ingress nor egress, a long brick corridor affording a glimpse of the Strand and the lagoon at its terminus. The masker's footsteps stay close behind me. I grip the hilt of my dagger in case this chance meeting turns dangerous.

The masker nears, close, closer, and as he passes, he places his hand on my shoulder, and closer still, his lips on my ear.

"I've been waiting a long time for this."

The point of his dagger presses into my back. I twist, and the point of his dagger cuts my flesh.

"Drop your dagger," he says.

I drop my dagger.

"Good boy," he says in a too-familiar voice.

Vertigo spins me around. "But you're dead."

"No, I'm not."

Ruggiero's voice obliterates me.

"Aren't you happy I'm back?"

"I saw your dead body..."

"You saw a burned body and my dagger. You're not half as smart as you think you are. I crawled all the way to Santa Maria in Siaris. They have the kindest nuns, Poor Clares, who nursed me back to health. True miracle workers. In gratitude, I didn't leave a single virgin behind. What else could I do, flat on my back in a convent in the middle of absolutely fucking nowhere for months?"

If I move, he will kill me. My dagger—his dagger—lies at my feet. He doesn't know the blade bears a poison kiss.

"You screwed everything up, ballot boy. I had it all under control until you fouled everything. As soon as I think I can't hate you more, you up the ante. Where is she?"

He's after Alex.

"You'll never see her face again."

"Face. Ha." He spits. "She's my bank, little brother, a purse of endless fecundity into which I make deposits and withdrawals until I'm richer than Ziani. Without her, I'm dead in the water. I need her to pop out noble sons at 50,000 ducats a head. Where is she?"

Rage suffocates me. My schemes, stratagems, plans, purposes, reasons, excuses, my idea of who I am, my entire life, turn to ash. He touches my cheek with the tip of his finger like he's never seen a tear before, then wipes his finger on his doublet as if a bird shit on him.

"Fuck you, Ruggiero. Just kill me. I'm sick of this world and all the monsters in it. But if you kill me, you'll never find out where Alex is, and your father will kill you."

Ruggiero's eyes flash malice. "Did you see him at the selection? He saw you. He couldn't stop looking at you. It made me sick. You have the same eyes, the same mouth, the same complexion, the same fucking glow."

Even my features turn against me and bear witness to the unbearable truth.

"Your mother was ten the first time he raped her. Did you know that? He boasted of it, and she wasn't the only one. He buys them, damages them, and throws them away. Boys and girls."

He grimaces as if a sword pierces his spleen. "If only they had executed him on Crete, I might have had a chance. Like you. But it was already too late for me. You see, he's alive because he is so much cleverer than everyone else, which makes him more powerful, too powerful, inescapable. So, no matter how much I hate him, I'm forced to admire him. Few men stand heads above the herd, more audacious, braver, burning hotter. For ordinary men, the world is too big, but for a few it's too small. Men like Alexander and Caesar and Attila. Papa is one of them."

In thrall to a desperate torrent of words, he must imagine this is our final conversation.

"Your mother was so much prettier than mine. Look at you. Pretty, yes, but weak. Effeminate. Not manly like me."

"Does he know my sin?"

"He does! And he doesn't give a good goddamn. His love for you blinds him. When he talks about you, he gets a look in his eye that makes me vomit. He adores you. He wants you by his side, and the more he loves you, the less he loves me, until I'm nothing, a raging hothead, an out-of-control thug, a pathetic drunkard, a gambler too stupid to win, throwing my talents away on petty crime and idiotic vendettas, failing to grasp the whole picture. But you..."

He holds the advantage, but his mania weakens him. I feint so that I can reach my only advantage, the poisoned dagger at my feet. I go limp and sag earthward as if weighed down with a mountain of grief and terror. He rambles incoherently as I sink to the ground. Then he hunkers beside me, drunk with rage, spewing hatred, his eyes fixed on mine so that he doesn't see my hand grasp the hilt of the poisoned dagger from the pavement and conceal it in my sleeve.

"He swore to kill me if I touched a hair on your head; yes, he did. But I'm already dead, aren't I? This is how I make amends. I'm taking my toll. Setting this right. Behold my resurrection."

Another tear rolls slowly down my cheek. He watches it the way a seagull watches the wake of a fishing barge leaking offal. He points his dagger at my eye.

"Where is she?"

"I'll never tell you."

"Do you think I can't find her? I will. But you can make it easier and quicker. If not, I'll start with your mother, then Mother Barbanegra, then your pathetic little slave friend, and I'll keeping going until my bride is strapped to my bed. Too bad you won't be there to witness our connubial bliss."

I slump forward, pressing my head against his chest. "Do what you must."

"Aren't you enjoying our little reunion?"

In a flash, the stratagem springs forth full-blown like Minerva from Jupiter's head. I fish the chain with the doge's ring from my tunic and dangle it before his eyes. "You might as well take this."

He scoffs at the ring. "I'll wait for the one with my profile."

I tease the mercy-maker from my sleeve. "Hannibal stripped off the rings of all the noble Romans he slaughtered. When he returned to Carthage in triumph, he dumped thousands of them in the doorway of the Carthaginian senate."

"Fuck Hannibal."

I slash his exposed forearm. Stung, he instinctively licks the wound. The poison spreads quickly, his limbs grow numb.

"You won't die," I say. "You'll just lose control of your body."

He growls, a gored beast incapable of language, and tumbles onto the pavement. His eyeballs flicker senselessly as his jaw locks. He struggles to move, but his torso, arms, and legs are dead weight.

"Can you hear me?"

Drool, a spasm, a deep groan. He hears me.

"Good. Now it's my turn."

I hunker beside him, grab him by the hair, and stare into his eyes. "The poison will wear off soon, but it will be too late for you."

I tuck my gold chain, the doge's ring, and the gold dolphin with the ruby eye into Ruggiero's pouch.

"Now, I'm going to fetch lords of the night and swear you attacked me for the purpose of stealing the doge's ring."

I slash myself with his dagger where he punctured me.

"See what you did to me? By our law, murder for theft is far worse than murder for jealousy, love, hate even.

Crimes of passion reveal a disordered mind. Murder for theft marks a pure criminal trespassing the sacred line of property. A clever man can easily argue his way out of a crime of passion, but not murder for theft, not in Venice where merchants rule, and especially not with something as potent as my ring."

His eyes suggest he understands every word.

"And don't worry. Our father will be caught, and he will also pay the price. We know how to bait the trap. And whether you rot in prison or die in a cage swinging from the campanile, Andrea Contarini, doge of Venice, will continue to govern with wisdom and strength, justice and mercy."

Ruggiero's mouth foams. I kick him to see how he reacts. His fingers twitch. The poison will soon start to ebb. I dash to the Strand for lords of night to press my charges and watch them drag Ruggiero to jail.

THE DOGE'S COUNCILORS walk on eggs during Ruggiero's trial by the Ten. The doge is in a perpetual rage. The transcripts of the trial are secured in an iron box with three locks. The doge has a key; a procurator of St. Mark's has a key; and the head of the Ten has a key. The box won't open unless all three keys turn simultaneously. Of course, nothing is foolproof.

Everyone from fishmongers' wives to powerful senators hangs on each thread of gossip. Throughout the trial, Ruggiero's supporters and opponents fight it out in the square. As soon as the verdict is reached, the public heralds loudly trumpet the news in St. Mark's Square and Rialto. The lords of the night beef up the peacekeepers against riots, ferociously police curfews, and ruthlessly enforce the ban on weapons in public.

Ruggiero cuts quite a sympathetic figure in the courtroom, still striking despite his scars and splendidly defiant. According to him, I executed an old vendetta by framing him. Everything boils down to his word against mine. He is noble but lacks all credibility. I am common, but I am still the hero of Trieste. After contentious deliberations, the Ten exiles him from the lagoon for eight years. No rituals of shaming. No march through town with a severed hand around his neck. Only a stern warning that if he violates the ban, he will spend the rest of his days in prison. Supporters carry him on their shoulders from the Hall of Justice to the galley awaiting him at the wharf.

"He won't be behind bars," I say to Marino Vendramin, "but he will be in Crete."

"Crete is far worse," says Marino. "In prison, at least you're in Venice."

The doge, however, is furious. He would gladly strangle Ruggiero himself.

"I'm the doge of Venice, damn it." He kicks his ceremonial stool across the dais. "That has to be worth something around here."

He only succeeds in making his council smile.

"We elected you, Exalted Serenity."

"Then listen to me for a change."

The meeting collapses in wrangling.

Serenissimo has often told me, "When there's nothing you can do, don't." He grabs my wrist. "Let us pray."

In the Evangelist's crypt, he says, "I'm sorry Ruggiero wasn't hung or quartered. I did everything I could. We'll wait for things to quiet down and then deal with him, like Bajamonte Tiepolo."

He sighs heavily, sinks into himself, and pulls his robe around him, a weary old man.

"It's been a long time since we talked, you and I," he says.

He means it's been *too* long. Matters of state have overwhelmed him, rightly so, nor have I been able to concentrate on the business at hand. As long as Ruggiero breathes, Alex is in danger. She's naïve, and he's a boar snuffling for the fattest truffle in the forest. I know her so well. She shoots first, like me, and asks questions later. She's also hungry, like me, only she doesn't know what she's hungry for. She's lucky there. Knowing only makes it worse.

I know the cost of killing, of fighting and losing, of staring death in the face and surviving. Alex has learned none of those things and knows nothing of the world. I know how lethal thorns hide beneath the most fragrant flowers. She doesn't. She can be blithely cavalier about danger. She will only survive if she focuses her brilliant and subtle mind on overcoming the traps fortune sets for us all. I tried telling her, but she wouldn't listen. Telling doesn't work. We must learn certain things for ourselves. I exhaust myself with worry. All day long I'm so weary I can hardly sit straight, and at night, I toss and turn, half awake and half asleep, haunted by the hunger in Astolfo's eyes.

If Serenissimo brought me to the crypt to say something good, he'd be in a better humor. I prepare for the worst while he prays in silence to whoever he prays to. I still don't know. After crossing himself, he stares straight ahead.

"Venice is a big and important city," he says. "A hundred thousand people, maybe more. But it's still a small town with small town ways and manners. Absent the foreigners who come and go, there's just us, and we all know one another; we see everything, and we love to gossip. Trumpets on high could announce the Day of Judgment, and people on the Rialto would still be trying to find out what happened to Ruggiero Gradenigo's runaway bride. Everyone has an opinion. Many say that you are obsessed with Ruggiero in an unhealthy way, that maybe you're the one who should have been tried, or that you killed Alessandra Barbanegra or pirated her out of Venice. I suspect her father won't stop searching, and I wouldn't want to be in her shoes when he finds her."

"That's all hogwash, sir."

"But I'm doge. What I know doesn't matter. I'm worried about you. You can't afford so many enemies at such a tender age. It's downright dangerous. For all of us."

"What would you have me do?"

"Stop moping and make Venice proud of you again. God knows, I do everything I can to help you. But you need to do a better job helping me. Forget Ruggiero Gradenigo. Enough. It's over. Wipe his face and his name from your mind. Forget this tragic girl, as smart and sweet as she may be. Forget Marcantonio Gradenigo and pray that you never hear his voice or see his face again."

"It's constitutionally impossible for me to forget, Serenissimo."

"It's not a suggestion. It's an order. Focus on our pressing issues. Be brilliant."

"Eventually, he *will* come for me."

"Over my dead body." He lays his hand on mine. "I intend to see you become a great man."

The warmth of his touch and the strength of his affection comforts me. Mama kissed me a thousand times a day. Alex and I sat for hours, her back pressed against mine, our arms out, hands entwined, silent and happy. I miss the closeness. I miss being touched.

"Life is not fair," he says. "We stole you from your mother, like pirates. A cruel thing to do. I know it's very little consolation, but in this life we never asked for, we are tasked with great work of the highest order. We hold the destiny of nations in our hands."

His lips tremble, too moved to speak further.

"I will do my best, Serenissimo. I have no other life. Mama married Giasone, and he moved into her house. Their house. Too small for three. This palace is the only home I have, and even that is fleeting."

"I'm not that old."

"I don't know what I will do when this job is done."

"We do our job. That is what we do."

A canon of St. Mark's tiptoes into the crypt, bows deeply, and hesitantly approaches. He's young, new, terrified to interrupt the doge in his sanctum sanctorum. He wouldn't do it if he didn't have to.

THE PALACE IS aroar. A squad of pages pushes through the crowded arcades calling for the Great Council to meet. The *Marangona* rattles the glass, the one bell the nobles can't ignore, their bread-and-butter bell, the bell of destiny.

Everyone asks why the bell is ringing, but no one can say. The Great Council chamber buzzes until every noble in Venice is locked inside. Taddeo Giustinian steps forward, leading a lord of the night, two captains of the Arsenal, and a grimy general I don't recognize who appears to have run all the way from Padua. Giustinian nudges the grimy general forward. Awed by the magnificence of the chamber and the great men scrutinizing him, the little general is tongue-tied, and stands silent at the foot of the dais.

Giustinian clears his throat loudly, and the general bows deeply.

"Exalted Serenity..."

He speaks too softly for even young ears to hear.

"Speak up, damn it. There's a bloody carnival outside."

The general clears his throat and starts again. "Your Exalted Serenity, senators, nobles of Venice..."

The doge waves his hand. "Skip the salutations. What happened?"

"Giocomo da Mazzorbo, citizen of Venice, having fallen in love with Giovanna Buzzacarini of Padua, eloped with the said lady to Sant'Ilario to be married..."

"Yes, yes, we know all that. Has Giocomo been tried?"

"The Lady Giovanna's father put his case before the lord of Padua, and said lord of Padua, Francesco Carrara, exercising his jurisdiction over Sant'Ilario, seized said Venetian captain in Sant'Ilario, tried him in Padua, and publicly beheaded him on the steps of the Church of Sant'Antonio."

In the abrupt hush, Serenissimo rises slowly, as if stricken. Relieved, the general steps out of the center of attention.

Serenissimo, gaunt but adamant, speaks. "They beheaded our captain? Over an elopement? So that's the thanks we get. We made the Carraras lords of Padua, and this is how they repay us." Serenissimo stalks the dais, his gold robe a swinging pendulum.

"Nobles of Venice, I warned you this was coming," he says. "Trieste was nothing but a ruse, a diversion."

He speaks from his heart, which is broken, and this brazen breach of protocol immediately sets tongues wagging. He speaks true, but he speaks too soon, too loudly, and his own mind. Everyone else calls for meetings, committees of inquiry, investigations, embassies, letters, while Serenissimo struggles to keep his head above the tidal surge of bureaucratic wrangling.

I know him now. We will go to war. We have no choice.

Alex has jumped from the frying pan into the fire, only she doesn't know it yet. I must warn her, but I can't. Does knowing make a difference?

What do I know?

I know the order in which the constellations march across the night sky.

I know the compass points and how to find them.

I know my doge and my duty.

I am Niccolò Saltano, bastard of MariaGrazia Saltano and Marcantonio Gradenigo.

I am the fighting ballot boy of Venice, the best shot from Grado to Cavarzere.

One day, I will love a man with all my soul and trust that the preachers lie.

I don't know what will happen next, but at least I know who I am.

Acknowledgements

To the giants whose shoulders afforded me a glimpse of Venice in her golden hours: Galeazzo and Andrea Gataro, Daniele Chinazzi, Vittorio Lazzarini, William Carew Hazlitt, Horatio Brown, Frederic C. Lane, Paolo Sambin, and to Julius Caesar for showing me how. Deby Veneziale and Amelia Bonvini, who made it possible for me to live in Venice for five amazing years. Steven LaBore, who bided his time while I did. And Elaine Mellman Struhl, Laura Struhl, Phyllis Mellman, and Luke Mellman, whose love animates and sustains me. My editor Elizabetta McKay who embraced the manuscript for all the right reasons and made it a better book. And Sharon Roe, for your relentless encouragement.

About Larry Mellman

Larry was born in Los Angeles and educated in literature, political science, and life at the University of California, Berkeley. He has worked as a printer and journalist in Los Angeles, San Francisco, Chicago, and St. Paul, Minnesota. Larry also worked with Andy Warhol and the Velvet Underground on the *Exploding Plastic Inevitable* in NY, Provincetown, Los Angeles, and San Francisco, was mentored by Dean Koontz, and shared a palazzo in Venice with international opera singer Erika Sunnegårdh.

While living in Venice for five years, Larry also taught English, led tours, hosted a B&B, and immersed himself in the history and art of the Venetian Republic. *The Ballot Boy* was born in Venice and completed in St. Paul.

Larry is a lifelong social activist and writer, a voracious reader and researcher, an opera fanatic, and devoted walker. He currently lives in St. Paul with his partner of twenty-one years and his ex-wife of twenty-five years. His son is a pianist devoted to blues and jazz.

Email
larry_mellman@hotmail.com

Facebook
www.facebook.com/Larry.Mellman

Twitter
@LarryMellman

Websites
www.theballotboy.com
www.larrymellman.com

Also from NineStar Press

Dublin Bay by John Patrick

In 1939, the world tumbles toward war and the lives of two young men will be forever changed.

James Brennan grew up in the poorest of Dublin's tenements, turning adversity to advantage wherever he could. But he's nearly a man now—with a good education at that—and wants more from life than what he can get as a day laborer, or following his father into the factory.

Otto Werner is the privileged son of a German diplomat stationed in Dublin. Otto is destined for great things in the new Europe sure to arise after Germany's victory in the war. But he's a lonely young man, living in Ireland with only his father for company, cut off from friends and family back home.

The two teens meet by chance, and each sees in the other a means to advance his own interests. But they quickly become friends, and then—surprisingly, dangerously—more. As the globe spirals deeper into chaos, the love between the young men deepens; but their world is not a hospitable place for forbidden love.

As war comes closer and closer to home, everything they believe—about themselves, about each other, about the world around them—will be shattered. Will their love for each other survive the pull toward destruction in a world gone mad?

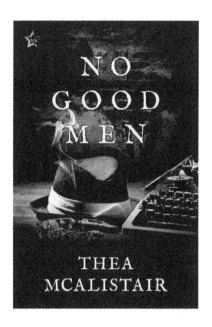

No Good Men by Thea McAlistair

In 1934, almost everyone struggles to pay the rent, and
Alex Dawson is no exception. To support his writing habit,
he moonlights with his mentor Donnie as a bodyguard for
the mayor. It's dull work, until the night a handsome,
golden-eyed stranger catches his eye—and both his boss
and his mentor are killed when his back is turned.

Jobless and emotionally adrift, Alex vows to find the murderer before the corrupt police can pin the blame on him.
But he soon discovers he's in over his head. The golden-
eyed stranger turns out to be a mob boss's cousin, and a
suspicious stack of money in Donnie's dresser leads Alex
to discover that his mentor and the mayor were involved
in something more crooked than fundraising dinners and

campaign speeches. As the death count rises amid corruption, mob politics, and anarchist plots, Alex realizes that the murders aren't political or even business. This is the work of a spree killer, and Alex and his new boyfriend are the only ones who can stop them.

Connect with NineStar Press

www.ninestarpress.com

www.facebook.com/ninestarpress

www.facebook.com/groups/NineStarNiche

www.twitter.com/ninestarpress

www.instagram.com/ninestarpress

Made in the USA
Las Vegas, NV
01 July 2022

50985888R00225